To Karen, my love, forever.

Above Libya   November 2010

The French Transall C-160 was on a scheduled late night mission from Khartoum in the Sudan to Marrakech on the west coast of Africa. The twin prop military plane was the equivalent of a U.S. Air Force C-130 tactical transport. The mission was a routine re-supply flight ferrying twenty-five large pallets of military supplies between French military outposts. With terrorist activities blossoming across the sub-Saharan desert the French were re-organizing support to their former colonies with manpower and supplies.

On this flight west the transport had only one passenger. He sat quietly in the web seats lining the fuselage in the cavernous grey metal fuselage. The only other persons were the loadmasters and they were busy making sure everything was squared away and remained strapped down as the plane traversed air stream variables. All three personnel had on cold weather gear and were breathing from portable air bottles strapped to their chests. The plane had climbed to its maximum service ceiling of 25,000 ft. The temperature in the fuselage had creeped below zero and was continuing to drop.

The tall passenger had on a cold-weather, high altitude, polypropylene jump suit, heavy jump boots, and a sealed helmet. His electrically heated jump suit had pockets crammed with gear, and an additional survival kit was held by web straps close to his body. Strapped to his thigh was a jumpmaster utility knife, making it instantly available if needed. Beyond that he was traveling light. He sat there quietly pre-breathing from a 100% oxygen bottle flushing the nitrogen from his bloodstream.

As the plane traveled at 150 knots high above the Saharan desert it approached Sabha, Libya, about 300 miles south of Tripoli. The pilot radioed his crew they would shortly be at the specified jump coordinates. He toggled off the plane's exterior running lights, rendering it completely invisible in the moonless night sky, and turned on an interior red light signaling three minutes to the drop zone. In the eerie dull light, the passenger stood up, checked his parachute rig for the third time, adjusted his helmet and gale-force yellow lens goggles and quickly switched from the loose oxygen bottle to the one strapped to his chest above his back-up chute. He adjusted his heavy-duty gloves to make sure the seal was tight. He would be jumping into minus 30-degree temperatures outside the craft even though he was flying above the Saharan Desert.

When he heard the whirring sound of the hydraulics starting to lower the rear cargo ramp, he grabbed a guide wire and started walking towards the rear of the plane balancing his weight to the plane's bobbing and weaving. At that point the loadmaster switched hats and became a jumpmaster attaching his static safety line to the ribs of the plane. As the rear gate opened a burst of frigid air raced into the bay and the plane momentarily bucked as it adjusted to the changes in pressure and air currents swirling around the tail section.

Josh Ranalli was about to exit the plane at 25,000 feet into the dead of night. It was like diving into a black hole. He was about to do a HALO, high-altitude–low opening jump. At the planes altitude, it would not even be noticed from the ground. On radar the plane was a scheduled military flight that would be ignored below. The jumper, once clear of the craft would use GPS coordinates to descend at 130 miles an hour for a pre-determined three vertical miles. Then at about 10,000 feet an automatic activation device, an AAD, would pop the canopy chute by firing a small pyrotechnic charge.

Josh Ranalli had done many jumps throughout his career as a Navy SEAL, and now as a covert operator for the Special Activities Division of the Central Intelligence Agency. He had been many things in the military and his skills had been utilized on many overseas black operations. This one was a recon mission.

He liked jumping into the abyss. It kept the adrenaline pumping and made him feel alive.

The rear platform fully extended and there was nothing to be seen except a few stars blinking above in the galaxy. At the appointed time the red light blinked off, replaced by an emerald green one. The jumpmaster signaled him with a go signal. Josh acknowledged with a short snap salute out of habit, took a couple of running steps, and launched himself into the pitch-black sky. He had trained for this countless times; it was always a leap of faith. But he knew what he was doing.

The freezing thin air penetrated the special jumpsuit he was wearing. He ignored the cold blast and concentrated on setting up his dive parameters. His helmet had a heads-up visual screen projected on the faceplate giving him his GPS readings, altitude and direction for the target objective below. Monitoring these visuals he made minor adjustments by flaring his arms and subtly twisting his body back and forth to keep the target coordinates centered on the helmet screen.

Hurtling downward there was no sound other than the violent flapping of his tight body suit being buffeted by the winds. He dropped like a stone. Monitoring his helmet gauges and digital altimeter, he glanced downward to search for lights below in the moonless night sky. The altimeter would monitor his rate of fall through the thin air.

He closed in on 7,000 feet and mentally prepared for the massive jolt he knew was coming. When the AAD device fired and the chute automatically opened above him he knew he would go from 125 mph to less than 10 miles mph in a matter of seconds. He actually looked forward to this 'body-hits-wall' effect because it meant that the canopy was functioning as designed and he might live another day. As he waited for the jolt he also eyed his main ripcord on the outboard side of his parachute harness. It was when that gut-wrenching concussion didn't come that you had to worry about a plan B. If the main chute did not deploy he would have to manually fire the AAD device to pop the canopy. Failing that, he would move on to plan C and go to his back-up chute nestled above his belly. There was a contingency for everything, and a backup for the backup.

He maintained a stable body stature with his legs and arms spread apart equally to prevent any tumbling at this critical point of the downward plunge. The AAD firing device delivered a massive jolt that broke the silence doing its job as the altimeter passed through the 7,000-foot level. Instantly bracing for the impact he hit the invisible wall as expected and his feet snapped out in front of him as if on a swing. Plan A was working.

Gathering his wits about him he looked up to see his pie shaped chute had caught the wind and deployed nicely without any foul ups of the parachute cord. He reached up to gather in the control toggles and gave them a few gentle pulls to make sure he had complete control of his new bird. The parachute reacted to his commands and he concentrated on maintaining a gentle downward spiral that zeroed in on the coordinates flashing in his helmet. He knew his chute had a four-to-one, lift-to-drag ratio. It would allow him to travel four meters horizontally for every vertical meter he dropped. Glancing down he could now make out a few lights from the desert city of Sabha. Josh visualized the map he had studied and started looking for the Libyan Air Force base that was south of the settlement about three miles out in the desert.

Descending to 1,000 feet with a gentle tailwind he identified the typical pattern of the dissecting airport runways in the desert night, white concrete imbedded in brown sand. He used that large X runway marker as a guide to search for a solitary road that led away from the airfield and toggled his canopy in that direction. The long black asphalt roadway stood out against the brown desert sand and led to a couple of low-rise buildings on the perimeter of the airfield. They could have passed for aircraft hangers except there were no runway approach aprons leading to them. With his target coordinates identified he passed the 800-foot mark and started looking for the airport fencing he knew would be there. Locating that perimeter marker he searched for a safe place to drop in for a quick visit.

Josh identified a broad tall sand hill that would provide temporary cover and allow him to bury his jump equipment should there be any patrols driving the fence line. He reached up for the toggles and steered his chute flaring the canopy at the last second to gently settle into the cold sand without having to tuck and roll. His boots slipped into the sandy gravel and he walked a few steps as his chute settled behind him. As it wafted to the ground he immediately kicked sand on it to hold it in place, and then stripped off his polypropylene suit. The thermal jumpsuit would quickly get very hot in the nighttime desert temperature. Five minutes earlier he had been freezing in −30-degree temperatures, now he was at the other end of the spectrum.

With the bodysuit hanging from his waist he put his heavy gloves back on and started scooping out a hole deep enough to accommodate his jump gear, except for his helmet. He tossed the gear in, covered it with sand and made an effort to smooth over the disturbance. He knew the blowing sand would render the spot invisible within a few hours, or, could do just the opposite, exposing his arrival. It was a crapshoot.

Glancing at his military grade watch he noted it was exactly 2:00

am. Right on schedule. Inching his way up the massive sand hill he pulled out a small compact scope with night vision capability and started scanning the airfield for any signs of life. He was in no hurry. To do this mission correctly he only needed stealth, to get in, gather intelligence, and then leave a laser marker that would allow a drone to follow up and take out the target. After a 10 minute glassing of the airfield and seeing no patrols or movement, he decided he could advance.

From the top of the sand hill he aligned his arms next to his body and let himself roll down the front of the hill sideways. This would leave less recognizable marks on the face of the hill that would quickly be covered with the drifting sands. He belly crawled over to the perimeter fence and then sat quietly again watching the interior base for signs of movement.

Withdrawing a small wire cutter from his thigh kit he snipped the chain link fencing creating a two-foot opening to slide under. Squirming through, he took out two black flexi-cuffs and in effect re-zipped the small entry point. Any perimeter guard making rounds would be less likely to notice the break-in.

He took off the top of his jumpsuit and pulled it down to his ankles. Letting it drag behind him, he belly crawled forward again dragging the jump suit to distort any path he left in the sand. Closing in on the darkest corner of the largest building he stopped to listen and scan the site. Seeing no movement he eased up to a doorway and tried the lock fully expecting to have to pick it. To his surprise it was unlocked. He quietly opened the door still lying on the ground. If there were guards inside, they would be shooting at a much higher trajectory.

Again there was no sound. He inched the door open and crawled into the building. Once satisfied he was alone he duck walked along the storage racks searching for his target weapons. He was looking for Stinger missiles that Gadhafi was known to have stockpiled in a variety of sites in the Libyan Desert. With the Arab Spring movement heating up Gadhafi's ironclad control of his country was in jeopardy, and it was critical that the U.S. find and destroy these weapons before they fell into terrorist or militia hands.

He quietly searched the whole building but found nothing. He moved out to search the other buildings in the cluster before he could call it a day. Following the same protocol he eased out of the building and crawled to another. It too was empty although he did find some long empty crates that could have held the five-foot long missile launchers.

As he approached the third and final building in the remotest part of the base he relaxed a bit knowing what he had come for was not there. That was a mistake. He eased through the doorjamb and walked right into a shotgun pointed directly at his head. A half-dressed soldier was doing the pointing, and he looked more scared than Josh was surprised.

Josh assessed the situation quickly and recognized his best option was to remain calm and passive as the soldier was more stressed than he was. With his arms up to signal compliance he noted the soldier was only five feet in front of him and the shotgun itself closed the gap another two feet closer. That closing distance was short enough that he could almost reach out to deflect the barrel. If he aggressively moved forward and shoved the barrel up and away he would be inside the arc, as he bludgeoned the man. Without moving a muscle he contemplated the move, but the man's black eyes suggested he too had realized the dangerous proximity. The soldier started to backpedal increasing the distance between them. Josh debated still taking the chance even though the gap was widening by the moment.

Just then, another soldier materialized out of the rows of stacked pallets and aimed a handgun at the intruder while rubbing his eyes. He too had been asleep. Josh instantly shelved the 'step in and throttle plan A' and processed information to move on to a plan B, although at the moment Josh was not sure what that plan B might be. There could still be more bad guys in the building. He decided to bide his time so they wouldn't just shoot him, because they could.

He continued to hold his arms high above his head in the universal sign for surrender. He noticed both men relaxed a bit when he demonstrated compliance. He put his hands behind his head to further relax them. As he capitulated they ratcheted down their alarm over the late night intruder. The soldier with the handgun motioned him deeper into the warehouse.

Josh walked slowly and did a quick eye scan of the square cinder block building. He noted there were no more soldiers lurking in the square building, just the three of them were attending this party. One dangling light bulb hung from the steel girder ceiling casting deep shadows on the many wooden crates and pallets stacked around the floor.

Josh broke the silence by uttering a question in Arabic, asking what was going on. It too had a calming effect on the two sleepy soldiers. He could see they were considering he was perhaps one of their own. He started to formulate plan B.

Before even settling on a plan, the handgun soldier in the torn t-shirt lowered his weapon and turned towards a chair where he must have been sleeping before being disturbed by the intruder. The man with the shotgun had again ventured in close to Josh. He had come back within striking distance. Josh didn't hesitate or debate his move further. He acted. Pulling both hands over his head and locking them together like a club, he swung his clenched fists towards the soldier's head with all the fulcrum power he could muster. Kind of like taking a homerun swing, but without the bat. The man saw it coming but was so close he could not duck to ward off the blow.

After smashing the man's head with his clubbed hands from ear to jaw, he grabbed for the shotgun barrel before it could fall and hit the concrete floor. The man went down in a heap. Capturing the long gun barrel ass backwards, he flipped the weapon in the air in one fluid motion, and then swung around to zero in on the torn shirt soldier still settling his butt into the chair.

    Roles reversed, the older soldier didn't even try to reach for the hand gun that was just inches from his hand. He finished sitting down and awaited his fate. Balancing the shotgun Josh stepped sideways around the seated man never allowing the gap to close. Behind the chair he used one hand to point the shotgun at the man's head just above his eye pushing hard enough so he could feel the muzzle. He carefully reached for the handgun on the table. As he backed away he feathered the safety to make sure the weapon was ready for action. Feeling the weight of the piece he was confident he had a full magazine. Stepping backwards to another table he carefully placed the shotgun down with the barrel pointing towards the sitting soldier. He racked the slide to chamber a round. He was more comfortable with a handgun in close quarters.

    Josh reached into his cargo pants and pulled out some more black plastic ties. He gave a command in Arabic and motioned for the sitting soldier to crawl over and tie up the motionless man on the floor. The man understood and took the plastic cuffs crawling to his partner. Showing complete compliance, he pulled the inert man's hands behind him and cinched them up tight. Josh pointed at the man's feet and they were tied as well. As the plastic cuffs were tightened the man stirred and shook his head as if he had run into a wall.

    He had the other soldier roll over and pre-threaded a plastic tie through the eyelet motioning for the man to assume the position. The man readily complied hoping that this was a good sign they were not about to die.

    Josh then sat down in the soldier's chair and asked him some questions. With his two hog-tied captives hoping to live through the night and see the dawn, the answers flowed to all of his questions. In no time Josh had as much intelligence as he was going to get from this remote bunker in the desert. The deadly Stinger man-pad shoulder missiles had once been in the storage building but had been moved just a week earlier to keep them out of the hands of the many insurgent groups challenging Gadhafi's iron clad rule. The two soldiers had no idea where the weapons had been taken. Josh believed they spoke honestly. There was no reason for them to die.

As he prepared to leave he saw some water bottles in a corner. He gathered four of them and poured them into a large bowl and placed it on the floor so the two men could drink. He knew they would be there a while and the heat in the building would be stifling in a few hours. He said goodbye in Arabic, took the handgun, and slipped out the door.

He could see the first hints of light in the eastern sky and knew the sun would rise in about an hour. He duck walked to the fence line and recut his plastic ties, slipping through in seconds. He didn't bother to re-tie them because the base personnel would soon know that someone had intruded.

Josh hiked up over the sand hill and gathered his helmet firing up his GPS. Punching in some coordinates he started walking straight south. The sand was soft and made forward movement difficult but he had been living in the desert long enough to deal with it. He had been there so often it was probably closer to home than back in DC. He kept up a steady pace. While it was still relatively cool in the desert he knew that would soon change when the sun started rising. His destination was about a two miles away.

In less than forty-five minutes he was at the designated coordinates and looked around. Spotting an anomaly in the otherwise smooth sand, he pulled a sand camouflaged tarp off an odd looking contraption. The machinery had a full metal framework with bike like struts connecting two flat metal fan-like objects. The machine had handlebar drive controls and a bike seat similar to a fat boy motorcycle minus the tires. The two large circles were actually twin-ducted rotors that provided lift. It was an Aerofex 500 Hover craft, a futuristic design bike that the military was exploring for use in desert warfare. It worked somewhat like the 'Star Wars' movie speeder bikes in "Return of the Jedi". Instead of racing through the forests of Endor, this hovercraft would fly across desert sands.

Josh had first seen the test vehicle in Nevada at the top-secret Area 51 military facility. He had tested it for a half-hour knowing he might get a future opportunity to field test it in the big sand box. He climbed aboard straddling the machine much like a motorbike, with controls just like his Harley back home. He put on his jump helmet and turned over the ignition. The machine was surprisingly quiet as the spinning rotors within the two-ductwork circles started spooling up. In no time he was hovering a foot off the sand.

Josh toggled the controls and used his body to create some forward pitch while maintaining horizontal balance. Like the much-heralded Segway standing bike, the Aerofex reacted to Josh's body movement and balance.

In moments the vehicle was levitating over the sand. Josh started moving forward as he gently leaned in that direction. He had seen the craft handle Nevada desert sands at thirty plus miles per hour but he kept the speed down to less than twenty because he only had the grey of dawn rising. The last thing he wanted was to crash into some sleeping camel or a desert oasis. When he wanted to navigate around a sand dune he leaned to the side just like on his bike and the hovercraft responded flawlessly. The machine would definitely have military applications in the deserts of the Middle East.

He traveled twenty more miles stopping only for a water break as the desert heat was rising and the machine kicked up a lot of sand and dust. He pushed forward because he wanted to see the next military marvel that was awaiting him. Rounding another sand dune in an endless sea of them, his GPS blinked that he had arrived at his destination. He shut down the machine and waited. He was 10 minutes early at the extraction point.

At the appointed time he looked to the southern horizon and a funny looking small helicopter materialized out of the blue. The machine was extraordinarily narrow from front to back, hardly enough room to hold a pilot or crew. In fact, it did not have a pilot; it was a full size drone helicopter, a K-Max 1200 made by Kaman Aircraft Company. The pilotless craft was capable of lifting a payload of six thousand pounds, which was actually more than the bird's empty weight. The helicopter had been first built in the 90's and had seen military service for years in Iraq and Afghanistan.

The helicopter swooped in and Josh waved although he knew he was waving at a pilot who was probably in Qatar. The craft hovered thirty feet off the ground directly above Josh and a strong cable was lowered with four nylon webs dangling. Josh already knew he was hooking up the entire assembly, to be winched up and carried away. The hovercraft was an exotic piece of hardware that wouldn't be left in the desert.

He hooked the four nylon straps to the built-in hooks on the four corners of the air bike and gave a thumbs up to whomever was flying the bird back in some trailer. The winch started pulling the bike up with Josh in the driver's seat. Once the cargo was positioned about fifteen feet under the pilotless craft, the helicopter gently banked and headed south for its remote base of operations in the southern corner of Chad. Josh Ranalli held on for dear life and tried to enjoy the scenery although all he could see was sand in every direction.

New York City, March 2011

The young man sat quietly in the yellow cab as it slogged through traffic and the throngs of tourists milling about in Times Square. His dark complexion was expressionless as he stared out the window ignoring the on-going prattle from the cab driver. He had a dark grey sweat suit with a white pin stripe running down the legs. He pretty much looked like a college student.

He had a square shaped backpack on the seat beside him with his hand resting on top of it. In actuality, he was ten years older than a typical college student. His hair was close-cropped military style, although it was pretty much hidden under his hoodie.

The cab continued north towards the Whitney Museum of American Art on East 74th. Pulling up in front the driver pulled to the curb and the passenger leaned through the glass divider to pay with cash. Hauling his backpack from the back seat, he started up the steps towards the Museum. As the cabbie went around the corner, the hoodied student stopped and reversed himself, back towards the sidewalk. There he headed west towards Central Park.

Crossing Madison Avenue, and then a block further to 5th Avenue he entered Central Park on the path that would take him past the Model Boat House. The park was crowded with families and nanny's watching their children. Following the paths he walked around the Lake, which was the second largest body of water in the park, and crossed over the famous Bow Bridge. He hiked like a college student on his way to class.

Continuing west he went through the area known as Strawberry Fields, made famous in a John Lennon song. The walkway led up to W. 72nd St., directly across the street from the exclusive Dakota apartment building where the same John Lennon was gunned down on its front steps. Without stopping to gawk as other tourists were doing, he continued his walk west towards Columbus Avenue, and then turned north for two blocks. At the corner he went right again, heading east back towards Central Park, as if taking a stroll. He casually slipped on a pair of flesh- colored driving gloves and pulled his ball cap down low shadowing his face. Midway down the block he stepped into an apartment building rear entrance and rang four of the doorbells simultaneously. Three of the building residents responded to the annoyance and buzzed him into the building. He entered with his head down to avoid a camera mounted on the wall above and took the stairs down to the basement. Seeing he was alone, he walked down a dark service corridor leading to the rear of the building.

At the end of the dank basement passageway he stepped into a freight elevator, pulled the birdcage door shut and pressed the buttons for the top two floors, eight stories up. The old elevator labored as it had for the better part of a century. Upon reaching the top floor he drew back the metal gate, stepped out and quietly padded down the hallway on soft rubber soled shoes. He moved to the south side of the building and quietly knocked on an apartment door. He didn't expect anyone to answer; it was more for show if anyone was watching. Glancing down the hall to make sure he was alone, he stooped down and quickly picked the lock on the old wooden door. He gained entry in less than fifteen seconds.

Slipping into the apartment he silently locked the door behind him and pulled out a .40 caliber Beretta Px4, in case someone was indeed in the apartment. The small handgun had been machined to accept a silencer, which he pulled from his other pocket. He threaded the two deadly components together and started a search of the premises. He smiled every time he said 'clear' to himself, checking each room of the lavish, though musty apartment. Satisfied he was alone, he moved into the ornate dining room, which had a large southern facing bay window. He set the Beretta down on a coffee table where it was close if he needed it.

Easing up to the window on 73rd Street, still in the curtain's shadow, he scanned down and east on the street below. Satisfied with the field of vision, he went to work. From inside his backpack he quietly ripped open some Velcro straps that securely held a number of matched metal and wood components that gave the backpack its structure. The components were amazingly compact and the backpack gave no hint of what was actually inside.

He started assembling a customized Galil SR 99 sniper rifle originally manufactured by Israel Military Industries (IMI). The weapon had a short 20-inch barrel. Without the muzzle break attached, the gun looked more like a long machine pistol. There was also a well-designed folding stock. He then mounted a 50 MM tactical scope on the receiver, which was a military grade mil-dot reticle that would assist in accuracy. The rifle chambered 7.62 x 51mm NATO ammunition and weighed a mere 14 pounds. Once the bipod stability struts mounted on the front of the receiver were folded down, the weapon was perfectly balanced and ready for action.

The young man then quietly moved some of the furniture around in the dining room. Using a massive 19th century dining table as a base he stacked another table on it scratching it in the process. The assembly offered a steeper downward shooting resolution. The temporary platform was set back a few feet from the window, which reflected the afternoon sun. He wouldn't be seen by the neighbors across the street. The young man stepped to the left bay window and opened the side frame that angled southeast towards Central Park. He cracked the window a mere five inches and returned to the platform. Sighting through the tactical scope he made some minor adjustments slowly dialing in his sightlines towards the corner of 73rd and Central Park West. By his reckoning his target would be about six feet above the sidewalk, within ten feet of the cornerstone of the Dakota building.

Three evenings earlier he had walked past the building and sized up the corner. While standing there, as if waiting for a bus, he had leaned back against the building wall. With a hidden piece of chalk in his hand he had casually passed his hand through his hair and touched the wall, marking the cornerstone six feet up. Then he casually walked ten feet west of that mark and repeated the process taking his time so as not to draw any attention. The ten-foot distance between the two marks would be his kill zone.

Satisfied with his shooting preparations he carefully searched the apartment for any of his fingerprints or bodily evidence that might have been accidentally deposited. Satisfied, he checked his weapon once more and sat down in a chair facing the door. His handgun rested in his lap. He had at least an hour to kill so he fired up his I-tunes using earplugs and listened to some heavy metal, and Frank Sinatra. He fancied himself an eclectic kind of guy.

Forty-five minutes later he stood and policed the entire apartment again for any personal items he might have deposited. He pulled out a piece of duct tape and wrapped it around his fingers, tape side out and patted the chair he had sat in for any wayward strands of hair that he might have shed. Finally he pulled out a red knit cap that had a long well- crafted rock-star black wig sewn into the lining and set it on the table.

Scaling his mini-tower gun emplacement he sighted through the scope on his subtle marks on the corner of the building and again adjusted his calibrations. Taking into consideration the windless day, he confidently thought he would only need one or two shots to do the job. With the safety engaged, he calmly sighted in on a number of people coming around the corner. He quickly settled his crosshairs on their foreheads before they had even taken three steps into the kill zone. He was confident he could hit his target within the ten steps he had measured. He tried re-establishing a second shot by moving the weapon and then re-sighting. It was not a problem and the narrow five-inch gap in the window did not distort the shot. He was ready.

At 1:00 pm the front door of the Dakota building main entrance on Central Park West opened and two private security guards, hired by the U.S. Marshall's Service, stepped out and surveyed the busy street. They were dressed in ill-fitting dark suits that shouted body armor and weapons. The security personnel stood there for a moment scanning the streetscape in both directions looking for any obvious threats. Satisfied there were none, they signaled their charge to step out of the building. An older man with curly grey hair joined them on the street. He was wearing a long black trench coat that also looked bulky enough to be covering a body armor. Right after him, two more guards stepped out. They formed up a tight circle around the old man and started moving north towards the 73rd St. corner where a town car was just pulling to the curb.

In the twenty seconds that had transpired, five van and car doors popped open on the surrounding street. A bunch of men and women carrying microphones and video camera equipment came scurrying toward the protective wedge.

These were the network news teams covering a story. Each of these reporters wanted to get a story for the 6:00 pm news that evening. They wanted an interview, or at least some sound bites, from the most infamous financial schemer that had ever lived. The grey haired old man had swindled thousands of wealthy, and not so wealthy, people out of their fortunes and life savings in a long-running Ponzi scheme. Finally brought to justice he was under house arrest until all his trial hearings were resolved. The judge had allowed him to remain in his home during the various phases of the trial. Today he was on his way to another one of those courthouse hearings.

The clamoring reporters descended like locusts trying to break through the security phalanx. They looked like NY Jet linebackers charging the quarterback. They shoved microphones and cameras in his face and blocked his path hoping to slow him down as he tried to get to the safety of his town car. The reporters clustered around him like they were in a huddle as he snaked around the corner. Eight stories up, the sniper realized he had a minor dilemma on his hands. Could he cleanly take the shot? Was he willing to cause collateral damage?

The reporters and cameramen were relentless. One actually pushed his quarry backwards to slow him down so they could take additional photos. The target fought back, frightened by his ambushers. Pushing one guy out of the way, his phalanx of guards tried to steer him towards the car at the curb.

The shooter watched through his scope and realized the reporters were helping to slow the procession to a snail's pace. He verified his target and settled the scope crosshairs on the man's forehead. Holding steady he flipped off his safety, took a cleansing breath and gently squeezed the trigger. The round exited the short barrel and passed cleanly through the five-inch gap in the window, racing to its intended target. A half-second later it had traveled the 1,500 ft. and hit its mark burrowing through the man's forehead and into his brain. The entry point made a neat, almost precise circular hole in front, snapping the target head backwards violently. The explosive power of the 7.62mm NATO round sliced through the brain like butter from the upper frontal lobe to the lower cortex. Upon entry the bullet started tumbling as it ran into resistance and exploded out of the back of the skull slicing the brain stem. The hardened steel round exploded out of the lower skull creating a much larger hole, sending brain matter and skull fragments scattering in a huge pie-shaped wedge of blood and gore. The exploding pink tissue and spray hit everyone standing behind the man. The financial schemer dropped like a stone disappearing in the middle of the horde of reporters.

Through his scope the shooter witnessed the carnage while effortlessly chambering a second round. In the process the ejected shell casing flew up and bounced off the table making a metallic ping sound as it bounced to the lower table and then to the floor. It landed on its side and rolled across the slightly uneven wooden floor and under an armoire. The momentum carried it to a flat metal heat grating where it silently fell into the ductwork below.

The shooter could see that a second shot was not required. Everyone in the tight circle was staring down in abject shock and horror. Registering what had happened; they were screaming and back peddling away from the scene. The reporters obviously had their story for the evening news. In fact, they were wearing it.

The gunman opened the breach and withdrew his second round dropping it into his pocket. He dismounted from his elevated perch and padded over to the window, staying out of sight. Using a handkerchief he eased the five-inch gap closed, hopefully before anyone would think to look up where the shot must have come from.

Moving away from the window he policed the floor looking for his ejected brass casing that had bounced to the floor. Not seeing it he got down on his knees and started scanning the floor and under the furniture. He still could not locate it but knew it had to be there. Moving the table and chairs he still could not locate the brass. Seeing the grating under the armoire, he realized he may have a problem.

Recognizing time was now a factor; he shrugged and pulled his rifle from the perch. In a practiced manner he broke the weapon down in less than thirty-seconds, storing the components in the backpack just as he had pulled them out. Reaching for his rock-star wig and skullcap he flipped it over his short cropped hair and pulled it down tight. With no one in the hall he quickly re-locked the door knowing that the resident wasn't expected home for another four days. Hopefully that would buy him some time and delay the assassination investigation.

Carrying his backpack in front to shield his handgun, he stepped into the hallway as if he didn't have a care in the world. He was prepared to say hello to anyone who might venture into the hall. Heading for the freight elevator, he retraced his steps back down to the lower level, and through the dark service corridor towards 74th St. Once outside, he turned west and walked two blocks towards the Hudson River and Sherman Square. In the distance he could hear a number of police sirens screaming towards the area. Still walking casually without a care in the world he made his way towards the subway entrance. Bounding down the steps he took the subway train south.

Riding four stops to Times Square, he climbed up to street level at 42nd and Broadway. Emerging he saw hundreds of people pointing up at the huge 24-hour video screens above the street. He knew what they were gawking at. Someone had just shot one of America's most hated financial criminals. Served him right!

He stopped to buy some roasted peanuts from a street vendor and decided to watch what would surely lead the 6:30 evening news. Knowing the storyline he quickly got bored and headed east on 42nd St. In a below ground parking garage he paid for his rental car with cash and drove out heading for the FDR Drive and a leisurely trip to Hartford Connecticut where he had booked a late flight under another name to Washington, DC.

Heading north out of the city he got off the expressway in Westchester and stopped at a huge storage facility. He had a permanent 10' X 12' foot storage space in one of those suburban storage facilities. Years before he had leased the storage locker after bidding on the contents of an abandoned unit, much like in the 'Storage Wars' television program. Bidding $400 for the unit, he retained the garbage he'd bought and used it for window dressing to hide the real contents of the locker. Buried under the trash was an elaborate safe storage box with two-inch locks and a number of folding shelf units. This was his New England gun locker.

Gaining entry to the gated 300-unit facility, he drove to Unit 1011 and parked his car directly in front of the pull-up garage door. This would prevent any other patron in the facility from just wandering up and in. He had a strong multiple tumbler lock on the door and quickly opened it. He yanked the garage door up and admired his junk.

Wading through the staged mess to discourage anyone who might break in, he threw some boxes that had miscellaneous junk in them aside and started unlocking the gun locker that also had fingerprint security. Making sure he was alone in the alleyway, he brought his backpack from the car. Inside the gun locker he had an assortment of pistols, rifles, and shotguns, each with different purposes for his unique line of work. There were also two large blocks of semtex and a couple of incendiary grenades safely stored away in a seamless metal box so rats couldn't get at them. He placed his sniper rifle backpack kit back in the arsenal, hooked his pistol on a peg with seven other handguns, and threw in his fake wig for good measure. Locking the arsenal box, he threw the same junk boxes over the locker almost burying it.

He had seven of these type storage units located across the U.S and Canada. There were two on the east coast, and two on the west, one in Chicago, one in Dallas, and one in Toronto. In his business you couldn't travel cross-country with weapons anymore so with this set up he could fly most of the time, rent a car, and only arm up when he needed to.

TOM RENK

    As he locked up the garage door he thought about the future storage war television guys who might one day bid for the contents of this unit and stumble upon thousands of dollars' worth of guns and ammo stored in it. He hoped he would continue to survive and pay the monthly rent for a long time.

New York City

Josh Ranalli usually didn't work in the United States. He hardly even had a residence in the country. By federal law his employer, which was an agency of the United States government, was not empowered by Congress to work within the U.S. borders. Domestic intelligence work fell upon the Federal Bureau of Investigation, the FBI. But on this day, Josh had been asked to do some domestic consulting at the request of Homeland Security and the NYPD. While he usually worked almost exclusively abroad, and alone, he was glad to be tasked to a case in the civilized world rather than some third world country. He had been away for a long time.

He was a trained covert CIA agent, and his usual assignments involved intrigue in that very large sandbox spread across the Middle East. He had been over there for most of the last nine years. As a battle-scarred former U.S. Navy SEAL he was a highly trained asset that was often tasked to the difficult off the books missions that the public never heard about. On this day he was being loaned to the New York Police Department's major case squad to get a better handle on an assassination that had taken place in New York.

He entered an upscale apartment building just off 72nd St and Central Park , on New York's upper west side, showed his credentials, and was told to take the elevator to the top floor. The agent in charge would meet him. Upon arrival he stepped into the hallway and could see the yellow crime scene tape just down the hall.

As he started down the hallway, he was met by a strikingly beautiful woman, with shiny blonde hair, and a perplexed look on her face. Josh liked that when he was home in the states the women really looked like women. He quickly estimated she was probably a few years younger than he was. But his age meter may have been off because he had been out-of-country for so long.

Josh noticed all women when he had been away for any length of time. He liked what he saw, even though he could tell that she was all business. She had on a standard black pants suit, the kind a woman on the job would wear. She had on sensible shoes, not the high heels you saw cops wear in the movies and TV. Her well-cut blazer covered a modest blouse that offered just a hint of things beyond. The blazer was long enough to cover the small handgun that was strapped to her side. She looked fit, like she was a runner in her off time.

"Mr. Ranalli? I'm Etta Petrini, with Homeland Security." She smiled and extended her hand.

Josh reached forward and shook hands when he really wanted to embrace her and get that first kiss he had been longing for. Her grip was authoritative and meant to show she was one of the guys. Shaking her hand he thought about getting her into the locker room to make sure she wasn't just one of the guys.

He realized he might be staring at her. He had been away a long time.

"Josh Ranalli, Ma'am, with the government, here to help you," he said, as he continued to shake offering a big smile. He liked to work with beautiful women. It rarely happened. They usually were completely covered up in scarves and burkas. Damn, he thought, it had been a long time!

She noted his enthusiasm but ignored it. Without further commentary, she turned and headed down the hall towards the crime scene marked by all the yellow tape. He followed, but hung back a few steps to gather in her features. He realized he was being a pig but couldn't help himself. He followed her slight hip swaying walk with his eyes and walked right into a candle sconce on the wall hanging at eye level. Almost poked his eye out. She looked over her shoulder and smiled. He returned the smile and continued scrutinizing the woman in front of him. Things were looking up.

"We're overseeing this case with NYPD," she offered. "They have the lead, but we have a concern this might be more than just a single anger killing. Although the shooter was probably justified, we believe this may be a professional hit. We just want to make sure the shooter doesn't have a longer list, if you know what I mean. It was suggested you might be able to lend some insight." She raised an eyebrow as if a question.

"Always willing to help a pretty lady," he said, and then wished he hadn't said it. How lame was that?

He had been briefed prior to arrival and generally knew about the case from the newspapers. He was intrigued to be analyzing another professional's work. But now, with Etta Petrini on the job he would be even more invested. He decided to look more professional and less showboat. She was interested in his professional opinion on who may have done the shooting. Getting to know her would have to come later. He reminded himself that he was just another soldier assessing the work of another.

Entering the police taped apartment where the sniper had set up for his kill shot, Josh silently walked the space. He examined the room as if he had been given the shooting assignment. After looking around and sizing up the steep line of sight required, he was impressed and respected the professionalism of the shooter.

Turning to Etta who had watched him silently he said, "This guy was clearly a professional, not some angry rank amateur who'd lost his fortune and wanted to get even. I'd estimate the shot was about

1,400 feet, give or take a foot or two. While his distance wasn't that impressive for a trained professional, he took the shot through a five-inch gap in the window."

Josh walked to the side window in the bay and pointed to the wooden sash where if you looked carefully, you could see the accumulated dust had been disturbed up about five inches from the flat sill. He asked if the sill had been dusted yet. Etta said it had been. He opened the window again. The five-inch gap proved to be a very narrow shooting line.

"Etta," he used her first name and liked the sound of it. He wondered if it was short for Marietta. He would like that too. "Etta, any chance you could get me some kind of a long gun or sniper rifle up here? What I would really like is something with a quality scope."

Etta Petrini had watched Josh analyze the room and figured maybe she could learn something from this guy. Besides him being a pompous ass. She nodded and pulled out her phone and hit a speed dial number. She walked away from the scene and Josh admired her profile again. He couldn't take his eyes off of her.

She returned and simply said, "Five minutes, they're bringing one up."

He was impressed. She got things done fast. NYPD Special Services brought a long gun up to the apartment in matter of minutes. Josh recognized the weapon but was more interested in the scope. Following procedure he made sure the weapon was unloaded and there was no cartridge in the chamber. Climbing onto the dining room table he sighted the weapon through the small gap in the open window at the corner below still marked with crime scene tape. The dried blood pool could still be seen on the concrete.

Scanning through the scope slowly back and forth he knew what he was looking for. With the scope focused in he spotted two almost invisible chalk marks on the corner-building wall about six-feet off the ground.

"Etta, do you have the CSI reports handy?"

Without a word she reached for a clipboard on a side table and rifled through the attached documents. She found and pulled out a four-page report and looked to the man standing above her. She was starting to feel like his secretary. And she didn't like it, she was usually the one in command.

"Can you check to see if they noted any telltale marks on the corner wall down there? Any mention of marks about six feet up on the wall?"

She scanned the report and said, "No, they didn't mention any."

"Well, there are two small marks on the wall down there. That was his killing field. I'm guessing our victim was about six feet tall?"

"So? We know that's where the guy got shot. Tell me something we don't know?"

She was getting impatient with this know it all.

He explained. "The killer would have made those marks ahead of time to square out his kill zone. It would assist him in sighting in the shot. If I had been doing the shooting I would have done the same thing. That means the shooter had to have been standing down there ahead of time to make those marks. I'd have NYPD take another look at all the camera video from the surrounding street cameras to see if your shooter appeared a couple days ahead of time to frame the shot. I'm betting you'll find a nice mug shot of our guy standing on that corner."

"Makes sense. I'll have them take another look." She was impressed. His tradecraft might help after all. She realized he was obviously a shooter himself evaluating the work of another. She decided to pay attention now. For the first time she noticed he was a good-looking rugged guy that carried himself well. Although, perhaps a little too lean. Knowing who he worked for she could guess what he's been doing all these years.

Next, Josh placed an empty cartridge in the chamber, gently

closed the breach and then ejected the shell from high up on the perch. The cartridge flew out in an arc and bounced off the dining table and then to the floor. It rolled under a large ornate armoire, probably because the floor in the old building had a bit of slant.

"Watch where that shell casing goes, would you?" he ordered.

Etta gave him a nasty look at the order, but was now invested enough in his knowhow that she watched the shell drop and then got down on a knee. She knew that the forensics team had already searched for any spent brass that might have been left behind in the apartment. That was automatic but she knew they had not found any. Maybe this smart ass guy had another trick up his sleeve.

Josh watched her duck down and admired the rear view. He noticed a flash of slender ankle hidden under the black slacks. Trying not to gawk and remain somewhat professional, he went back to work. Climbing down from the shooters nest, he moved next to Etta on the floor. He imagined they looked like two burrowing chipmunks. She smelled great too.

He checked under the armoire. There was an old metal heating vent close to the wall and the ejected shell had rolled next to it. On a hunch Josh pulled out his utility knife and quickly unscrewed two small screws holding the grate in place. He wiggled further under the armoire and with a small penlight looked downward. About three feet down there was a one-inch wide metal shelf sticking out that met a lateral vent. There, sitting on the narrow ledge, amidst some dust bunnies was a brass shell casing. Reaching down with a pen he was just able to stick the pen into the casing and retrieve it.

Checking out the casing Josh noted it was a standard issue NATO round, the same as he often used. There were no fingerprints, nor should there have been, that would have been too easy. But the casing did suggest that the shooter knew his stuff, and had probably used a true sniper rifle in his kill shot.

Etta stood up and dusted her pants and jacket off even though she was spotless. She reached for an evidence baggie. She was again impressed that this man had found something the CSI techs had not, and in a matter of minutes.

"I'm impressed Mr. Ranalli. What is it you do for a living again?"

He smiled as best he could, and said, "Same as you Etta, I'm here from the government and I'm here to help you."

She gave him another crooked smile acknowledging the old joke and said, "Well, I appreciate the assistance. Maybe we can crack this case together. I wish I had you around all the time."

"I'd like that Etta. Glad I can be of help," he said, falling in lust. "Let's go downstairs and see if we can solve this little murder before this guy decides to shoot someone else."

Josh continued to stare and offered a sincere smile. He liked this lady. He was obsessed with her beautiful blue eyes. But he reminded himself that he had always had a thing for eyes. Once the eyes roped him in he'd look beyond them to check out all the other important features. This woman looked like she filled the bill in all categories. He started thinking maybe something could come out of this professional encounter. He'd like that.

"How about some lunch. Homeland Security agents eat don't they?" There is a great deli over on 11th Ave. I'll buy"

Etta realized that this swarthy, good looking Italian CIA agent was asking her out. She was flattered and willing to play along. It had been a long time since she'd been on a real lunch date. But she decided that today maybe should be the day.

"Let's go cowboy, but I'm buying, you earned your lunch!" This time she gave him a real smile. Kind of an off the clock smile.

The forensics team had also identified a single long hair in the hallway right outside the apartment and had it analyzed. It was found to be a man-made synthetic material with traces of glue suggesting that a hairpiece had been worn. That too would have been standard spy craft. Change your appearance going in and coming out so people would not notice you and make a connection. The surrounding street cameras would have a number of things to look for that might help identify the shooter.

Wadi Hadramawt, Yemen

The old stake truck with the tattered canvas cover had left the two-lane macadam highway a half-mile back. The driver was carefully following the instructions from the man who had hired him for the job.

Wasi Habrel had been a Yemeni dockworker for many years. By saving his money he eventually was able to buy an old wreck of a Mercedes Diesel stake truck. It wasn't pretty but it had a good engine and had been a stable workhorse providing livelihood for his entire family. With his vehicle he took transportation work wherever he could find it. Recommended for a two-day transport job from the Aden docks to an inland desert location about one hundred miles away, he gladly took the job. He needed the rials.

He'd been directed to drive a load of heavy crated boxes from Aden Harbor cast into the mountains to the ancient city of Shiban. He knew that whatever he was carrying must be important, because it had been unloaded from a tramp freighter that had armed guards on board. Setting out that afternoon, he'd driven east and then north without incident. There was a good two-lane asphalt highway along the coast, in some places even divided roadway. Traffic was light and when he saw the night shadows creeping down the mountains in the east, he found a level area on hard packed sand just off the highway where he could stop safely and rest. He was tired enough that he fell asleep in the driver's seat in a matter of minutes. He slept soundly until almost first light.

With the sun rising, he got out of the old truck to relieve himself. He then reached for his prayer rug so he could do his morning prayers next to the vehicle. After he finished his morning routine and ate some bread and bottled water, his curiosity got the better of him and he climbed into the back of the vehicle. He wanted to know what he was carrying.

His consignment was packed in ten, identical, five-foot square wooden crates bolted to pallets. They were wrapped with strapping material, some of which had sprung as the load shifted. There was no contents identification or shipping manifest. He'd simply been told to drive to Shiban, one hundred miles inland from the Arabian Sea. Once there, he would be given further instruction.

He was very curious about the load. Reaching for an old claw hammer lying in the back he found a crate that had already snapped it's webbing when the load had shifted. He started working on the corner nails trying to ease up the lid without leaving any serious gouge marks. He finally got a corner loose enough that he could pry up the lid and shine a flashlight into the narrow opening. The light bounced directly back into his eyes and startled him. The light had bounced off the objects within. Intrigued, he forced the box open a bit more and recognized what he was looking at. The wooden crate was filled with glass in frames much like you would find in a window. The items were nestled side-by-side with perhaps ten or fifteen in the crate. They were well packed with wadded up paper nestled between the panes of glass and frames.

He thought the contents were a bit odd. Why was he hired to bring windows way out here in the middle of the desert? Perhaps he was making a delivery to a hotel in Shiban. The tourist trade was picking up even though terrorist activity was also increasing.

He checked a second box and found more of the same. Satisfied he had a legitimate load of goods to be delivered, not guns or other contraband, he used the hammer to reset the nails and seal the crates. Climbing back into the cab he started the engine, disengaged the old parking brake, and moved back onto the deserted highway heading north. He drove another three hours to Shiban.

Once he was in the Shiban valley, he found a well-tended farming community surrounding the ancient trade route city. He headed for the old walled city and the town square as he had been told. Driving through the centuries old gate, he marveled at the hundreds of four and five- story sand colored brick and adobe tenements that were stacked tightly together, many of them over 300 years old. They rose vertically out of the desert as if an apparition. He wondered how he would find the man who would assist him on the next leg of his delivery.

Entering the central square, he drove past one of the Mosques that had been a part of the trade route city for centuries. Afternoon prayers had just finished and many men were milling about and heading towards the coffee shops in the central square.

As he drove past the shopping bazaar, he noticed a man running towards his truck. The man continued his converging path and jumped onto the running board on the passenger side. The man had a well-trimmed beard and clean robes. He smiled and said hello to Wasi by name. Holding on to the rearview mirror, he reached in and unlatched the door, climbing in as the vehicle continued to move. Wasi saw that the man had a small handgun tucked into his cloth belt underneath his loose tunic.

At first Wasi thought his dory was being high jacked by a road thief, but then he realized the man had called him by name. He relaxed a bit, as much as anyone can when a gun is brought into the equation. Just to be safe, Wasi reached down to his own belt and reassured himself that his Jambiyah, a curved blade knife was still nestled in his belt. The curved knife had been his father's and had been in the family for at least a century.

"Mr. Wasi, I have been waiting for you. I missed afternoon prayers because I was afraid you would drive through town while I was praying. But I am glad that you are here. Have you had anything to eat on your long journey?"

The driver relaxed at the mention of food and decided this man was indeed his contact.

"I have not had anything since morning when I had some water and dates beside my truck on the highway."

"Then we must stop for some food. There is a small shop up ahead on the right. I think the truck will be fine and we can eat in the courtyard and keep an eye on it."

"That would be good brother. What may I call you?"

The new passenger thought about that for a moment. He decided to be honest. "I am Khalid, a farmer from a valley just north of Shiban."

Wasi thought it odd that a farmer needed hundreds of windows but decided to not let on that he had peeked into the cargo crates on board.

The two Yemenis enjoyed a simple lunch of rice, chicken and dates and washed it all down with the local tea. Hot liquids in the summer sun made you feel cooler both inside and out.

After lunch they got back in the vehicle and started driving north out of town. Wasi was relaxed by this time, as the man had been cheerful and talkative in the small shop. He had even paid for the lunch. They drove north into the hills. About three miles out of Shiban, the road got much rougher. Another mile and the road turned into nothing more than a rutted pathway into the foothills of the surrounding mountains. His passenger encouraged him to drive carefully as the road would get even worse, but said they only had another two miles to travel. Wasi again wondered what they would be doing with glass windows up here in the hills away from the city.

They took their time driving because of the rutted and missing roadway. Following instructions he drove up the dry riverbed, circling around massive rocks and outcroppings as they kept rising from the valley floor. Looking at his somewhat accurate speedometer, he noted they had traveled a total of about eleven miles from the city when they broke into a clearing and saw some people standing in the shadow of a massive rock formation.

"We are here my friend, you have done well since we left the road," Khalid said, as he stuck his head out of the passenger window and waved at the men standing up ahead.

Pleased they had arrived wherever they were going, Wasi responded lightheartedly, "I hoped we would not have to travel too far off the road, or your glass would have all broken."

As soon as the words came out of his mouth he regretted having said it. He had admitted knowing what was in the cargo bay. His new friend and guide did not react to the statement. Instead, he turned and stuck his head out of the window, again waving the small group of men over towards the truck. Wasi again noticed the gun in his belt and a shiver went down his spine even though it was over one hundred degrees in the desert sun.

Khalid directed him to park the truck in the shade of a massive rock outcropping and climbed out. He walked over to the men who all looked somewhat out of place. They were obviously western men dressed in Arab clothing. Most of them were tall and lanky, with somewhat lighter skin tones, but all had scruffy thick beards. They were clearly not from this region.

Wasi went to the back of the vehicle, opened the tailgate and climbed in to pull the tattered canvas cover back. Three men climbed into the bed with him and started muscling the first crate towards the rear tailgate. Four additional men approached and slid some broad planks of wood, thicker than two by fours, into the pallet-like bottom of the box. They each took a corner and step walked the box off the back of the vehicle at shoulder height.

"Be careful with that crate, it has some valuable, breakable objects in it," Khalid said, as he helped muscle the second box into position on the tailgate. In a matter of minutes they had all ten crates unloaded and sitting in a stack in the shade of the rock outcropping.

"Come my friend, we have finished. I will return to the city with you. Here is your pay. We thank you for your travel. I will even buy you a good dinner if you like when we get back to Shiban. Wasi again relaxed at the mention of food. He waved goodbye to the many young men standing around and climbed into the vehicle.

Carefully driving down the dry riverbed, it was easier because the load was lighter. He kept thinking about another meal. And he had money in his pocket. Rolling over the rocks and deep rutted tire impressions he debated if he would start driving after the meal, or would wait for morning.

When they got to town, it was mostly deserted as everyone was again at prayers in the Mosques. Khalid directed Wasi to drive behind a building that turned out to be a tight alley between two taller buildings. Because of the deep shadows created by the tight walls, it was almost dark in the narrow corridor.

As he pulled the brake, Wasi looked over at his new friend and dinner mate and saw a handgun being pointed at his face. Before he could react, the gun exploded and a bullet penetrated his forehead just above the right eyebrow splattering pink brain matter on the driver's door, and the adobe wall behind him. His head snapped back against the door as he died instantly.

Khalid wiped the blood spatter off of his weapon with the dead man's tunic, stuck it back in his hemp belt and reached for the bag of money that he had given the driver. Looking in the rearview mirror and then forward, he eased out of the door wedged against the wall and snaked his way to the back of the truck. He then walked down the alley, rounded the corner, and walked towards the restaurant where he had promised to take his driver for dinner.

Shiban, Yemen

The slight, average height man with horn rimmed glasses, and a neatly trimmed beard sat quietly on his prayer mat and stared out the open window at the many sand-colored brick and adobe buildings that were sandwiched together in a tight cluster. Like children's building blocks, he thought, in the middle of the desert.

Anwar al-Awlaki's flowing white robes billowed in the hot breeze keeping his body dry as he contemplated his next move. He had curried favor with al Qaeda leader, Osama bin Laden by opening a new front for al Qaeda in Yemen. Bordering Saudi Arabia, this strategic location would allow bin Laden to wage holy war on the House of Saud.

He had been in the desert for some time now on a mission that would pay dividends in the near future. He had set up a training camp that was producing sniper/assassins. The eventual targets would be various Arab leaders from around the world. Once these marksmen were trained, they would be sent out to stir up anarchy throughout the Islamic world, by taking out various dictators and political leaders, and creating chaos and turmoil throughout the Middle East. The plan called for all of this to be blamed on Israel and its Zionist partner, the United States. Bin Laden had given his seal of approval more than a year ago from his hidden encampment.

Since that time U.S. Navy SEALs had found bin Laden's hidden compound and killed the leader of Al Qaeda in his compound. He had fallen to the Satanists and his death now needed to be avenged. With the sniper mission proceeding well, Awlaki had become bored and wanted to get back into a more active battle against the Satanists of the West. It was time to avenge the leader. Thus, he had come up with an even more audacious plan that would take the battle back to America. He had the knowledge and the capability to open a new battlefront. He just needed approval to move forward. He was confident he could hit America harder than the 9-11 attack on the Twin Towers.

Having stayed in touch with his followers in the U.S. he was well aware of what was happening on the political front. The winds of change had come to America. They had elected their first black President. He looked down at the piece of paper in his hand. It had only a few notes on it, but that was all he needed. Underlined in red were the words, kill the new President, the one who had ordered Osama bin Laden's assassination!

A bodyguard entered the room and said a meeting had been arranged with Ayman al Zawahri for the following day on the coast of the Gulf of Aden. It was day's drive but the cooler weather from the sea would be a welcome relief.

Al Mukalla, Yemen

The journey south was uneventful although he occasionally looked to the sky wondering if the American drone ships were watching his movements. Anwar al-Awlaki did not like his travel arrangements but they were necessary so as not to draw attention. He hoped the drones and satellites would not be interested in a lone vehicle crossing the deserted mountains. Especially one that looked so decrepit it might not complete the journey.

In the past he could have traveled in a comfortable Mercedes sedan with air-conditioning, and a convoy of bodyguard vehicles in front and behind him. But now the ever-present eyes in the sky watched for such convoys crossing the desert. So he traveled in a single old car to stay alive and fight another day. He sat up front with the driver. A single bodyguard was asleep in the back seat. They drove into the coastal city of Aden and picked up an escort car that led them towards the eastern edge of town.

Driving east along the coast on a modern asphalt two-lane highway they came to an almost unmarked drive, turned and drove up a winding dirt road. They reached a level plateau overlooking the Gulf of Aden, and the two cars pulled into a gated courtyard.

Set back from a cliff overlooking the sea was a small but nicely appointed brick and stone villa, with a commanding view of the Gulf of Aden. Below the cliff was a golden sand beach, with a soft two-foot surf washing in. It was an idyllic location of peace and harmony.

Anwar al Awlaki got out of the old car and walked towards a shaded portico where his host awaited him. They greeted each other with a slight bow and embraced for a moment. The large rotund man then led his guest to a patio area beneath fig trees that offered protection from the equatorial sun. Pleasantries were exchanged and tea was poured from an ornate silver pot.

The two white-robed men enjoyed their drinks, the fresh air, and the sun filtering through the leaves of the fruit trees. They watched the many freighters and bulk carriers plying the Gulf of Aden just a couple miles offshore. They were in no hurry to get down to business.

"It is normally so hot in Yemen that I am greatly enjoying the cooler breeze and the smell of the salt air in the wind. It has been invigorating these last few days. I am pleased you have come for a visit my friend."

"I agree Ayman. This is a welcome change of pace from the stifling desert heat in the camp."

"So tell me Anwar, how does the training go? Have you been able to show our people how to handle the sniper weapons we obtained for your school? Can they compete with the Americans?"

"Ayman, you flatter me. I do not personally show our warriors how to handle these deadly weapons. But we have been training a number of assassins that learned their craft in the streets of Ramadi and they are training every day. No, I am but a general manager making sure we are moving forward. And we are, it goes well. As long as we can keep the desert camp a secret we can train our people for work all over the Arab world."

"That is good my friend, Osama would have been pleased to hear we are having success.

We must try to avenge his death at the hands of these Americans." He quieted for a moment and then said, "So why did you want to meet with me, other than getting out of the desert for a few days?"

"Ayman, you are wise beyond your years. I have come to ask for a new assignment. I have set up the camp and it is running as we hoped. The program progresses well, but I have become bored. I want to do more to avenge the assassination of our leader." Anwar stopped talking and waited to see if he could elicit a response from his elder.

"That does not surprise me my friend. We all want to make the Americans pay. If the camp is running well, then perhaps we can talk of another assignment. What might you have in mind?"

Anwar Al-Awlaki was pleased. Zawahiri was smart enough to see that he could be more helpful to the cause. He glanced out to the ocean for inspiration and then turned back to his senior.

"Having originally come from America, I lived in San Diego and in Washington D.C. on the east coast. I have traveled the country, walked in the streets. I know America well enough to take the attack directly to them. I also have followers there who await my command. They will help us to achieve our goals."

"Ayman, Osama talked about taking the battle to America again as we did with the Towers in New York. With his death it is even more important that we strike again, and strike them hard. So what do you propose?"

"The U.S. has killed our leader. Thus, I think we should kill their President, the same President that ordered the Seal Team attack in Abbottabad. Killing this man would be the ultimate symbolic victory for al Qaeda and it would truly avenge the death of Osama!"

Shiban, Yemen

This second class of terrorist trainees was completely isolated at the remote camp hidden in the rugged foothills north of Shiban. They experienced a hard life, living in caves, sleeping on straw mats, and eating meager rations. But they had been recruited for a specific cause and accepted their situation willingly.

There was never any downtime in the camp except when the satellites were known to be overhead. They were either training in languages, listening to indoctrination speeches, practicing spy craft, or sweating in the heat of the desert sun. They had been carefully recruited from Arab countries all over the Middle East, but mostly from Iraq and Afghanistan because their hatred was already so intense. Many were seasoned fighters that had already spent years making life miserable for Americans in whatever country they were in.

It was an extraordinarily hot day with little air movement. The young recruits were exhausted having lugged many window frame units up the hills and cliffs one by one. Adnan Menaj, the most storied sniper in Iraq, was the man in charge. He was teaching the twenty journeymen the fine art of shooting custom sniper rifles over great distances, hitting targets more than a half-mile away.

"Jamal, set up another firing position on that next cliff over there." He pointed to an outcropping another hundred feet up the cliff. I think that will give us just short of a 700-meter distance to the target. When you get there we will take a reading to get an accurate distance. We must be good at multiple distances to hit our targets."

"Adnan, I understand the importance of these different elevations, but must we always drag these heavy windows up there as well?"

"You do if you have to take the shot through a window glass to maintain cover, and live to talk about it afterwards. We must learn how to shoot through window glass. In a city, if you have the window open, the security people protecting an important target will come to investigate. Shoot through the glass and they will have no warning of your presence. The challenge is to still hit the target when the bullet must first smash through the glass. Do not question my authority."

"I apologize, Emir." He used the Arabic word for leader to show how contrite he was. He continued dragging the window frame up to the higher level on a protruding cliff.

The other student terrorist shooters were doing the same thing from other vantage points, all aiming at a killing field set up on the valley floor. They had created a dozen shooting lanes ranging from towering cliffs down to the equivalent of two and three story buildings. Each student had been taught how to build a snipers nest that he could hunker down in until the appointed time. They had been taught to be tough, to go without food and water, to pee where they sat rather than crawl away from their hole and relieve themselves. They were not allowed to drink coffee or the strong Yemeni tea to help steady their nerves so they could shoot straight and true.

Adnan Menaj thought they were getting better. With more practice they would know how to take out a target on the first try, and still live to fight another day. He looked about and saw that everyone was in position on the twelve different shooting levels. They were using relatively decent equipment to work with, purchased on the black market from the Chinese. No questions were asked when the one hundred weapons were purchased.

China's military were first class entrepreneurs. They had a well-established back door sales policy to anyone that had the cash. They had been arming South Asian countries for years. First, they had sold weapons to the Bangladeshi Army, and that led them to the Indian military. Once the Indian armed forces had established a relationship for special ops weapons and training, the Pakistani Army had come calling asking for such equipment as a deterrent against their archenemies. It was the domino theory all over again. The Taliban got into the game and al Qaeda followed quickly all seeking better arms to fight the Satanists from the West.

The weapons had arrived by ship just a few weeks before this class of sniper students had assembled. These students were working with JS 7.62mm sniper rifles with conventional bolt actions that weighed just over twelve pounds. More important, the weapons could be broken down into a small carrying case that made them easily transportable. The barrel was only 23.6 inches long and the stock was about the same. The rifle had a fixed butt stock, but had been reworked to break down along with adjustable cheek rests and recoil pads. The weapon was manufactured for a maximum range of 800 meters, over 2,400 hundred feet, about a half mile.

Adnan looked around at the class of shooters perched on various rock outcroppings. Some were close and shooting at steep angles and others were further away shooting relatively flat trajectories. All were sweating profusely with the moisture glistening off their faces in the hot sun as they waited to shoot.

The instructor gave a command with a small battery powered megaphone that still echoed off the canyon walls. They couldn't use radio devices fearing they could be electronically monitored. The single shooter was given the signal to proceed. The terrorist waved his hand to acknowledge and chambered a round. He started sighting his weapon on the target on the valley floor. He was shooting through a single plate glass window that was perched just five feet in front of him wedged between two large rocks to hold it in place. He sighted through his scope and brought the crosshair image to the head of the body target. Using a formula that had been hammered into his brain, he calculated his target size in meters X 1000. Other factors he would normally consider were wind and elevation adjustments but there was no wind in the desert on this day, just stifling heat.

Satisfied he had correctly dialed in his distance, he flipped off the safety with a thumb and slowly eased his finger into the trigger guard. Then he focused on his target and gently squeezed off a shot trying to minimize his body movement, which would transfer to the weapon. The striker slammed into the .308 shell casing of the 160-grain bullet. The compressed tungsten-powder ignited and sent the round screaming down the barrel. In the bright sunlight there was a minimal muzzle flash and very little recoil.

The bullet instantly smashed its way through the plate glass window frame just a few feet in front of the barrel's muzzle break and took flight into the valley below, at about 1,450 feet per second. The bullet held true and smashed into the body target in the vicinity of the neck, clearly about eight inches lower than the shooter had hoped for.

"Mahoud, it was a good shot but eight inches low from your planned head target," Adnan barked into his megaphone. He wanted to encourage his shooters not defeat them. "Set up another window and try again. Factor in the drop in elevation better and you will learn from your mistakes."

A minute later Mahoud had wedged a new window frame between the rocks and settled into his prone shooting position. He signaled when he thought he was ready. Given the go ahead he sighted in his weapon as before paying more attention to the elevation drop.

Taking a deep breath and exhaling it to settle himself, as he had been taught, he inhaled another breath and slowly exhaled as he gently caressed the trigger. Again the weapon barked with a sharp retort echoing through the surrounding canyons. The glass shattered and a millisecond later the bullet found its target. This time it caught the front of the face just above where the eyebrows would have been if a man had been tethered to the backstop. Adnan spoke into his megaphone for all his students to hear.

"Mahoud, you have hit your target well. It is dead beyond a doubt. In fact your earlier shot would have been a kill shot as well, but this time you have left no doubt. Come down out of the sun. You have done well."

He looked to the next shooting position, this one set up at a higher angle some fifty feet in the air but only 500 yards off in the distance. "Ozan, it is your turn to show us you have become a true marksman. Do well and you too can come off the mountain and out of the blazing sun."

The others sitting in various sniper nests in the cliffs circling the targets had hoped they would be next. They groaned to themselves as they realized they would be baking in the sun for many hours as the deadly class went on and on.

Washington DC, Chinatown

Just a few blocks from the FBI Building on Constitution Avenue, Josh Ranalli walked by the Spy Museum and silently snickered his disgust, thinking if they only knew what really went on. This museum dedicated to the covert spy world had been functioning as a tourist attraction for at least fifteen years. It actually had a Board of Directors made up of old Cold War espionage agents from the U.S., the old Soviet Union, from Europe, and from the famed MI-6, James Bond's secret agency in the UK. But it was not a game.

Josh had never ventured inside the two-story, block-long building. He figured it would further trivialize the futility of his work over the past ten years. Plus, the ticket prices had risen to astronomical rates since its early days when people waited for hours in lines to get in. It was all too plastic and Hollywood for him. He'd heard there were all sorts of exhibits including a mock Checkpoint Charlie and Berlin Wall in the basement, and James Bond's, original Austin Martin that Sean Connery drove in the movie Goldfinger. Josh did admit that the twin 50 caliber machine guns mounted under the headlamps would have been a great addition to some of the cars he had driven on assignments.

He just shook his head and moved on down the street heading for Chinatown. While it was not as large as San Francisco's, or New York, it still had the traditional street threshold entrance announcing you had arrived. Once there you could smell the live fish and skewered frogs, the recently hacked chickens, and the fragrant Asian produce and spices. The shops were colorful and full of tourist trinkets. But most important you could still get real Chinese cuisine.

He walked up to a restaurant he knew well and stopped at the Chinese and English menu posted in the window. Looking at the reflection in the window he surveyed the street both ways seeing if anyone was following him. Out of habit he glanced up and down the street noting everyone and everything surrounding him. Then he purposefully moved into the Red Pagoda Restaurant. Without waiting for the old Chinese gentleman to greet him, he headed towards the rear of the restaurant and a sat down at a corner table that gave him a clear view of the front and the side kitchen service doors. A waiter immediately came over, bowed and offered him a menu. Without looking at it he ordered green tea and a couple of egg rolls to keep occupied until his guest arrived.

Ten minutes later, after consuming the egg rolls smothered in sweet and sour sauce, he saw his guest through the front window doing just as he had done before entering. The tall man casually scanned the window menu and utilized the window glass as a mirror to scan the streetscape. Satisfied he hadn't been followed, he too ducked into the restaurant. In the doorway he slipped off his sunglasses, and quickly scanned the room, already knowing where his contact would probably be sitting. He walked over monitoring the surrounding luncheon crowd. It was basic spy craft habit.

He slid into the high walled booth nodding a simple hello. The waiter reappeared and they both ordered some lunch. Josh ordered some shrimp with lobster sauce and the other ordered beef and pea pods, and green tea. Josh ordered another pot as well.

"Thanks for meeting me Josh," Derek Flynn said, as he poured himself a cup of tea.

Derek Flynn was an Assistant Director of Covert Operations

with the Central Intelligence Agency. He'd been a field operative for years before the Wall came down and the Soviet Union decided to cease operations. For the last ten years he'd come in out of the cold and was driving a desk, managing covert fieldwork all over the globe.

"Good to see you Derek. It's been a while. I haven't been back to Langley for a couple years now. But I don't miss having to check in for debriefings."

"We've missed you, Josh. Welcome home. You should come out just to see who isn't there anymore."

"Nah, it's been so long I think everyone's better off if I don't show my face around there. People might think I'm a spy!"

"Well?"

Changing the subject, Josh said, "I appreciate you meeting me here in the city. And I'm glad you keep sending those paychecks to the bank. So how is your family?'

"Courtney is fine and the kids, well, they aren't kids anymore. Logan is in his second year at Georgetown and playing shortstop on the Varsity already. Taylor is just finishing high school. She is seventeen going on twenty-seven if you know what I mean."

"Yeah, I do," Josh said, again doing an automatic scan of the room. "I bet she is a charmer too. I seem to remember she was a beautiful little girl who knew how to twist daddy around her finger," Josh laughed at the thought.

"She still does. Gets me every time. She can't do it to her Mother so she doubles up on me and gets everything she wants just by saying …Papa. I'm just hoping she turns eighteen soon!" He sighed. "How about you, any special woman in your life?"

"I've been wandering in the desert for the past few years. What do you think? The only women I've seen are dressed in black from head to toe. That can be a hell of a buzz kill. The only thing I have acquired is a highly developed eye fetish."

"Yeah, I could see that happening. What about back here? No ladies lined up?"

"I met a delightful lady in our game in New York. She's with Homeland Security and just recently took a new Managing Director job in the Chicago DHS. She was something else and we hit it off well, at least from my perspective. If we ever get a case that could get me to Chicago, I'm all in.

"Yeah, well you know we don't actually work on this side of the pond, so I doubt that will happen. You may have to look around here in DC."

Josh laughed. "When I am here, I live like a monk in a second story walk-up above a bakery. It is like a cell. I have a dorm room refrigerator, a microwave, a double mattress on the floor, and a clock radio that I think still works. Yeah, the ladies are lined up to come to my place.... in the bakery down stairs. And I don't like sugared doughnuts."

"Sorry I asked. Maybe you need to work on that.... the doughnuts I mean."

"Especially since my employer is about to send me overseas again?" Josh inquired.

The waiter brought the two meals a few seconds later. In Chinese restaurants it seemed they had your plate already prepared before you walked in. In actuality, the food was all pretty much interchangeable and all they needed to do was choose the pre-prepared components and stir fry them up for a few minutes. Josh said thank you in Mandarin and they both dug in.

"So Derek, what's on your mind? We haven't met like this for years. The last time we had Chinese you sent me on a two-year assignment into the deserts of North Africa where I craved Chinese food and got none."

"Josh, I guess you could call this our own little foreign assignment lounge."

"I'm not complaining, I actually like Chinese food! You know," he said cheerfully, "over there they just call it food." He smiled at his lame joke. "But getting here, I did almost spit as I walked past the Spy Museum on 9th."

"Don't get me started. My neighbors all want autographs now. I'm thinking of getting some baseball type cards for the neighbor kids, like the cops have. Whatever happened to the word covert?" Not waiting for a response, Derek leaned in closer and said, "I hear you were involved in catching that New York assassin who took out the Ponzi guy. Too bad really, the guy really needed to be taken out."

"But we tend to frown on such domestic violence in the news. Yeah, they did call me in. In fact, that is where I met the lady from Homeland I was telling you about, the one I would like to meet again. But that is another story. She needed a sniper's perspective. I was able to check out the nest, and make some observations that led them to the guy. He was Croatian, and was using an Israeli Galil to throw off the investigators. He actually knew what he was doing and his kit was really compact allowing him to move seamlessly through the city."

"Almost sounds like you're idolizing the guy?"

"Not really, just one shooter appraising another's work. And I don't think anyone has really been mourning the loss, have they?" He paused a moment and then added, "Except maybe the reporters gathered around him that day. I guess they were all covered with his blood and brains! Those guys and gals will probably be scarred for the rest of their lives."

"But they got a hell of a story for the effort. You know, exclusive, live from the scene, blood and guts," Derek said, chuckling as he contemplated the carnage.

Josh leaned in close. "This is not for publication but they caught up to the guy here in DC. It was a contract hit and Homeland Security has the guy in a safe house sweating him to track down his sponsor. They are concerned the guy had a larger list."

Both men contemplated that thought for a moment and then Josh cleared the air by saying, "So what's on the Agenda. Don't I get a couple weeks off for helping catch an assassin that probably did the U.S. a service?"

"A vacation does sound nice. I wish I could make that happen but something's come up in the Middle East that needs your particular touch. How about a desert vacation?"

"Why am I not surprised? The Middle East has become one of my favorite places. Spicy food, veiled, formless women, and weapons in the hands of crazed people who know how to use them. They will kill you just because you look at them funny."

"You've got to love our work, think of all the fringe benefits," Flynn said mockingly.

"I figured that might be the direction you'd be pointing me with what's going on over there. The entire Arab world is self-destructing before our eyes. And the scary part is they may take all the oil with them."

Derek Flynn leaned in again lowering his voice. "We're concerned al Qaeda in Yemen is behind all this Arab Spring anarchy. God knows we have no love for all those tin badge dictators getting roughed up and tossed out of their countries, but we're concerned with who's coordinating the mischief. And who may step into the void that is left behind. We need to know what's going on, and who is driving the bus."

"This is the same crap we ran into when we took out Saddam Hussein in Iraq. All sorts of religious infighting cropped up. It's the same thing the Soviets found when they gave up in Eastern Europe and let the people have a say. But why Yemen?"

"Well, as you know the regime is teetering and there seems to be a large contingent of al Qaeda jihadists waiting to take over. If Saleh goes we lose our eyes and ability to keep them in check. We think al

Qaeda will step in and take over."

"That all makes sense. It's hard enough to keep the Yemeni's in line these days," Josh said, as he reached for another egg roll.

"With the bad guys in Yemen, right in the Saudi's backyard, it presents a whole host of new problems. If al Qaeda takes over Yemen we'd be fighting a country instead of a bunch of nutcases. And that would mean another war zone we don't need at this point. How many conventional wars can we fight at one time? We're spread pretty thin already."

"That's an understatement, what did our President promise? We'd get out of Iraq and Afghanistan right away, bring home the troops and concentrate on domestic policy. Yeah, right,....now we're adding Yemen to the mix. Pretty soon it will be the Sudan, Egypt, Syria and Libya going nuts."

"Alright, I'm game for a new adventure, but what am I looking for this time?" Josh said, as he pushed his plate away.

"We've been getting reports of a well-coordinated campaign to eradicate the Arab leadership all over the Mid-East. Tunisia has blown up. Mubarak is already out. And look what's happened. Then look at what happened to Gadhafi. We're getting reports that some people don't want to wait for the natural order of things. Supposedly there's a group out there training snipers to take out all these dictators. We figure its al Qaeda trying to reclaim the high ground." Derek let that sink in for a moment.

"So would that be all bad?" Josh asked, intrigued with the idea of taking out all the bad guys at once. "Hell, there were a number of times I wish I still had my old M40A1 with me when I was within shooting distance of many of those bastards."

"Well, it is a pleasant thought until you think about what might replace them throughout the Arab world. Over the years these guys have maintained their power bases with patronage, fear, private armies, and military strong-arm tactics. Once they're taken out of the picture with a bullet to the brain, we might see even greater anarchy. Conventional wisdom suggests al Qaeda might be able to step into such a void and offer the masses a different path based on their crazed interpretation of the Koran."

"Yeah, I can see that," Josh nodded and poured himself another cup of tea. "Ok, so you want me to go investigate Yemen and then what?"

"As I said we think al Qaeda is running this sniper training camp up in the mountains. They're supposedly training recruits to shoot the eyeballs out of hummingbirds on the fly. Supposedly they're spreading out across the Middle East and have a green light to take out various Arab leaders whenever they can."

"So my dark Italian good looks come into play again? Am I supposed to try and get recruited by these assholes, and determine where the target practice is going on? And when I do, what are the rules of engagement? Can I paint the rocks with a big circular target and call in some B-1 bombers from Diego Garcia and call it a day?"

"That might be an option, but we haven't got that far yet. For now we need to get some good field intelligence to determine what is really going on, and who's driving the ship. Up to this point our drones haven't been able to locate the place. We need boots on the ground."

"Yeah, I can do that. So when do I leave?"

"I've got three full sets of documents for you." Derek pulled out a manila envelope from his briefcase and tossed it across the table. "One will get you to Yemen as a Naval Attaché assigned to the Embassy. We'll have a contact there for you to communicate with on a direct basis. That will get you in country. Then you can slip away when you're ready."

Josh opened the seal and saw that one was for Naval Attaché, Commander Joshua Moseby. One was for Mohamar Atari, originally from Libya, and now living in Rome as a cab driver, and the third was Egyptian, also a cab driver, from Cairo.

Josh nodded. He tucked the folder in his jacket and said, "How soon?"

"I can have you on a commercial flight tonight unless you have personal affairs to take care of?" Derek said, knowing what the answer would be.

"I've been a ghost for the past four years, why should I start paying taxes, a mortgage and car payments now? The girls can wait another few months."

"That's what I figured. Your ticket to Rome is for 19:00 tonight. You'll get a couple days there to do some research. I got you a nice hotel close to the Vatican. Then when you're ready, book your flight to Sana'a." He smiled as he handed him the first class ticket on Air France.

"Smart ass, yeah, it should fit fine, if anything, I lost weight in the Sudan."

"Once you're settled in and get a Yemeni refresher course, disappear and see what you can find. Just set up a communication code to keep us posted."

"Done, Thanks for lunch Derek. See you!" Remember, if we ever get anything in Chicago, I'm in." Josh stood up and left without paying. He figured the CIA could pick up the tab. They were sending him into battle.

Rome, Italy.

Josh slept most of the way across the Atlantic. With his military background, where you were taught to sleep any time you could, his work and frequent travels he'd learned how to sleep almost instantly whenever he needed to, recognizing there could be long stretches when no sleep would be available.

The Air France flight 927 landed on time at Leonardo da Vinci–Fuimicino Airport and with his military credentials he passed through customs without a problem. Knowing Rome well, he hailed a cab and threw his gear in the trunk and climbed in. He also knew how Italian cab drivers drove, challenging the roadway like it was a personal racetrack, so he insisted on finding a cab with seat belts in the back. He braced himself for the white knuckled 19-mile trip into the city and his driver did not disappoint him. Driving on Hwy A-91 the driver was weaving in and out of traffic and using the centerline as if it was his own personal pathway to the ancient city. He constantly honked his horn as if that would make things right. This self-styled Indy driver made fast work of the distance perhaps hoping he would be that much closer to a lunch plate of spaghetti after this American fare.

The driver knew where he was going and climbed the hills to the Intercontinental Hotel just a few miles away from and overlooking the Vatican. As Josh exited his motorized chariot he looked at the

Tower of St. Peter's Basilica rising above Rome and blessed himself for having survived the drive.

He checked in and found himself in a nice suite overlooking the city. Not one to bask in the rooms finery or the distant view of the Vatican gardens, he quickly changed into some Libyan cab driver street clothes, grabbed his new identity and walked out the door. He walked down the hall finding the back stairway without drawing any attention, and took it to the ground floor. He walked out a service exit and away from the hotel towards some restaurants at the end of the block.

Wandering down the street he found what he was looking for, a taxi stand with four vehicles waiting for a fare from the lunch crowd. He walked up to the last cabbie in the queue and thought he looked Arab so he stuck his head in the passenger window and asked in Arabic if he could bum a cigarette. The older driver was half asleep and seemed startled for a moment but recognized the dialect and started pulling a smoke out of his pack. He invited the stranger to climb in the front seat. Doing so, Josh thanked the driver for his hospitality and took a deep drag and sighed as if he had the entire world on his shoulders.

"Brother, you are Libyan, no?" the driver said to his new acquaintance.

"Aye, and I thank you for the smoke. I have run out of money and there are no jobs to be found, even washing dishes."

The old driver understood as he too had had a difficult time first finding work when he had come over on one of the boats many years ago. "It will get better my friend. What is it that you do?"

"I have been a driver as you are, but back in Tripoli, before coming north. With all the unrest that goes on at home now I cannot care for my family, so I come to make money and send it back to them."

"I understand, I was from Benghazi before coming here many

years ago. Where are you from, what village?"

"I am from Gadhafi's home town of Sirte, on the Gulf of Sidra. I was drafted for his personal military unit and was made a part of his Revolutionary Guard. While that lasted it was good pay and my family was well taken care of. Now I am too old for that business. They let me go. It is a young man's game, the war business."

The driver listened attentively. The front cab in the line picked up a fare and all three taxis moved forward. The driver again turned off the engine to save fuel. "So what was that like? I have heard many stories of the Colonel's exploits. I have heard he likes the Scandanavian women bodyguards with the big breasts?"

"They were big mean women that could kick a man's ass, and often did so on Gadhafi's order, just to amuse him." He used his hands to emphasize the big breasts of these women and got a hearty laugh from his new friend.

"No, I was a trained marksman and had little to do other than practice. There was a lot of sword rattling by the Leader but often we had no one to actually fight except the insurgents in the south desert. It was boring work for the most part, but I was good at what I did. Now I must wash dishes to make a living for my family."

The driver looked at his new seatmate and sized him up. "Perhaps I can find you some work my friend, in our trade, if you are willing to work. Or perhaps even in that war business you talked about."

"That would be good, as I would like to pay you back for the cigarette." Josh said as he smiled at the driver. He looked out the window and considered what had just been said. The driver's comments were leading and it might be worth the time to explore what he meant by this war business comment. His travel to Yemen might have to take a back seat for a few days. The cab driver started his vehicle and pulled away from the curb without waiting for a fare. He had found a new recruit for the cause.

West of Tripoli, Libya

About 45 kilometers west of the capital of Libya the flat coastal lands covered in sand started rising into the mountains. The double-lane blacktop roadway narrowed down to a single lane as it approached the town of Zuwarah.

Just outside of town, a small group of Libyan Berber rebels from the western mountains sat in a darkened room to minimize the sweltering heat of the day. They talked about the next incursion they hoped to make. It would be on one of Gadhafi's secret munitions dumps squirreled away at a remote air force base about 50 kilometers south on the desert road to Jadu. The rebels discussed how they could organize a covert attack on the remote site late at night and overpower the bored troops who were more interested in staying in air-conditioned barracks than walking perimeter fence lines.

The consensus was to move forward because such weapons would command hard currency on the black market and would help to fund the insurgency. Gadhafi was going down. It was just a matter of time. The people of Libya had enough of the crazed dictator. A civil war was brewing.

As night fell the small group of rebels took their few weapons and drove out of town towards Jadu in a number of pickup trucks. There was no one on the road at that late hour and they drove with their headlights out using the half moonlight to guide them. When the road split, they took the southern spur and drove on over an even rougher road towards the munitions arsenal.

Two miles from the small base they pulled off the rutted dirt road and hid their vehicles behind a large sand hill. The ragtag group of rebels walked the rest of the way to the outer perimeter fence about 2:00 am. Using a bolt cutter they made a few cuts to the chain link barbed wire fencing, just enough for each soldier to slip under. The group silently made their way the last 300 meters crawling on their bellies looking for signs of sentries, or any life at all. They saw none.

Creeping up to a group of squat one-story buildings the Berber rebels spread out and each took a building to enter. Using stealth and the element of surprise they eased into each building without a sound. Instead of using their guns, they silently dispatched each guard in their sleep using their tribal knives. The arsenal had been taken without a shot.

Once all the guards were dealt with a short message was sent to the pickup trucks in the desert and they were brought forward to the compound. Presuming no 'under attack' message had been sent out to the nearby Nafa Air base down the road, they had some time before Gadhafi's people might come looking.

The leader had his men spread out to gather all the weapons they could carry. They broke into the locked armament vaults and started gathering hundreds of AK-47, some still in crates. They filled up the five vehicles quickly and realized they had a major cache of weapons. One of the rebels found a stake truck parked behind one of the buildings and hot-wired it to assist with the transportation effort.

The rebel leader started searching every room for other intelligence and stumbled onto a major find in an unlocked office completely separate from the weapons arsenal. Stacked neatly in a corner, covered by tarps, he discovered a number of crates filled with weapons that he had seen pictures of and had heard about. They were Stinger missiles, in military vernacular, MANPADS, Man Portable

Air Defense Systems. He did not know how they actually worked but he knew they were deadly and that he had made a major discovery.

Quickly realizing these weapons were even more valuable than the AK-47s, he called his men together and they started hauling out the crates to the four vehicles. He made them pull off some of the small weapons and load the missiles first. Then he allowed the other weapons to be stacked on top of the crates as best they could.

In another ten minutes the trucks were racing through the gate and into the night with a massive load of weapons. The insurrection had just taken a quantum leap!

Rome, Italy

Looking out the window of the cab as they passed into the Arab slums of Rome Josh felt somewhat uneasy being driven into the unknown. But he also had an inkling that this would go well and might assist in his immersion into the Arab terrorist underground movement. He remained calm and ran over his cover story to get it clear in his head. His driver was not talking as he drove so Josh was able to gather his thoughts.

The cab driver moved further into the Arab slums with its narrow streets and alleys. He knew where he was going. The clustered overlapping buildings and apartments sandwiched together had seen better days. The cab turned into a dark alley that was covered with tarps and blankets and went another quarter block before turning into a fenced courtyard area at the back of a two-story sandstone building. Outside stairs led up to a flat roof. He followed his new friend up the stone staircase and found himself in front of three robed men sitting at a table on four pillows. They were drinking dark aromatic coffee that he could smell from a distance.

One man motioned for the new arrivals to sit, and they approached the table. The host offered coffee and Josh accepted asking if he could have it black in the Libyan manner. He was on stage now and had a part to play.

Pleasantries were exchanged and Josh could see that they were gently trying to explore his background without actually asking direct questions. They made inquiries of his past in Libya and he was able to respond in Arabic with a Libyan accent. He felt he was being tested and offered good information and confident knowledge about the country and Gadhafi's dictatorship. He could see that they were becoming more comfortable with him so he let it slip that he had been a sniper in the Revolutionary Guard. This got their attention and all pretense of courtesy disappeared, as they wanted to know everything that he had been involved with. They were obviously interested in his background. He asked for a second cup of the bitter black coffee and settled in for the continued grilling.

Twenty minutes later he felt confident he was being welcomed by this group of elders. He also recognized he was being recruited to join them. They asked if he could demonstrate his ability with a rifle and Josh shrugged and looked around as if to say where and when. He presumed they didn't mean here because they were still on a roof- top in the city of Rome.

But a rifle was brought forward and presented to him. They suggested that he take a shot at a wooden electric pole that was on the roof of a building about 50 yards away. While Josh examined the long gun to determine if he could make such a shot with an unproven weapon, a minion was dispatched to the other roof to set up a target and monitor the spectacle. Once the man was on the roof a couple alleys over Josh was instructed to hit the pole. He was told he would only get one shot because they were in the city. One rifle shot would draw no attention, while multiple shots would draw the local authorities.

Josh set up a firing position using the back of a table and then noticed two plastic water bottles were sitting on an adjacent metal table. He asked if he could have some water and they brought him a bottle.

He took a swig and then poured the remainder onto the flat tile roof. Without asking, he twisted the narrow plastic bottle onto the end of the rifle barrel and sighted down the line at the pole out about fifty yards. He noted that there was no wind to speak of and that the rifle looked as if it had been well taken care of. Taking a breath and then exhaling, he gently squeezed the trigger. The rifle barked, but there was no sharp crack of the controlled explosion. Instead, a greatly muffled sound emitted from the rifle caused by the silencer effect of the plastic bottle. It was a noise that could have been a car back firing.

The Arabs and the cab driver jumped back at the splintering plastic, but then looked across the roofs towards the young man spotting on the other end. Josh took one quick look, set down the rifle and sat back down on his pillow. He was satisfied he had hit the mark.

The young man on the roof of the other building examined the pole and ran his hand over it until he came to the splinter that was dead center in the pole just about five feet off the ground. The smashed bullet was wedged tightly into the entry hole. He turned and signaled that the bullet had met its intended victim.

The Arabs jaws dropped and they turned and looked at Josh for a moment. Then the leader walked over to the side table with the other plastic bottle of water. He drank the last of the water and asked for a second shot. He said the first shot had been quiet enough that no one would have taken notice. He wanted to see more.

Josh was asked to hit the same pole but this time standing and not using a rifle support to steady his shot. Josh stood up accepting the challenge and the makeshift silencer. Why not he thought. I'm not sure where this is going but I can definitely hit the damn pole. He went through his normal sighting routine. The shot was somewhat difficult because the bottle on the end of the barrel prevented direct line of sight, but he adjusted. He asked whether the next shot should be above or below the first and was told to put it a foot higher on the pole.

He steadied himself knowing that this was the ultimate test. He inhaled and exhaled, inhaled and gently caressed the trigger. Again the bottle exploded with more of a swish and pop. Everyone stood there watching the young man three alleys over. He ran to the pole and quickly signaled that the second shot had indeed hit the mark.

Josh was in, but in to what? He waited to find out if this would take him off mission or actually help him.

The three Arabs sat down and congratulated Josh on his fine shooting. They admitted they were impressed with the quality. And they told him they had a job for him. Would he be willing to train Arab snipers how to shoot like he could shoot? In Yemen?

"I actually did that kind of shooting at much greater distances in the Guard. We used to use the water bottles just to lessen the sound, make it more interesting and a bit of a challenge." Josh said in Arabic.

"We are impressed brother and we believe that we can find you good work with such skills. We would need you to leave Rome even though you have just got here, and go to a faraway place, and I am sorry to say to the mountains and deserts again. We will need your skills in Yemen."

Josh tried hard not to react although he thought they might have seen a smile. But he recovered instantaneously and asked what he would be doing for the cause.

"Now that the Americans have killed Osama bin Laden we are trying to establish a new front. We are training snipers to assist us in moving forward. While I am doubtful that you need sniper training I think you could be a big help in training our recruits. We have a camp in Yemen that has already graduated a class of twelve snipers and these terrorists are spreading out to do what they do best. You will help train and become a part of the second class."

Josh was beside himself but concealed it. "From one desert to another, as long as I am fed and paid for my skills, I can be of service. I suspect driving a cab in Rome is probably more dangerous to my health than being in the Mountains of Yemen."

His cab driver friend laughed out loud and agreed that he was making the better decision.

Marrakech, Morocco

Mahoud Asiri had graduated from the desert sniper course and had been given his first assignment. He had flown into Marrakech the day before on Italia Airlines on a direct flight from Rome. His passport said he was Italian. He was to be a student on holiday traveling to see the exotic sights of the fabled trade routes and the famous spice markets.

It was his first time in the ancient city and he was about to meet his contact. Booked into a five star hotel, the Royal Mansour, he was astounded by the luxury of the establishment. It was very different from his misery in the desert. The place was fit for a king, not a lowly assassin. He found out that the hotel was actually built by King Mohammed VI, the current reigning Monarch of Morocco. He had commissioned the showplace utilizing 1,200 master craftsmen laboring in the desert. The Hotel was more a private resort than a standard hotel. Within the walls and behind a 2.5 ton bronze door were 53 traditional Moroccan style three-story riads. These individual homes offered privacy with rooftop plunge pools to ward off the desert heat, enclosed-courtyards and butler service for each of its guests.

Mahoud settled in to wait for his contact to arrive and thought this could be a lifestyle he could get used to. It was certainly better than the horrible heat of the desert.

He lounged by his private pool on the roof and waited. Out of nowhere a neatly appointed butler appeared with an iced tea drink. He quietly approached and bowed presenting the beverage. Accepting the drink Mahoud turned back to view the sunset settling in the mountains.

But the butler did not turn and leave. Instead he pulled up another chair close to Mahoud and gave a password that announced he was the contact. The assassin expressed surprise at this turn of events.

The butler explained he was in the employ of al Qaeda and had taken this position because it afforded him access to the highest circles and guests of all sorts. As a butler he could come and go as needed to meet his contacts without suspicion. The 53 riad suites were all interconnected with employee service tunnels to serve all of the guests staying at the hotel.

He went to his employee service door and pulled out a backpack that he presented to Mahoud.

"I was told that you would need this backpack and would need Spanish money for your travel. Other than that I have no knowledge of your itinerary. Please enjoy our hospitality and if I can offer you any service please ask."

With that he bowed, and slowly backpedaled towards the service door, and then disappeared.

Mahoud looked about and noted no one could see him from any of the other verandas. He opened the backpack carefully noting that it contained a sniper rifle that was extraordinarily disguised to look like the metal frame of a backpack. In and around this disguised framework he would be able to pack his clothes and look like an innocent student tourist from Italy.

The following day the newly appointed terrorist left the hotel and walked through the labyrinthine Medina, or the Kasbah, as most people called it. It was lined with market stalls selling food, spices and linens. He walked with purpose towards the central plaza and the bus terminal ignoring the aggressive sales people in the stalls.

Using his new student identity he booked passage on a tourist bus that would take him east and north to Rabat and then to the city-state of Ceuta on the northern tip of Africa. This destination city was directly across from Gibraltar and the continent of Europe.

The bus drove into the Atlas Mountains and the Ounila Valley with its picturesque villages, oasis pastures and cool mountain breezes. Heading north the bus entered Fes, once one of four imperial cities in Morocco dating back to the 12th Century. He tried to read a travel book on the area but found it did not do the sights justice. Instead he looked out the window.

Beyond Fes, the bus headed straight north through mountains and valleys before entering Ceuta, an autonomous city of Spain, situated on the North African Coast. This historic trading city had been a volatile battle zone dating back to Roman times, first settled by Carthaginians, then the Romans, Vandals, Visigoths, and finally as an outpost of the Byzantine Empire. Muslims had claimed this peninsula landmass since 700 AD and used its strategic passage to Europe throughout the Holy Wars. In current times it had become an international city with major populations of Christians, and Muslims, mostly Berbers, living side by side. There were also small minorities of Jews and Hindu's to further internationalize the city. It has always been an international trading port because of its importance at the entrance to the Mediterranean through the Strait of Gibraltar.

Mahoud entered this international city-state without problem showing his student ID and immediately went to the port to book passage to Gibraltar. He bought a ticket for a ferry departing the next morning. Walking over to the Mediterranean Marine Park, which surrounded three manmade lakes, he booked a room at a small Ceuta Hotel and settled in for the night. This resort area had swimming pools, nightlife, a casino and restaurants and he enjoyed his evening before his actual mission started.

Early the next morning he checked out of his less extravagant room and walked to the harbor a few blocks away to find his ferry boat. There was minimal boarding security for the hourly ferries, checking passports and verifying that a ticket had been purchased. Even though it was early the ferry was relatively full and he blended in as a tourist, taking photos and enjoying the sights as he cruised across one of the most congested sea routes in the world. From the boat he could see ships lining up and passing through the Strait of Gibraltar as far as the eye could see. It had been this way for centuries, long before Christopher Columbus and even Hannibal's armies had crossed this passage on their way to Italy.

Once he arrived in British Gibraltar the security seemed to ramp up. He was now on European soil and the Europeans paid more attention to overall security. But as a tourist with a backpack he was mostly ignored as he stood in line taking photographs of the Rock of Gibraltar looming almost above them. He blended in with the thousands of other backpackers that would pass through this customs checkpoint each year. He cleared customs without a second glance and headed for a nondescript hotel he had found online out on the peninsula close to the airport.

Tunis, Tunisia

The truckloads of strategic missiles were driven out of western Libya before the Army knew anything about the attack at the mountainside munitions dump. When the next shift of soldiers drove up to the base, they found the devastation to be complete and radioed in the news. By the time the military arrived at the arsenal, the Berber pickup trucks were racing across the border to Tunisia and heading north on the P-19 Highway towards the Port of Tunis.

The trucks did not drive together but stretched out over two miles as they headed north. The vehicles arrived in Tunis about midday and made their way through the vast city to the La Goulette Warehouse District next to the deep-water Port of Tunis. Once the trucks backed into the loading dock, the missiles and other weapons were off loaded in a rundown waterfront warehouse just a few hundred feet from one of the industrial piers. The delivery trucks immediately made the return trip south towards the Libyan border where they were abandoned and would be found by their Libyan pursuers.

Covert arrangements to sell the weapons started immediately, with calls put out to known middlemen representing all sorts of black market arms dealers. In no time a number of bidders had been lined up, interested in what was being offered for sale. One middle-eastern representative of al Qaeda was especially interested in the stinger missiles. It had been his primary objective to ferret out these air-to-ground missile systems he knew Gadhafi had buried in his desert arsenals. He advised the seller that price was no object, and that he needed the complete cache of missiles launchers, immediately.

The al Qaeda operative called his superiors with the news. They did not hesitate in wiring money to a bank in Tunis the same day. The transaction was to be paid for in Euros early the following morning and the weaponry was again picked up from the warehouse before the other arms dealers even showed up for the auction. With two enclosed panel trucks and four armed guards, the hand-held missile systems were quickly driven across town away from the waterfront. Now that al Qaeda had purchased this cache of weapons they would need to decide what to do with them.

British Gibraltar

British Gibraltar is a unique place because it was built on a huge rock that spirals into the sky. The Straits of Gibraltar is a strategic waterway, a narrow passage of international water between the Atlantic Ocean and the Mediterranean Sea. All Mediterranean traffic passes through this pinch point between Europe and Africa. The land mass is rugged rock with mountains rising almost directly out of the sea. The usable land mass is minimal with 90 percent of it covered by the Rock. The city at the rock's base utilizes every square inch of flat land. Everything is tightly crammed into this narrow sprit of peninsula, even the airport.

The Gibraltar Airport crosses the narrow peninsula at ninety degrees from east to west through a natural valley between two towering peaks. It has but a single jet runway, half of which is built on landfill jutting out into the Mediterranean. To complicate matters most of the city of Gibraltar is situated on the southern side of the airport connected by a single roadway that crosses right over the very active runway. Winston Churchill Avenue is six-lanes wide and all commerce has to use the road to get from one part of town to the other side. When planes are arriving or departing all street traffic is stopped behind large barricades with lights, much like at a railroad crossing. All traffic stops while the planes land or takeoff, and when clear, cars and pedestrians cross the active runway in either direction.

It is a sight to see with people getting out of their vehicles, watching and waving at the planes arriving and departing.

Mahoud was up early and carefully sanitized his small hotel room of every trace of himself. He walked the five blocks to the center of town and then joined a group of tourists who were waiting at the airport barricade for a plane to land on the runway that split the city in two. When the plane roared past landing to the east, he thought, as did the others waiting, that they would be able to cross. But the barricade did not rise. On the west end of the runway another plane was spooling up its engines from an idle and was about to take off once the first plane cleared to an approach apron. The terrorist shifted his backpack and continued to wait with the tourists.

A few minutes later the Air Morocco jet went screaming by and the barricades were raised. Traffic and pedestrians from both sides streamed across the runway with purpose so they would not have to wait for any other plane interruptions. Mahoud Asiri joined the crowd. The pavement was well marked separating the pedestrians and cars and trucks from each other, but it was still unnerving to be walking across a major aircraft runway.

Staying on Winston Churchill Drive he walked on towards the border between British Gibraltar and Spain, a distance of perhaps 500 meters. The border checkpoint loomed ahead. The metal fence was eight feet high and strung along concrete posts with concertina wire strung along the top. Multiple car and pedestrian gates handled the ebb and flow of travelers crossing into Spain. He knew where he was going and concentrated on looking like the tourist he was supposed to be. As before he was quickly scrutinized and given a two-question interview by a red jacketed security agent and quickly waved through the security gate.

Now in Spain he looked to his left and identified a five-story building literally sitting on the international border. In fact he already knew that one edge of the building was actually across the fence line. Walking past a British red telephone box outside the front door of the building he entered and walked to a side stairwell without drawing anyone's attention. He climbed the five flights of stairs without effort and slowly opened the door to see if anyone was in the hallway. It was empty.

Knowing about an empty office space in the corner of the building he quickly picked the lock and let himself in and then locked the door again. Walking halfway to the window, but not so close as to be seen, he scanned the vista of the entire Gibraltar Airport. From this vantage point he could see the entire length of the single runway in both directions, and the entire terminal building along with the planes parked on the tarmac.

Looking around he gathered a number of tables that would become his shooting platform. He stacked two of them somewhat in the middle of the room about five feet from the large plate glass window. Then he covered the stacked tables with a white painter's drop cloth. As he stood behind the tables this would afford him greater cover from anyone looking into the buildings windows.

Using the first table as an assembly area he began unpacking his weapon. It was a Chinese JS 7.62 mm bolt-action rifle just like the one he had practiced with in Yemen. He carefully examined his 7.62mm NATO rounds that had been sewn into the metal framework of his backpack. He chose three cartridges that looked perfect and loaded his magazine. Unfolding the stock and mounting the telescopic scope on top of the receiver, he placed the weapon on the top table and started his sighting efforts at the airport across the street.

He slowly scanned the area and made mental notes about what he was seeing. Another plane had just landed and was taxiing into the terminal. He followed the plane to the end of the runway and then back to the terminal. He patiently waited while the plane spooled down and preparations were made to pop the doors. When the boarding ladder truck was driven up, he zeroed in his sight on the doorframe of the plane and watched as passengers started exiting the craft. With his scope he felt that he could almost touch their heads even though he was about 400 hundred meters away. He became comfortable looking at faces and then mentally pulling the trigger. About forty passengers exited and walked down the stairs entering the terminal building. He took the rifle down to the lower table and pulled up a chair.

Reaching for his wallet he pulled out some photos of his girlfriend, which he did not have, and a photo of his parents standing together. The photo was actually a photo of his target that would be flying into Gibraltar in the next hour. He stared at it to make sure the image was clearly in his mind and he would recognize the man without fail, the man he was about to kill. The hour passed slowly.

Taking out a clean cloth he started wiping down every spot that he may have touched in stacking the tables, pulling up the chair and leaning against the door. He would need to depart fast after the shot because the broken glass would bring the authorities quickly. He had an escape already planned and it would take him only a minute to vacate the building.

At 11:30 am a Saudi Airlines 737 jet landed from west to east and rolled out to the end of the runway jutting into the Mediterranean. It slowly taxied back towards the terminal. Mahoud was up and tracking the plane's movement every step of the way. Once it crossed into the terminal area, the ground personnel started to waive the plane into a corner of the airport that would not offer him the shot he had planned. He scrambled to see if he could get the angle by moving both tables towards the window. As he started to push the tables with a screeching noise across the concrete floor, he noticed the plane had stopped and looked as if it did not know where it was supposed to be going. Then the shooter noticed two black limousines driving onto the tarmac and heading for where he had first expected the plane to dock. He watched as the ground crew started waiving the plane back in that direction. Mahoud relaxed for a moment but then realized he had moved his sniper perch towards the windows at least a foot or two. He frantically started pulling them back so his shot would perform as he had expected. Luckily his chair was in the same position it had been before the table moved. He pulled the table one more time and felt it was where he had started.

Grabbing his rifle he started sighting in on the plane as it stopped moving. The ground truck with the attached stairwell immediately pulled up and a few dignitaries and security men congregated around the base of the stairs.

The door of the plane was pushed out from the fuselage and turned backwards as the stair platform nestled against the plane. Mahoud focused his rifle and adjusted the scope on the doorframe. A man poked his head out of the door and quickly scanned the area. Then he disappeared back into the plane. It had to be one of the Sheik's bodyguards assessing the situation. He had verified security was in place and the limousines were at the base of the stairs.

A number of personnel exited the craft one at a time in a slow and methodical order. As each face appeared the sniper had time to settle in on the face features and determine it was not his target, and wait for the next person. Then two black suited passengers came out both with earpieces hanging from their ears that disappeared into their jackets. They each took up a position on the raised platform ready to bracket Crown Prince Ahmed – Nayef, of the House of Saud.

Mahoud thought the bracketing was a good way to announce the VIP entrance, his quarry. He steadied his rifle and took a couple of full breaths like he had been taught.

The next person out of the hatch was a man in flowing robes and a colorful ornamental headdress. He looked down at the small crowd gathered at the base of the stairs and offered a wave of his hand.

The terrorist zeroed in and scanned the face and recognized his so-called 'father' just like the photo in his wallet. Only it wasn't his father, it was his target. He settled the crosshairs on the man's forehead just below the headdress, and made the mental adjustment to factor in the single paned window five feet in front of him. He knew the trajectory would be off slightly but he had learned how to shoot through glass and still hit his target, even at greater distances.

It was time. He took his last calming breath and squeezed the trigger as if caressing a baby. The window in front of him shattered in a blast of splintering glass as the bullet passed through and went down range. The bits of glass plunged to the street below. Without waiting to see if his target had caught the bullet, he worked the action loading a second cartridge and made another mental adjustment noting the absence of the glass and that he was shooting straight away. As he began to zero in again on his quarry's face, he saw that look of shock when someone did not comprehend what was happening. The Sheik's hand shot up to his neck as blood spurted and gurgled out in big globs all over his white robes.

Mahoud knew a neck shot could mean many things so he sent another bullet screaming down range as the man started to collapse. This round caught the man in the back of the shoulder as he was falling to the platform. It passed through his right shoulder blade down through the body piercing the heart. Both security guards drew their weapons and searched for a target to no avail. No one had yet realized the two shots had come from over 400 meters away outside the airport perimeter.

The sniper did not savor, nor gloat over his kill shot. He did not watch the commotion and fear that erupted on the stair platform. He was already packing his weapon. In less than a minute his weapon was broken down and stored in the backpack. At the door he checked for anyone in the hall, silently stepped out, and relocked the door. Passing a small towel over the handle he turned and walked down the hall with his backpack casually thrown over his shoulder. He took the elevator to the second floor rather than the first floor lobby area, and then walked down the back stairwell.

With a large reflex camera hanging around his neck he stepped out into the sunshine, turned left and walked away from the building and the airport. He knew a public beach and a yacht club was just a block and a half to the west. He stopped at the breakwater wall and took a couple photos of the many boats in the harbor and the people who were enjoying the midday sun. Then he casually strolled down to the beach and found a spot between two families with small children. He dropped his pack on the sand and took off his shirt and shorts draping them casually over his gun bag. In swimming trunks he walked to the water's edge and then turned around to take a photo of the beach from the water. He was actually scanning to see if anyone had followed him, or paid any attention to his beach arrival. He scanned and saw that no one was looking his way. He took some more photos of the beach as a keepsake. In the distance he could hear a number of police klaxons wailing as they rushed to the airport.

Walking out of the water, he kicked sand up as he went back to his beach spot. He picked up a beach ball that rolled to his feet and threw it back to the kids playing nearby. He placed his camera, which had all sorts of tourist photos recorded on the drive, inside the flap of his bag. Then he raced back into the warm surf to cool off, and more importantly, to wash off any gunshot residue that might be on his arms and face. After cooling off in the warm surf for ten minutes, he returned to the beach, stretched out in the sun to feel the burn, and started reading a history book about Spain and Gibraltar. Much of it had to do with Islam and the Moors coming across Gibraltar centuries earlier. He had his tourist alibi set.

Rome to Sana'a, Yemen

Josh was surprised at how quickly they organized the flights necessary to move him from Italy to Yemen. They were obviously in a hurry. He hardly had time to disappear for a couple of hours. Knowing the city of Rome he slipped away casually walking through a number of tourist areas. He knew he was not being followed. He returned to his room. He left a coded message for his handler advising he had made contact and was on his way to Yemen. He packed his other identities, clothes and uniform, knowing they would be cared for and available in case he needed them again. Then he left the hotel going off the grid.

He met his new friend, the cab driver, who took him to the airport for a scheduled flight to Cairo. It was an uneventful flight but he clearly felt that he was being monitored the entire way as they crossed over the Mediterranean Sea. Perhaps, it was because he had disappeared for a few hours earlier in the day. He settled in and enjoyed the tea service.

He was met and escorted out of Cairo's International Airport and was driven back to the Mediterranean coast and Alexandria's airport for the next flight. It left on time and took him over the Red Sea to Sana'a, the capital of Yemen. He had been there before but he did not let on. He presumed he was still being followed so he gave no one any cause for concern.

Disembarking, he gathered his worn carpeted satchel in baggage claim and looked around. Within a minute a bearded man in well-worn street clothes approached and used his Libyan name so he knew he had the right man. Without further discussion he was escorted to an old black Mercedes at the curb. He was encouraged to sit in front with the driver and could see there were already two men in the back seat.

"Welcome to Yemen, Mohamar Atari. We have heard that you bring us special skills that we can utilize. Please tell us of your background with the Colonel in Libya."

Josh / Mohamar half-turned his head and offered a greeting in Arabic. He did not stare at the two travelers; rather he sized them up as muscle, not the brains of this outfit. He also glanced at the driver and noticed the outline of a pistol stuck in his loose shirt. He presumed that at least one of the men in the back had a gun trained on him as well.

"I am a just cab driver from Tripoli," he said. "I looked for work in Rome, but now I am here. I am told you have work for me."

"Yes, we know about the taxi driving. We are more interested in your military service. We have been told you can shoot the eyes out of Jewish pigs. Tell us where you learned such things?"

Josh had studied his Libyan documents well and he knew his layered background story backward and forward, but he didn't want to be forthcoming. He would let them draw it out of him. He had studied detailed maps all the way across the Atlantic Ocean and he was confident that he could give them what they were asking about. In his undercover work he had posed as a Libyan before. He knew the language, the country and its customs quite well. With his dark complexion he could pass easily for a Mediterranean type and he was confident with his assumed persona.

He figured they already knew who he was so he recounted his work in the Republican Guard. They were mostly interested in the training he had received as a sharpshooter, so he slowly told them all the details as he had before.

"But tell us about Gadhafi's women, those Scandinavian Amazons that protect him?"

Mohamar wasn't surprised with the question. It seems everyone in the Middle East must have heard about these tall blond women security guards that Gadhafi had in his employ. Luckily he knew all about them as well, and rolled out a juicy story from the viewpoint of a Republican Guard soldier observing them from afar, with much desire and envy. That was what they really wanted to hear from him. He gave them mouth-watering descriptions of the blond amazons and filled their brains with detailed images that violated every rule of Islam. They ate it up for over an hour of driving. Eventually that line of questioning died down as they drove south on rutted two-lane highways towards the port city of Aden on the Arabian Gulf coast.

Every now and then the lone vehicle would come upon a military checkpoint, but the car was always waved through without fanfare, as if dignitaries were aboard. That was troubling to Josh as this was the established Yemeni military, not al Qaeda.

After a couple of hours, but before getting to Aden, the car turned and headed east into Abyan Province, long known to be an al Qaeda stronghold. Hours later near Shiban, the driver turned off the highway and the vehicle labored to carry them over dusty trails and up a number of wadi's, the dry riverbeds heading into the mountains. They eventually arrived at a desert encampment with surrounding cliffs on all sides.

As the car pulled to a stop, they were warmly greeted by a number of western looking young men who had western clothes on their bodies. Standing in the background was a bearded thin man in his 40's, dressed in flowing desert robes. He had gold wire rim glasses perched on his nose. He looked more like a college professor from

Cairo University than a known terrorist. He also looked as if he did not want to be out in the desert sun.

Josh / Mohamar sucked in his breath but was careful not to let on that he knew whom he was staring at. It was Anwar al-Awlaki, a U.S Muslim cleric who was about as high up in the al Qaeda organization as someone could get. Josh was inwardly excited but couldn't show his pleasure at what he was seeing. He may have stumbled into a two for the price of one mission. He knew that the President of the United States had already authorized the capture or killing of this terrorist thought to be responsible for a string of terrorist acts.

The young men welcomed him with little caution. Josh felt his shooter's reputation from Rome must have preceded him. He was encouraged to join them in a tent set up under a large rock outcropping. Inside he shared in food and water sitting on hand made carpets stretched into the corners of the tent to minimize the sand grit invading the meal. Awlaki joined them but stood back and said nothing drawing no attention. Josh ignored the terrorist, although he wanted to wrestle for one of the bodyguard's weapons and blow the man's brains out.

After a light meal with rich bitter coffee, the men all stood and went outside into the late afternoon sun. Others in camp started gathering around the newcomer. A tall man, with a sunbaked, weathered look from being in the desert sun all his life, stepped forward and presented Josh with a rifle. He then led the growing group over to what served as a shooting range in the middle of the desert.

Josh estimated the range to be one hundred yards with just a glance. The man who was obviously a leader asked him to demonstrate his craft as a trained shooter. He examined the rifle and noted that again it was well taken care of and the sights seemed to be well aligned. The weapon was of Chinese manufacture. He had fired such weapons before but he was not that confident in them. He examined the action noting it was well maintained and had not been abused. He decided he could do this. Looking to his host, he asked matter-of-factly.

"What would you like me to shoot at? How would you like me to shoot, standing, sitting, or lying on the ground?"

The instructor handed him a single cartridge and pointed at the targets. He encouraged him to sight in his weapon. Josh was grateful they at least would allow him to do that.

Without asking he sat down in the dirt and took a shooters stance, folding one leg under him and using his knees and elbows to balance and steady his shot. He knew this to be a typical sniper's stance that was taught by the Libyans. Taking the single cartridge he loaded the weapon and made sure he kept the rifle pointed downrange. The last thing he needed was for some trigger-happy yahoo to put a bullet in the back of his head.

He sighted downrange and made some adjustments before slowly squeezing off his shot. The retort echoed off the cliffs and hills surrounding them. Near the target area a bearded man in camouflage tunic tentatively stepped out from behind a large boulder and went over to the target. It looked like he didn't want to be there. He examined the target and placed his hand over the bullet hole and then turned and signaled with his hand to body that the torso target had taken the round in the upper center chest. It looked as if it would have been a potential kill shot. Without waiting to be told, he then quickly ducked behind the boulder where he had been hiding, expecting another round.

Josh was handed another single round, this time by the head instructor, Adnan Menaj. Without a word he loaded his weapon to repeat the process. This time he adjusted his aim based upon where he had hit the target on his first shot. Before settling in to steady his shot he looked up at his host and tapped his left chest signaling he would aim for the heart. Breathing in and out he gently squeezed the trigger. The bullet exploded from the barrel and a half second later a puff of smoke could be seen rising from the target. He had fired true and the spotter came out from behind the rock, trotted over to the target and placed his hand on his heart.

"I'm impressed, Mohamar," Adnan Menaj stated. "That is indeed good shooting. You have adjusted to the first shot well. Do it again, please?

Josh stood up and accepted the cartridge. He chambered the round and with his hand signaled he would go for a head shot this time by tapping his forehead. He half-turned and spread his legs taking a stable stance. Leaning into the shot he rolled his arm through the sling for stability and settled on his target. He gently squeezed off the round. Looking down his sight he could see that he caught the target in what would have been the brow area between the eyes.

The terrorists were equally impressed and they showed him so by cackling their appreciation. Josh looked at the group and off to the side saw Anwar al Awlaki signal to the instructor. The man brought Josh a magazine with five rounds in it. A new target was being placed downrange, and the man placing the target moved far to the left to get out of the line of sight.

Josh was asked to fire all five rounds at the target as fast as he could. Josh decided he would shoot from top to bottom and pointed to his body where he would try to place each shot. The surrounding men all smiled, and then grimaced as he pointed out his last shot location. Sighting his Chinese rifle, he sent the first round into the forehead of the new target as he said he would. The second shot caught the unfortunate target in the throat as predicted, the next in the heart, and the fourth was a gut shot to the middle of the torso. Finally, he adjusted and put the last a shot right in the center of the groin. Everyone watching groaned again and a few men grabbed their genitals.

"Adnan, I think we have found our second instructor," Anwar al-Awlaki said as he stepped forward to pat Mohamar on the shoulder.

Josh privately shuttered at the touch and gave serious thought to swinging the weapon into the terrorist's face. "We can now train our people faster and put more teams out there to stir the Arab world. Come my friend we have much to talk about."

Josh was steered towards a private tent off to the side. He was still considering killing Awlaki right on the spot but three other men with weapons followed them including Adnan Menaj, the instructor.

Inside the tent they all sat down and talked for an hour about what was being done in the desert. They explained that they were training terrorists to go after any and all Arab leaders, key personnel in the dictator armies and anyone who would get in their way. Josh found out they had already dispatched one class of snipers into the field and they were very interested in putting out additional shooters as fast as they could be taught how to make the kill shot. As they were talking Josh noticed a satellite phone in the corner that had a blanket haphazardly thrown over it. He would need that phone to get a message out.

Aden, Yemen

Mahoud had executed two more Arab leaders since Gibraltar, one in Syria, and most recently in Karachi, Pakistan. He'd been lucky to escape with his life in Karachi because the ISI in Pakistan was quick to descend on the site. He had to hide on a tramp steamer for three days before it left port for a trip to Aden, Yemen.

Once in the Port of Aden, he was summoned to meet with an unknown leader. Driven to a hilltop home overlooking the Gulf of Aden he had just sailed through he noted security was high. A black canvas bag was placed over his head and he was led into a dark room. The bag was removed and as his eyes adjusted he saw that he was sitting with Anwar al-Awlaki and Ayman al-Zawahiri, two of the top al Qaeda leaders, second only to Osama bin Laden.

"Mahoud, you have done well since we sent you out to kill those who would stop al Qaeda." Awlaki said as he bowed to the assassin. "Both Ayman and I have been impressed by your work. You have greatly helped the cause."

"I am honored to be with you and al Qaeda. You have taught me well, Anwar. But I have become spoiled as you place me in such places as the Royal Mansour in Marrakech, Morocco." His eyes had adjusted to the semi-darkness and he stared at the bi-speckled man sitting next to Anwar. "How may I serve the leaders of al-Qaeda? What is my next target?"

"You have moved about well brother. You have learned how to move across borders and through cities not drawing attention to yourself. Thus, we are in agreement that you are ready for an even more important task."

"How may I serve?" Mahoud said, excited that he was being chosen for a greater task.

"With the killing of Osama by the infidels we need to re-establish the initiative. We must take the battle to them as we did in 2001. And we have a plan that will make the Americans fear us again. For this we need you to go to America. For the next few weeks you will study here at this compound. I have brought some of my brethren that support me in the U.S. to assist in your training. We will make you an American, but just on the surface so you can blend in. Then in a few weeks you will have to spend a week in the mountains again for some special training."

Mahoud reacted with a slight frown, which he tried to hide. He did not like the mountain desert camp environment anymore. Since he had started his assignments he found he liked the travel, the cities, and the hotel rooms.

"But it is only to learn about a different weapon system that you will use in America."

"Leader what shall I be doing in America that is so important that I do not continue what you trained me for?"

For the first time Ayman al-Zawahiri spoke. "You will assist us in killing the U.S. President! That will be our ultimate victory."

With that statement the meeting was over. Mahoud sat there in shock. He was going to America to kill the President. And he would not be using a sniper rifle to do so.

Shiban, Yemen

Josh had settled in to life in the sniper camp. He was teaching terrorist soldiers how to shoot. His rationalization was that they were not yet killing real people, only shooting out window glass, scarring boulders, and shredding targets. He was biding his time to find out as much as he could about the shooters already in the field. Once he had that information he would call in a strike on the terrorist camp, and hopefully Anwar al-Awlaki as well. That would be a good day's work.

With the sun settling he came down from his perch on the 20-meter cliff where he had been training on high-angle shooting. His students were getting better. That meant that he would not have a lot of time to take out the camp before they dispersed.

As he walked passed the Awlaki's cave he noticed that his car was not parked under its usual rock outcropping which was carefully camouflaged. It was nowhere in camp. He looked about and realized that he was also completely alone and that no one was observing or monitoring him. It's now or never, he thought.

Waving to the cave entrance like he was acknowledging someone, he made a bit of a scene inquiring if he was being called over to the entrance. Hopefully, anyone watching would think he was being summoned. He carried on a conversation with himself as he walked the twenty yards to the entrance. Stopping outside he gestured with his hands, and then set down his rifle and gear behind a rock that made it disappear and stepped inside.

Unarmed, he proceeded carefully, unsure that someone else may be in the cave. Once inside the mouth of the cave, he called out to Awlaki in case anyone was in there. He was mentally prepared to give a summary of the day's instruction and who had excelled at shooting.

No one responded, so he continued forward quietly. Stepping around a broad curve in the hollowed out rock cave, he came to a larger cavern. It was large enough to hold a bed and mattress, a simple table and chairs, and prayer rugs off to the side. As his eyes adjusted to the dark room, having come from the bright afternoon sunlight, he started searching for the satellite phone he had seen a number of times before. It would allow him to make an emergency call to one of his handlers at the Consulate. His plan was to turn on the phone long enough to mark his spot in the desert. That would send the phone's coordinates for the camp so that aerial surveillance could be established with drones and satellite observation. With any luck he hoped to be able to talk directly with his handler to coordinate the strike on his signal. At least that was the plan.

As he continued his search of the pitch-black room, he heard voices outside the entrance. It was casual talk and not an immediate cause for alarm but his instincts told him to develop a plan B to seek cover in case the terrorists did in fact come into the room. With his eyes now acclimated he saw that Awlaki was not a tidy housekeeper. His bed-roll was haphazardly hanging from the bed. Perhaps there was enough room under the bed to hide.

Just then the voices started coming closer and Plan B became Plan A. Josh looked carefully at the bedroll and how it hung from the wood frame of the bed. In the half-light he noted the darkest position under the bed. Crawling in, he drew himself against the cold cave wall as far back as he could. With the voices getting louder he took some full breaths knowing he would need to keep his breathing as shallow as possible in a few seconds. Doing so he also laughed at himself, a trained CIA field operative, hiding under a bed so he wouldn't be discovered. Not the stuff of James Bond novels, but any port in a storm. The voices entered the room.

Josh could hear one set of feet move to the table and presumed he was lighting a kerosene lamp. He wondered if he would be seen once there was a light source in the room. He willed himself deeper against the wall. Luckily, he was wearing black fatigues.

"Adnan, we must consider breaking camp soon. I am fearful that those infernal drones are getting closer to finding us. How well are our snipers trained? Could we turn them loose with the training we have provided?"

"I have heard our first class has done well with some targets already eliminated. This class will also do well, and I think they are ready. We have been lucky with Mohamar sharing the instruction efforts. He has helped us to move forward much more quickly."

"That is good my friend, I've come up with a new plan to avenge the death of Osama. And we will again take the battle to U.S. soil.

"Anwar, I am pleased that you have a new assignment in America. May I join you on this journey? I am tired of this desert rat hole?

"I am afraid not. We already have the plan in motion and the people have already been chosen. Some are already in position. No, we will find another important task for you, my friend. You have served us well."

"Let's talk about breaking camp at the end of the week. We will shut it down and give out assignments to the class. If you would like I can save a couple of kills for you? Would you like to be in the field again?"

"I would like that very much. The desert dulls the senses and I feel that I am losing my skills only teaching. I would like some assignments if for no other reason than I would like to sleep in a bed again."

Adnan sat down on the bed and Josh held his breath. He realized that Awlaki was probably looking directly at the bed. Adnan rested a hand on the cotton bedroll that was heaped beside him, and leaned back on the wall directly over Josh. He asked another question of his leader.

"May I know of your plan in America?" he said respectfully. "I would still like to be a part of it."

"I am sorry my friend, but this is too big to speak about with anyone. Only a few people know of it. It must stay that way. But I will tell you this much. We will greatly avenge the assassination of Osama bin Laden by the Seals and the President of the United States. It will make the world take notice of al Qaeda again much like the World Trade Center did. This time we will not kill thousands. It will only be a few, but a very important few. It will involve a killing that we have wanted since we started this holy war. Every news outlet, TV and newspaper in the world will cover this act. You will hear about it the moment it occurs and you will know it to be what I cannot speak about now."

"Then I will be with you in spirit. All ahu Akbar!"

"Come let us have some food. We must make plans to get out of this place, and give out assignments in the next three days."

With that the two terrorists stood and left the cave. Josh could see their boots leave the room and he could hear them talking as they went to the cave entrance. He dared not to move a muscle but his back was cramping because he had literally bent himself into the cave wall. He silently stayed frozen for a couple of minutes and then slowly rolled onto his stomach to ease himself out from under. Doing so he almost struck his eye out on a thick metal wire dangling just behind his head. Reaching up to push it away he realized it was the antenna from the hidden satellite phone that had almost poked him the eye. He had found it.

He noted its position and crawled out trying not to move the bedroll still hanging from the bed. He stuck the phone in his belt in the small of his back and pulled his loose tunic over it. Slowly inching his way down the rocky corridor towards the light, he watched for any people moving about outside. Now he was squinting to block out the bright light ahead.

Trying to blend with the cave wall he looked left and right and saw that everyone had gone to the far left chow cave. Taking a leap of faith, he stepped backwards out into the brightness. He again waved to an imaginary person in the cave as if saying goodbye. Shouldering his pack and rifle he ducked around a large boulder away from people moving in the other direction.

Without waiting to see if anyone had noticed, he crossed over a low ridge and then headed for a path that would take him up the mountain towards the various shooting platform ridges. He kept walking until he reached the 100-foot platform, on the highest cliff. It was about the furthest point from the camp and valley floor below. To make sure no one would observe him, he burrowed backwards into a rock outcropping. In the shadows of twilight he became almost invisible.

He fired up the satellite phone. It was a western style military field phone that had probably been used in Iraq or Afghanistan so he knew how it worked and what the likelihood of raising a friendly was. He dialed in a known CIA line that should be monitored 24-7. He would leave a carefully worded message knowing it would be scrambled and could not be listened to without some extraordinary additional hardware.

As the phone lit up, a strong GPS signal automatically went out to stationary satellites focused on this part of the world. Josh would be able to mark the spot for the terrorist encampment without saying a word. To be certain the camp's location was triangulated, correctly he would leave the signal on as long as possible.

Next he carefully prepared a clear and concise message. He knew he would not get a second chance to broadcast or clarify anything. He advised his code name. That alone would get the contents of the message to the right people. Then he stated the sniper camp was closing so a strike was required within two days. A heavy strike to obliterate the encampment and the entire terrorist cell.

He knew they would proceed, not worrying about his welfare. Only he needed to worry about that. Next, he advised this phone was in the possession of a very high valued target and should be monitored any time that it was powered up. If the phone moves after the strike, follow it and take it out as well. Finally, he said to kick this up the line as fast as possible so it got to the right people. Out!

Josh left the phone on as a beacon for the satellites above. Lifting his head, he scanned to see if there was any movement around him or in the camp below. There was none. Now came the hard part. He needed to go down and back into the cave to put the phone back in its place. He eased out of his rock cubby and duck crawled over to the path that would take him back down to the valley floor. The phone was again hidden in the back of his waistband, but it was still on and sending a signal.

Once he was on the path he made no effort to conceal himself. Carrying his rifle over his shoulder he casually walked down the hills as if he was coming off the hill for the first time. He ran into no one as they were all eating dinner.

As he walked he knew the hard part was coming. Reversing his steps he walked to Awlaki's cave entrance and seeing no one looking his way he again slipped into the cave. Stealth was less an objective. He needed to get the satellite phone back under the bed.

Entering the large caved room, he could see it was empty because the kerosene lamp was still lit. At the bed, he pulled out the radio, turned it off and crawled under the bed to place it where he thought he had found it. In doing so he knocked the blanket off the bed and swore to himself. Spy craft 101 required everything to be as if it had not been touched.

He grabbed the blanket and draped it over the bed like he thought it should look. Turning around he went for the cave entrance. As he passed the rough table being used as a desk he looked down and saw a map of the United States partially folded. Before reaching for it he looked hard at how it was folded. Then he carefully opened the panels that were hidden. On the map he saw a large circle drawn around the City of Chicago. It was the only pencil marking on the map. He carefully folded the panels back to where he had memorized them being and headed for the cave entrance.

This time he just walked out the entrance and saw that Adnan Menaj was walking across the dusty field with his head down. He waved and walked up to him hoping he hadn't noticed where he had come from. He had at most three days to clear the area before the strike.

Chicago, Illinois

The British Air international flight 1232 was just 2 minutes off scheduled arrival time after an 8-hour flight from London. As the Boeing 747-800 flew over some of the worlds' tallest buildings in downtown Chicago on final approach the pilot lined up the craft following instructions from the control tower. Due to the prevailing winds coming out of the west, the huge jet was landing east to west and it would be a straight-in approach on Runway 27 L.

Because it was a clear, crisp day, late in the afternoon, with the sun beginning to set in the west, many of the passengers were leaning towards their windows and staring at the impressive skyline and the city spreading out for as far as the eye could see. Joe Mazzoni sitting in Coach Seat number 33A was doing the same thing getting his first look at Chicago, soon to be his new home, after years of working in Italy and England. At least that is what his dossier and passport stated.

The jet aircraft slowly descended, almost floating towards its destination runway that only the pilot and co-pilot could actually see. As the plane closed the distance the strobe lights flashing a beacon of 'here you go' to the pilots, the passengers looked out over the miles of streets, the neighborhoods, the shopping strips, and the typical afternoon rush hour on massive freeways below.

Crossing the outer perimeter fence the plane lined up perfectly with the center of the runway, sweeping past nine jet craft queued up to take off after the arriving flight cleared the runway. The massive eight wheel assemblies touched down on the concrete sending small puffs of smoke into the air as the tires went from rest to a thousand rpms, in less than a second. The pilot next concentrated on bringing his front wheel assemblies down.

At 200 mph the plane continued its rush down the runway straight and true. With steady downward draft from the wing flaps the pilot eased the nose down until the front assembly touched concrete with the less visible puff of heated rubber. The plane continued down the runway reducing its speed with engines reversed and full flaps slowing the craft. Only when the pilot was close to his assigned turnout did he apply some light pressure to the brakes to slow the craft further.

The 747 maneuvered along its designated path following instructions from the ground traffic controller. The route took them around the entire airport, past the United terminal buildings, past the seven story parking lots and the airport power buildings. The large plane turned onto a massive bridge that crossed over traffic streaming in and out of the airport. Ahead was a separate International Terminal where the passengers would be processed through customs and sent on their way. Waved into their parking slot the pilots stretched and began their shutdown procedures as the doors were sprung and the passengers disembarked.

Walking out the plane's main compartment the passengers crossed the gangway and were herded like cattle into a series of corridors that only permitted one-way passage. Quietly monitored by customs officials, they followed feeder corridors that took them down a couple of levels and eventually entered a cavernous hall that had multiple processing lines for passport and immigration control. A good number of international flights must have landed just before them because there were about 900 passengers in a dozen lines being processed by their friendly customs officer.

Joe Mazzoni was tall enough to see above the heads of most of the people trying to determine what to do next and observed a less crowded line to the left. He confidently started heading that way. He had been instructed to look bored and confident, as if he had done this sort of thing a dozen times. In fact this was his first pass through an international customs line. He had been schooled for a week on this very transition process in a Mosque in London. He could do this.

As his particular line moved forward he fumbled for his travel documents, passport and declarations, just like everyone else was doing. He had even been instructed to look at the occasional girl standing in the other lines. While this was foreign to what he had been taught about women, he was on a mission and was advised this would be normal activity for a young virile Italian.

Ten minutes later he had made it to the front of the long customs line. He stood casually behind the white painted strip on the floor and waited his turn to approach the immigration cubicle and his passport officer. He tried to control his breathing and ran down the list of what would probably be asked and his planned responses.

"Next." the officer said, casually glancing to his next customer and waving a hand to bring him forward. Joe stepped forward. The customs officer took the proffered documents, opened the Italian passport to the photo page that had all the personal information coded into the document. He quickly glanced at the photo and then up at Joe, noting that the image and the man were one and the same. He then inserted the magnetic strip into a machine below the counter and waited.

"So Joe, what do you know?" he said, and smiled as he waited for the machine to do its work.

Joe's head snapped up. He didn't know how to respond, they

hadn't covered such a question in his training. What did this man mean?

Thinking quickly, he pulled his best Italian accent out and said in fractured English, "I do not understand, Sir. What should I know for you?"

The Officer looked up and smiled, raising a hand to calm his Italian visitor. "That is what my Father always said to me every night at the dinner table. I'm a Joe too, and I was often as confused as you are. Joe what brings you to America?"

Back on script, this question Joe knew how to answer. With practiced ease he said, "I come to work for my brother's Italian restaurant." He waited a moment and said, "He needs my cannoli recipe, his are not so good."

The officer chuckled. "I can understand, good cannoli's are hard to come by." Just then the magnetic passport-scanning machine flashed a small green light. The officer flipped through the hand-stamped pages of the passport looking for any bad entry stamps. There were none, just Italy, France, and the United Kingdom. He grabbed a U.S. entry ink stamp and found an empty page, whacking the passport with the ink impression.

He handed the documents back and said, "Welcome to America, and Chicago, Joe."

Joe said thanks and gathered his documents and headed for the door and his luggage in the next large room. He found his two pieces of luggage circling on a baggage carousel and pulled them off. He knew he had nothing of concern in his luggage. His trial was almost over.

The baggage officer asked him to open up the bags and stand back. He made a cursory look at the contents and then took a white cloth tissue and rubbed it along the zipper lines. The officer made a motion to wrap it up and started moving down the line towards a young woman in a mini-skirt that was just walking up dragging two large suitcases.

Joe headed for the door and walked out into a crowd of expectant people, some holding signs and flowers for arriving loved ones. He looked about and saw a man standing somewhat back who had a small sign saying J. Mazzoni. He acknowledged the man with a nod and walked over. Saying nothing the man assisted Joe with his bags and they left the international terminal walking to a beat-up cab that was parked at the curb. There was another Italian looking guy standing next to the vehicle. He didn't say anything, just pointed towards the trunk and got in the taxi. The two men loaded the two bags, slammed the trunk door, and climbed in the back seat.

As they pulled away from the curb, Joe Mazzoni let out an audible sigh and quietly said in his native language, "I'm glad that is over."

"Welcome, Mahoud," the driver said, over his shoulder as he drove towards the highway, "We have awaited your arrival. We hear we are about to embark on a new plan."

Atlantic Ocean, 30 degrees W, 50 degrees N.

The large container ship was stacked with over five hundred boxcar sized shipping containers in orange, blue and brown corrugated metal. It was plowing through the swells west-northwest making good time due to excellent weather conditions. The ship was headed towards Toronto, Canada with a mixed cargo of auto parts and oil machinery destined for the Canadian provinces of Ontario and Alberta.

Once the ship passed into the St. Laurence Seaway the passage became even calmer and the international crew became relaxed with their daily chores on board. No one noticed that two Indonesian crewmen had disappeared from their regularly scheduled duties. They worked their way forward between the cargo stacks looking for a particular container that was buried under eight stacked containers near the bow. The non-descript unit marked # ZX 77 639442 was finally identified far forward away from the superstructure and most of the crew working on the stern of the ship.

They broke into the sealed container and used some large flashlights pointed at the ceiling to light the entire box. Closing the container doors behind them, they scanned the container contents searching for a series of crates that were marked as corrugated steel plates building materials. Finding the boxes, they broke them open, revealing long flat plates in some and the missile crates in others. In another box they found heavy-duty drills, screws and bolts to work with. Rearranging cargo boxes away from the deep end of the container, they cleared a large space and stacked the missile crates vertically from floor to ceiling. After they finished lifting these crates into place they assembled a new wall with the large corrugated plate sections from floor to ceiling. In effect, the missiles crates had disappeared and unless someone was looking closely they would not recognize that the inside of the container had shrunk by five feet.

Against this newly created wall the two Islamic Indonesians worked up a sweat re-stacking additional automobile parts and oil equipment crates to even further conceal the false wall. The whole effort took less than three hours. Satisfied with the work they had been charged with, they resealed the container and went back to their regular crew duties.

Once the ship docked in Toronto, the unloading process began and in less than two days the longshoreman had lifted and pulled every container from the ship. As scheduled by the shipping documents and manifests, all the containers were loaded on trucks or railroad flatcars to be forwarded to appointed destinations. About one in fifty containers were opened for inspection. Container ZX 77 639442 was not inspected and was loaded onto a truck destined for a Ford auto plant outside of Toronto.

Shiban, Yemen

Josh was still marveling that it had been so easy to penetrate the terrorist camp. He had figured it would have taken take weeks and perhaps months to gain the confidence of al Qaeda and find a way into their midst. Most of it had been sheer luck, and his ability to 'shoot the eyes out of Jewish pigs' had certainly played a part as well. That part had come from years of training with the Seals.

He had been equally shocked when coming face-to-face with Anwar al-Awlaki in Yemen. Langley had been looking for this top-ranked terrorist along with Ayman al-Zawahiri since they had taken out Osama bin Laden. These were now the top dogs, and dogs they were. While they suspected Awlaki was in Yemen, they had not been successful in tracking him down. Josh was elated he might get a two for the price of one out of this undercover operation.

"So Mohamar, you have helped us move this program forward much faster than we figured. For that I thank you. Our assassins are progressing well. No?" Anwar Awlaki said to his now favored sniper instructor.

Mohamar looked up from his mid-day meal and smiled at the man he would like to strangle.

"Your sniper recruits were good soldiers before they came here. Now we teach them focus and patience, and I think they learn well now so they can get out of this mountain furnace."

Awlaki laughed. "I think you are right, my friend. What about you, does this heat bother you?"

"Heat is heat no matter where it is. I think Yemen is about the same as in Libya. We are close to the Equator and the sun is above us regardless. I can sweat here the same as in Libya. Although here I do not get to see Gadhafi's women guards," he said smiling. He hoped to divert the conversation again by simply mentioning the Amazon women in Tripoli. He hoped it would work on Awlaki as well, but it didn't.

The Imam was focused and women were not in his script. "Yes, I understand that our surroundings are not the best in the world, but we must do our work away from all those prying eyes of the CIA. No one bothers us up here and we can teach in peace."

"As long as I am paid for my teaching I can put up with the heat and the hard beds."

"Perhaps you do need a change of pace. I travel tomorrow to the Gulf of Aden. Set up your schedule with Adnan and let him handle the men tomorrow. Join me. You can help me as a bodyguard. I must visit someone to plan our next effort. We leave at dawn and I wish I could offer luxury but those CIA drones hound us so we travel in an old truck with no air. The sacrifices that we make."

"I'll appreciate the change of scenery and look forward to a breeze in my face even if it is 100 degrees desert air. I will speak with Adnan."

Anwar al Awlaki went back to his cave, which was 20 degrees cooler once you went 30 feet into the interior.

Josh looked around for the other instructor and advised him he would be traveling with Awlaki the next day. He asked him to work his shooters from heights of over 75 feet. Adnan was impressed with is new instructor and readily agreed to the request.

Josh figured more activity in the hills at the highest points around camp would make it easier for the drones and satellites to see and pick out the encampment movement. The countdown to the strike was on. And he now had an excuse to be out of camp and away from the carnage that was forthcoming. The only problem was that Awlaki would also be absent from the strike. That meant that he might get to deal with the terrorist himself.

Sault Ste. Marie, Ontario, Canada

Christian Morrow sat in a metal folding chair on his dock on the St Mary's River staring at his large cabin cruiser. It was tied up and bobbing in the wake of a passing iron ore ship that had come through the SOO Locks linking Lake Superior to Lake Huron. His boat was primarily set up as a fishing boat, one that had all the bells and whistles and could also attract tourists for Coho salmon fishing excursions. He liked his life.

But Chris, as he was known, was actually Algul Zafir, from Turkey. His real first name, Algul, was Arabic for vampire and he was a sleeper agent working for the terrorist organization al Qaeda. Just before 9-11 he had been asked to immigrate to Canada and set up a fishing operation in a border town with the United States. He was given substantial financial support to purchase a large, well-appointed boat and now lived in a nice riverfront house with his Canadian wife and two children. The young children attended local school and his wife made regular trips to the mall. He was playing the part of a Greek immigrant who had traveled to Canada for a new beginning. He had developed a solid commercial fishing enterprise supporting a small retail store on Main Street. In addition, he supplied Coho salmon and perch to a number of restaurants and grocery stores throughout the area.

The most important factor in his relocation was that his riverfront home and dock was a mere 500 feet from the United States border, which was out in the middle of the shipping channel. Only water and an imaginary line in 50 feet of water separated him from the United States.

After many years of quietly residing in Canada, waiting for a follow-up contact, out of the blue, he finally received an assignment from his financier. A large shipment was being sent to his business address. He would need to covertly transport it to the United States. He had been advised the items would need to be artfully concealed in the boat for the crossing so as not to be discovered if inspected.

He climbed back onto his boat, the 'Native Son', and went down the four steps to the galley and salon. He had considered naming the boat Incognito, but he figured that might actually draw attention rather than making him invisible. Native Son suggested roots.

On the far side of the cabin a large forward berth with a queen size bed filled the room. The bed's mattress and supporting wood platform was wedged up against the ceiling with a two by four stud exposing a series of storage drawers and compartments. All of these inner components had been ripped out leaving a large cavity over eight feet long and seven feet wide. Back in the Galley the cabinets under the sink and along the stove and refrigerator walls were also exposed with the shelving pulled out. Additional items would be stored behind the kitchenware and provisions. He estimated he had created hundreds of square feet of additional storage space.

On the stern deck two Harley Davidson Motorcycles were lashed down fully visible to anyone walking by. Algul had decided a good cover would be a pleasure-fishing trip through the Great Lakes, and on to Milwaukee, Wisconsin to visit the Harley Davidson Motorcycle Plant and Museum. In the past few years he had taken a liking to biking in the north woods.

He was aware that another person would be accompanying the

shipment and that he too would travel to the States. Algul asked if the man had a Canadian passport and was advised that he did. He requested the man's photo be forwarded so he could create the necessary Immigration and Naturalization Service (INS) papers that might be inspected on the boat trip.

Aden, Yemen

As dawn was rising over the eastern mountains in central Yemen, the old truck left the dirt roads and pulled onto the two-lane asphalt highway to the south. The truck bed was half covered with an old, ripped canvas tarp that had seen better days and was lashed to the framework. It flapped in the dry wind. In the truck bed close to the cab, tucked under the more viable part of the tarp were two cloth seats that had been bolted to the floor of bed. Anwar al-Awlaki and Mohamar sat silently somewhat protected from the hot winds swirling about them. For the most part they were invisible to anyone or anything flying above. From that vantage point it just looked like a farm truck driving to market.

With the increased drone activity in Yemen east and north of Aden, it was necessary for the terrorist leaders to travel this way if they wanted to live another day to fight the Americans. A number of terrorist leaders had been killed in recent days by unseen attacks from the air. The Americans seemed to have taken a much more aggressive path to fighting the terrorists, with the blessing of the Yemeni government

Awlaki was lost in his thoughts as he stared at the passing desert. He was excited because he had been given approval to take the battle back to American soil. His mission would allow him to leave the infernal desert and return to clean beds, better food and civilization.

He was elated the sniper school mission was winding down and had already accounted for four kills. When this next class was sent out there would be a total of twenty-four assassins doing the work of al Qaeda in Arab countries all over the world.

Josh sat quietly next to the number two man in the al Qaeda terrorist organization. He was again contemplating reaching over and strangling the bastard with his bare hands. He knew he could do it and could possibly take out the driver as well. But he was thinking long-term and realized he might gain greater intelligence by biding his time. Over the years and many missions he had learned patience. Some new mission was already in progress and it involved an action that would take place in the States. If his guess were right, it would center on Chicago. And it would involve some major people. Perhaps he could find out more before dispatching this asshole with the reading glasses.

They drove in silence because they would have had to shout at one another to be heard. Each man took a nap while the other stayed awake, acting as sentry.

In a couple of hours they came to the outskirts of Aden and were met by two other vehicles that pulled in front and behind them as an escort to wherever they were going. Josh could see the Port of Aden ahead. He knew it well because he had been on the investigation team that came to investigate the terrorist attack that had taken place on the USS Cole as it sat in the harbor seven years earlier. They drove past the harbor on the expressway and headed east out of town without stopping.

A few miles outside the city where the road narrowed back to a two-lane coastal highway they turned towards the Gulf of Aden and snaked their way up a narrow driveway. The escort vehicles stayed behind at the highway turnoff. Up over the crest of a hill and then down towards the water they drove to a garden villa that sat on a rise over the bright blue water of the Gulf of Aden. This close to the water the air temperature had dropped at least ten degrees and the winds were blowing stronger.

The truck stopped short of entering the walled compound and both Awlaki and Mohamar Atari jumped off the back tailgate. The truck immediately drove back the way it had come. Awlaki led the way to the house encouraging Mohamar to follow for some cold refreshment. He looked as if he was a man with a purpose.

Inside the courtyard they saw another older man with horn rimmed glasses sitting at a table and again Josh had to take a deep breath to stifle his excitement. He was staring at the current leader of al Qaeda, Ayman al-Zawahiri. Josh's insides broiled as he contemplated what he should do. He could charge forward and lop off the heads of both of these al Qaeda terrorist leaders in a matter of seconds if he wanted to. No guard would be able to stop him. But he would die in the process. Perhaps it would be worth the sacrifice. But he decided to bide his time and play this out.

"Leader, I bring you greetings from the desert and thanks for inviting me here to this cool oasis. I would like to introduce Mohamar Atari."

Josh bowed slightly but otherwise made no attempt to approach the leader. This was the way an Arab would respond to meeting an elder. He remained quiet and averted his eyes. He was afraid to look and give away his hatred and contempt for the man who had orchestrated the killing of three thousand Americans in the World Trade Center attack.

Awlaki continued, "He is the Libyan soldier and sniper I was telling you about. He has helped us to move our program in the mountain encampment forward greatly. We now have a second class of assassins ready to be sent out."

Zawahiri waved them towards the table and a guard appeared from the shadows with some glasses of cold water and hot tea. His AK-47 weapon was slung haphazardly over his shoulder. But he looked as if he knew how to use the weapon. Josh had made the right decision not to attack the new head of this terrorist organization. He was also pleased to hear that he might be asked to go to America for the next strike. He hoped to learn more.

The conversation was mostly about potential Arab spring targets around the globe. Josh was surprised by the numbers being contemplated and even some of the names on both sides of the Islamic movement. It seemed no one was to be spared, Sunni or Shia. Obviously they would be encouraging chaos within the entire Arab world with the hopes that al Qaeda would then rise in the power vacuum created by all these assassinations. He sat quietly and mentally filed away all the target names and countries. Such intelligence would be invaluable for the CIA and U.S. to build new relationships and alliances with Arab leaders, if they weren't already being targeted or killed.

Josh sat there drinking first the ice water, as if he was dying of thirst, and then started in on the tea until his bladder was full. He quietly signaled that he needed to relieve himself, and a guard stepped forward to escort him to a water closet in the beautiful villa overlooking the Gulf.

Because he had been so meek and quiet while sitting with the leaders, the guard quickly became bored monitoring the man peeing. He stepped outside the room and gave the man some privacy. Josh tucked himself away and carefully opened a second door from the toilet. It led into a nice office and study. He stepped in and saw five cell phones stacked up on a side table next to an easy chair and the window looking out to the Gulf. It was Zawahiri's office where he was doing his calling, he thought. He wished he had a listening device to plant. Checking to see his guard was nowhere in sight, he quickly scooped up a cell phone and pocketed it. He also grabbed a plastic bag with a zip seal that was on the table. Looking out the window he could see the flag of an Iraqi oil tanker passing in the

Gulf of Aden just a quarter-mile off shore heading east for the Indian Ocean. He made a note of the time. He would pass the info about the Iraqi flagged tanker and the exact time on to his handler. They would be able to match the ship's exact position to the exact time and vector into Zawahiri's little villa on the hill overlooking the Gulf water. In no time they could have eyes on the terrorist and take him out.

He now had a phone to make that call. All he needed was some time to make it. More importantly he needed to pass along that the next al Qaeda Op was going to be on American soil.

August 4th, over Chicago

The large custom white with blue trim Boeing 747-200B, tail number 28000 was on final approach into O'Hare International Airport. Its Air Force designation was normally VC-25, but with a very important passenger on board, the planes radio call sign was officially 'Air Force One'.

All air traffic around and near the airport was on-hold, either circling in the air at the outer reaches of O'Hare airspace, or completely grounded on the tarmac. There was zero plane movement while the President's plane squared up to Runway 27 L, east to west. The huge plane crossed low over the surrounding neighborhoods, the I-294 expressway, and the outer perimeter fences and made a perfect landing two minutes ahead of schedule.

Everyone knew who was coming to town. In the terminals, waiting passengers were lining the windows to get a look at Air Force One and the world's most important passenger, the President of the United States. In numerous planes already loaded sitting at the gate, or out on the tarmac in holding areas, passengers craned their necks to see through small porthole windows as the famous jet raced down the runway.

The President had come home to Chicago for a Birthday party, his! He was 50 years old and was planning on having a celebration with his many friends from Chicago, where he had got his start in politics. It was not a working weekend.

Air Force One taxied to a remote corner of the huge airport where a large number of dignitaries, and security, were waiting for his arrival. Rather than using his armored limousine, which had arrived earlier on a C141 Star lifter Cargo plane, he would transfer to his Hyde Park residence aboard two Marine Helicopters standing by. After visiting with his arrival party, he boarded the helicopter now officially designated as Marine One.

This was the twenty-first time the president had come home to Chicago since taking office.

Sault Ste. Marie, Ontario, Canada

The container truck arrived late in the afternoon on the appointed day. It pulled close to the door of Morrow's fishing market business almost at the corner of Pim and Bay Streets. Across the road was a large empty lot that fronted the St. Mary's River and the Water Aerodrome, home of the Bush Pilots Plane Museum. There were bush floatplanes coming and going all the time taking fishermen into the northern woods and lakes.

The truck driver opened the container and not wanting to participate in the unloading, process said he was hungry and went looking for some dinner down the block. He advised he'd be back in two hours to depart for Alberta with his next delivery of oil machinery parts. He headed down the street towards a bar.

Hamid Aziz bowed and introduced himself to Christian Morrow. Very exact pleasantries were exchanged, and each person verified they were talking to the right person. Once that was done, they quickly started unloading the crates. Away from prying eyes they used the same drills to dismantle the false corrugated wall exposing the missile crates stacked to the ceiling. Working together they pulled the top crates off the stack and carried them into the warehouse stacking them near the door. In no time they had removed all the weapons from the container. They also pulled out all of the false wall components and stacked them with some scrap metal at the rear of the storefront.

A couple hours later the truck driver returned from his dinner, swaying a bit from a number of cocktails. He got the necessary waybills signed and stumbled to his cab. He drove away none the wiser about what had been unloaded. He pulled down Bay St. towards Hwy 17 north. His next stop was the tar sands oil fields in Alberta.

Algul and Hamid watched the truck pull away and then went into the warehouse. Still not knowing what he would be transporting into the U.S. he handed Hamid a second crowbar and together they started popping open the crates. When the first lid was sprung and the packing materials were pulled back Algul gasped at the weapons tightly nestled in the crate. Four Stingers, air-to-ground, hand-held missile launchers were nestled front to back.

He looked at his new friend searching for an answer to an unasked question. Finally he said, "What are we going to do? Start a war?"

Hamid was prepared for the question, "I do not know that, Algul, our task is simply to get these weapons into the United States. By the way, where is this Satanist country?"

Christian pointed out into the river. "It is 500 feet that way. The middle of the river is the border. But what are these for?"

"Again, I don't know, all I know is that they are destined for Chicago and I'm traveling with them. It is our job to get them there."

"How many of them are there?"

"I believe we have 30 of them in these crates."

Algul was greatly troubled by all of this. After all these years of living in peace he was feeling more Canadian than terrorist. This was more than he bargained for when he accepted the assignment to travel to Canada. He always thought that he would be asked to deliver someone to the U.S., not bring weapons into the country. No matter what happened this was going to have a bad effect on his life and family. The hairs on his neck stood up and he shivered.

Hamid must have been reading his mind. "Algul, this is what you signed up for many years ago. What do you think they wanted you to do, learn how to fish and become a westerner? Your mission is for the cause and it comes from the highest circle of al Qaeda.

Come, we must get ready to go. Where is this boat of yours?"

"I know, I know. I guess it is what I have been fearing ever since arriving. But I had no idea that it would come to this."

Hamid ignored the comment and started opening another crate. Algul stood there for a minute wrestling with his conscience and then picked up his crowbar and started working again.

"We will have to take these weapons to the boat after midnight. There should be no one around at that hour. I've prepared a secret chamber that should accommodate all of these weapons. After we get your INS papers filled out we will begin our journey."

Shiban, Yemen

Air Force Colonel Mike 'Hammer' Peshia, of the North Dakota Air National Guard, adjusted his joystick with a gentle pull to the left to begin another run. He watched the five 21inch monitors in front of him as he guided his drone in a sweeping turn over the Yemeni desert. But he was not actually flying over the desert. He was comfortably sitting in a trailer on a NORAD Air Force Base outside of Minot, North Dakota. Inside the air-conditioned trailer were two additional pilots and technicians 'flying' their different un-manned drones above the desert 12,000 miles away. The war on terrorism had dramatically changed in recent years.

He was flying a remote-controlled Predator C Avenger Drone some 10,000 feet above the Yemeni mountains searching for a desert encampment nestled somewhere near the small city of Shiban. He had been tasked to this search from an intelligence report that had been received a few days earlier. All he knew was that there was an al Qaeda camp somewhere nearby that was supposedly training sniper assassins, and it was his job to identify it and pass the intelligence back upstairs.

His jet-powered bird was invisible at that height and could travel over 200 miles per hour, about 50% faster than the turboprop-powered Reaper series. It was large enough to carry two, 2,000 pound bombs and a rack of Hellfire missiles, although today he was just on a reconnaissance mission using extraordinarily high definition cameras and sensors that could look through clouds and pick up heat signatures from on high.

In recent years putting traditional fighter forces into battle had been so costly and dangerous that the Air Force started developing drone aircraft to take the human loss of life out of the equation. The drones were much cheaper than traditional aircraft, were unmanned and could loiter overhead for many hours without refueling, and offered an extraordinary viewpoint for any required military action.

Having set up a 200 square mile aerial search the drone was flying an up and down grid-pattern scrutinizing all the terrain below. Peshia was looking for any vehicle or individual movement on the desert floor and in the rolling hills and valleys of central Yemen.

Next to the forward-looking camera screen was a heat signature monitor that showed hot ground anomalies as red blobs on the almost constantly yellow surface temperature. The monitor noted a number of small red dots standing out on the top of some higher mountain cliffs and immediately locked into the position allowing all other systems to zero in and explore what was being seen.

The visual cameras scanned down and recognized human beings walking about the area and clustering on some cliffs. The heat signature screen was able to identify some instant explosive heat registrations, which could be rifle fire. The various cameras on the drone all focused on the site gathering information and taking pictures that were immediately relayed back to the drone's operators, both pilot and technician.

Colonel Peshia recognized what he was seeing and immediately called for his boss to come over and take a look. They analyzed the tapes again and agreed that they had found the camp that was supposed to be in the area.

The news was transmitted to the resident CIA analyst assigned to this remote base. He reviewed the tapes and photos and sent them on to Langley for confirmation that this was the terrorist camp they were looking for. In no time Langley confirmed its agreement and noted that their information said the camp would be closing down within days. They got the necessary approvals to destroy the camp and everyone within it for the following morning at 6:00 am. Colonel Peshia was ordered back to base as another drone took up position to monitor the target for the next 15 hours.

Aden, Yemen

Josh walked back to the courtyard with the guard trailing casually behind. The stolen cell phone was tucked in his bulky desert fatigues hip pocket. He knew that eventually the missing phone would be discovered and that he had only a limited time before he was exposed as the thief.

He wandered over to the courtyard wall and gazed out over the Gulf and the beach below. He was within earshot of the two terrorists talking at the table, but he tried not to show too much interest in what they were saying. He did hear the words 'force one' and he thought he heard the word 'missiles'.

Since he wasn't being called over to the table, he decided he would remain where he was and continue to covertly listen. The talk changed and he heard them angrily announce vengeance would be theirs. The meeting must have been over. A chair scraped on the stone patio and he looked over to see Awlaki coming towards him.

"I will be going back to camp in a few minutes to get it packed up and closed down, but you will be staying here. We may have a new assignment for you that will get you out of this infernal heat. But it will require you to learn a different weapon system, unlike your sniper rifle. It is a weapon that is less exact but can do a great deal of damage to what it is aimed at."

"I am honored to do such work. May I ask what you will have me do?"

"In time my friend, in time." Awlaki followed his gaze out to sea and said, "I see you are eyeing the ocean. With all the dirt we have been eating for weeks in the mountains, perhaps you would like to jump in and cleanse yourself of the grit, huh? It is only a short walk to the beach, I have done it myself when I have been here before. Go, get the desert out of your hair. I will send for you by another truck tomorrow. Today rest and enjoy."

Awlaki turned to the guard and told him to go with Mohamar to the water. "Nawaf, show our guest the beach and allow him some rest time before the sun sets."

Josh couldn't believe his luck. He might have some time to be relatively alone and make a call to his Aden handler. If he could do so he could take out Awlaki, Zawahiri and the terrorist camp. It would be a good trade even if he were discovered.

The guard looked eager to change his venue and walk towards the beach. He swung his AK-47 around his body and pointed Josh towards a gate and the wooden stair path that snaked back and forth down to the beach and water. They walked as compatriots rather than adversaries. The beach was more stone and pebble than fine sand but Josh was fine with it. It reminded him of his favorite coral island in the Bahamas where he often went between assignments. If he could get away from here before they bombed the crap out of it, he decided he would go to his own beach again.

The guard made no effort to swim in the water. He must have liked how he smelled. But Josh had enough of the desert and wanted to cleanse himself. He pulled his fatigues off, first the tunic which he spread out like a towel and then his pants. These he rolled up, careful to make sure that the cell phone was near the top of the pocket but still hidden from view. He placed this on top of the shirt much like a pillow.

In his white shorts he turned and walked into the surf, allowing the water to reach his thighs before diving forward into a wave. Surfacing, he combed his hair back over his head and cleaned out his ears. He rubbed his arms and legs and the back of his neck washing the desert off of him. The guard casually watched him and then looked left to watch a couple of freighters passing in opposite directions out in the Gulf.

Josh noted his disinterest and decided it was time to make the call. He came out of the water and stood watching the same freighters. The summer breeze quickly dried his body and he turned to walk over to his clothes. He was about twenty yards from where the guard sat on a rock staring out to sea. Kneeling down he fell forward on his spread shirt and grabbed his pants like it was a pillow. Laying his head down he turned to see that the guard was getting up and walking down the beach a bit.

Josh pulled out the cell phone and fired it up hiding it on the side of his head away from the guard. Out of the corner of his eye he punched in his controller's memorized number in Aden and heard it connect. He turned his head again and noted the guard was now 35 yards away.

As soon as the call was answered it went to message, which was expected. It was a scrambled call. Josh began talking.

"Code Derek,... I'm out of the camp,... take it out as soon as possible. Awlaki is not in the camp but he is on his way back there. He is alone with just a driver, in an old truck with a tattered canvas cover on the highway between Aden and Shiban. Take him out for me, I will not be with him. Third, at 2:15 pm local Aden time today, an Iraqi oil tanker was in the Gulf of Aden heading due east. Match the timecoordinates with the ship's exact position. From that point draw a line directly north and find a large villa set up on a cliff overlooking the Gulf. If you do this fast you will be able to take out Ayman al-Zawahri. That's all. I'm clear of the site. Josh."

He looked back at the guard who was now coming his way. He put the phone back in the plastic bag in his pocket and sealed it. He debated burying it in the sand so it could continue to send a signal but he had no time. He placed his head back down. The guard returned to his rock and sat down oblivious to the call that had just been made. Josh laid there for fifteen minutes soaking up the afternoon sun. He went over in his mind if he had covered everything completely in the message. He had, and now all he had to do was get away from the Villa before they bombed the crap out of it. Not worried about himself he hoped the message would get the priority it needed to get the number two, now number one man in al Qaeda.

As he continued to lie there he sifted various options through his mind. Then, he heard a car door slam on the top of the hill some 60 yards away. Tires screeched in the loose gravel of the courtyard above. Someone was on the move. Without moving or lifting his head too much, he looked over towards the cliff and the catwalk stairs leading upward.

At the top of the cliff by the gate he saw movement. It was three of the guards with their AK's at the ready starting down the wooden step path. The jig was up. They must have realized he stole one of the phones. He also bet that tire sound was Zawahri getting out of Dodge. It was time for him to get out as well.

He casually turned towards his Guard some 20 feet away and slowly got up and stretched, pulling his shirt on. His bored guard had not heard the commotion up above, he was facing out to sea and close enough to the water that the breakers were masking sounds. Josh moved casually towards the tall man putting his fingers to his mouth, suggesting the universal signal for 'Gotta a smoke?'

The guard acknowledged the man approaching and reached into his jacket pocket for his pack of cigarettes. Josh ignored the three men descending the steep stairwell and resisted the urge to look that way. All he needed was a few more moments and the AK-47 on the guard's back.

Arriving in front of the now friendly guard, he suddenly drew the guard's attention towards the three men charging down the stairs shouting to their compatriot. The guard looked surprised and concentrated on what the three were shouting.

Without warning Josh threw a full-on haymaker punch with all his strength at the man's head, catching his jaw solidly. The guard never saw it coming and dropped like a stone, luckily falling sideways exposing his weapon. Josh yanked it off the guy's shoulder and checked its status. The weight of the banana clip suggested it was full, so he clicked off the safety and turned towards his next challenge.

The three guards saw what had happened. All three started shooting haphazardly as they continued racing down the stairs. Bullets started kicking up sand and plinking off rocks all around Josh.

He estimated he had about thirty seconds to get into the water and swim away. The three guards would be slowed slogging through the dry sand and stone to the beach. But after that he would be chewed up in a hail of bullets.

He took hold of the AK to aim carefully and started placing single shots as close to the three men as he could. He doubted he would hit them at the distance because the AK-47 was notoriously inaccurate at almost any range. But the weapon could spit a hail of bullets pinning aggressors down. His well-placed shots did the job and slowed the guards even more. They obviously wanted to live. Continuing to shoot selectively, he backed towards the water. With the water lapping at his knees he emptied the banana clip magazine at the three slowly advancing guards.

When the banana clip was empty, he threw the AK-47 over his head into deeper water, turned and high-stepped further into the surf as fast as he could. As the water got deeper his pace slowed. When the surf reached his thighs he dove in and started swimming a strong free-style stroke out into the Gulf. He churned through the water like an Olympian. He wanted to take a look behind to see if they were coming into the water but figured it would break his pace. His prior Seal training and countless miles of swimming were paying off as he put distance between him and the pursuers.

The guards must have reached the shoreline, because he heard their weapons start roaring. He was obviously still in range. The guns were spitting metal and the shots were dancing in the water all around him. As the noisy barrage continued nothing hit him as he plowed through the surf. Just as he decided their aim was lousy, a bullet flew past his head catching the very top of his ear cutting the soft tissue. With his adrenalin pumping the ear sprayed the water with his blood. It was time to dive.

Without looking back he knifed downward at the waist. His legs went up in a powerful kick three feet out of the water and another bullet caught him in the lower thigh above the knee as he slid under the water. He winched in pain, but knew it had not hit bone because the leg continued to function as he dove deep. He continued to pull downward with his upper body.

He went down at least ten feet to stay away from the bullets whizzing into the water around him. Leveling off beneath the surface he used a strong breast stroke to propel himself further into the Gulf. He zigged sideways to escape the barrage at the surface. His Seal training had taught him how to hold his breath for an extraordinary amount of time. His eyes stung from the salt water but he was used to that as well. He stayed down for almost a minute continuing his underwater breaststroke. Perhaps they thought they had got him.

Still underwater he changed directions to the west so they would be surprised when he surfaced elsewhere. Just about out of breath he stopped and tried to determine where the beach was. He then slowly kicked his way to the surface feathering his upward progress with his arms to just break the surface enough to get his eyes out and inhale another good breath. He was about 50 yards off shore. He could see the three guards; they had spread out along the beach in twenty-five yard intervals. They were searching the surf but with the incoming wave action they still had not seen him bobbing almost under water.

Taking another deep breath he reversed the arm pull to propel himself downward without breaking the surface. Five feet down, he kicked over and started swimming again with his leg still bleeding profusely in the salt water. After another five surface breaths like that he was winded but still determined to get away. He had information he had to pass on.

Knowing he was leaving a blood trail, he thought about sharks looking for an easy meal.

Surfacing gingerly, he noted the guns had stopped firing and his three pursuers were retreating up the beach towards the stairs. Figuring they might be going for a boat, he floated on his back and pulled out the cell phone sealed in the plastic bag. It was still dry so he made a call to his handler in Aden, by his estimates less than 10 miles away.

The call went through and he asked who was on the line. His handler responded asking where the hell he was.

"I'm bobbing in the Gulf of Aden a couple of miles away. Bleeding from two bullet wounds and looking more and more like shark bait," he said as he looked at the beach and stairs in the distance. They were retreating over the ridge and out of site.

"We have a bird up now with some Marines heading that way. Can you keep this line open so we can draw a fix on you?"

"As long as the battery lasts on Zawahri's phone it will be pinging. Semper Fi! Tell them guys to get here quick and to call up a secure line. I have to pass some important Intel up the food chain."

"Done. Advise where they should be looking for you."

"I'm about 300 yards off shore, so have them hug the coast line heading straight east. I'm not sure how far but I'll stay on the line. It will help take my mind off the sharks. When I see them I'll talk them into my position."

"Roger that, I'll patch you through to the crew now."

Lying on his back, he treaded water trying to maintain his position 300 yards out. He kept an eye on the Villa on the hill to make sure the bad guys didn't find a boat and make a second effort. He reached up to his ear and noted that the salt water had kind of cauterized the soft tissue wound through his earlobe. It wasn't bleeding much. Now he was the man with the forked ear!

He reached down to his leg wound and felt around. The bullet had gone through the fleshy part of the leg missing bone and arteries. But it was still pumping blood into the surrounding water from both the entry and exit wounds. He took off his old shirt and wrapped it as tight as he could around his leg to create some tourniquet pressure. He hoped the sharks had a good meal that morning.

Off in the distance he saw a helicopter before he heard it because of the wave action all around him. He pulled the phone out again and hailed the crew.

"Hey guys, you're a sight for sore eyes and bullet ridden body. Keep coming directly east on that compass heading another mile. I'm the guy in the red pool of blood with my thumb out. Can I hitch a ride?"

"Yes Sir. We don't have you in site yet but we got a bunch of eyes looking for crimson in blue."

"Yeah, that'll be me. You're half a mile out, turn three degrees, to your right. Yeah, that's it."

Closing the distance, the Marine pilot said, "Gotcha, Sir, it really is crimson. You have any blood left? We'll put a man in the water. All you have to do is smile. We'll haul you in."

"I'll appreciate that Captain. That, and I need a secure line as soon as I hit the flight deck."

The chopper came in swiftly and hovered twenty feet above him. A rescue swimmer dropped down feet first splashing just ten feet away. He swam over and appraised the situation. A winch and cable, which had a small plastic platform attached was lowered. With no immediate threat in the area, they brought Josh up first and started tending to his leg wound. The cable was lowered back down for the Marine swimmer and before he was even inside the helicopter bay the bird elevated and rotated moving west picking up speed.

Josh asked for a secure line while still bleeding all over the open cabin floor.

CIA Langley, Virginia

CIA Director Logan Taylor sat in his seventh floor office looking out over the forested countryside that seemed to reach endlessly. The view always pleased him and allowed him to put aside the hundreds of challenges that he was facing each day, if only for a minute.

His private cell phone rang and he reached for it immediately. It was Derek Flynn, Assistant Director of Covert Operations from the sixth floor.

"Logan, I have to see you now, we just hit the mother lode. We may win the terrorist trifecta and the war after all. I'm on my way."

"Fine Derek, come ahead." but he was talking to a dead phone line.

Three minutes later Derek walked down the hall to the Director's corner office. He acknowledged the security guard sitting outside the office, nodded to the Director's personal assistant, and pushed through the glass door.

"You won't believe what I have to say," he said breathlessly. "Since we got the upper hand with the bin Laden mission, I put Josh Ranalli on another assignment to check out this sniper camp we keep hearing about in Yemen. He went to ground a month ago and we haven't heard from him at all. Two days ago he called with the camp location, sending us a signal from a satellite phone. Guess who the phone belonged to?"

"Well, it couldn't have been bin Laden? So, don't tell me we found Zawahri?"

"Almost as good. It was Awlaki's satellite phone. He's the guy running the sniper camp! Josh called it in because the camp is closing up shop soon, tomorrow in fact. They are mounting some new mission that will target the U.S. stateside. I think that's why Josh has not killed the bastard himself."

"So let's get him and the sniper camp," Director Taylor said. "Call in the Seals or drop a couple of bunker busters on the bastards. Let's send a message that al Qaeda can't hide anywhere."

"I've already set up drone surveillance of the entire area and pre-scheduled a drone attack subject to your approval. But it gets better. Just thirty minutes ago we got another communication from Josh. He is near Aden and clear of the camp so we can blast the crap out of it. He advised that Awlaki was also outside the camp but he's now on the highway heading back towards the camp. He's in an old pick-up truck. I've got two more drones up looking as we speak."

"That would be great news to take him out. The President would be pleased."

"There's even more," he couldn't contain his excitement. "The most recent message came from a stolen cell phone. Now guess who that belongs to?" He looked at the Director smiling, and waited for a response.

"You're shitting me. Zawahiri? Our guy does get around doesn't he?"

"Josh gave us a specific time and told us to pinpoint where an Iraqi oil tanker was sailing at that exact time in the Gulf of Aden, east of the city. When we have those coordinates we are supposed to look directly north to the coast of Yemen and a specific villa up on a cliff overlooking the Gulf. Zawahri has been basking in the sun there for some time, probably since we got bin Laden."

The Director started to reach for his phone.

"I've already put up another bird to scour the coast once we have that tankers coordinates." Derek Flynn said. "I've got two more Predators on standby with enough firepower to send Zawahri to meet his dead leader."

"Keep me posted. This would be a big one worth a trip to the White House."

Sault Ste Marie, Ontario

It was after midnight when the sleeper agent and the terrorist started transferring the weapons to the Native Son fishing boat. At that late hour the docks were deserted and Bay St. was poorly lit. The missiles were carried in blankets two at a time across the empty lot to the boat. The two men passed the blankets across the rear transom and then down the stairs and into the forward berth. When the first three were nestled in the bed frame they could see that most of them would fit nicely. By 2:00 am they had the 30 missile launchers on board. Packed tightly with blankets to keep them from moving or banging into one another, the bed frame and bed quilts were lowered back down. The forward berth looked as it always did, an inviting nest to sleep away the night.

Next they carefully carried the missiles themselves in a number of boxes with boat provisions on top should any one wander by and see them loading. These were put in the cabinets under the sink and cabinets. Once they were all stored he stacked dry goods, cereal boxes, and pots and pans in front of them. Anyone looking in would have a hard time seeing the shells behind all the kitchen gear and food.

They tidied up the boat and brought over all their Coho salmon fishing gear stacking it on the rear deck for the world to see. Then they called it a night.

The next morning Algul started his computer and went on-line with the U.S. Customer and Border Protection (CBP) Service. He answered the various questions that were posed giving his boat registration number, boat name, length and his CBP decal number. He had completed this process many times before.

Next, he listed the name, date of birth, passport number and NEXUS card data for himself and his passenger, now posing as his brother visiting from Toronto. Having all this information entered on-line made sailing into the United States easy. Their only other responsibility would be to check in with one of the video telephone terminals along the way to verify all this information. But he intended to go one better. He would actually stop at the Rock Cut Coast Guard Station, on the southern leg of the St Mary's River, which he had done many times before to say hello and check in personally. He figured presenting themselves for inspection would most likely allow them to pass without a boat search or any greater scrutiny. And even if they were boarded and examined they had artfully concealed the contraband.

After the paperwork was filed they loaded the last of the provisions on board. They brought on a bunch of frozen fish for the coolers to look like they had been fishing along the way and made sure they had a couple cases of beer on board. After all it was a vacation.

That afternoon, they eased away from the dock just east of the SOO Locks and within ten minutes were out in the channel invisibly crossing the U.S. Canada border that ran through the center of the St. Mary's River. Staying in the deep water channel with all sorts of large iron ore boats and container ships, the Native Son made its way east for one nautical mile and then turned south with the River heading towards Lake Huron.

The St. Mary's River is a major shipping corridor that can handle deep draft ships. As they neared the Rock Cut waterway, Algul called ahead on his marine radio to the U.S. Coast Guard Station abutting the cut and asked if they could stop to clear customs. The Station crew recognized the Native Son skipper and waved him in. In the first hour of the journey Algul had schooled Hamad on what he needed to know and say about the trip to the States. They went over the possible questions a number of times. His new brother seemed comfortable enough so they threw out the boat bumpers and eased into the Coast Guard Station dock. He positioned the boat so the on-duty personnel could clearly see the boat, the fishing gear and the two motorcycles strapped down on the rear deck.

Both men jumped ashore and walked into the station with their papers.

"Hi, Chris, you haven't been this way in a couple of months, don't you like us anymore?"

"Hello Dave, nah, I've just been fishing the other side of the locks. Canadian fish taste better, don't you know?"

"Yeah, yeah, so what brings you this way?" Dave said, as he accepted their papers and took a cursory glance at them. Then he looked out the station window at the boat below and saw the two Harley bikes lashed down and the fishing gear.

"My brother-in-law and I are taking a holiday to Milwaukee to see the Harley plant. We heard they have a terrific museum. The wives didn't want to tag along on a boat for that long, don't you know. So they're flying down and meeting us there."

"Makes sense, I heard that Harley museum is pretty cool. Wish I could join you."

"We're also going to give your U.S. fish another chance, which is another reason the wives didn't want to come with us," he said laughing. Hamad followed suit although he was very uncomfortable. He wanted to kill all of them. He continued to wander the public part of the station looking at the nautical maps, allowing Algul to do the talking.

"Papers look fine Chris, do I need to board to search for cigarette contraband?"

"Be my guest, but I'm not smoking anymore, so the worst you'll find is some Canadian beer which we are not importing. That, we're drinking."

"Another reason to join you. You should have clear sailing. We aren't expecting many ore boats coming north this week. How about a beer for the road? I'll walk you out."

The three men walked out to the boat and stepped aboard. The Coast Guardsman stepped over to one of the bikes and straddled it like he was driving the open road. Chris opened a cooler and pulled out three Canadian beers and distributed them. Dave dismounted, slipped the beer into his pocket and stepped over the gunwale onto the deck.

"For later," he said. "Have a great trip. Get any good pictures I want to see them on your way back." As a courtesy he released the forward line and then did the same on the stern.

"You got it Dave, I'll see ya, when I see ya." Chris turned over the engine and pushed the throttle forward. The Native Son eased away from the dock.

Hamad stood on the rear deck and watched Dave go back into the building. He shook his head and muttered quietly, "It can't be that easy?"

"It can, and it is. I knew the boat would be part of my assignment and I have been nurturing these relationships for years in this direction towards Lake Huron, and the other way through the locks to Lake Superior. All that effort just paid off. We are on our way. Dave will enter the boats data in his computer for us and now we are legally in the U.S., for the time being."

"Why didn't I come this way earlier? I'd be a U.S. millionaire by now."

Chris steered the boat out into the middle of the channel and the rock cut. He eased the throttle up to a nice low wake cruising speed. The St. Mary's River emptied into Nicolet Lake further south, and then into Munuscong Lake, which eventually merged with Lake Huron. As they traversed these bodies of water they passed a number of ships going in both directions.

Once in Lake Huron they turned west into the setting sun and made for the cut between Mackinac and Bois Blanc Islands. Mackinac was a famous resort area now, but originally it was a strategic fort and battle site in the war of 1812 with the British.

The boat cut between Mackinac and the much larger island that was mostly uninhabited virgin forestland. Passing through the deep water cut Chris turned into a small cove on the dark island where they could anchor for the night with little probability of seeing anyone.

Sharorah, Saudi Arabia.

Twenty miles north of the Yemeni border with Saudi Arabia, a covert, U.S. drone base had been established in the middle of nowhere. The closest road was five miles away and it was nothing more than a packed dirt road scraped into the earth. It was often impassable because of the blowing sand. The base had been setup with secret approval of the Saudi government and the House of Saud to help combat the growing terrorist threats in Yemen directly to the south.

Situated about 150 miles north of the Gulf of Aden, the entire base was almost invisible to the outside world. The base was not large. It didn't need to be, as it was only used to launch surveillance and combat drones. They required little space and only a short runway for take-offs and landings. The command and sheltered bunker buildings had been flown in by helicopter from the USS Wasp, a LDH-1 Landing Helicopter Dock Carrier on station in the Gulf providing service support for the base, and quick strike capability to the region. The ship also participated in pirate watch duties to protect shipping traffic traversing the narrow Gulf of Aden.

At the completely camouflaged drone facility deep in the desert, Air Force ground technicians loaded ordinance on two Predator C Avenger drones. A full complement of 2,000-lb guided bombs and Hellfire missiles were being secured beneath the wide wings. As the morning's first light announced the sun, a launch signal was given and the two drones taxied into position and took off into the light dry wind. The pilot-less crafts started rising quickly with small but powerful jet engines.

In North Dakota, half a world away, Colonel Peshia and his co-pilot, Sensor Operator Nicole Sweigart, had the stick of one of the drones. They had earned the right to fly this mission having first located the secret al Qaeda camp in the mountains of central Yemen. As their craft clawed its way into the clouds he ran a battery of tests to make sure that the drone was flying at optimum parameters. The second drone pilot did the same at the next double console just a few feet away. Both craft headed south and crossed into Yemen in a matter of minutes.

The two remote pilots took the drones up to 10,000 feet, the equivalent of almost two miles and leveled off, vectoring towards the terrorist campsite that had been identified earlier and was now painted on their screens. It would not be a long flight. They knew exactly where they were going.

'Hammer' Peshia had been flying a long time dating back to the First Gulf War in the early 90's. He had even been involved with the first effort to go after Osama bin Laden, which failed. His F-16 squadron didn't have this kind of technology back then and while they blew the Afghanistan terrorist camp to kingdom come, bin Laden had already left the mountain hideout and gotten away. The Colonel was looking forward to making this second chance mission count.

Coming up on his pre-determined coordinates, his cameras locked and recorded the images of the valley camp and surrounding mountains. There was not much to see, they were very well camouflaged, probably squirreled into caves. His photo images cut right through the clouds and he re-verified his coordinates were on-point. The terrorist camp was directly below. He had his written orders and approvals to attack so he armed his considerable ordinance hanging below the drone wings and locked in the ground coordinates of the target. The screen showed a target box straddling the valley floor in the center of the encampment. He moved a second box on the screen about three hundred feet to the left and locked in that coordinate as well. Looking first at his drone wingman sitting in the next cubicle, then his commanding Major General and the consulting CIA officer in the trailer, his technical officer flipped up her weapon button covers and toggled release of one 2,000-lb bomb, gave a silent five count, and then released the second one.

His wingman would go through the same procedure but he would first give the initial ordinance a chance to hit the targets before releasing his. He set different coordinates in the other direction three hundred feet to the right and then 300 feet to the south of ground zero. Watching his downward camera monitor he saw the blinding lights of the first two bombs smacking into the valley floor in succession. He then flipped his toggle switches and sent his guided bombs on their own path of destruction.

Everyone in the trailer watched the monitors as the screens went ballistic white with the flash as the first two-thousand pound bombs exploded. Then a good ten seconds later two more hit their targets, one after another. The pilots looked away to keep their eyes sharp, as they were about to enter a second phase of the attack.

The destruction below took a long time to come back into focus on the camera monitors with all the smoke and burning fires distorting the images they were seeing. The two pilots moved their joysticks and sent their drones into a wider downward circle around the terrorist camp. Stealth was no longer required. Those four bombs would have woken up everyone within 20 miles. As they spiraled down their cameras were now searching for survivors who might have lived through the carnage and might try to escape into the desert. Survivors would be doubtful because the bombs would have had a concussive force that would have turned internal organs into jelly. The only possible survivors might have been deep in the surrounding caves, but even they would have succumbed to the concussive force shooting into the cave entrances.

Both planes continued circling downward looking for movement. The heat signature cameras were not as useful at the moment because there were too many small fires burning, throwing heat in all directions. At 1,000 feet the drones leveled off and continued their search. After ten minutes of circling and looking for signs of life, the mission was officially terminated and the two drones started climbing for greater altitude. They knew that Yemeni ground troops would be arriving in a couple of hours to assess the strike, verify terrorist losses and clean up the devastation. CIA personnel would also be in attendance to ascertain if the planned targets were taken out.

As the drones came back on station at 10,000 feet Colonel Peshia was handed new map coordinates that he programmed into his primary screen. It was an overview map of Abyan Province in southern Yemen between the port city of Aden and the terrorist campsite they had just vaporized. He was ordered to vector in on the only highway leading from Shiban towards the Gulf of Aden. He was looking for an old pick-up truck traveling alone. It would have a tattered canvas cover flapping in the wind.

Peshia thought he was on a wild goose chase looking for a needle in a haystack but he did not question the order. He swept his craft into a wide turn and got over the highway at 10,000 feet and started searching for any road traffic. Using his forward-looking cameras and radar he found that there was actually was some traffic on the highway. His Predator Avenger drone flew over two cars that were hauling more stuff than he thought was possible to carry, but no truck.

A few minutes later with the cameras searching far forward he spotted what looked to be an old truck driving north on the two-lane asphalt highway. Knowing he would not be seen or heard overhead because of the drones small signature, he toggled his console joystick and started descending to the 5,000-foot level making a wide sweeping turn to fall into line behind the vehicle. As he got closer the cameras verified the truck did have a canvas bed cover flapping in the wind, just as he was instructed to look for. He maintained his altitude and locked onto the target vehicle.

Nicole Sweigart, his Sensor Operator and co-pilot started focusing her camera and video equipment zooming in for a more detailed look. She also initiated a laser system that would tag the moving vehicle and lock onto its heat signature. The two Air Force personnel worked as a team just as they would have in a real jet cockpit. The people standing behind the 'cockpit' leather armchairs in the North Dakota trailer stared at the video feed and the images being processed by the computers.

As the cameras continued to zoom in on the back of the truck and the flapping canvas, they saw what they were looking for. Sitting on a semi-hidden bench was a bearded man in white robes. His body would appear and disappear as the canvas moved back and forth. In a couple of frames the personnel could see the man reach for something and pick up a phone, which he held to his ear.

The CIA analyst immediately reached for a phone and dialed a number. He spoke a few words and then waited for the better part of a minute. On the other end of the line Langley contacted their Aden station to confirm whether the phone belonged to Anwar al Awlaki and was in fact currently being used. The Aden office came back advising the phone was indeed on and transmitting from central Abyan Province.

"That's him! It's confirmed. They've been tracking the signal since it lit up."

"Sir, we are tracking whom?" Sweigart inquired, realizing that she was about to be ordered to send a missile downrange.

"That lone man sitting in the back of that truck is a highly desired al Qaeda terrorist, Anwar al Awlaki, the number three, or four, leader of al Qaeda. We keep killing them off so I'm not sure how high up the ladder he is at the moment. We believe he's heading up al Queda in Yemen. He's the instigator of the sniper training camp we just took out, and is planning some sort of U.S. soil terrorist mission."

Sweigart was completely satisfied with the answer. "Your orders, Sir?"

The two senior men in the room looked at one another. They knew they already had approval to act once the target was verified. The approval came from the White House.

"Take him out"

"Yes, Sir," Sweigart said. She glanced at her seatmate. He nodded as she locked in her laser guidance system on the vehicle traveling below. She reached forward to her armaments board and switched a toggle sideways, arming a Hellfire missile hanging from the drone. Signaling the systems were green, the Sensor Operator Officer settled her hand around the joystick and trigger mechanism and waited for the order to shoot.

"Fire."

The Hellfire missile weighs one hundred pounds and is laser guided directly to the target. Triggered, it dropped from the drone's rack with a quiet whoosh as the fuel mixture ignited, and started downrange on its singular mission. Acquiring its GPS-guided laser coordinates it made small corrections and in a matter of seconds dove straight towards the target. The missile took a steep trajectory and slammed into the vehicle from above in a colossal explosion in the middle of the desert. The vehicle was encompassed in fire, with a super-heated cloud of smoke and flying metal shrapnel expanding outward. The vehicle's forward movement carried what was left of the molten mass off the road and into a culvert where chunks of asphalt and sand rained down. The tires, the truck cab and whatever had been in the truck bed burned with a thick black smoke.

"Hopefully that and the camp bombing will put an end to any new terrorist act he was planning on American soil."

"Let's hope so, but there are lot of angry Islamists out there. Nice job people."

The two drones turned north and headed for the desert of Saudi Arabia.

Lake Michigan just east of Door County

The Native Son was a good deep sea vessel and handled the rough seas crossing Lake Michigan without any problems. They traveled from Grand Traverse Bay in Michigan west across the Lake, passing North Manitou Island before hitting open water. Their destination was the storied Washington Island on the tip of Door County, Wisconsin. From there they would hug the coast and move to the south towards Milwaukee, Wisconsin, the home of Harley Davidson.

As they motored across the sixty miles of open water they put up their fishing lines and trolled to see what they might catch. They had already caught a number of Coho Salmon near Beaver Island further to the north. The fish were added to the freeze box. If they were stopped and boarded their story would hold up. Plus they had their motorcycles to flesh out the storyline.

Hamid was relaxed now, almost as much as Algul. The plan was being executed flawlessly. Everything was going almost too easily. He found he liked being on the boat even though he had spent the first day throwing up before he found his sea legs. Algul had explained that the waters of Lake Michigan were often rougher than the ocean because the deep water constricted between two landmasses was always being blown by hearty winds. He said ocean seaman would be on the Lake and often get seasick when they had never suffered such indignities on the high seas. On the ocean the water rolled in large evenly spaced swells that a ship could ride up, over, and then back down again. On Lake Michigan the water moved in short, choppy waves that constantly broke across the bow slamming into the ship for a much rougher ride.

The weather was supporting their effort and they made good headway. Once they crossed the Lake they headed south passing Sturgeon Bay and then Algoma, Two Rivers and Manitowoc. Nearing Milwaukee they pulled inside the breakwater and headed for the port entrance. Passing under the Lake Freeway Bridge, I-794, they motored up the River until it broke into north and south branches and turned south on what was called the Kinnikinnic River. Passing all sorts of industrial buildings and old lofts that had been converted to condos and apartment with their own floating docks, Algul kept heading south slowly in the no wake zones.

Passing through this re-gentrified zone of downtown Milwaukee's south side they moved into a turn of the century industrial sector with warehouse type buildings lining the river's edge. What once had been a major waterway now showed its age with crumbling docks, weed infested lots and a number of boat yards with huge cranes that lifted boats from the river for winter storage. Slowing even more they entered the 1st Street basin, about as far down the Kinnikinnic River you could go with a flying bridge boat.

Across the river from the Horny Goat Brewing Company, Algul effortlessly eased the boat up to some pilings and an old wooden dock. He had pre-arranged to moor his boat in this location next to a salvage yard. For $100 dollars a day he could tie up and offload his motorcycles easily for the trip to the nearby Museum. The manager of the salvage yard apologized for the lack of amenities, but did provide a hose line for fresh water and an electrical line to run power to the boat. But the best feature of this unlikely spot was the cycles could be offloaded and driven right up a shallow boat launch. Even better for Algul's purposes, an enclosed van or truck could also back down the same old boat ramp. At night the boat would be almost invisible under the 1st Street Bridge above them.

Schiller Park, Illinois

Joe Mazzoni, aka Mahoud, wasted no time in organizing his operation and team. He set up an office in a small retail-shopping strip on west Lawrence Avenue, one that had seen better days, signing a two-year lease for the space. He paid cash for the security deposit and the first two months' rent. The commercial broker didn't ask any questions because he had five empty storefronts in the small strip and welcomed the cash. Joe advised the broker he would be opening a residential real estate office. Signage was being arranged and office furniture would be delivered in a couple days, with an opening scheduled in a week. This was all true.

Once the broker left counting his cash, Joe signaled to a car parked across the street to pull up to the storefront. Three dark complexioned men of Mediterranean or middle-eastern origin got out and brought in a couple boxes of painting equipment and three gallons of paint. Without saying much they spread out some drop cloths and prepared both the outer and inner offices for a fresh coat of paint.

Once Joe had the three men working on the office painting effort he grabbed a Google map he had downloaded and left the building. He started driving around Schiller Park and the neighboring towns checking out what residential real estate looked like in the areas surrounding O'Hare International Airport. He took the better part of the afternoon driving up and down various streets, cutting back and forth down dead-end streets that butted up against airport perimeter fences and major highways surrounding the airport. He had a thick notebook on the passenger front seat and made notes on many of his observations.

He put in over twenty-five miles driving around that day never straying far from the large international airport circle. In working his way around this huge landmass he eventually passed beneath major approach routes where arriving jets were landing into the wind, coming in fast, one after another, and less than a minute apart. They were so close to the ground that the roar of the turbine jet engines drowned out all sound. He tried to estimate how high these aircraft were when they passed over various points. In some cases the planes were only a couple hundred feet from touchdown on the runways. The planes were so close he felt he could reach out and touch them.

Moving on he came to some huge parking lots surrounding a convention center and a large arena, as well as commercial and industrial buildings facing the north side of the International Airport. Again the fencing and crossing side streets were within spitting distance of runway approach paths. Huge marker lights were lined up with bright lights and strobes to guide the airliners in during evening hours. He took note of the addresses and which businesses had for sale or lease signs up.

Nearby there were rows of small commercial buildings that had seen better days. They had commercial storefronts but most of the space was dedicated to warehousing and each had loading docks in alleys running behind the buildings. He noticed that a number of these warehouse operations were for sale or lease and recorded the contact information.

He continued his drive around the Airport heading to the far west side. On York Road, which runs north and south on the west side of the airport, he passed a two-story grey block building that had no windows. The name out front read Heavenly Bodies and he wondered what that could be. He decided to investigate because it was late afternoon and the gravel parking lot was filled. Parking amidst the vehicles he walked towards the single door. Up the ramp he opened the door and saw a large bored man who gave him a once over and stood aside.

There was a single window bay down the short hallway and a young woman was kind of hanging out of it, like she was waiting for someone, perhaps a customer. She said that it was ten dollars to get in and that covered the pizza that was always available. Still unsure where he was Joe fished out a ten-dollar bill and paid the young lady. The big guy watched the transaction but said nothing. Obviously he was a guard, or perhaps a bouncer.

Turning the corner he entered a dark room that had lights near a bar on the far wall and a bright red heat lamp shining down on a paper-thin pizza that looked like it had been there a week. As his eyes adjusted to the darkness he saw that there was a young lady with very little clothes on gyrating next to a brass pole on a small stage. It was strip club!

Somewhat surprised, he tried to act casual, presuming that people were probably watching him. As his eyes adjusted to the darkness he identified the bar and headed that way trying not to step on the men sitting at tables all around the room. He found a bar stool and ordered a beer. Then he swiveled around to watch the show. There were a couple of small stages just a bit larger than a kitchen table. Half of them were filled with young and old men all drinking beers waving dollar bills in their hands for the exotic dancer on the mini-stage above.

He was amused by the scene, but kept quiet. So this was how the business world spent their afternoons sitting in a dark bar throwing dollar bills at scantily clad women. The girls were indeed beautiful but he did not enjoy the spectacle. But at the same time this place might serve his needs when his people needed a reason to be in the area.

He took mental notes about the building, gave thought to how his men should act while they would visit such a place and tried to watch the patrons to see how to fit in. After watching a number of men approach the dancers on the stage with a couple dollars in their hands, he thought he too would give it a try if for no other reason than to experience the thrill of being close to these almost nude young dancers,

He waited until no one was seeking the attention of the dancer and walked over to the edge of the stage. The young blond looked over and slowly sauntered his way. She squatted down to his level and spread her legs with a come hither look on her face. All he saw was a dead bored young woman that was offering a peek for a buck. She swayed her hips from side to side. Having watched the other young men he held up his dollar and the blond pulled her skimpy thong out a half-inch. He understood that he was to slip the bill under the edge of the waistband. For his efforts he got a caress on the cheek and thought that her hand was cool and moist to the touch. He tried to smile back and backed away as she was already scanning the stage for another mark. He returned to his beer and watched as she did the same thing to two more young men. One guy gave her a five-dollar bill and she rewarded him with a kiss on the cheek for his efforts. He wondered what twenty dollars would have gotten the guy.

That was enough excitement for him so he stayed by the bar and ordered another beer. He watched the stream of men come and go as various girls took them into a private room that said VIP on the curtain. He guessed they were getting private dances for much higher fees. That must be the twenty dollar room, he thought. It was an interesting place.

Finishing his second beer, he decided to head out. At the door he noted the pizza under the heat lamp had shrunk another half inch and now looked like cardboard. Exiting, the bouncer eyed him once more and turned his attentions back to the window lady.

Stepping outside he was blinded by the bright sunshine and had to stand there a half- minute while his eyes adjusted. At that moment a large 747 jet aircraft roared overhead, closing the distance to the airport a few hundred feet from the outer perimeter fence across from the strip club. It was just 200 feet in the air and defied explanation as to how such a large metal-bodied plane could stay in the air. He squinted and watched it pass overhead and smiled.

He next drove south on York Road paralleling the Airport. Ahead, he could see another American Airlines 737 jet clearing the outer fence line on a different runway. The plane was also less than 200 feet in the air. One block south of Foster Avenue, running east west he turned on Beeline Drive, which was an industrial street leading into a commercial business park. The road was pitted and bumpy due to the heavy truck traffic. He pulled into an asphalt parking lot and turned off the engine. His car was parked so it faced west looking into the late afternoon sun. He pulled out his dark sunglasses and stared into the western sunlight. In less than a minute he could see another jet aircraft approaching his position. When the jet got closer it too was only two hundred feet above his car. Except for the bright sunlight shining in his eyes Joe thought he could see the pilots through the cockpit windows.

As the plane passed over his position he heard the engines throttle up to full power for the final three hundred yard dash to touchdown. He knew that was procedure to give the plane the necessary speed and power to lift off again if the landing was aborted. The plane howled as it flew right over the car. Joe again felt as if he could reach out and touch the wings.

He sat there and again focused his attention on the western sky. In about 30-40 seconds another jet aircraft came into view barreling down the same path. Again he thought the plane would hit his car. Satisfied that this was an excellent spot to monitor plane traffic he looked around to see what the buildings near this point might offer.

Just a few hundred feet away was a warehouse building that had seen better days. There was a small retail storefront at the front of the building on Wolf Road and it had a sign offering the place for lease. The sign was in enough disrepair that he could tell it had been in the window a long time. He pulled out a pen and added the contact information to his log book.

As he slowly drove by the entrance he noted that it had been a carpet business. Out front in one of the parking spots facing the street was an old step van that had carpet advertising on it. The tires were flat and he suspected it had mostly been used to advertise the carpeting business to passing vehicles. He made a mental note of that as well.

His notebook was full and he had not yet completed his complete tour of O'Hare International Airport. He called it a day and started back to the Schiller Park real estate office that was being painted.

Aden, Yemen

Josh Ranalli was quickly taken to the U.S. Consulate compound in Aden. His wounds were bandaged and he was given an arm full of antibiotics and a fresh set of clothes. He sat in the interior soundproof office in the middle of the building. The room emitted a steady humming sound that muddled all conversation. He was talking to his superiors at Langley on a closed circuit television.

"Josh, we had no idea where you were, but I was confident you'd eventually surface. Glad to have you back," Derek said, as he sat across from the CIA Director's desk.

"Yeah, I'm sorry I couldn't contact anyone, Derek. I kind of stumbled into the mother lode that first day in Rome. It was unbelievably easy and almost comical how fast I was able to make contact. They thought I was a former Libyan soldier who had seen sniper service in Tripoli. I got to use the Swedish big boob's security guard bullshit again."

"That's always a good story for those introverted bastards. They eat that shit up."

"Every time I needed to change the direction of their questions all I had to do was mention those Swedish breasts and give them a mental image to think about. It works every time, except with Zawahri, but he's an old codger. Anyhow, they were interested in me because I could shoot. I demonstrated for them right in Rome's

Arab quarter and before you know it they invite me to work for them and shiped me off to Yemen. I became a sniper instructor at the camp you wanted me to find. Go figure!"

"Well, you do lead a charmed life, don't you? With your considerable Intel we were able to blow up that sniper camp, and we got Alwaki as well, but we missed Zawahri. He must have bugged out about the time you called us."

"That's about right, timing wise. I was on Zawahiri's beach taking a little R & R, when I heard a commotion by the villa. I'm guessing they realized I'd stolen one of his many cell phones. All of a sudden there were squealing tires above and then his security guards came charging down the hill shooting at me. So I had to bug out and figured a good swim would give me an exit. I would have made it too if they hadn't winged me. Thank God for the Marines."

The Director had quietly listened to the conversation up to this point. "Josh, are you well enough for a trip home soon? While you have personally helped to eradicate another two layers of al Qaeda, it still sounds like they may be mounting something new back here. Can we see you soon?"

"Sir, The leg will be fine, just another scar. And the Doc tells me the ladies will love my new split ear. Yeah, I'm fine. They say they can get me up to 'the Deid' in the next three hours and then on to Aviano. From there, I'll jump the first commercial flight out and be back in DC in less than 24 hours. I should be there by tomorrow evening, raring to go."

"Anything else to report?"

"When I was hiding out in Alawaki's cave, don't ask,..... I noticed a map of the U.S. with a big-penciled circle drawn around Chicago. I also heard them talking about missiles and some sniper they had sent on this new special mission."

"Ok, we'll put our ears to ground and start checking around. Fly safe and get some sleep. Make that leg of yours better because you may have to hit the ground running again."

"Roger that, Sir. On my way, Out."

Josh limped out of the room and headed for the stairs to catch a nap before his military flight to al Ideid, a large U.S. Air Force base in the middle of Saudi Arabia.

On the Kinnikinnic River, Milwaukee, WI

It was past midnight. The salvage yard manager had left hours earlier but had given his temporary renter a key for the padlock gate into the yard. Algul and Hamid had rented a step van earlier in the day and had some large color magnetic signs made at an area sign shop. Two signs said 'Al's Motorcycle Repair', and two other signs said 'Al's Expert Carpet Installation. All four signs had fake phone numbers and websites listed in smaller type.

As Hamid backed the van down the boat launch towards the rear deck, Algul laid out some motorcycle tools he had brought along on the boat and on the launch deck. If anyone did come along the story was the motorcycles were being worked on. Both men rubbed some grease on their hands and coveralls to look as if they were indeed working on the bikes. Algul removed the lug nuts holding the front wheel assembly on one bike and pulled the wheel off.

Seeing that no one was around and very little traffic was crossing the 1st Street Bridge above, they opened up their secret stash and started carrying the weapon systems out one by one, wrapped in blankets. In no time they had the windowless van loaded. Locking up the boat, they both hopped in the van and drove out of the salvage yard locking the gate behind them.

They drove in silence to an old road motel on 27th Street near the Milwaukee airport. They had reserved a room on the first floor so they could park the van right outside the door. The van now had the signs announcing Al's Expert Carpet Installation. They figured that would make a break-in less likely.

The next morning Hamid made a phone call to Chicago on a burner phone. He verified the voice was the person he wanted and said hi. He stated he was coming home to see his brother and would be there in the following day. He hung up and broke the phone's spine. Grabbing a second phone, he called a different number, which was answered by the same person he had just spoken to. He gave him an address in a suburb of Chicago. They hung up again.

The following morning Algul said goodbye to his long lost brother who would drive the carpet van to the Chicago area. He called a cab to take him back to the boat. He would return to Canada and await another mission.

Chicago, Illinois

Joe Rizzoli now had a bankroll. Actually, it was a sizeable transfer that had bounced around a half dozen countries and banks before being deposited in his name in a local community bank in Schiller Park, a small suburb just down the road from O'Hare International Airport. He transferred some of the money to another new account in his real estate company name. Now he had funding to buy some real estate.

His first purchase was an industrial building just north of Runway 22 R from northeast to southwest in Rosemont. It was a building just behind the Allstate Arena, where a basketball team played, rock bands had concerts, and circuses came to town. It had an office / industrial / warehouse feel to it and a loading dock that could accommodate a mid-size truck. Perfect for his needs. He planned to set up a small business selling air-conditioning equipment and was having a half-dozen used units being delivered in a couple of days.

Heading west he drove down York Road and into an industrial park with various one and two story warehouse buildings lining the streets. As he worked his way deeper into the area he came upon a number of building parking lots that abutted the outer perimeter fence of the Airport. The fence was six feet high and topped with barbed wire, but that did not bother him. He parked his car amongst others and sat there watching his surroundings.

Looking out onto the large airport he could see two major runways crossing from the west to the east and another to the southeast. That would be runways 9 L and 14 R. He could see planes landing from the other side of the airport coming out of the east. That was today, the wind could change and the same planes would be landing out of the west and flying almost over his head. He made some notes and thought about having a plumber's panel truck parked in this position. The truck could pull up just moments before a plane was landing. A gunner could step out of the side door and shoot in moments. He marked his map and made some additional notes.

Just then a man in a dark suit carrying a briefcase approached the car from behind and 'Joe" reached for his pistol lying under a newspaper on the passenger seat. He disengaged the safety and waited. The man nodded to 'Joe' and then got into the car next to his. He started the engine, backed out and drove off. Joe re-engaged the safety and slipped the gun under the newspaper. The businessman wasn't the least concerned that a man was sitting at the airport perimeter fence. That too was a bit of intelligence.

Next he drove to the old carpet business he had found further south on York Road. The building owner was waiting for him and grateful someone was interested in his dilapidated building. They toured the small office and large warehouse, and after a little dickering they agreed upon a great one-year lease. The landlord even offered to have the old truck towed away, but Joe said no. He explained he hoped to use the truck as a mobile advertising sign out front. He said he would fix up the old truck and get it running again. The landlord was pleased he wouldn't have to haul it away and left. He had a lease and three months' rent so he was a happy man.

Over the next few days, 'Joe', the new real estate man started purchasing some homes in a number of different neighborhoods surrounding O'Hare Field. First, they were not that expensive because of the close proximity to the airport. Second, they were working class neighborhoods where different types of people would be tolerated without any great scrutiny. And third, the airplanes flew as low as 300 feet above the roofs.

One house was in Schiller Park on Linn Avenue. The street was a short one-block long stub with a few small bungalow homes stuck on a tight wedge of land between I-294 and the railroad yard to the east. Chase Realty had it listed on the market for over six months without a sale. People didn't like the noise levels as the planes would come overhead every 30 to 40 seconds. The house was a small wood and brick veneer two-bedroom bungalow. It had a deep driveway and a separate garage that had a large door allowing entry of a van or medium sized truck. Joe made a low ball offer and the realtor jumped at the chance to unload the dog.

There were only six houses on the block and all had small garages at the backs of the yards offering seclusion. The homes were close to a 12-foot high block wall that abutted the expressway and lessoned the sound of the thousands of cars passing every hour. At this point I-294 had twelve lanes of traffic six in each direction because of its close proximity to the entrance to O'Hare Field. It was a perfect home for his needs and he had a renter all lined up, painter number 2.

Moving north to the suburb of Des Plaines, he found another home for sale on the corner of Greco and Lunt Avenues. It too was the last home before the expressway fence and the airport perimeter across twelve busy lanes. It was on a tree-lined street that offered an almost solid green canopy. It had once been a thriving neighborhood but with the growing airport and surrounding expressways the homes had seen better days. It was a nondescript small reddish brick bungalow that had a four-foot high chain-link fence around the entire lot, probably to contain a dog or children. Set back on the lot was a dilapidated beige garage that had an old power boat on concrete blocks next to it. It was perfect for his needs so he made a ridiculously low offer, which was immediately accepted.

Moving southeast he drove to Franklin Park and looked at a commercial business on Franklin Street. He found a small business that was facing north towards the airport. As he stood there outside the door he heard a growing rumbling that kept getting louder. He actually ducked as a 757 American Airlines jet flew directly over his head a mere two-hundred feet above him. He smiled and then watched the plane cross the airport perimeter.

He was shown the large warehouse and the tall truck freight doors and noted that a number of trucks were parked in the alley. Two of them looked as if they were permanent fixtures. Every other minute he had trouble hearing the landlord because of jets just above the building. The alleyway behind the building was remote enough that you could not see traffic from Franklin Street or from the crossing Wolf Road. And it was directly on the flight path for Runway 32 L.

After a week 'Joe' had leased or purchased twelve properties at the head of every runway heading into O'Hare Field. The sellers or landlords had been easy to deal with. They were grateful for the interest and even more pleased with the up-front rent. They weren't asking questions and had no intent of queering the deal.

Langley, Virginia, CIA Headquarters

Josh's flights got him to DC quickly. Years ago he had learned how to sleep anytime, anywhere, and he used full advantage of his first class passenger status to catch some shut-eye. It had been harder to do on the military flight legs to Rome, but the final six hours had been in Lufthansa's new lay-flat First Class service. He was refreshed and only when he stretched was he reminded that a bullet had gone clean through his leg.

"Nice forked ear Josh, is that a new Yemeni tradition?" Derek said, as he stepped into the briefing room.

"Yeah, I think I like it. Doc said it will probably heal that way. Haven't been able to try it out on the ladies, though. They may find it attractive in a kind of satanic way. So what do we have?"

Derek laid out a series of paper files and started rifling through them. He found what he was looking for and flipped it over to Josh.

"That's NSA's summary on any traffic they have picked up about Chicago and terrorists. Not much to look at, but they've flagged the lead now and will scrutinize anything they hear. Once our ears are tuned in at NSA we'll zero in on any mention of the key terms both here and overseas."

Josh figured there would not be much to go on but a nugget is a nugget.

"On a separate red flag they did pick up some leads about missiles going missing in Libya. With that civil war raging all over the desert I'm guessing the militias are breaking into all sorts of remote stockpiles of weapons Gadhafi had, especially after they took him out. I'm guessing all sorts of bad guys have stumbled onto these caches of weapons buried in that Libyan sandbox. There are even stories in the news that Stinger missiles are out there for the highest bidder. We even have a buyback program in place to get the weapons back."

"We knew that was going to happen." Josh said, "Gadhafi had weapons squirreled away all over the damn country. I dropped in on one outpost a way back and only found empty pallets. The bad guys had already taken them."

"Well, keep me in the loop. I'm grabbing some shuteye and I'll be heading to the windy city to see if I can kick up anything on that end."

Tunis, Tunisia

Mike Barron was the resident CIA Officer in Tunisia. He received a message that asked him to see if there was any shipment of arms passing through the Port of Tunis. In no time he had made contact with three of his confidential informants that were on the payroll. They had nosed around the waterfront and two of them had stumbled on an interesting piece of information. Talking to various sources they heard there had been some sort of open auction of Gadhafi weapons and missiles brought across the Libyan border by Berber militias. All sorts of gunrunning assholes had showed up to bid on the weapons. It was supposed to have happened less than two months ago. All these guys had showed up looking for a large cache of weapons but found someone had beaten them to the punch.

With that nugget of information Mike Barron starting combing the various waterfront bars seeing if he could substantiate what he'd heard. In the third dive bar he found a known Egyptian arms dealer who was three sheets to the wind leaning heavily into the well-worn bar. He could hardly maintain his balance on the barstool.

The CIA agent eased himself to the bar and sat down next to him ordering a drink. In no time he was commiserating with the man to see what he could find out. He bought the man another drink and let him know he too was an arms dealer, from France, who had heard about the lousy auction. After another cocktail they started becoming old friends and shared stories of missed opportunities. The drunk was still pissed that he didn't get a chance to bid on the missiles. He was angry that some al Qaeda asshole had beaten him out.

The agent bought another drink but slowed the pace a bit to keep himself sharp and the drunk alive for a few more questions. He slowly drew out whatever information he could and eventually heard the weapons had been loaded on a container ship that was bound for Canada. The drunk's head hit the bar with a thud and everyone looked up. The drunk was alone at the bar and he fell off his bar stool hitting the floor hard. The agent was already half way out the door.

The next day the agent went to the dock foreman's office and offered a nice-sized 50 Euro bribe for access to recent shipping records. The foreman pocketed the money and left the small office to his guest while he went for a smoke.

Mike Barron found a quiet corner and did what spies do best. Over the years he had learned how to investigate shipping records and manifests so he started pouring over the books zeroing on the dates in question. He did so until his eyes hurt.

Eventually he identified two ships that had been in Tunis on that same weekend that were scheduled for passage to Canada. One was a bulk carrier that was deadheading back for more Canadian grain. The other was a container ship that was carrying oil field components, auto parts and smaller mixed loads. The second ship had made port in Toronto.

He pulled the ships manifest information, cross-referenced ownership, and pulled individual shipper names, container numbers, consignments, and intended delivery points. They would have to comb through the data back at Langley and try to figure out what was in each of the containers and where they ultimately were shipped. He was glad he was in the field and only had to gather the information.

He felt sorry for the poor slobs that would have to scrutinize and track down each of the shipment containers.

Leaving the dock shipping office, he drove over the U.S. Embassy. Going to the communications room he sent the information back to Langley. Then he went home to nurse his headache from too much drinking during the day.

CIA Langley, 3rd Floor Mid-East Section

Mideast analyst James Mallory sat in his cubicle looking at the data that had been dropped on his desk. It was a stack of shipping manifests and container logs for a ship that left Tunis, Tunisia and traveled to Toronto, Canada a couple months ago. It was his job to find a needle in a haystack. He was searching for weapons that were not logged that may have been in a container amongst 500 similar containers the size of trucks.

It was another day of unglamorous spy work. But he rationalized, he was helping the James Bonds of the clandestine service do their jobs in the field. He had always admired the James Bond character and read all the novels. He had seen all the movies over the years and insisted on sitting through the long film credits to absorb the whole experience. He paid attention to detail and that was probably why he was stuck in a CIA cubicle analyzing data all day.

He organized the stacks of gathered data and started searching the accompanying shipping manifests to see what was being transported, where it was going and to whom. By afternoon he had made numerous stacks of information and started narrowing his search by calling companies to ask about the shipments and deliveries. Since he was mostly talking to clerks who managed shipping traffic for a living he was confident in their responses. If he got straightforward responses about the container contents and destinations he separated them into one stack. If he got evasive responses or pushback he separated them for additional follow-up. It was a slow and arduous process of looking for anomalies, looking for something that did not add up or make sense.

By late afternoon he had determined that almost all of the shipments were legitimate and had been received where they should have been going. He had whittled his stacks down to a few miscellaneous containers that had mixed loads, meaning they had gone to a number of locations for partial deliveries.

In examining these manifests he found numerous metal parts shipments going to a number of Canadian addresses. They were shipments of specialized pipe lengths, thick metal couplings, generators, and oil derrick equipment. That all made sense because the bulk of the ship's containers had been destined for the shale oil fields in Alberta. But one container had a large order of corrugated metal building sections that were shipped to a commercial fishing company in Sault St. Marie. That was an anomaly. He questioned why anyone would ship heavy corrugated metal building components across the globe to Canada, when such metal building materials were probably readily available locally. That warranted further investigation and Mallory reached for a phone.

He dialed the Canadian company phone number on the shipping manifest.

"Hello, Morrow's Fish Market," a woman answered and cheerfully offered, "How may I help you?"

"Good day, Miss, I'm calling about the shipping materials that were delivered about three weeks ago. Just checking on the status of the delivery. Did you receive all the boxes as ordered? We're you satisfied with the building materials?"

"I'm sorry, you must have the wrong number. We haven't received any building materials delivery. We're a fish market," the pleasant sounding Canadian woman stated.

Bingo, another anomaly, Mallory thought. He tried another follow-up question.

"I apologize, the shipment was sent to a Christian Morrow in Sault Ste. Marie. The shipping manifest says it was delivered on the 9th last month? My records show that he signed for it."

"Well, this is Mrs. Morrow, and Chris is my husband, but I am unaware of any shipment. Although he may not have told me about it."

He considered that response. It seemed odd, a wife that doesn't know about a truck-sized shipping container delivery to their business? Next question. I'll ask for Christian.

"Might Christian be available? All I need to do is verify his satisfaction," Mallory said, hoping to elicit some additional information.

"Well, he's not here at the moment. He's out on a boat trip with his brother," the woman said.

"Could I reach him tonight, or perhaps tomorrow?" The analyst inquired.

"I'm afraid not, he's on a fishing vacation. He went Coho fishing in Lake Michigan with his brother. They were also going to visit Milwaukee as well, to see that Harley Davidson Museum," she offered helpfully, trying to be nice. "He's been gone a week already and probably won't be back for another."

"Well, that's fine. I'll probably check back in a week or so. Thank you," Mallory said, and cut the connection. Luckily she had never asked him who he was, or from where he was calling. Better left unsaid, especially if this was the lead they were looking for.

He decided the anomaly was worth following and placed it on the top of the stack. He dialed his supervisor to report his day's work and the possible lead. He knew that now some poor James Bond type would have to go out and do the fieldwork, but at least it was off his desk.

Chicago, Illinois

Josh Ranalli sat uncomfortably in his first class seat looking down at the many skyscrapers spread out all over downtown Chicago. He was still sore from the bullet wound in his thigh, but unless you were looking for it you could hardly notice his slight limp. He was pushing himself so the healing process would take its course. The forked ear was another story. He noticed the first class flight attendant looking at him a number of times and she was always smiling. Maybe this rather unique disfigurement would have a plus side.

The United flight was on final approach into O'Hare. As they got lower and lower he watched as they cleared the Forest Preserves east of the airport, flew over the Rosemont Convention Center and then the Interstate highway. The plane soared about 300 feet above the homes just east of the expressway. He thought about how wonderful it must be to sleep under that day and night.

Once the wheels touched down on the runway they taxied over to the outer United Terminal block and he disembarked. He got his bearings and headed for the elevator to the underground passage leading over to United's main terminal building. The moving walkways were tempting but he needed the leg exercise so he cut to the right to walk the quarter mile in the ever-changing lighting that created strobe like patterns on the long hallway ceiling. He guessed it made people forget they were walking underneath 200-ton airplanes.

In baggage claim he grabbed his bags, turned around and started to look for his local liaison. By Congressional mandate the CIA was not authorized to do its work domestically. That was the realm of the FBI. But after the 9-11 terrorist attack those rules had been pretty much thrown out the window because of the constant terrorist threats. It was at that point that the many competing alphabet federal agencies were told to play nice with one another. A new organization was created, Homeland Security. It was charged with the responsibility of coordinating with all federal agencies to assess and resolve all terrorist threats, domestic and foreign.

Looking around he spotted the agent before she spotted him. He recognized her instantly. It was Etta Petrini, the attractive women he had met a year earlier in New York on his sniper liaison. Things were looking up, he thought. Perhaps he would get a chance to get an assessment on his new forked ear sooner rather than later.

"Mr. Ranalli, I believe?"

"Good memory Etta, you spotted me quickly, perhaps I made an impression in New York?" he asked, regretting it as he said it. What a jerk, and right off the bat. He flashed a smile to make up for it and turned his head to show off his new ear crease.

"But Mr. Ranalli, was my Dads name, I'm just Josh." He proffered his hand to keep everything professional even though he would have liked a hug. It had been a long five months in the desert.

He closed the distance and shook her hand. As he gawked at those beautiful eyes again he was reminded she was a stunning woman. In an instant a number of thoughts flashed through his brain. She was still hiding a great figure in another business suit, but grey this time. She looked great in gray too! She had obviously been an athlete in earlier years. A runner? Or maybe even a body builder? He needed to drill down a bit more on her background this trip. He also noticed she still had on those sensible shoes, ready for field action. He wondered what was under all that professionalism.

"Josh, good to see you again. I wondered if our paths might ever cross again." Now she was doing the smiling.

That's a good sign, he thought. "I volunteered for this assignment once I heard you were on the job," he lied. He thought for a moment and decided this lady deserved the truth and decided to fess up. "In truth, that's a lie." he said, "I didn't know you were going to be here. But I'm very pleased to be working with you again." He smiled his best again.

Throwing his bag over his shoulder they started for the door. He drifted behind because of his limp and followed her out the door and across three lanes of traffic. He walked just slow enough to again admire the view he had remembered from New York. And this time there were no candle sconces in the way.

He had been holed up in a cave for too long. They walked up to a standard issue black four-door sedan that was illegally parked under the shuttle train concrete pylons. A cop was also heading that way eyeing the vehicle, but she held up her credentials to wave him off.

"So, Josh, what do we have here? Another terrorist plot that will scare the crap out of me and our good citizens?" the agent inquired. She tossed the question over the roof of the vehicle and then gracefully slid into the driver's seat.

"I hope not. That's why I'm here to explore what may turn out to be just a wild goose chase. But I'm pleased that you are going to be my handler. I'll enjoy being handled."

He realized that must have sounded pretty lame as well. "Thanks for picking me up."

"Just remember you CIA types don't have official jurisdiction or status here stateside. But I make you legitimate." She again smiled and started the car. "I am lead, so no cowboy stuff, Ok? You follow me."

Josh reddened up as he thought about her backside. He decided he would try to enjoy this temporary assignment. Things were looking up. Most cops didn't look like this striking woman. They were usually a lot less attractive, both the male and female.

As they buckled up he saw that she was packing and all of a sudden felt naked. He made a mental note to ask for a loaner. He figured he was safe at the moment. What could happen on the expressway?

She noticed he was staring but chose to ignore the looks. She was secretly pleased to be partnering with this guy too. As she maneuvered through the airport she looked over at her temporary partner and gave him an inquisitive look.

"So what happened to your ear?" she asked, changing lanes. "Do you also speak with forked-tongue?"

Josh fingered the split soft tissue and casually said, "Do you like it? It's a recent war wound compliments of the bad guys overseas. Let's just say that I ducked just in time."

"I guess so! I presume that's all that you can tell me about it, right?"

"Pretty much. If I told you more I'd have to kill you, and that would be a terrible waste of a beautiful woman,….who is packing, I might add! Which reminds me, can I get a loaner for this little investigation? I feel kind of naked without a weapon."

It was her turn to envision that naked image for a moment and she blushed as she thought about it. Shaking it out of her head she said, "We'll see. I'm not sure why you are even here yet. Once I have some idea of what's up, we can talk about armaments. The car is secure, so how about filling me in. What's going on? All we have so far is you might have stumbled on a major terrorist threat focused on the city of Chicago."

"It's a long story, but if I remember Chicago traffic correctly we have at least an hour before we get downtown. I'll give you an abbreviated summary."

"That would be fine except we aren't going downtown. Homeland's got its own building out here now, just outside the airport. We'll be there in less than 10 minutes, so give me the cliff-notes version."

"Or maybe we could catch lunch somewhere?" he asked hopefully. "Let's get re-started where we left off in New York."

"Well, we could eat something." She thought for a moment. Someplace quiet. She exited the airport at River Rd and then turned on Bryn Mawr Rd. heading west. Turning south she entered a parking garage and took Josh to the Five Roses Pub, part of the Rosemont Entertainment District. At lunch time the restaurant would not be too crowded and they could get a booth in a corner away from other guests. Things were looking up.

As they walked in Josh was pleased with the location. It would allow him to get to know Etta. They ordered some drinks. Noting she was working, Etta ordered an iced tea. Josh would have liked a beer but wanted to be professional and ordered two Diet Cokes. He didn't need the diet, he just couldn't handle the sweetness of the regular stuff in his throat. Having been in the desert for months, he couldn't get enough of the brown liquid. He drained the first Diet Coke in a matter of seconds.

They ordered burgers and Josh started telling his redacted story about his recent mission, at least the parts that he could share. He didn't mention specifics but alluded to having looked the bad guys right in the eyes as he heard about terrorist plans for America and possibly Chicago. He was all business although her beauty kept throwing him off his game as he talked across the table.

Etta listened quietly trying to connect the dots linking the possible terrorist threat to Chicago. She asked a few questions to zero in on the threat level. By the time lunch was finished she knew that this would become a legitimate threat. She also knew she was sitting across from the real deal. She thought she needed to get to know this undercover operator better.

"So is that where you picked up the forked ear?" Without waiting for an answer, she said, "Well, I'm glad you made it and can fight another day. Was that you by any chance that set up Awlaki in Yemen? I heard we almost got Zawahri at the same time." She looked over and smiled to show she didn't actually expect an answer.

"Well, let's just say that I was recently bobbing in the Gulf of Aden, bleeding like a stuck pig, trying not to become shark bait. The bastard hi-tailed it out of town before we could drop the hammer. He's a slippery fox for such an old guy." He too smiled at her and knew that he would enjoy hanging with her.

"On that leg limp, did they get you good?" She hoped not!

"You picked up on that, huh? Just a thru and thru to the thigh. Nothing vital. As you said, I'll live to fight another day, just need to get the muscles exercised a little more. Turning to show his ear again he said, "So what do you really think of my new ear look? Do you think women will like it?"

She appraised the red-scabbed wound. She didn't want to look too interested. She didn't know this guy yet. But she might want to get to know him.

"I'd say you would get some questions. They may want to know how it actually happened. If you tell them the truth that a bullet cleaved your ear, I'd say they'll like it. Otherwise, they will think your just some old hippie who pulled out a cheap body piercing by accident." Her eyes twinkled.

"Old?" he laughed. "My flight attendant on the plane wasn't turned off. She even tried to whisper her number in my ear. And it was the cut ear. I think she thought it was cool."

"How young was she? You know tattoos and body piercing are in vogue now. Did she ask you your age?" Again, she chuckled.

"I was in first class and the young ones don't have enough seniority for up there. She had a few years on her, about like you, and she was interested. I could tell. Maybe I should have gotten her number. She said she was based out of Chicago."

Etta didn't respond. She was still evaluating his comment 'old, about like you'. Was that good or bad. She reached into her breast pocket and retrieved her business card handing it to him. "There, now you really do have a card and number for all that effort. Enjoy."

They left the restaurant and drove south a short block to Balmoral Avenue and turned right heading back towards the airport. Josh could see planes landing almost directly overhead and the terminals in the distance. They crossed over the Tri-State Expressway and turned north on a side street with a number of office buildings lining both sides of the street. At the end of the block he saw a large 'Bandits' sign proclaiming the home of a professional woman's softball team and a huge bubble dome that looked like a sports facility. Across from the baseball field was a large office building that had all sorts of privacy signs marking its entrances. If you looked closely you could see a number of federal agency crests were posted on the primary entrance doors.

Etta Petrini drove behind the building into a large parking lot that had a perimeter metal fence with concertina barbed wire topping it. There were dozens of federal cars, SUV's and vans parked in rows with agency names on the door panels, including AFT, Border and Immigration Control and Homeland Security. She turned off the ignition. At the door an armed uniformed guard looked at their credentials and let them pass.

Racine, Wisconsin

Hamid drove the carpet van at about three miles over the speed limit along I-94 heading south. He wished he could drive faster but was told not to draw any police attention. The cars flying past him at 75 and 80 mph were angry with him as he bottled up the free flow of traffic. A couple people even pointed fingers at him. He ignored them and paid attention to his driving.

Moving down the highway he saw signs announcing a 'Mars Cheese Castle' and wondered what on earth that could be. His immersion training had explained Wisconsin was famous for its cheese, and that its people liked being called cheese heads, but did they actually have a castle built of cheese, he wondered. A second sign heralded the marvel again so decided he had to see for himself.

Breaking all the terrorist rules, he angled off the highway and started looking for the 'castle'. Beyond the stoplight he saw it. It was huge, and indeed looked like a real castle with turrets and huge stone walls. Could it actually been made out of cheese? He turned into the vast parking lot, already crowded with cars. Everyone wanted to see this marvel.

He parked near one of the entry doors in a handicapped spot. Backing in he thought maybe they would think he was unloading carpet. After locking the van, he turned and touched the building behind him. It was not made of cheese. It was made of concrete block. So much for that theory, he thought.

Entering the castle he was dumbfounded to see hundreds of people shopping for cheese and everything that went with cheese. There were huge rounds of cheese displayed, along with large refrigerated display cases with hundreds of different cheeses spread out for sampling. There was even a wine bar area and racks and racks of cheese related products.

Hamid was clearly amazed. He did not have such things at home. Sampling a few cheeses he knew he had to buy some for the remainder of the trip. There was even some cheese from his native Turkey on display. He knew what they tasted like so he concentrated on the local Wisconsin cheese, which was supposed to be so good. Everyone was happy and buying cheese like it was the last thing on earth. This was something he would need to tell the people back home. America was astounding, he thought.

Finally satiated with his exploration, he made some purchases using the American dollars he had been given for his travel. Leaving the store he noticed a police car parked in front of the van.

Hamid stopped in his tracks. The officer was writing up a ticket. Proceeding forward he walked up to the Officer as he had been trained for this situation. He thought quickly and said, "Officer, I apologize, I was just making a carpet delivery."

"Look Mister, I'd believe you if you didn't have cheese crumbs on your beard and a bag full of goodies behind your back." He ripped the ticket off the pad and handed it to him. "Move the van now, or I'll give you another ticket for sloppy eating habits. Have a good day."

Hamid looked at the ticket and saw it was for $150 in U.S. dollars. He decided not to say another word and got in the van as quickly as he could. When the County Sheriff squad car moved out of the way he pulled out, took one more look at the incredible cheese castle towering above him, and drove out of the lot.

At the stoplight he looked at the ticket on the dashboard. Having no intention of paying such a fine, he ripped the ticket in half and tossed it out the window. The two pieces fluttered to the road surface and caught in the curb. The light changed and the ramp to the Interstate and Chicago was straight ahead. Gaining speed he settled in at 67 miles per hour and opened his cheese curds and started popping them in his mouth.

Schiller Park, IL.

In the last few weeks Mahoud had brought together a rather dedicated group of Muslims from around the country. They were all committed to jihad and were prepared to do as they were told to move the mission forward. Even he was surprised at how many contacts Awlaki had developed in the United States. They were showing up because they had heard of Anwar Awlaki's death in Yemen at the hands of the American aggressors and they wanted retribution for their Imam's death. Once the calls had been made these 30 plus individuals, both men and veiled women, had arrived in less than a week coming from as far away as San Diego and Washington DC.

As they arrived, they checked in at the real estate office purporting to look for housing, and they were each assigned to live in various houses Mahoud had assembled in the last two months. At each house they were instructed to move in and become familiar with their area. Each person was given background stories and encouraged to make acquaintances with their new neighbors. They were told to blend in and become a part of the neighborhood and local community.

In addition, he assigned them to new jobs at the various businesses he had purchased or leased. Some of them were to become carpet salesmen, others became equipment repairmen, or warehouse men. In these local business operations they had to set up the businesses, creating showrooms, building storage racks, setting up loading docks, and creating waiting rooms. The businesses needed to be functioning, at least to the casual observer. At these workplaces these new employees were also encouraged to blend in and become familiar with their neighbors and the area surroundings.

The common denominator for all these people, both their homes and businesses were located within spitting distance of the major runways approaching Chicago's O'Hare International Airport. Mahoud's new recruits realized that fact very quickly. Depending on which direction the wind was blowing, large commercial aircraft would be flying directly overhead, sometimes with only 200-300 feet of clearance as they touched down at one of the largest airports in the world. With planes flying overhead almost every minute of the day these people would duck as the jets thundered by above their heads. They were in fear of the planes actually landing on top of them. Later, as they became more used to the constant noise they started wearing earplugs and ear protection equipment. Many of them found it hard to sleep

Homeland Security, O'Hare Airport Field Office

Josh Ranalli and Etta Petrini were getting familiar working with one another. In a professional way, to Josh's great frustration. They had been pouring over all sorts of terrorist data trying to find some links to Chicago for days.

"Josh, we may have a break," Etta said, walking in and sliding next to him. "Langley just sent us some Intel they have been chasing down. Your guys have been trying to track some of those arms shipments from Libya, that went through Tunisia on a ship bound for Toronto."

"Great, where is the ship now?"

"It docked in Toronto and was unloaded about a month ago," she said, as she scanned down the CIA report summary. "That seems like old news to me."

"What else, why is that ship important?" Josh said, scratching his nose. He wasn't sure he smelled something yet. He asked for more.

"It says one of your guys uncovered a shipment of missiles that were stolen from one of Gadhafi's arsenals by some Berber militias and spirited over the border into Tunisia. There it was sold to a known Al Qaeda arms buyer. Since it was missiles they followed the trail and ultimately found that the weapons had been loaded on a container ship headed for Canada. By process of elimination at the port of Tunis they think they found the container and the container number, and tracked it after leaving the boat."

"Go on" Josh said, as he grabbed a map of Canada from a drawer. "Where was that container going?"

Etta kept reading the report. "The shipping containers were primarily full of auto parts for Ontario and oil processing equipment for the Alberta oil fields up north. But it says they also had an interim stop at a retail fish market storefront to deliver corrugated metal siding in Sault Ste. Marie, Canada."

"So there's your anomaly." Josh offered. "Why does a retail fish market in Canada need corrugated metal siding from Tunisia? I'm guessing that stuff is readily available locally at the ACE hardware store."

"Yeah, that makes sense. One of your analysts said he called the manifest phone number and talked to a woman who owns the store. She didn't know anything about it. She suggested talking to her husband, but he was away on his fishing charter boat on his way to Milwaukee, WI. He's still gone for another week." Etta looked up. Josh was already reaching for a phone.

He called Langley and was put through to James Mallory, the analyst. He wanted some additional insight. He wanted to know if the wife gave off any evasive vibes, tried to overly protect her husband, or seemed out of sorts or uncomfortable with the conversation? The analyst responded she was helpful and honest, as much as she knew. He believed she had no knowledge of anything out of the ordinary. He thanked the man and promised an update.

"Etta, do you have any good contacts with the Mounties up north?"

"Yes, I have a security liaison who I could call. What are we asking?"

"Call and ask him if he has someone up in Sault Ste. Marie, which I see is right on the U.S. Canada border, that could swing by our local fish market and quietly see if anything is smelly, besides the fish? Oh, and ask him to see if there was any corrugated metal siding recently put up or lying around the area. I know it may be nothing but it's worth taking a look.

"You got it. What else?"

"If this guy is a Canadian, what does he have to do to come down here by boat? Is there some filing, boat registration, or paperwork that needs to be processed? There must be some alien or visa entry data available for him to be down here. Maybe we can find him that way, or his flight plan, I mean boat plan."

"Again, I can do that, but I'm starting to feel like your personal secretary again," she raised her carefully cropped eyebrows but smiled sweetly. "Remember, I'm the one packing a weapon."

Josh looked up and duly noted her comment. He was reminded he still didn't have a weapon. He smiled back innocently asking for forgiveness. Then he thought of one more question.

"One more thing, might you have enough pull to get us a plane or a helicopter ride north on short notice? This guy may be delivering contraband to the U.S. right now. Maybe we can catch him in the act. If my memory serves me, the Coast Guard flies Blackhawk's don't they? It would be my second chopper ride in two weeks."

"Actually, they fly Dolphins up here mostly for search and rescue," she said, pleased that she knew the answer and he didn't. She reached for the phone.

Bailey's Harbor, Wisconsin

Chris Morrow had motored out of the Kinnikinnic River and under the Milwaukee harbor bridge heading north. It was a relatively calm day but he paralleled the eastern shoreline of Wisconsin to avoid the chop in open water. Passing Sheboygan and Two Rivers he made good time and had the shoreline to look at. Late in the day he decided it was time for safe haven. There was a marine bulletin predicting bad weather rolling in from the north. He knew of Bailey's Harbor Marina and decided the protected bay would be a good place to tie up for the evening and also get a good meal.

The following morning he cast off as planned and slowly cut through the no-wake dock area to exit the marina. Once outside the breakwater he revved up the engines and started cruising east at 10 knots towards the twin Manitou Islands. From there he would head north past Grand Traverse Bay and Beaver Island, and then east again through the Straits of Mackinac.

The water was again calm after the night storm and he made good time in the open water. Setting his cruise control apparatus, he went below and dug through the lower cabinet for something to eat. As he rooted around he was stunned to see one of the missile launchers back in the corner. It had not been removed from the boat. It was wedged behind a long sleeve of cardboard. Next to it was a single rocket nestled in a blanket.

He was stunned. What the hell, he thought. This can't be. Hamid said he'd done an accurate count and transferred all the weapons. He had readily accepted that count. He sat there on the salon floor in a complete state of shock. What was he supposed to do now? Should he turn around and go back to catch up to Hamid? No, that would be impossible. He had no idea where the shipment was being taken in Chicago.

He considered his options. Should he toss the deadly missile launcher over the side and let it sink into oblivion? He knew Lake Michigan was over 900 feet deep in some places. While that was a possibility, he couldn't do it in the heavily traveled Straits. Someone might see him dumping the weapon.

Sitting there, he also thought about Hamid returning once he realized one launcher /missile was missing. That thought chilled him, as he was concerned for his family. He sat there thoroughly perplexed with his situation. He didn't move until the boats cruise control signaled a programmed compass adjustment was forthcoming. Forgetting about his hunger he shut the cabinet door and climbed up to the deck. Making the directional adjustment he sat there staring at the horizon lost in a fog of uncertainty. What was he going to do?

Later in the day as he approached the high span of the Mackinac Bridge connecting Michigan with its separate Upper Michigan land mass, he heard the sound of a helicopter off in the distance. He didn't pay much attention to the noise because there were all sorts of tourist attractions in and around the area. He just assumed it was a tourist flight from Mackinac Island.

He started his run under the Mackinac Bridge staying clear of two bulk carriers passing in the opposite direction. The helicopter beating sounds started to get louder and again drew his attention. He looked back over his shoulder. The chopper was a large one, bright orange and black, the colors of the United States Coast Guard. It seemed to be homing in on his heading. Passing a huge concrete bridge pylon he looked back again and saw the helicopter seemed to be following his boat. It looked as if it would fly under the six-lane highway span.

He became concerned, but was unsure what he should do. If they were homing in on him he had a new problem. Easing his twin 200 horsepower in-board engines forward to maintain speed as he rode over the bulk carriers wakes, he remembered the quiet cove where he had spent the night at Bois Blanc Island on the way down. To see if they were following him he started a slow starboard turn towards the Island. Glancing over his shoulder again, he saw the orange helicopter make the same directional adjustment. That was not good.

He maintained his speed as the helicopter passed around him making a wide three hundred yard circle. He could see someone was hanging out of the open side door looking down with binoculars. That chilled him even more. Normally he was practiced in dealing with authorities and could handle himself in such a situation, but this time he had a stinger missile launcher buried in his boat. That was considerably worse than having a handgun in the glove box. If he was boarded and searched they would find the weapon and the jig would be up. He scanned the water's surface. What could he do? Just as he entered the island cove and calmer waters he heard a loud voice on a speaker call out. He throttled down.

"Ahoy, Native Son, this is the U.S. Coast Guard, we'd like you to weigh anchor and shut the boat down for boarding. We'd like to ask you some questions."

Christian backed off the throttle, but did not turn off the engines. He stepped tentatively out from beneath his cockpit canopy and looked up at the hovering craft just fifty feet above him. He wasn't sure what he should do. The wash from the copter pushed him back under the canopy. He looked about in terror. So this is what it felt like. He felt like a rat stuck on a ship. At least it wasn't sinking, not yet.

"Native Son, please come about and comply with our orders. Shut down the engines and prepare to be boarded," Josh Ranalli barked into his portable bullhorn. "We would like to check your papers as a Canadian in U.S waters. It's a routine inspection, Sir."

Christian was now completely terrified. His controller had never asked him to fight any terrorist battles. He was only supposed to fish and drive his boat. He had not bargained for this. What could he do?

Then he thought about the lethal weapon hidden below. He wished he had pitched it three hours earlier. His mind was racing under the pressure. My God, he thought, maybe he should defend himself. If he shot down the helicopter he could make a break for it and run the boat across the Strait to St. Ignace on the Upper Peninsula. Then he could commander a car and drive north over the Canadian border, maybe thirty miles away. Maybe he could make it before more authorities showed up. He thought about his chances. He didn't like the odds but then he thought about his family in Sault Ste. Marie and decided he had to try something. The bullhorn bellowed again.

"Native Son, this is our last request. Please shut down your engines. We will lower a person to look over your papers and inspect the boat. You can be on your way in 10 minutes."

The boat captain made the decision he wasn't going to be caught. He would fight. But first he stepped out from beneath the canopy and waved a signal that he would comply. He gave a thumbs' up signal and then stepped back under to throttle down the engines to a whisper, signaling compliance. The engine turbulence from the twin screws stopped churning the water behind the boat.

"He's complying," Etta said. She put her SIG Sauer 516 assault rifle down on the seat, "Now what?"

"I'll go down on the cable and take a look at our potential

terrorist. Captain, can you get me into position over the boat?"

"Roger that, do you know how to handle yourself on the winch seat? That small seat will start spinning around due to the rotor wash as we lower you down."

"Yeah, a couple weeks ago I was hanging on one of these lovely swings overseas. I know about the wash blowout. I just hate to mess up my hair."

"What hair," Etta said. "You have a weapon on you? You never know. I'll cover from up here." She reached for the SIG assault rifle and wrapped the sling around her arm.

"Is the Pope Catholic, yeah, I have one, …now," Josh said emphasizing the 'now.' He looked down but could not see the man on board. He figured he was under the canopy to escape the constant blast from the rotor blades.

Des Plaines, IL.

Hamid had made a single call ahead and been given directions on where to go with the carpet shipment. He exited I-294 at Touhy Avenue and headed west to Mannheim Rd. At the stoplight he waited to turn south. A large 747 United Jet roared overhead a few hundred feet above and then passed over the Allstate Arena arched roof, touching down on Runway 22R a half mile away. That was close, he thought. Then it dawned on him how his missiles would be used.

He sat there for a moment thinking what these weapons could do, until the car behind him honked. Turning and ignoring the angry look as the car behind him roared past, he drove towards the arena, and then down a side street parallel to the large parking lots surrounding the massive building. On his right were a number of one-story warehouse buildings, and he found the address he was looking for. Parking out front, he locked the van and walked into the business. It had the smell of new and old carpeting just like his van.

"I have a delivery for Al?" he said, to the dark complexioned man standing behind an old glass counter that had seen better days

"Al is not here at the moment, but we can help you with your delivery, we were expecting you," the man said. He jerked his thumb towards the back of the shop. "There is an alley out back with a dock area. You can pull up there."

Hamid was unsure if he should just deliver the goods or wait for his contact. He hesitated.

Just then another dark complexioned man in a sports coat walked in and said, "Hamid, welcome my friend, I'm glad to see you made it. Do you have those special order carpet rolls I wanted?"

Hamid relaxed. The man knew his name and they knew he was coming. This is the voice he spoke to and had given him the delivery instructions. The two men embraced even though they had never met.

"Mahoud, I'm very glad to be here. It was an interesting journey. I do have your merchandise in the van. I think you'll be very happy with it."

"Good, let's drive around back to the dock. My employees will be happy to assist you in unloading. I'm anxious to see what you have for me."

They both went out to the van. "Hamid, did you have any problems on the journey? Did you handle the boat travel ok? How about seasickness?" he laughed out loud.

"As I said, it was an interesting journey. If I had known it was that easy to get into the United States, I would have done so years ago. We even shared a beer with one of those damn border guards. I really couldn't believe it." Hamid decided he wouldn't mention the handicapped parking ticket while driving down from Wisconsin. The man would never find out.

They drove around the block and down the alley to the last building suite on the southern end of the block buildings. Hamid backed the van up close to the dock. He knew with the van doors open no one could see what was being removed. As he got out of the door, another large jet roared over the Arena building just a block away. He stopped to watch. So did Mahoud.

"Beautiful, isn't it. It's almost like you could reach out and touch them they are so low."

"I suspect that we will be touching them soon," he said, as he started unwrapping the blankets that were thrown over the Stinger missile launchers.

Mahoud called four of his men over and they gingerly picked up each carpet section and carried them into the warehouse. A separate rack was utilized and each carpet was stacked side by side. Once the carpets and hidden missiles were unloaded, Hamid drove the van around the block and parked so the alleyway was not blocked for other tenants.

As he walked back into the warehouse he heard Mahoud yell, "Count them again!" The leader pointed at another man, and said, "You too, count."

Hamid stopped walking as Mahoud turned to him. "There were supposed to be thirty of them. I only count 29. Where is the 30th one?"

"I counted them myself when we took them off the boat. There are 30, I'm sure of it." He walked over and started counting too. He completed the count and looked perplexed. He counted again and again came up with 29 launcher tubes and 29 missiles.

Mahoud stood there with his arms folded tightly across his chest. He was furious.

"Ok, you and I both get 29, not 30, so where is the other one? Did you decide to keep one for yourself?" His voice rose a notch. "Did you hope to sell it on the black market? You'll be dead before that happens." He pulled out a gun and pointed it at the man.

Hamid took a step backwards and raised his hands in fear. "I did not take the weapon. I swear. Maybe it was Algul, the fisherman. He was upset once he saw what he was being told to deliver."

"Then why would he keep one? That makes no sense. I was told I have thirty weapons coming. I received twenty-nine. Where is the other one?" he pointed the gun at Hamid's head just three feet in front of him. Everyone else in the room took a couple steps backwards. They knew what was coming.

"I swear on Allah that I have not taken it, Mahoud. I don't know where it is. We should contact Algul and see if it is still in the boat." Hamid started to put his hands down.

Mahoud didn't care there was one less weapon. He wouldn't need it to complete his mission. But he was furious that this one unit could be discovered and prevent him from killing the President. He ran these thoughts through his mind. As another jet roared overhead he pulled the trigger and shot Hamid, the deliveryman through the forehead. The projectile propelled the dead man backwards and he fell in a heap onto a thick oriental carpet.

"Wrap him up and get rid of him," he said disgustedly. "In fact, drive him and that van back to Milwaukee. Find a quiet spot and burn him and the van up there.

Bois Blanc Island, Michigan

When Algul slowed the engines to a whisper he disappeared down the steps to the cabin, unseen by the hovering craft above. He wished he had a handgun but didn't. And he recognized that a handgun wouldn't solve the problem. It would only anger the hell out of the guys above him. He reluctantly knew the missile was his only chance to escape.

He opened the cabinet and quickly pulled out the light green metal casing of the launcher. He loaded the long slender missile into the tube. When the shipment had arrived at the fish market he had done some Internet research to see how such weapons worked. He was glad he had done so. He was actually going to shoot the weapon. He fired up the battery pack and homing mechanism, and let the weapon power up. All in, he thought.

Climbing the three stairs he looked out to see that the helicopter was nowhere in sight, thus it was still overhead. Still sheltered, he glanced around the roofline and saw that a man was swinging out from the bay door under a winch. Here they come, he thought. It's now or never.

Forty feet above, Josh swung out on the cable and adjusted his weight so he was balanced. He reached to his waist to be sure there was clear access to his sidearm. He signaled the crew chief he was ready and the winch started lowering him down. The helicopter's rotor blades were beating the air straight down where it buffeted the boat and water creating concentric ripples on the surface. Josh kept looking down trying to actually see the man. Etta released her seat harness so she could lean out and cover Josh from above. But she kept her rifle arm hidden from view.

On the deck Algul gave up to his desperation. He knew it was now or never. Making sure the Stinger had powered up, he peeked out again and saw the man getting closer. He made his decision. Stepping out from his cover he looked through the rangefinder and all he could see was helicopter, there was almost no range to be determined. He couldn't miss. About to pull the trigger, he realized if the missile did hit the huge target above, it would come down directly on top of him. He hesitated, hoping the craft would veer away before he pulled the trigger.

Everyone above saw what the man was doing at the same time. Josh saw the weapon poke out from beneath the canopy and instantly recognized what it was. "Shit," he said out loud, but no one could hear him with the helicopter noise from above.

Etta saw the missile launcher but didn't initially comprehend what she was seeing for a moment and then her training kicked in. She started pulling her weapon up to protect the ship.

The pilot trying to hold the craft steady couldn't see what the all the commotion was but his crew chief screamed into his communications gear, "Gun… Missile!" The pilot with years of flying combat missions in Iraq, reacted almost instantly, yanking his stick and trying to move the craft up and out of harm's way.

That sent Josh swinging wildly to the left as the chopper pivoted. The rotor wash changed directions and sent him swinging on the end of his tether. It also threw off his aim as he had drawn his weapon and was about to defend himself. Grabbing the cable with both hands he banged the plastic Glock 17 against the metal cable. His weapon dropped away before he could regain control. He hung on for dear life as the chopper climbed wildly and rolled out, pulling away.

Algul got the effect he had desired. The chopper was no longer above him. It had flared out and could be downed without fear of it falling on his boat. The heat-seeking missile would cut through the helicopter like butter at this distance.

He aimed again and pulled the trigger. The weapon system ignited and the rocket exited the tube with a loud whoosh. The back blast filled the tight cabin area and the kick threw the shooter off balance and he went down the salon stairs.

The rocket traveled the 80 feet to its target in less than two seconds. As the helicopter bucked wildly, the rocket missed the primary cabin but tore into the tail assembly, blowing the entire stabilizing unit cleanly off the screaming craft. With the tail rotor assembly gone, the helicopter was nothing more than a dead weight, a large chunk of metal about to fall out of the sky. The overhead blades continued rotating in a blur but couldn't hold the heavy craft in the air. The pilot lost all control. In a practiced manner recognizing his plane was gravely injured he shut down the engine and calmly released his harness.

The crew chief also knowing the bird was dead weight reached under the jump seats and pulled a three man bright orange inflatable raft from its storage area. He jettisoned it out the open door. It inflated immediately drifting down towards the water. He tapped the pilot on the shoulder and together they turned their attention to their passengers.

As the craft violently swirled in the sky trying to maintain altitude, Etta Petrini lost her balance on the bench seat and was pitched out the bay door. She began a fifty-foot fall to the icy water below. She screamed loud enough that Josh heard her flying by. He didn't hesitate. He snaked himself out of his sling and dropped into the water following her.

In her fall Etta had enough time to get her legs under her and she knifed into the water. But with the rifle sling still wrapped on her arm, the weapon violently jerked her arm and shoulder upon impact. The weapon also came up and smacked her in the forehead knocking her unconscious as her body sank eight feet under.

Josh hit the water a moment later and sank ten feet down before his buoyancy became a factor and brought him back to the surface. He quickly scanned for Etta. She was ten yards away doing a dead man's float head down.

The helicopter came crashing down as well, just 20 yards away on the other side of him. Coming down on its side, the rotor blades were still spinning at a high rpm. They slammed into the water with such ferocity that the water boiled from the impact. Each blade plowed into the one before it churning the surface. Simultaneously, the body of the huge craft slammed into the water. With both bay doors open, the water rushed through the cabin in a matter of seconds and the helicopter disappeared beneath the surface.

Josh frantically swam towards his new partner. At the same time out of the corner of his eye he saw the boat they had been trying to board pulling away fast, creating a huge wake. Josh kept swimming and promised himself he would get the bastard.

He approached Etta who was still bobbing face down in the water. He grabbed her and unceremoniously flipped her over. She was starting to turn blue. He reached up and smacked her hard across the face. No reaction. He checked to see if she was still breathing. In the water he wasn't sure if she was, so he supported her head from below and started mouth-to-mouth as he kicked to stay afloat.

It was not easy to do. After ten breaths, without chest compressions, which would have drowned her in the process, he got a reaction. She spit out a mouthful of water, started sputtering and coughing. She flailed about with her one good arm. The other one just floated there not obeying any of her commands. He recognized she had a possible break and could see she was in great distress. But she was alive!

He looked around and saw an inflatable boat bobbing 25 yards away. The crew chief was trying to pull his pilot aboard.

The cabin cruiser that had just shot them down was racing off in the distance and the water was now calm and serene. Josh yelled to the crew chief.

"I need some help over here, she's hurting badly."

"Were on the way," he yelled back, as he hauled the pilot's butt into the small craft. "What the hell was that all about?" was all he could think to yell back."

Josh didn't want to wait for them to come to him. He grabbed Etta's flak jacket collar trying to stay away from her separated shoulder and started dragging her towards them. As Josh swam a weakened sidestroke with a bum leg, he heard a boat motor coming towards him. Was the son of a bitch coming back to finish them off, he thought. He stopped a moment and reached down for his weapon but remembered he had just lost it.

The boat turned out to be a fisherman in a 20-foot Boston Whaler, which had been fishing in the nearby cove. He heard the explosion and saw the helicopter go down, so he had come out to see what was what. He motored around the crash site and saw a man hauling a woman in the water. They seemed to need his help the most. So he cut his engine and glided through the debris right up to them.

"What the hell happened out here?" the fisherman asked.

Josh ignored the question. "She's hurt, help me get her into the boat," Josh said, not asking, ordering. "I think she's dislocated her shoulder so be careful."

The man assisted him and gingerly pulled the woman out of the water. She groaned from the handling. Josh pulled himself up.

"I'm a federal agent, do you have a radio?"

"Yeah, right there," he said, pointing, "next to the wheel, who do you want me to call?"

"The cavalry. How do I get the Coast Guard and the marine police?"

"They're marked on the radio. Press the button and start talking," the fisherman said. He took a life preserver and gently eased it under the woman's head. She moaned and coughed up some more water.

"Mayday, Mayday, A U.S Coast Guard helicopter has gone down in the Straits at Bois Blanc Island. There are survivors in the water. They are hurt. Send help immediately."

"Roger that, who is this?" a woman's voice inquired. Josh ignored the question.

"The helicopter pilot is OK but we have a woman who is hurt badly. We need help now. I can see the bridge from here. We are about a mile due east."

"We are at the Air Station Traverse City and have a helicopter spooling up right now. Help is on the way. Should be on site in 15 minutes. I'm also dispatching help from Mackinac Island. Again, whom am I speaking to?" the woman asked. She was calm but trying to follow protocol.

The pilot and crew chief tried to crawl into the boat but Josh stopped them.

"I need this boat guys. Help is on the way. Can you take Etta here in the dingy?"

They understood. Etta was carefully moved to the smaller boat. Josh unwrapped the assault rifle still wrapped around her arm as gingerly as possible and jumped back into the Boston Whaler. He looked over at the fisherman and told him he needed to borrow his boat. He didn't say why but the assault rifle in his hand said it all.

"I promise I'll take good care of the boat or buy you a new one if I mess it up."

The fisherman didn't even question the authority. He started moving towards the dingy.

"Captain, you know the drill. No one knows what went on out here. We have to keep this quiet at all costs. Say it was malfunction and the chopper just went down. You take the heat and I'll make good on it later. Also, keep our friend here on ice for the moment."

He pointed to the fisherman. "Thanks for coming to our rescue." He looked at Etta who was sputtering and groggy but coming to. "Take good care of her and tell her I'm chasing the bad guy. Hell, tell her I love her!"

With that he gunned the inboard engines and the whaler took off out into the Strait.

As he pulled away Josh looked back and saw that Etta was moving again. He hated leaving her but the bastard had to be caught.

As he raced across the Straits of Mackinac Josh checked his assault rifle to see if the water had damaged it. It looked waterlogged but ok. He pointed the assault rifle over the side rail, set it on single shot and pulled the trigger. It fired. Satisfied, he set it down and turned to search for his quarry ahead. The terrorist had already passed under the bridge.

Josh crossed the Strait and paralleled the massive bridge deck to dodge another tanker passing beneath. He headed for St. Ignace on the tip of the Upper Peninsula of Michigan. He knew it was a tourist town, from which you could catch a ferry to historic Mackinac Island. He also knew that St. Ignace would be crowded with tourists. The terrorist would be able to blend in with the crowd and disappear. He had to catch the guy. It was still more than a half-mile ahead of him entering the breakwater but he was closing fast.

Josh looked about the boat and spied a duffle bag long enough to conceal the automatic rifle. Holding on as the craft bounced over the waves, he reached for the bag and emptied it. He inserted the rifle. And put the strap over his shoulder. He headed for the main pier.

Des Plaines, IL.

The carpet shop next to one of the world's largest airports was busy. A lot of carpeting was being sold and the two man installation crews had jobs every day in the immediate surrounding area of the airport.

Once Mahoud's many homeowners and business employees had settled in, they each received a visit from Al's Carpeting Van delivering new carpeting compliments of their leader. The carpeting delivery crew usually arrived late in the day and would carry large carpet sections into the houses or businesses. All of the residents and businessmen were pleased to receive the new carpeting.

Mahoud would visit each delivery at the same time as his carpet installers arrived. After the shades were drawn he would unroll the carpet and show them the stinger missile launchers and missiles that had been delivered. His guests sat around in a circle as he explained what they were looking at and how the weapon functioned. They all began to understand what their mission was to be.

He explained that in the next few months they would have an occasion to shoot this weapon at a jet airplane that would be flying over the house or business. They would be given a clear signal as to when that day and time would come. On that day they would maintain phone contact and arm the weapon inside the house. When told to do so they would step out the door just seconds before the plane would be rocketing overhead at tree top level. They would simply take the shot. Then their job would be finished and they were free to jump in a car and leave the area for good. For each home and business Mahoud presented maps showing marked highway entrance points that could be accessed quickly to allow the terrorists to get away.

At each house those gathered sat quietly listening to the instructions being given. No one dared to question what was being said. They understood the orders and had already committed themselves to jihad. They had been given their mission.

St Ignace, Michigan

Josh pushed the throttle of his borrowed boat to full speed towards St. Ignace. It was small tourist town but one with a storied history dating all the way back to 1671 when Father Jacques Marquette first established a mission there. He came into East Moran Harbor under full power searching for the cabin cruiser that was still a quarter mile in front of him. He saw that there were numerous cabin cruisers in port all tied up along a number of pleasure craft piers. As he searched the Star line Mackinac Island Ferry dock he saw a man running off the long pier and disappear into the crowd of people queuing up for the next island ferry.

Josh kept the throttle full forward and headed for a somewhat sandy beach next to the commercial pier. It was late in the day and there were no swimmers so he cut his engines at the last moment and ran the boat right up on the shore grinding into the sand. Josh grabbed his weapon bag and jumped off the side running up the beach towards where he last saw the terrorist. Drawing a crowd because of his entrance he had to push through them to get to the road.

He arrived to see a black SUV screeching away from a very agitated family. A man was chasing after the vehicle screaming and waving his hands. Josh realized his man had just stolen the SUV and was getting away. He was heading north out of town.

He scanned his surroundings trying to identify another means of transportation. Across the local business highway he saw an old guy on a Harley motorcycle pull up to a gas station pump. He looked like an old Vietnam Vet with his American flag dew rag tied over his flowing gray hair. He had the standard black leather riding gear from head to toe with at least a dozen club patches stitched on.

Before he could open his motorcycle gas cap Josh ran up to him and recognizing a U.S. Marines patch, said 'Hoo Rah' to get the man's attention. The man looked up searching for a fellow Marine. Josh said he was a policeman and needed to borrow the bike to chase a fugitive. The grizzled Vet looked like he was lost in thought for a moment, so Josh flashed his credentials. The Vet absorbed the situation and got off the bike.

"There's still enough in there if you aren't going too far, should be good for another 75 miles." the Vet said, as he handed over the keys.

"Yes, Sir, that'll do." He started the bike, and pushed off the kickstand, "I'll take care of it Marine. I have a soft tail at home. Stay here, and I'll have it back in no time."

"I am not a Sir, young fella. Just call me Ralph." He pointed across the parking lot. "I'll be getting some lunch at that deli over there. Go get the son of a bitch."

"I'll do that Ralph. He is a son-of-a-bitch." He goosed the throttle and the rear tire spun on the oily concrete. The bike raced forward, and he rolled onto the street heading north. Gunning the bike through its gears he was quickly cruising at 60 in a 35 mph zone through the small town, heading straight towards Business Highway 75.

Weaving in and out of traffic he watched ahead to see if he could spot the fleeing SUV. As he past side streets he searched to see if the guy who had shot him out of the sky had diverted off the main drag. He figured he was still heading for the border.

Business 75 eventually merged with Interstate 75 and Josh shot up the ramp blending in with northbound traffic. His gas gauge was registering pretty close to empty but he knew how miserly the bike burned fuel. He figured that would be enough for the moment, unless the guy made it to the border and into Canada. He advanced the throttle and felt the bike take off. Without helmet or glasses the wind started to bite. Squinting to avoid the bugs, he tried to search for the vehicle somewhere up ahead.

He shot up the road passing the County airport on his right and noticed the sign said Sault Ste. Marie and the border was only twenty-eight miles away. Ahead at the Gane's Road exit he saw the SUV drive up the exit ramp. Presuming his terrorist knew the lay of the land Josh slowed down a bit to let the guy show him where he was going. The vehicle turned left crossing over the expressway. Josh followed at a distance.

The terrorist took his time obeying the various stop signs thinking he wasn't being followed. Once across the expressway he turned north again on a frontage road called the Old Mackinac Trail Road, and followed the speed limit. Josh followed at a casual pace just keeping his suspect in view. He would bide his time until there weren't any civilians around or the border came into play. He didn't want to put anyone in jeopardy because the guy could still be armed.

The two parties traveled north about a mile and then the SUV driver turned west across some railroad tracks onto a Forest Road. The sign said welcome to the Hiawatha National Forest. There was nothing but conifer forestland as far as the eye could see in all directions. Jake initially went by the turn, but then doubled back and crossed the tracks just in time to see the SUV make another turn to an even less traveled path. Perhaps it was a back road to the border.

Josh decided it was time to close the gap. There weren't any people around, just forest and maybe a bear or two. He gunned the bike to catch up and it jumped instantly. God bless the Marines, always ready! Closing fast he pulled out his gun and switched off the safety.

He didn't plan on taking additional chances.

The SUV driver noticed the bike coming up fast and realized he was being chased after all. He stomped on the accelerator and raced down the rut-covered road trying to outrun the motorcycle. The SUV with its four-wheel drive handled the potholes better than the two-wheeled cycle did. He increased the gap.

But Josh gunned the bike again and closed in. As he came within 200 feet he decided to shoot at the wheels to see if he could slow the guy down. The first shot was close but caught the back taillight and shattered it. Josh tried again and blew out part of the rear window. The third shot caught the driver's rear passenger tire, which exploded from the impact. The van swerved to the left but the terrorist must have taken an evasive driving course because he held the vehicle on the road. He was weaving back and forth, running on a rim as the rubber flew off, but he maintained control. Josh came closer.

Still doing close to forty the SUV came around a blind bend in the soft gravel and the driver realized the road was coming to a T intersection in less than 100 ft. He slammed on the brakes and tried to control the fishtailing SUV so that he could steer through the ninety-degree turn to the right. He was hell bent on making the border. The SUV slowed for the impending turn but not enough. It was too top heavy with a blown tire. The rutted road added to its instability.

The vehicle tilted on two wheels as he entered the tight intersection. While his speed had dropped the SUV continued its drift sliding towards the culvert. The large vehicle caught the edge of the loose gravel and its momentum carried it over the edge. Slipping into the drainage ditch it started tipping even more and that forward, sideways movement rolled it over on its side. The vehicle snapped through a couple of saplings and then completed two full rolls before coming to a stop wedged against a massive downed tree.

Josh was 100 feet behind him as he watched the vehicle tip and roll ahead of him. He downshifted and squeezed the brake levers as tight as he could to prevent the same fate for his Marine's bike. The accident noise shattered the silence of the forest and birds jumped out of the surrounding trees with the violent intrusion. In the T intersection the Harley fishtailed but Josh maintained some level of control and skidded to a stop short of the culvert.

He could see through the downed trees that the SUV had righted itself on the other side of the culvert in about a foot of water. The vehicle was covered in mud and grass. The engine block was still running although it sounded as if it was choking and would soon expire. It smoked and sputtered and made grinding sounds in the otherwise quiet forest.

Josh kicked out the bike stand, turned off the engine and removed the key. He dropped it on the ground at the edge of the road rather than putting it in his pocket. He checked his weapon and started advancing, angling down into the culvert. He hoped this guy was still alive. Stepping through the shallow water he saw that the driver's door had sprung open from the rollovers. That meant his man could have been thrown from the vehicle.

Scanning the immediate area he advanced carefully from the rear of the SUV, but he found the front seat empty. Josh presumed he had been thrown free in the crash. As Josh considered his options, a heavy metal object hit him from behind. It was a glancing blow landing mostly on his shoulder, but it was enough to cause him to lose the grip on his weapon. It squirted out of his shocked hand and fell into the murky swamp water below. So much for a weapon!

Turning around he found the crazed terrorist standing there with blood running down his forehead. He had a tire iron in one hand and a sharp hunting knife in the other. Josh tried to focus from the shoulder blow. He realized the hunted had now become the hunter. He shook his head to clear his thoughts and prepared to defend himself. This guy had already shot him out of the sky, tried to drown him, and injured his partner. He obviously intended to finish the job.

Being an expert at hand-to-hand combat, Josh shook off his shoulder pain and stepped toward his attacker. The terrorist lunged swinging the tire iron over his head for a head blow, probably to be followed by a knife lunge to the midsection. Josh parried the tire iron swing by sidestepping left, outside the arc and delivered a vicious open palm punch to the elbow joint of the attacker. The arm snapped as he pushed it in the direction it wasn't meant to go. The attacker screamed from the pain as his snapped elbow joint dropped to his side no longer accepting commands.

As his attacker's charge faltered, Josh wrapped his arms around the man's head and started squeezing the life out of him. The terrorist did not give up. With his knife hand he tried to stab backward to break the hold. Josh released the strangle hold for a moment and grabbed the knife wrist, twisting violently. The man had no choice but to follow his twisting arm and did a body flip over the log. Josh came up with the knife in the process. He could have used the knife but he wanted this guy alive. He flipped the knife in the air, catching it by its handle and drove the knife straight down through the fat of the man's hand. The knife went deep between the bones and pinned the hand to the log digging in at least three inches deep.

The man started screaming and tried to pull away from his pinned hand. He flayed about with his other arm, but that was of no help because the cleanly broken elbow just hung there by skin and muscle. Without either arm available, the fight drained out of him. He wasn't going anywhere. Josh stepped back to assess the carnage. The man continued to scream from the pain.

"Get a hold of yourself," Josh yelled over the racket. "And stop that screaming. You'll draw every wolf and coyote for miles with that kind of wailing. They'll come to investigate a wounded animal that must be dying. You'll be their next meal!"

The terrorist stopped screaming immediately. He scanned the

clearing looking for any predators. But every time he moved a muscle the pain of his hanging broken arm and nailed hand reminded him of his predicament.

Josh recognized the fear the tough guy was exhibiting and decided he would use that fear to his advantage to get the answers he needed.

"So before the coyotes come to investigate, I think we should talk. Ok?" He splashed around in the water beneath him and found his gun. Letting it drain he checked to see if it would still function. He was confident that it would.

Then without warning he took the butt of the gun and hammered the knife head stuck in the man's hand. Just one very focused blow. The sharp knife vibrated from the concussion and the terrorist started screaming again, glaring at his captor. Josh definitely had gotten his attention. Calmly he said, "You answer my questions and we can get out of here a lot quicker and have that elbow and hand looked at."

The terrorist whimpered. He tried not to move to alleviate the pain radiating up and down his body.

"So whom do you work for?" Josh said, as he raised the butt of his gun again.

"I'm a fisherman, from Canada, for God's sake!" Algul said, trying to claim his innocence. His voice betrayed his fear as he watched the butt of the gun rise.

"I know that Christian. You're also the guy who just shot a U.S. Coast Guard helicopter out of the sky with a dangerous weapon and almost killed five people. I'm more interested in your benefactors, the people who bought you the boat?"

"I paid for the boat myself," he said defiantly, trying to mask his pain.

The butt of the gun came down hard again. The pinned man screamed from the pain as the knife vibrated with the blow. His broken arm flailed about useless to stop the blow.

"Keep that up and you will probably draw a bear as well. They all home in on wounded animals. Three or four coyotes can chase down a larger animal, and then pick a carcass clean in less than an hour. Now, enough of this bullshit, whom do you work for?" He again raised the gun above his head.

Algul would have physically collapsed but he couldn't. He was nailed to the downed log hanging there by his skewered hand. He decided to try a version of the truth.

"I don't know who sent me here. I was just told to make a quick trip to the States." He looked up hopefully and tried not to move. He also made a quick scan of the surrounding woods to see if he was attracting any predators.

"That's a better answer, we may get out of here yet. So where did you go in the States?"

"I was fishing. That is what I do."

"So why is there two motorcycles on the boat?"

"I was trying to fix them when the fish were not biting," Algul said, trying to divert attention from the firing of a missile.

The gun butt slammed down on the knife twice making the metal blade quiver back and forth even faster. Algul howled from the searing pain of the knife's vibration and instinctively tried to reach over with his broken arm to protect himself. That movement just transferred the electric jolts to his shoulders and chest. The pain made every muscle ache and he thought he might faint. His head was ready to explode. Then he heard a coyote howl off in the distance, but how far away? Was it close? His face registered the terror.

Josh recognized he had this guy and soon would have his answers. The coyote howled again and was answered by another off in a different direction.

"You thought I was kidding, didn't you? They heard you screaming like a wounded animal and will be homing in on that sound.

Once more than one of them get here they will get brave and I won't be able to hold them off. They will tear you apart."

"Why did you have a Stinger missile on your boat? Where are the others?" Josh looked him in the eye and raised his gun hand as if he was ready to strike again with a less than forthright answer.

The man was in complete agony and heard another coyote announce he was coming into range. At that moment he gave up and recognized he was defeated. His head was ready to explode from the pain radiating through his body. He realized he would never see his wife and child again.

"I was told to deliver the missiles to America and then go back to being a simple fisherman," he said truthfully. He froze and watched the gun butt hovering above his hand. But it did not drop.

"Where did you take the missiles? Where did you drop them off?"

There was no fight left in him. "I was told to take them to Milwaukee. I had a passenger who was supposed to be my brother. He rented a van and we offloaded all the weapons." The words came gushing out in between strained breaths as he tried to deal with the shooting pain in both of his arms. His eyes never left the gun butt.

"But you fired one of them at me in the helicopter. If you offloaded them why were you able to shoot us down?"

"Hamid miscounted and only took 29 of them off of the boat in Milwaukee. I didn't even realize there was still a missile aboard until I was half way back." He cowered from the blow he expected to reign down on his skewered hand."

"Why Milwaukee?" Josh asked, trying to comprehend the path of the deadly weapons. His gun butt stayed in the air over the man's hand

"Our cover was to visit the Harley Motorcycle Museum in that city. That is why we went there. Hamid was then supposed to drive the weapons down to Chicago. From there I have no idea where the weapons were going. That is the truth." Algul feared the strike of the gun butt but it did not come. A coyote came into view standing on a rise at the tree line. The ragged animal stared at the spectacle before him and appraised the situation.

Algul, the sleeper terrorist was now frantic. He knew he was completely helpless nailed to the log as he was.

Josh saw the animal as well but calmly pressed his inquiry "How many weapons?"

"We had thirty launcher tubes and thirty missiles stowed away," he said, totally defeated. He knew he would either die in these woods or would survive to rot at Guantanamo. He would never see his wife again.

Josh was done being nice. "How were they transferred to Chicago? Who drove them there?"

"Hamid took them in a white step van that had an Al's Carpeting sign on it. I truly have no idea where he was going. He did not say and I don't know what they were going to be used for." He looked down and winched in pain as he tried to adjust his back against the log. It only made him scream again.

A second coyote joined the first on the small hill.

Josh realized that his questioning had gone about as far as it could for the moment. With two scavengers already circling it was time to secure the prisoner and get some help.

"It's your lucky day my friend, I believe you. Let's see if we can get that bleeding stopped or the coyotes may still get you." He pulled out the knife and the man collapsed dragging his hand off the log. Josh flipped him over and pulled off his own belt wrapping it around the man's good upper arm. He then tied it in the back to the man's belt so that his good arm and bleeding hand was immobilized behind his back. The other arm hung limply as it was broken at the elbow, swollen and useless.

He used his gun to fire a single shot into the woods. The two deadly predators reacted by bolting into the woods. That would give the coyotes something to think about. It would only buy him some time but that was all he would need. Opening a suitcase in the family's demolished SUV he found some shirts. He tore them into strips and used them to staunch the bleeding from the terrorist's hand wound. The first couple wraps turned red before he was finished.

"Pull on your belted arm and it will act as a tourniquet to slow the flow of blood, but release it every now and then, or you'll lose the arm." Josh explained, as he immobilized the broken arm with another shirt, tying it to the man's waist. Then he dragged the man up and placed him in the front seat of the wrecked SUV. He locked all the other doors and set the windows to almost closed, allowing air to circulate.

"I've got to get help so you sit tight. Your screaming drew enough attention that the coyotes will be out here waiting for an opportunity to have you for dinner. They are very patient animals, they'll wait all night if need be. Thus, I'd suggest you stay in the vehicle until help arrives. You try to get out and they'll drag you down in a couple of minutes." He reached across the terrorist and buckled the seat belt to keep him seated. The man had no operable arms so he wasn't going anywhere. The man looked terrified with his predicament.

Picking up his gun he walked to the Harley parked on the road without looking back. He picked up his keys from the ground where he had tossed them. It was a bit of basic spy craft so it was harder for someone else could to use your vehicle, in this case the Harley. He stood the bike up, toggled the engine start and gunned the engine. In a moment he was racing down the path he had come in on.

St. Ignace, Michigan

Josh drove back into town at a much slower pace than he had left. He headed directly to the gas station. He found his Marine sitting on a bench with a cigar and beer in hand. He pulled up to the pump and opened the gas cap.

"Regular, I presume?" he yelled over to the Vet, who was getting up to walk over. The Vet debated what to do with the cigar and decided to pour a bit of beer on his cigar ash. Then he tucked the stogie in his vest pocket for later.

"Did you get the bastard?"

"I did. He's cooling his heels a couple miles north of here."

"I hope he knows we don't like that kind around here?"

"He does now." He topped off the gas tank and resealed the cap. "I owe you big time Ralph. Let me buy you this tank of gas."

"No need, it was my pleasure. It felt like I was contributing again."

"You were, Marine, more than you will ever know. Can I ask one more favor? Do you know where the police station is? Would you give me a lift over there?"

"Sure it's just a couple blocks away. Mount up."

They drove the six blocks to the small police station with a single cruiser out in front. Josh dismounted and thanked his new friend again. If he only knew, he thought.

Josh entered the station. It was a standard small town sheriff's office. A high front counter, a couple desks and an office in the back. It was small enough that he could see where he needed to go. The sheriff's office was clearly marked and there were a bunch of people inside. He didn't stop at the desk and walked into the office.

"Josh, are you ok?" Etta said, from a side conference table. She slowly tried to stand up but was still pretty unstable and returned to her seat. Her arm and shoulder was completely immobilized in a sling strapped to her torso.

"Don't worry about me, what about you? When I left, and I truly apologize for leaving, you were half conscious and turning blue in the water. He walked over and lightly embraced her, careful not to cause additional pain. He wanted to lean in, give her a tight hug and kiss her on the lips, but he didn't trying to look official. He was quietly impressed that she had rebounded so well.

"I'm fine. They popped the shoulder back in and drugged me up. I should be up to speed in a day or so. Did you catch the bastard?"

"Yeah, I got him thanks to a Marine and a Harley." As he turned to the sheriff he saw there was another uniform in the room. The insignia said Coast Guard. He introduced himself and found out it was the Coast Guard Commander from Air Station Traverse Bay. He had come to find out why he'd lost a multi-million dollar helicopter.

"As Ms. Petrini probably explained, this is a Homeland Security operation and we were chasing a terrorist when he decided to shoot our ride, your helicopter, out of the sky. Is your pilot and crew OK?"

"They're fine, wet and angry, but not hurt, other than their pride," the Commander said.

"They expect that kind of action in Iraq and Afghanistan, but not in Michigan. Just wondering what the hell happened?"

"We have a national security threat here and we need to keep the entire thing under wraps. I mean a tight lid on the whole matter.

We're still trying to catch up to the rest of the bad guys. If any of this gets out they may go to ground and we'll never find them."

The Commander and the Police Chief looked mystified and obviously wanted more. They were not even sure who they were listening to, just a disheveled guy from out of nowhere.

Etta decided to take command. "Gentlemen, what he means is this whole thing didn't happen, at all. Commander, you'll have to announce the helicopter went down due to mechanical failure so it doesn't draw any further attention. We'll clean up the mess later." She turned to the sheriff. "I have to ask you to put a complete lid on this as well. You'll all be part of the hero bandwagon after we catch these guys. Can you bury any inquiries for the moment or at least contain them?"

"I think so, but I have one very angry vacation family in town that lost their SUV, and the local press is wondering what happened with the chopper. I also have a fisherman cooling his heels in an interrogation room."

"Sheriff, tell the family to rent an SUV and finish their vacation. I'll personally guarantee the rental cost and the SUV replacement." He looked at Etta for agreement. She nodded almost imperceptibly.

"Then invoke the national security thing on the fisherman and tell him we'll pay for the boat if I damaged it running it up on your beach. That guy saved our lives and got us back in the game. He's a hero, play it that way."

The Sheriff seemed satisfied and said he would take care of it. "So where is this terrorist fugitive?"

Josh realized he hadn't mentioned his injured prisoner in the woods yet. "Sheriff, I have the guy handcuffed in that stolen SUV about six to seven miles north of here on a forest road. It's in the Hiawatha Forest. The van went off the road at a T intersection near some swampy ponds. I think the vehicle is beyond repair."

"I know where that is. I hunt out there. I can have some deputies out there in ten minutes."

"You may need to send an ambulance as well. Our bad guy is hurt pretty good. He's tied up with a fully snapped elbow, and a deep knife wound completely through the hand. He also has cuts and bruises from the rollover. Tell your deputies, and I'd send at least two, to be careful, there's a bunch of hungry coyotes in the area circling the vehicle because he was screaming quite a bit. They, and he, are both thinking he's dinner."

Etta raised an eyebrow. She imagined what Josh had done to get the information he needed to move forward. She didn't say anything. He'd brief her later.

Josh ignored her inquisitive look and said, "There's also a duffel bag with an assault rifle in the back of the SUV. It's not loaded but you may want to collect it, property of Homeland Security."

The sheriff understood and reached for his radio. The Air Station Commander still looked perplexed about his downed bird, but recognized that a Homeland Security stamp trumped everything. He moved to a phone and started making some calls.

"I've got a plane coming to pick us up, along with our prisoner. I figured we're going back to Chicago? Etta stated rather than asking.

Josh nodded. He then reiterated the importance of the tight lid on the whole matter. The mission was only beginning. He knew they had to find the 29 other missiles.

Then he went to take a leak and clean up the mud and blood.

Over Lake Michigan

The unmarked Lear jet was cruising at 25,000 feet in a couple of minutes heading for suburban Chicago. Josh and Etta sat forward quietly discussing the day's events and nursing their wounds. Etta was hurting all over but she hung in there and tried to understand what Josh had found out. Obviously something was about to go down in Chicago.

Algul, the terrorist, was strapped to a gurney in the rear, lightly drugged for the transfer. The two agents had interrogated him further while waiting for the plane and believed they had all they were going to get out of him. He was only a minor piece of the puzzle. The sleeper agent would now be sent down the rabbit hole.

The plane was heading towards Chicago and scheduled to land at a suburban airport in Sugar Grove, IL. The two agents would be dropped off, and the plane would then proceed south with the other passenger to Miami, and points beyond.

The Sugar Grove Airport was chosen because it was 42 miles west of the Chicago Loop and would draw no attention. A lot of government clandestine work was done at the third tier airports around the country. They were small enough that people could be moved around without fanfare.

It also happened to be close to Etta's home. Both of them needed some recuperation time. They also needed to digest what they had learned from the terrorist just captured. In no time the plane was approaching Chicago metro airspace and swung west to line up for the 5,000 foot long runway. The plane's wheels lowered and locked into place. The plane dragged a bit with the wheel assemblies exposed. They prepared for touchdown.

"I'll look forward to sleeping in my own bed this evening if I can get to sleep with this throbbing shoulder."

"You'll be fine. I got some great sleep aids." He showed her a couple bottles of Jack Daniels he had lifted from the cabin cruiser mini-bar. They had never been opened. "Muslims don't drink. "It will help you sleep like a baby." Josh said as he looked at the area below. "Can we get a car way out here?"

"Certainly, we have all the conveniences out here in the boonies," she said playfully. "You know, this is the airport where the President's limousines and equipment are often sent ahead of time when he comes to town. It's also a Chicago area back-up landing zone that can handle a 747."

Josh stared out the window watching the approach as they crossed the outer markers.

"What was that?" he inquired. "What about the President?"

Etta repeated, "I said the President's support team flies into this airport whenever he comes to town. He may land at O'Hare International Airport but everything else comes here first, to Sugar Grove. The Air Force brings all the equipment in on Hercules 130's. You know he still has a home in Chicago in the Hyde Park Kenwood neighborhood on the Lake, don't you?"

Josh searched his mind to remember what he had heard and seen in his immediate past. A number of things started falling into place as the planes wheels touched down.

"A while ago I was in a remote desert cave in the middle of absolutely nowhere Yemen. I happened to be hiding under the bed of a certain al Qaeda nutcase. When he finally left the damn cave,

I noticed he had a U.S. map on his worktable. It had a single circle drawn around the city of Chicago. And it was the only mark on the map. Then a few days later I overheard a few words that Awlaki was speaking to Zawahri. All I heard were the words 'force one' and 'missile'. I'm beginning to think they were talking about Air Force One and these same Stinger Missiles we're looking for."

"So you were there,"…she said. "You're the one that got Awlaki?" It was more a statement than a question, but it confirmed her suspicions. "You do get around don't you, soldier?"

"Yeah, but that's not for public consumption." He thought for a few more minutes as the plane taxied towards a private hanger on the far side of the field.

"Etta, I think that's what the missiles are for. They are going after the President. They intend to get even for us killing Osama bin Laden and Awlaki. Tit for tat! ….. Son of a bitch!"

Etta tried to put together what Josh was saying. Linking the missiles to Chicago, the President and Osama bin Laden might be a stretch, but if you connected all the dots, it could also make sense. She sat there stunned as the door to the plane started unfolding. "If that's true they have 29 Stinger missiles to make good on the threat. Or heaven forbid, they could try to take out 29 airplanes and thousands of people."

"Ok, we have our work cut out for us. If nothing else, we try to disprove the premise. But either way we have to find those missiles. Any idea when the President might next be coming to Chicago? We should check on that right away."

"I'll make a call up the food chain tomorrow morning, but they'll want to know a hell of a lot more as soon as we call.

"That makes sense. They probably won't believe us two drowned rats. So we better come up with a plausible scenario first. You must have a kitchen, how about I cook us a nice dinner before I put you to bed. With a couple glasses of wine you'll sleep better and tomorrow we should be able to come up with a spellbinding terrorist plot."

He liked this woman and wanted to get to know her better. Without waiting for an answer, he got up and checked on the drugged terrorist. He patted his drugged head and wished him safe journey on his trip south.

Etta got a rental car and Josh drove out of the airport following her directions. They could hear the Lear jet engines spool up and roar down the runway. Driving down Highway 30 and then north on Hwy 47 they drove for a couple miles and turned into a nice subdivision set back in the woods.

The house was literally shoehorned into the woods. Upon closer inspection on the back deck Josh saw that the trees were all lined up symmetrically across the backyard. Etta explained that it had been a black walnut tree nursery in an earlier life and the now tall fifty foot trees had never been harvested.

It was a beautiful home, not large, nor small, just right for a couple of people. It had a main floor master suite and a couple bedrooms upstairs. Josh set the tone for the evening by carrying his bag upstairs and throwing it on a double bed. As he came back down he noticed a double-sided fireplace between the family room and the kitchen. He rubbed his hands together and Etta pointed to matches and the gas jet.

Etta started searching for food but Josh stepped in quickly and found a couple of steaks that weren't frozen, some potatoes for baking, and fresh green beans. Then he saw a grill out on the deck and stepped outside.

The backyard was indeed beautiful. Fully forested, the grounds were covered by hundreds of large leafy hosta plants, in all sorts of colors. There were a number of meandering mulch covered paths leading to various points in the yard. Way in the back there was a well-used fire pit in a large stone circle. "This is beautiful Etta, did you do all this?"

"My husband and I built this together over the years. It was his labor of love. Now with the stressful work we do, this is where I wanted to be at the end of the day. The peace and tranquility is mesmerizing. The only other place I'd want to be is the Equine Humane Center."

At the mention of the husband Josh reacted but said nothing. Etta must have noticed.

"My husband Pete was killed in a car accident five years ago. This yard was his baby and has become my refuge from the world's turmoil. You should have seen the yard when we built the house. It was a thorny mess with chest high brambles and weeds everywhere. It took years to tame the forest and build this quiet restful setting. Now it's my personal refuge from all the craziness in the world. But I've had less time to maintain it with our work."

Josh didn't probe the husband equation any further. She seemed ok with her position in life. Time had hopefully healed that wound. She was now obviously married to her work just like he was. But she also had this private refuge to keep her grounded and sane. He didn't, and wished he did have such a place, and perhaps such a woman. This place made him want to know Etta even better.

He jumped up and told her to relax on the deck. He went inside and got the steaks, some wine and glasses, and started cooking dinner. They enjoyed the peace and quiet. He gave her a back rub being careful not to touch the injured shoulder. She accepted his touch, drank her wine and enjoyed the pampering. She began to unwind.

Rosemont, Illinois

Mahoud entered the Westin Hotel on Mannheim Road and asked the front desk clerk if he could be shown the hotel suites on the top floor. He explained he was a photographer and had been told the view east from the top floors was astounding, especially in the morning when the sun was rising over the lake. He intimated he might rent the suite in the future to shoot the sunrises.

The clerk called a hotel group sales person who was more than happy to show the rooms that were not occupied. On the top floor the sales lady dutifully knocked on a door to make sure no one was in the suite and then let the man in for a look. Mahoud walked directly to the large window and pulled back the privacy curtains. He looked out over a huge forest preserve laid out before him and could see downtown Chicago's skyline clearly in the distance.

The sun had already risen to a ten o'clock position. To carry his story he used his hands to frame the pictures he would be taking. As he went through the motions of looking east and framing pictures, he watched as four distinct lines of jet planes materialized and came into view. The spacing between the lines was at least a mile apart and the approach distances between jets was four to five miles.

As he kept framing his future downtown photos, he timed how long it took for the most distant jet in view to reach the hotel area.

The runway they were approaching was a mere half-mile behind the hotel.

He turned to ask about rates for the suite and stated he may want to set up a shoot on relatively short notice. The sales person was most accommodating and suggested rates. She also gave him her business card and said she would make sure he got the suite facing east. He asked to see one more suite on the other side of the hotel property facing the Airport. Looking out he could see the entire airport perimeter and the multiple runways crisscrossing the grounds. He would be able to film the entire terrorist attack from this vantage point.

He thanked his tour guide and promised to send her a print of the sun rising over Chicago when they were done with the shoot.

Next he drove to the Hyatt Hotel on Mannheim Road a half mile down the road. This landmark hotel with it turret like towers in the four corners of the building would offer a different view and perspective. He repeated the process here asking to see a tall tower room facing east, this time not a suite. Equally impressive views offered site lines that brought the planes in almost directly overhead, roaring across the building and highways just before touchdown at O'Hare.

He repeated this process with other hotels and a couple of tall area office buildings for all the other approach routes into O'Hare International Airport. No matter what direction the wind was blowing on any given day, his team would be able to identify a single incoming jet and determine which runway would be utilized. Since he had a couple of missiles underneath every runway approach he only needed to know which one to activate and give the signal. With this setup he knew he would not miss regardless of which way the President and Air Force One arrived in Chicago.

He next drove to a Gander Mountain store in the far western suburb of Batavia and placed an order for 12 pairs of high-powered binoculars. He asked for glasses that didn't reflect light back much and would be good for sighting elk across a canyon. The clerk was most helpful and had him set up in no time. Next he checked out field radios that would allow him to isolate a frequency for a group of hunters spread out over a ten-mile circle. He asked if the equipment could offer multiple frequencies that could be changed quickly.

He then drove back to his Schiller Park real estate office to begin training his spotter teams. He would need fourteen of them to cover all access points to the many runways at O'Hare.

Later in the day he went to the library to do some research and looked at recent Chicago Tribunes stacked up in the reading room. Surprisingly they went back for a month. Then he switched to the archive machines and started looking at a few older months but he was careful not to do a search for anything to do with the President and the White House. He figured there were people who monitored those kinds of inquiries. He didn't want to draw any attention at this stage of the game. Instead, he started looked at Tribune front pages going back a year looking for any mention or articles stating the President was coming to Chicago, or was coming home for a few days rest or some political fundraiser. He was already aware the President came to Chicago quite regularly because it was his home. He wanted to see if there were any predictable patterns he could benefit from.

The plan was coming together nicely. All he needed was the President of the United States to come home for a visit.

Sugar Grove, Illinois

Etta woke up with a start and groaned as she started to roll over on her pinned shoulder blade. It was daylight and the sun was just starting to stream into the bedroom bay window.

She tried to shake off the fog from the wine the night before. Looking down the bed she realized she had on a nightgown, but didn't remember putting one on. She pulled up the front of the gown with her good arm and saw that the discolored flesh from the shoulder dislocation had lightened from a deep purple, and mustard yellow to a lighter red as the badly bruised muscles started to heal. She also noticed that except for the sling immobilizing her arm she was naked under the gown. The girls were roaming free!

She thought about that for a moment. She didn't remember much about what had happened the night before. Josh and she had enjoyed some wine on the deck and throughout dinner, but had she had that much to drink? She peeked under the filmy nightgown again, shrugged her good shoulder, and then smiled to herself. She had enjoyed the company and the massage last night. It had been a long time since she had been that rested. She just wished she remembered something, anything!

There was a soft knock at the bedroom door and Josh walked in balancing a breakfast tray full of food. "Wake up sleepy head. Time for breakfast, then after we are fortified, we have to go catch the bad guys." He set down a tray that had bacon and eggs, wheat toast, and steaming black coffee.

She smiled and realized she could get used to this treatment. It had been a long time since she had been so pampered. She started to ask a question but Josh interrupted her.

"I probably shouldn't have let you have so much wine on top of the pain pills they gave you, but I figured maybe that way you would sleep better. How about it, besides the hangover, how do you feel?" He sat down on the edge of the bed.

She offered a thumbs up signal and started to ask another question, but again, he beat her to the punch.

"You know I could have taken advantage of you last night," he said, with a sly smile on his face. "But that might have caused an inter-agency problem neither of us wants. Instead, I was a gentleman and only assisted you to bed, although I did take a quick peek when I helped you into that nightgown. Luckily, I found a loose one, so I didn't disturb that arm too much. And before you ask, I slept upstairs. There is an even better view of your yard from up there." He changed the subject and handed her a napkin.

She blushed, the color almost as deep as her red / purple discolored chest. That hadn't happened for many years. She again considered asking a pointed question but decided not to. She figured that would say a lot.

"I do feel much better." She again lifted the nightgown, and said, "I actually think it's healing quite nice."

He started to ease forward to take a look for himself, but then thought better of it. He didn't want to push his luck. There would be time for that in the future. He knew that this was a person he wanted to develop a long relationship with, not just a toss in the hay.

"We have to talk to a whole slew of people today. And formulate what we think these guys are going to do with the missiles. Before you nodded off you said my assessment made the most sense. Do you still think so now that you are bright eyed and bushy tailed?"

"You did look didn't you?" she said, blushing again. Then she smiled. "I'm embarrassed, I drank so much, and I don't remember a thing from last night." She thought for a moment and then said, "Maybe it is better that way. Or," she paused for effect, "perhaps we'll have to have some more wine when we catch these bastards."

Josh was truly intrigued with this woman. "Let's eat up, get dressed, and get to HS. We have a long day." He backed out of the room to change.

As he left she whispered to herself, "You could have helped me dress too." And then felt wicked for thinking such things.

After eating her breakfast Etta tried to get dressed on her own but realized she would indeed need some assistance. She had taken off the sling and pulled on panties and pants with her good arm. But she was having trouble hooking her bra. She called out to Josh for some assistance. She decided two could play this game. She positioned herself with her back to the door.

Josh entered the bedroom and stopped in his tracks. He admired what he saw before him, a half-clothed woman with an exposed beautiful backside. He was tempted to walk around in front of her, but again decided not to push his luck. Besides, he had already admired her beautiful breasts the night before. Now the back side image before him suggested that everything would indeed be worth seeing.

"Can you give me a hand? You took the bra off last night, the least you can do is help me get it back on."

Though he hadn't done such things for quite a while, how hard could it be? He remembered when he was a young man and how he could pop the clasps open with world record speed. But he had never reversed the process. So he stepped forward and tried to be as professional as he could. After a moment of fumbling he was successful. One shoulder strap was twisted so he straightened it out and enjoyed the touch of her silky skin.

Etta reached down to the bed for a white blouse next, and handed it to him. He carefully helped her slide it onto her arms from behind and enjoyed her smell. He stood behind her as she labored to button the blouse. Giving up, she turned and asked him if he could help again. He readily assisted but realized this too was foreign to him. The buttons were on the opposite side from a man's shirt. He tried to maneuver the small shell buttons through the buttonholes but looked like an idiot doing it. He figured she thought he was dawdling, which he wasn't.

She enjoyed the attention, his clumsiness, and his closeness as he labored with the buttons. He also smelled good after his shower. She smiled and gave him a quick peck on the cheek for his efforts.

Now he was embarrassed. "I'll get the car started," he said, and backed out of the bedroom bumping into the doorframe.

"That was sweet," she said to herself, "I like this guy."

On the forty-mile drive to the Homeland Security office at O'Hare they talked shop. They created a checklist of what needed to be accomplished on Etta's I-Pad. Once she got it fired up she was able to type with her good hand.

"First, I'll make an inquiry to see if the President is traveling to Chicago soon. That will give us a timetable." Etta said, typing in a note.

"I agree, but let's not shout wolf to the White House just yet. Let's do it through channels so no one gets crazy, before we can prove we have this threat."

"But you said you know the threat is in Chicago, and involves missiles and Air Force One. That is one hell of a threat in my mind."

"Granted, but we can't prove it yet. All we have is a map memory in my head, a shipment of missiles that we know have been brought to Chicago, and a crazed terrorist threat coming out of Yemen."

"Ok, so what do we do to tighten this up?" Etta said, as she looked at her almost empty checklist.

"We have to try and find that van, our fisherman terrorist said the missiles were loaded in a white van marked Al's Carpeting. Maybe they are dumb enough to leave the vehicle out where we could find it in the open. That would get us closer to these guys."

"Good, how about we do a State Patrol traffic cam search on I-94 from Milwaukee to Chicago and see if we can pick out anything. I'll call up a search around O'Hare as well. What else?" Etta said, as she added to list.

Josh ran though his mind. "Next, we need a good map of O'Hare and all the runway paths so we can see where the flight lines are coming into Chicago. We need to know what the planes typically pass over. Those missiles fire quickly and are hard to defend against especially when they are shot at a low flying plane."

"I've been told that Air Force One has all sorts of defensive, evasive capabilities and can create false heat signatures to trick any missiles."

"I've read that stuff too, but if a missile is fired at the last second before a plane is landing, any defensive efforts of Air Force One would have a hard time reacting. A Stinger gets turned on, spools up, and the bad guy shoots. The missile travels fast and if it only has to travel up 500 feet to hit a target, how can anyone activate defensive and evasive measures in such a short time. That's when I'd do the shooting," Josh said as he worked it out in his mind. "If it takes three seconds to push a defensive button the missile is already there. Even if the defense is automatic with a threat detected it would hit before anyone could react. Look how fast that bastard shot our helicopter out of the sky."

"Don't remind me," Etta said, as she rubbed her shoulder and thought back to her recent terror. "I may never get in a helicopter again." She searched the O'Hare Internet information on her I-Pad. "Did you know that planes land at O'Hare about every thirty seconds? They often have four active runways handling arriving traffic at the same time. And each runway is about a mile apart."

"Yeah, but when the Grand Pupa's plane comes into an airport they put a stop and ground hold on all traffic in the area." Josh stated, as he changed lanes in the heavy traffic heading east.

"I know. I've been sitting on the field in a plane," Etta said. "They usually don't even tell you what the deal is. All you can do is sit there for a half hour trying to figure out what is going on. The guy next to me told me the President was coming to town and then we all watched to see when Air Force One would land through those tiny windows."

"I haven't had the pleasure, thank you. But what this means is Air Force One is a heck of a target on final approach. That's when I'd shoot it down, when it's low and vulnerable," Josh said, feeling guilty for the thought.

"So perhaps we should drive the neighborhoods around O'Hare looking for the kinds of places the bad guys could take such a shot. We should figure out where all those runways cross over neighborhoods."

"I hate to say so but this all makes sense," Etta said, "How about we also pull all the entry visas and plane manifests for the last couple of months. We can run them against known bad guys and maybe we get lucky and find a few terrorists hiding in Chicago."

"You think they would buy houses? Maybe we should look at real estate transactions too. Maybe we can find a pattern." Josh said, as he headed up the Balmoral ramp.

"That should give us a good start. I'll drum up some DHS help to run all this stuff down," Etta said, as she closed her I-pad. "We also have to find out how tight a timeframe we have and when the president might be visiting Chicago again."

Josh pulled into the unmarked building's parking lot entrance in the shadow of O'Hare. As they got out of the car and started walking to the building a United 787 Dreamliner went thundering by just 250 feet above them. Both agents looked up. Josh put his arms up like he had a Man-Pad on his shoulder and shuttered.

At the door he flashed his badge and the guy let him through without a glance. He was more interested in looking at Etta. Josh agreed with the man.

Elk Grove Village, Illinois

On the far west side of O'Hare International Airport Mohoud sat in a broken chair in the window of Johnny's Carpet Emporium, another building he had just leased. The empty building was on Wolf Road, directly across from the airport perimeter fence. He could see through the filthy plated glass window, obscured by all sorts of overlapping sales posters. Out front was an old enclosed box truck with flat tires that had seen better days and had been parked there for years. It too once advertised Johnny's defunct business.

He sat there listening to the constant plane traffic roaring by overhead. He figured that was why the business had closed its doors. Having observed landings for weeks now he knew more likely than not that Air Force One would approach the airport from the east coming in over downtown Chicago. About sixty-five percent of the time the prevailing winds came out of the west blowing east. The wind direction determined the path of all plane landings. The planes needed the wind lift to assist with both landings and takeoffs.

Keeping that in mind he was debating doubling, or even tripling his terrorist bet. He already planned to have back-up teams on all four sides of the airport to take second shots if the President's plane was able to evade the first missile shots as they were landing. If the first missile missed, he assumed that the pilots would follow standard protocols to protect the President and immediately go to full power to get away from the threat. When a President has been shot the Secret Service immediately spirits him away from the threat. Why should the Air Force be any different?

Thus, he would need to position and train his other field teams to wait for such an eventuality happening and then step outside and take additional shots. All of the stinger missiles would seek the strongest heat signature and home in on the target. Since the President's plane would be the only craft in the sky, the missiles could converge on Air Force One as it tried to escape the attack. It would be a spectacular light show with thousands of people in the airport watching.

More importantly it would avenge the assassination of Osama bin Laden and Anwar Awlaki.

Homeland Security, O'Hare Airport

Etta Petrini was the center of attention in the office all morning as her fellow agency employees heard about the terrorist threat and her close encounter with Lake Michigan. They were all thankful that the inter-agency stranger had been available to save her life.

After a morning de-briefing by her boss and a number of other agency counterparts, Josh and she were finally able to settle into desks and start looking at the data that had been assembled from their morning drive checklist. A lot of manpower had been tasked to the checklist and the mountain of paper was growing. There was a note that the Director had a confidential file for her eyes only.

The CF had a short summary about the President's travel plans for the next two months. The most immediate event listed advised the President was scheduled to attend a major fundraiser in Chicago in four weeks' time. While it had not yet been announced, the event would be one of those million dollar fundraisers that would bring out the city's elite with big checkbooks. Invitations were being sent out this week. At $20,000 per plate and $150,000 per table there would be all sorts of news stories popping up in the next week or two about the President's visit.

With that impending newspaper exposure the press would start regularly reminding the general public that the President was coming home. That meant the terrorist would also know and have a confirmed target date. More importantly, Josh and Etta could now build a backwards timetable. With just under a month to work with they would have to move fast. Once the visit was publicly announced, the President and his staff would be reluctant to cancel on sketchy information. They had their work cut out for them.

Presuming that they understood the terrorist's plan of attack Josh started looking at a large map of O'Hare International Airport and a list of all the runways traversing the field. He quickly realized it would be a lot of ground to cover. Calling up the same satellite information on his laptop, thanks to Google, he started zooming in on the various runway tips. Identifying them on the master map he then used his cursor to drag the view across various roads, outer perimeter fences, local streets, businesses and highways into neighborhoods and industrial parks. There were all sorts of homes and businesses that abutted the airport. The detail was extraordinary. He could see garages, out buildings, alleyways between buildings, and numerous parked cars and trucks. There were a lot of places to hide and by his estimates there would only be a couple hundred feet of airspace between these locations and the fuselage of any arriving jet. He had to get out there to see for himself.

Etta was directing the setup of five computer monitors on a bank of tables. She was instructing five staff members that they would be looking at highway and red-light cameras for the past couple of weeks. They were specifically tasked with looking for a white panel van that had the name Al's Carpeting on it. They started with I-94 cameras heading south and eventually looked at cameras set up in the communities around O'Hare Field. Even she was astounded how many cameras were out there. Hopefully they could spot something before they all went blind staring at the monitors.

Another staffer was assembling a long list of real estate and leasing purchases that had been recorded in the last four months in and around O'Hare airport communities. They were told to look for any transactions that showed property being exchanged, new leases being signed, new resident names, etc.

Once Josh and Etta had everyone working on the initial information dump they decided to go take a look for themselves. They drove an unmarked car out of the lot, turned onto Balmoral Ave. and crossed the Tri-State Expressway driving east to River Rd.

"Where to first?" he asked, as he identified where they were on the map. "North or south?"

"I say we go south, and go clockwise around the entire airport. You're the secret agent, you tell me where you would hide if you wanted to shoot down the president's plane!" Etta said, smugly. She decided to take command and give the orders. She was feeling much better and feeling less pain in her arm.

"So now, I'm a terrorist?" Josh said, looking back down Mannheim. He actually thought that was a good idea.

"You hunt them for a living, so I figure you are kind of like one of them. Let's go, that way."

Josh drove south and kept his window down so he could hear the planes arriving overhead every minute. Passing between the many tall hotels surrounding the Rosemont Convention Center he pointed at a couple of them.

"I'd need a spotter or spotters to tell me when the President's plane is on final approach. They would see a hell of a lot more to the east if they were high up in one of those hotels, but not on the roof. I'm guessing that the Secret Service watches for that kind of thing."

"They do, I used to have a friend who was part of the President's advance team and they have those things covered." Etta said, offering some input to be a part of this exchange.

Yeah, I'd create a nice little hidey-hole in one of the top floor rooms, maybe not the top floor, probably one floor below the top. I'd sit back away from the window in a comfortable chair with my feet up. With a good set of binoculars I could spot Air Force One maybe five miles out and that would give me the time to determine which runway the president's plane was lining up on and mobilize the shooters to get ready."

"They'd definitely need to communicate with one another so I'll see if we have had a run on radios and binoculars in the Chicago area. Since they won't know which direction Air Force One is coming from until it gets within airport range, they would have to activate their shooting team. We should also think about the possibility of jamming their comm's."

Again, Etta added notations to her tablet. "I'll look into that. Maybe we could prevent them from actually communicating the shoot order."

"If they use this approach they will have to cover all airport approaches, but with 29 missiles at their command that is probably exactly what they intend to do," Josh said. His mind was racing now. He knew what he would do if he was the terrorist. But he worked alone and this was a massive operation.

Another jet aircraft flew overhead heading west to the airport. It was already down to a few hundred feet as it passed over a neighborhood of very small brick homes with garages at the back of each small lot. Josh turned down a side street and drove into the neighborhood. It was a small enclave of working class homes that were sandwiched between an industrial park and the expressway abutting the airport. Josh drove two blocks and had to turn when a large wall of concrete and wood fences prevented further western movement. The walls were highway abutments to deaden the sound of the traffic. He could hear traffic buzzing past on the other side of the massive wall and then heard the reverse thrust of the jet engines that had just past overhead. He stopped by a small pocket park with some children's playground equipment and spread out the map on the dash again.

"We are right here and runway 27L is just beyond that wall across the highway. This is a kill shot area right here. I'd rent one of those homes and wait until I get the word to shoot. Then I'd step out the front door, or maybe the garage a couple seconds before the plane arrives overhead. And pull the trigger. Look how low the plane is coming in."

Both Etta and Josh got out of the car and sat there. An American 737 came roaring in for a landing and passed overhead about 400 feet above them. The noise was incredible and neither could speak for a couple seconds.

"Now listen, you'll hear the plane touch down, that's how close it is, and then the engines will reverse a couple seconds later. There, see," Josh yelled, over the car's roof, "That is how they're going to do it."

"Not if we can help it," she yelled back.

They got back in the car, made some notes about the homes, wrote down some addresses, and drove towards the next runway pattern to the south. All afternoon they drove through neighborhoods and business parks, down dead-end streets abutting the airport perimeter fences, and in between buildings and warehouse alleyways.

Josh made notes and diagrams of the various intersections, the surrounding businesses, houses and buildings where he would set up a kill zone. He understood the terrorist's objective and applied the same thought process they would employ to accomplish it. He realized they had found a kink in the armor and that the terrorist act was very doable, especially with the deadly Stinger missiles. He had confirmed they had them and that they were somewhere here in Chicago. Now he had to figure out how to stop them.

Andrews Air Force Base, Maryland

Inside a huge hexagonal aircraft hangar in the southwest corner of Andrews Air Force Base, just southeast of the District of Columbia, a majestic blue nosed and silver bodied aircraft was being prepped for an overseas trip. The aircraft being worked on was assigned to the Air Mobility Command's 89th Airlift Wing. This was the home of Air Force One and the Presidential Maintenance Branch crew was preparing the craft for an overseas flight to Mexico City. The President was going to discuss immigration legislation with the President of Mexico. While it would just be a three-day trip the planning efforts had been underway for the last week. Every detail of the plane and the flight plan was checked and rechecked.

Air Force personnel had already prepared and sent three C141 Star lifter cargo carrier planes ahead. They were toting all of the president's equipment including his motorcade bulletproof limousine, support team vans and Secret Service SUVs loaded with weaponry to protect the President while on the ground. Once this cargo was pre-positioned the President would follow. After such a trip all of the cargo would be re-packed and returned to Andrews to be prepared for the next flight of the President of the United States.

On trips to third-world countries even the fuel required for the return flight was brought along so there could be no tampering with the aviation fuel sources. In those situations large balloon like heavy rubber bladders were transported and stored at the forward site.

Inside the hanger there were actually two identical customized Boeing 747-200B series aircraft. They are officially called VC-25A's and have tail codes marked 28000 and 29000. But when the President of the United States was using this custom aircraft its' official designation is Air Force One. For that matter, any fixed wing United States Air Force plane carrying the President was designated Air Force One.

This jet aircraft is a mobile flying White House, able to transact all the business of the Office of the President wherever it is located. The plane has unlimited range with a capability to refuel in midair, and could stay in the air indefinitely, or as long as food stores would hold out. Its communications and onboard electronics are considered the best in the world. The systems are all hardened to protect against cyber interference or even the electromagnetic pulse of a nuclear weapon. The plane can fully function as a mobile command center in the event of an attack on the United States or the President.

The three level craft has over 4,000 square feet of space available to the President, his senior advisors, military support and office staff. The President's private suite features a large office and conference room, lavatory and sleeping facilities. There is a full operating medical suite adjacent. There is staff seating and a press area with the plane able to comfortably carry 75 passengers and a crew of 26.

Its internal communication capabilities are transmitted over 200 miles of shielded cable and wiring allowing the plane to be in contact with any country or person in the world. There are multiple onboard secure telephones with air-to-ground capability, plus radios, faxes, televisions, computer connections, and weather related equipment making it a flying command center.

The plane has the most up-to-date advanced avionics and defensive capabilities available, all of which are highly classified. Outfitted with an array of electronic counter measure (ECM) systems, and directed infrared countermeasures (DIRCM) the plane can jam enemy radar, create false position signatures, and defend itself from heat seeking missiles, by ejecting metallic chaff and flares to throw off any enemy or terrorist device homing in on the craft. In addition, a recent countermeasure addition is the Large Aircraft Infrared Countermeasures (LAIRCM) system, which automatically directs a high-intensity modulated laser beam at any missile threat shot at the plane. This is an active/passive system that does not require overt action by the pilots. The system simply reads a threat, responds to it, and then advises the pilot the threat has been detected and dealt with. The pilot then takes additional evasive action to remove the President from the threat.

The 28000 craft was being readied by its dedicated crew. These Air Force service men and women were specially trained to look and crawl into every nook and cranny, test every bolt and piece of sheet metal, examine every engine component, stabilizer and elevator system, and do exhaustive diagnostic checks on everything time and time again. Every component needed to be functioning at optimal levels in order for an air-worthiness stamp of approval to be given for the Presidents plane. Late in the morning the crew finally finished its work and Air Force One was approved for its flight to Mexico. The maintenance branch crew finished their cleanup and headed for the hanger kitchen.

"So when will she be back?" asked one of the engine mechanics walking back with his Master Sergeant supervisor.

"It's a quick trip. She'll be back in the hanger in five days. Then well have her for two weeks, so we can do some additional diagnostic work on the outer starboard engine and work on that internal elevator wiring issue," the Master Sergeant said, closing his maintenance log. "Then she's off to Chicago for some fundraising trip."

Sugar Grove, Illinois

Driving west on I-88 in bumper-to-bumper traffic Josh and Etta agreed not to talk about their pending terrorist plot for an hour or two. While time was of the essence, they felt they could spare a few hours just to clear their heads and get some sleep.

"So what made you decide to live way out here," Josh asked. He looked over at Etta who was driving again and admired her beautiful profile in the setting sun. "This has to be a 35 mile drive each way?"

"It is actually 41 miles, but it allows me to decompress. Dealing with security issues all day wears you down. By the time I get home I've purged my mind of all the bad guy terrorists and crazed militias we have to deal with. Way out here it's a sanctuary where all you hear are the birds and an occasional coyote howling in the night."

"I've had my fill of coyotes thank you, although I'm thinking they could be used as a great interrogation technique if we could cage a few to howl at terrorists chained to a wall." He chuckled to himself remembering the look of fear on the boat guy's face when he threatened to leave him in the woods stuck to a tree.

She ignored his comment fearing it would again take them back to shop talk.

"I love it out here because it's quiet. I love horses and can ride almost every week of the year when I'm around."

"Haven't been on a horse since Afghanistan, but your right, they are noble animals and ask very little of you. Where do you have this love affair with horses?"

"I have a good friend that runs an Equine Humane Center in Big Rock, just down the road from my house. She has loved horses all her life and a few years ago set up this horse rescue facility. They care for abandoned and rescued animals helping to rehabilitate and nurse them back to health. Then they try to find them new homes where they will get the care they deserve. It's a labor of love. She's been doing it all her life. I volunteer there because I don't have the time to have a horse of my own with this damn job."

"That would be tough. So what do you do?" He liked this lady more and more.

"Oh, it's very glamorous work. I muck the stalls, groom and feed the horses, exorcise them when they're injured and generally try to show them someone cares. Like I said, it cleanses my mind and it's nice to have someone love you with unadulterated love."

"I can readily agree with that," Josh acknowledged, "our work doesn't offer much peace and quiet, just terror and frustration. Now, if you would walk and feed me occasionally, I'd offer the same kind of unadulterated love and follow you anywhere," he said playfully.

She looked at the man in the passenger seat and sized him up a bit more. This was a good man, a lonely man, married to his work just like she was. She realized she wanted to show him there was more to life.

"So, how about we get you fit for a bridle, throw a saddle on you, and I'll see if I can break you?" She couldn't believe she had just said that. She blushed as she tried to steer the car to stay in her lane.

Josh saw her cheeks light up and decided to throw it right back at her. "Only if you promise to ride me hard and put me up wet. Maybe I could use some breaking." He leaned over and started to give her a kiss on the cheek.

Etta saw the kiss heading her way out of the corner of her eye.

She steadied her hands on the wheel making sure the car was centered in the lane, and at the last second turned to meet him full on. She didn't want a peck on the cheek, she wanted the full Monty.

He enjoyed the kiss, slowly pulled back and then whinnied like an appreciative horse getting an apple.

Then they both blushed. Two adults that carried guns and hunted terrorists for a living were acting like school kids. Both settled back in their seats contemplating what had just happened. Josh figured it was something to do with the fresh country air. He liked it.

Homeland Security Office

The Homeland Security task force assigned to the potential threat on the President had grown from a few people a week ago to over twenty spread out in the offices around the largest conference room in the building. The interior hallway windows had been masked over to keep the exposed research materials away from the uninvolved. All sorts of data was being researched, analyzed and shared between task force members. On the hard cushioned walls around the room numerous aerial maps of the greater O'Hare International Airport were pinned up. The maps had a variety of different colored pushpins noting various types of information.

The largest map was a satellite view eight feet square and highly detailed. It showed all the runways crisscrossing the nine square mile international airport circle with large directional arrows showing final approach paths to and from the airport. With the airport being so large, O'Hare had multiple parallel runways that could accommodate landings and takeoffs simultaneously from different directions. This helped to accommodate the ever-changing wind direction in the Windy City. It was an extremely busy airport with landings and takeoffs every thirty seconds during peak times and that was almost all day and into the night.

The international airport had been at this site for over 65 years. During World War II the Federal government had purchased 1,000 acres of farmland northwest of Chicago for $450,000. The government moved in and built a huge Douglas Aircraft plant, manufacturing and assembling Douglas C-54's, at that time the largest U.S. troop and cargo plane being made. Adjacent to this plant site there was a small Orchard Field that was used almost exclusively by the military to fly the planes out. Thousands were employed in the complex.

After the war ended, the plant closed but the runways and hangers remained. In 1947 the City of Chicago annexed the massive site and converted it into a commercial airport. To physically connect the remote airport site to the city limits, the city annexed a narrow strip of land, actually a 200-foot wide drainage waterway. This came about before anyone thought the airport would grow into one of the worlds' busiest. They named it O'Hare Airport, in honor Edward H. O'Hare, a fallen Congressional Medal of Honor winner who had been a U.S. Navy flying ace. Two years later it was designated an international airport.

There was a second large map of the O'Hare area on another wall. The locations of all recent real estate purchases and leasing transactions dating back a year were being identified. Different colored pins noted sales and leases in residential neighborhoods, commercial buildings, high-rise office buildings and industrial warehouses surrounding the airport. There were hundreds of these transactions and the task force had gathered names and companies looking for anomalies and perhaps connections.

At another desk analysts reviewed the names of all persons flying into O'Hare from international destinations. They were matching points of origin, with known terrorist names and faces to see if they could identify any connections. They were also cross-referencing these lists of travelers with real estate and leasing transactions in and around O'Hare Field. It was like looking for a needle in a haystack.

The information gathering was ongoing. The next step would be to merge the various databases to see what might match up, whose paths may have crossed and where, and what might be deduced from all this assembled information.

In a side conference room team leaders were discussing the overall threat and the possibility of canceling the President's fund-raising trip to Chicago. There was concern that canceling the trip would raise even more questions with the media that would eventually cause panic with the general public. Everyone agreed the larger concern had to be to locate and neutralize the Stinger missiles. A single Stinger missile, aimed at any domestic jet aircraft, could easily bring down a plane full of innocent people creating a major terrorist incident and a public relations nightmare. The public would determine it was not safe to fly and the economy would be dramatically affected. Such an act would be like 9-11 all over again.

"All right people, let's gather round and see what we have come up with thus far," Etta announced to her charges. The buzz in the room quieted down and everyone tried to find a chair at the table. Josh sat off to the side. He was just a liaison. Etta was running the show.

"Reports?" Etta said, and looked to the team working on the terrorists' movements.

JR Strok started the discussion. "As you know we've been watching video tape of highway traffic coming down from Milwaukee and all the traffic cams we could get a hold of in the suburbs around O'Hare. I think I have permanent double vision, but we did find something. We saw an 'Al's Carpeting" van pass a couple of highway cameras in Wisconsin. The driver even got off the highway in Racine and stopped at a Mar's Cheese Castle business up there,… don't even ask,… he even got a parking ticket for his efforts. And it hasn't been paid.

Down the table someone asked, "Who would have thought terrorists were cheese heads?"

"The van was spotted again getting off at the I-294 Touhy Avenue exit and headed west. The last camera that picked him up was at Mannheim and Touhy."

"That puts him in our theatre. No luck after that?" Etta inquired.

"Well, one of my other guys was still watching the highway tapes and we saw the same exact van going the other way two days later. We were watching the southern lanes and the van was seen in the background heading north back towards Wisconsin."

"We made some additional inquiries with our people and the police agencies in Milwaukee. They just called advising that a burned out step van had been found in an abandoned warehouse. It had been torched and they did a pretty good job of burning it out. There was a male body inside burned beyond recognition. Forensics couldn't find any prints but they were able to identify enough of the magnetic sign to know it was the carpeting van

"Thanks JR that pretty much confirms that our contraband is now down here in Chicago, and they're tying up loose ends.

"So we have 29 missiles to account for. What else do we have?"

Doug Roth, one of the analysts assigned to the real estate review spoke next as he handed a report across the table to Etta.

"We've been looking into real estate transactions. Believe it or not, we've actually matched some buyer names on real estate property transactions to people who flew into Chicago in the last year from various domestic and international destinations. We also matched two sales for commercial space in the immediate area. The transactions don't seem to be clustering in any one place, but they are all close in to O'Hare."

"That's great. Check those transactions and locations against the runway approach maps. I bet well find them hunkered down under the flight paths into the airport," Etta said, "I'll need those addresses. We'll do a drive by today and see if there's anything hinky going on." She nodded to Josh and he made some notes.

Doug shuffled his papers and went on. "Another anomaly we identified is that five of those transactions involved a small independent real estate sales office in Schiller Park. In two cases they helped arrange financing as well. And the storefront business only opened up shop a few weeks ago."

Marty Thekan, a meteorologist assigned to the task force, offered a short report about prevailing wind conditions that could be expected in the next month. He had analyzed all past data and projected future weather patterns, high-pressure systems and jet streams coming out of Canada. He said he was confident the majority of the landings and takeoffs would be using the east to west runway configurations for the immediate future. That helped to narrow the field where they should look for the missing Stinger missiles, at least as it related to the President's Air Force One.

Near O'Hare International Airport

Josh and Etta secured a non-descript white van for this reconnaissance trip. The vehicle had no rear windows and would allow them to make some wardrobe changes in the field so they could do some covert neighborhood searches without drawing any attention. The task force had agreed that spooking the potential terrorists would create an even greater challenge. They needed to identify all the terrorist suspects and all the weapons before charging in. They still had a few weeks before the President's plane would arrive.

Etta had borrowed a postman's outfit including the blue/gray shirt and slacks, along with a summer jacket from the Des Plaines Post Office. She had also borrowed an old brown mail sack that was stuffed with magazines and circulars. She also brought a business pants suit to change into should the need arise.

Josh had secured a gas company meter reader's outfit with an authentic looking name badge that would allow him to walk through yards reading meters. His second outfit was some soiled jeans and a sweatshirt along with some charcoal to roughen up his appearance as if he had just stepped out of an industrial plant. Neither was sure what the plan was but they hoped they might get a closer look at some of the target houses they had identified in the preliminary drive-by.

In Des Plaines they drove down a side street one block from a dead end road that abutted the twelve-foot expressway retaining wall, and the airport runway beyond. One of the suspected homes there had been recently sold to a person of interest that had flown in on a student visa just two months earlier. The transaction had been handled by a suspect real estate office in Schiller Park, one of their future stops. Etta said she would give the mailman ploy a try and see what she could see. She stepped into the back and started changing into her uniform.

Josh sat in the driver's seat monitoring the streetscape and taking occasional glances in the rear view mirror at the beautiful woman stripping to her skivvies. He was smitten with his new partner. She bounced around trying to pull on the blue pants and then sat down to tie the heavy black shoes. She put her long hair in a ponytail and tucked it under and thru the back vent in the postman's cap.

In no time she was a United States postal employee. That was when she noticed Josh's eyes in the rear view mirror.

"You bastard. You're supposed to be watching the street?"

"I was," he said smiling.... and all the hills and valleys too. It's beautiful country. You could be my mailman any day."

She ignored him but was pleased that he was showing interest in her. That hadn't happened for years. "Meet me a couple blocks over. I'll make a pass at the end houses for three blocks each way from the runway."

"Make sure you walk up to all the other houses around our target. They may have someone watching movement up and down the street."

"Yeah, I know, buckaroo. This isn't my first rodeo."

She looked up and down the street for any pedestrian traffic and then stepped out of the passenger side of the van. She threw the sling over her shoulder and wished she hadn't brought as many magazines in the sack. Her shoulder still hurt from the dislocation.

Heading down the street she started walking up to every door mailbox. She had a number of pieces of mail in her hand and when she opened a box she would rustle around making an effort to look like she was dropping mail in. Then she would move on.

As she approached the target house she started making mental notes of everything she was seeing. The front steps, a screen door and a sturdy looking wood front door, the number of windows, the chain link fence surrounding the property, a dilapidated garage at the end of the driveway, and a large dog house in the backyard that looked like it might be being used.

As she stepped up on the front door porch she saw that there was a woman looking at her through the front window on the right. She ignored her but noted she was wearing a dark burka but without the veil. She opened the mailbox with her right hand that had sorted mail in it. Knowing she was out of range from the woman, she reached in and grabbed a an existing piece of mail and put in a Good Housekeeping magazine that had an occupant address on it. She turned and walked away without looking back.

Figuring she was now being watched she made a point of going to the neighbor house and repeated the process. Just then a large 747 thundered overhead and twenty seconds later she heard the tires squeal as they touched down on the runway. Turning, she glanced back at the suspect house and saw the woman was now standing on the front stoop watching her. She ignored the woman and as casually as possible went on her way. She turned the corner and decided to visit a few more houses in case the woman decided to follow her around the corner. She didn't.

Etta did the next block at the end of the road as well. Both she and Josh agreed that any of these homes would have a good line of sight to the planes that were thundering by overhead. Satisfied with her reconnoitering, she headed for the white van that had moved and was parked up the block. Her mailbag was considerably lighter.

Once in the vehicle, Josh drove off and went a couple blocks before pulling to the side of the road.

"I should have wired up a small camera for the bag. Next time, I'll do that. There was a Middle Eastern woman in the house and she watched me the whole time I approached the door, and then as I walked around the corner and down the block."

"I hope you left her some mail?" Josh said, like a teacher to a student.

"You really think I'm an idiot don't you, of course I left some mail. I'm sure she will truly enjoy her complimentary copy of Good Housekeeping. Ok, smartass, it's your turn to undress and walk the minefields."

Josh climbed in back and started disrobing. Etta started driving to their next stop about a mile away, near the next runway approach. Driving, she tilted the rear view mirror when he wasn't looking, muttering two can play this game. She admired his muscled physique and noted a past bullet hole on his lower back that she had not seen before. She decided she would have to give him a better inspection next time she had the chance.

Josh came forward looking like a gas meter reader and attached his name badge to his shirt pocket. He grabbed a clipboard and got out of the van. He walked down the street. He took some shortcuts through the backyards and across lawns searching for gas meters. At every house he would make like he was taking a reading, tap the gauges, take some notes on his clipboard and then move on. When he got to the suspected target house, he made like he couldn't find the meter and went around the entire house the long way.

He glanced in the windows as he made his way around the house and finally came upon the meter. He tried to take a reading and gently banged on the metal receptacle trying to see if he could draw a resident to a window or outside. That didn't work so he looked like he was puzzled and marched to the back door of the house, all the while taking in his surroundings, noting the garage, the doors, and the windows. This house had an abandoned step van in the backyard that had three flat tires and had seen better days.

Knocking on the door he waited for someone to answer. A dark skinned man came to the door and drew the white window drape back a little. He seemed annoyed but eventually opened the door.

"Good afternoon, Sir, gas meter reader." He held up his badge for scrutiny. "Just taking a reading. Your gas meter seems to be really flying, almost spinning. Have you smelled gas in the house today?"

The man looked confused but said in broken English no, he did not understand.

Josh made a face sniffing the air, but that got no reaction either. "May I come in and check for any leaks?"

The man understood enough to know that the meter reader wanted to come in, but he again said no and shut the door. Then he heard the man say to someone inside the house that it was a gas workman but I sent him away. He said it in Arabic.

Josh had what he wanted, confirmation that the house was indeed occupied and possibly by some bad guys. He went back to the exterior house meter and fiddled around with it some more in case anyone was watching from within. He presumed they were. He decided he would go a number of additional houses until they couldn't see him anymore.

Ten minutes later he was back in the van and recounted his findings. The house was definitely on their list.

Josh and Etta spent the afternoon alternating incursions into various neighborhoods all around O'Hare. At about 4:00 pm they were parked in a hotel parking lot in Rosemont finalizing notes when Josh suggested they should go pay a visit to the local real estate office in Schiller Park, the buyer or seller of many of these homes and businesses.

"How about you be a woman executive that has been transferred here, and I'll be the factory worker husband that follows you like a puppy dog."

"You just want to watch me change clothes again."

"It never crossed my mind,….. but now that you mention it, put on that low cut blouse. Let's see if we can get a rise out of them while we're there."

"I can't believe you can use a terrorist operation for your own personal depravity. You must be really horny."

"Always my lady, always. Now get in back and take off your clothes!" He smiled as he said it.

"You're sick. You know this is a two way street. I'll strip if you do."

"Then we won't be able to keep an eye on the road and accomplish what we set out to do."

"Which is what? Tell me again." Etta said, as she took off her postal uniform and stood there in a low cut bra and panties.

"I…uh, what did you ask?" he again smiled, and leaned forward to give her a kiss.

"She accepted the kiss and pushed him away. "Put your pants on, buster."

They drove towards Schiller Park, just three miles away, and worked out a scenario to present themselves as potential house buyers. Josh had slapped a magnetic sign on the sides of the van that advertised 'Steel Industrial Supply' which would explain the van.

They pulled into the small, retail strip mall off Irving Park Road, and parked right in front of the real estate office. The storefronts lining the parking lot had seen better days, but the office looked freshly painted. The real estate office also had the obligatory house listings pasted to the windows and it looked like there were a number of people inside.

Etta got out first and strutted over to the window listings looking like a determined lady. Her husband followed behind. She was all business and dressed accordingly and he looked like he had just come from his factory job.

They made a show of pointing at some of the window listings and then walked over to the door and entered. Etta had to open her own door because her man was oblivious.

A woman sitting at the reception desk greeted them. She was dressed in a black hijab, but had no veil. Her coal black eyes scrutinized the walk-ins. She didn't rise from her chair but greeted them in passable English.

Etta said hello and took command of the conversation clearly exhibiting she was the party to be dealt with. Her husband ignored the counter exchange and wandered over to look at more house listings posted on the sidewall. This gave him an opportunity to scan the interior and to look behind the countertop. It also mimicked what he had been doing outside. He could feel the people in the outer office watching him as he moved about.

The smartly dressed businesswoman explained that she had been transferred into the area and wanted to explore any fast sale housing opportunities because her husband had found a job in Franklin Park, the next suburb south.

Josh reached into his pocket and palmed a small microphone transmitter. It looked like a typical plastic stickpin, very similar to the ones that held the house listings on the board. He made a point of pulling off one of the house listings and walked it over to his wife to show her the photo. She acknowledged the listing but continued her conversation with the woman behind the counter. Josh shrugged, and took the house photo back to the wall, and reposted it to the board, this time using his miniature microphone pin. He made sure that it was directionally pointed towards the counter.

The receptionist excused herself and went over to the office doorway behind the counter. She opened the door and spoke to someone in a low voice in Arabic. Josh listened carefully. She was asking someone if he wanted to talk with the pigs in the office. That was revealing, he thought to himself.

Still looking at the real estate listings he noted that a number of them were marked sold. In fact, they included a number of houses on their suspect list. There were also some commercial buildings marked sold or leased. Josh made a mental note of the addresses for later follow-up. He bet they too would be near the airport runway approaches.

A man dressed in a suit came out of the back room straightening his jacket. He smiled at his new customers at the counter. He was clearly Middle Eastern. Both Etta and Josh looked at him casually, but scrutinized every detail of his face as they were trained to do. He welcomed his guests, introduced himself as Joe Mazzoni and asked if he could be of service. He waved the potential customers into his office and asked the receptionist to bring in some coffee. She tried to hide the face she made, but silently went to a coffee maker on the other side of the room.

As trained agents, both visitors absorbed all there was to see within the office, even looking back towards the front counter to see what was behind it. They took in every detail of the manager's private office. Josh was already thinking they would need to come back at another time, so he looked for security cameras, checked out the door locks and windows that could be unobtrusively observed from his vantage point.

The office manager directed them to a small conference table and poured three cups of a dark roast coffee for his guests. "How can I be of service?"

Etta took the lead. Josh continued to play the subservient role, acting less interested, which allowed him to keep fidgeting and looking around the office. He found an MLS real estate book and started flipping through it, and played with a pen he found on the table.

Etta patiently told her story. "We need to find local inexpensive housing in the immediate area because of our work here. In a few years we will be able to save enough to move up a bit. We also want to look at any rental units? Might that be an alternative?"

"I have had great success moving both home sales and rentals in the area, in spite of the recession and the airport being so close by. You have probably noticed that some planes pass overhead above these neighborhoods. That can be a problem but it also offers some great values. I'm sure that we could assist you in finding a home to buy or rent."

We drove the Schiller Park neighborhood before we came here and they do fly right above here don't they?" Etta said, raising an eyebrow. She wanted to see if she could elicit any comments steering the conversation to the planes and airport to test his knowledge.

"Yes they do, but only some of the time. You actually get used to the noise, or I wouldn't be able to sell homes here at all. Some days the wind direction changes and the planes use different approaches and flight paths. Then you wonder where the planes have gone and marvel at the silence."

"Well, the pricing for homes in this area is certainly attractive, I guess that is a tradeoff," Etta said, looking at her husband and admonishing him for not paying attention.

"I think the planes are cool. I could sit outside and watch them thunder overhead all night long." Josh said to no one in particular.

"I've done the same thing. It's like you could almost reach out and touch them as they fly above you. But you do get used to it."

The manager decided to seize the moment. "How about I draw up a list of properties in the immediate area. I can even show you a couple of rentals that I am managing if you don't mind looking past people's personal belongings. None of the rentals are long term and they could open up at any time."

"That would be great. Could we get some spec sheets on what these homes have in them? We could look them over on the weekend and then narrow the list to look at a few next week after work?" Etta said, reeling her suspect into the game.

"I would be pleased to do that. Give me a few moments to pull some properties and rentals together. Have another cup of coffee. It will only take a few minutes," he said, as he headed for the outer office.

Josh and Etta covertly smiled at one another when he exited the office.

"We may have to come back here later tonight to take a look around. Can we get some supplies on short notice, Josh whispered, watching the door.

"Yeah, we have what we need at the office. And a few more microphone pins as well. I'm also thinking cameras, I'd like to see who else comes in here?" Etta said. She lowered her voice as she heard movement outside the door.

The manager returned to the office and she said out loud, "So maybe we can put up with the noise and get settled sooner than we thought."

Josh just shrugged and flopped back in the chair.

"Here are some listings that might get you started. I could arrange a showing for next week. The bottom three listings are rentals which have people in them at the moment but they all may become available within a month so, I'll show them to you if you would like to see?"

"That sounds great. Let me look these over and I'll get back to you by Monday."

They all stood. The man shook Josh's hand but bowed to the woman, preferring not to touch as was his religious custom. With a bunch of listings in a brown manila folder, Josh and Etta left the office. Outside Josh made Etta look at one more property pasted to the window. He wanted to show her he was invested in the process.

They got in the van and drove away heading east. About a mile away they drove into a large forest preserve area and parked the van to discuss the day's events.

"Well, I think we found one of our bad guys," Josh said. "He's pretty slick but the situation there screams dirty. I couldn't tell you, but when we arrived the receptionist asked him in Arabic if he wanted to talk to us pigs. It's kind of like connect the dots. I've gone on less in the past."

"I agree," Etta said, scanning the house listings they had been given. "If I recollect the house addresses we've been targeting, most of these are houses directly under flight paths, and these rental properties are too. What if we could play this out and actually get a look inside some of these houses before the president's plane comes to Chicago?"

"That makes sense. I was going to suggest that we pay a moonlight visit to our friendly real estate office tonight, but maybe we should wait so we don't wear out our welcome just yet. This guy even said the rentals might open up next month, which would be after the President's visit, when he doesn't need the locations anymore."

"Ok, so before we go home, let's swing buy all these houses and see if they really are under the flight paths. I'll put them in suburb order. You start driving. Then I'll take you home for a good soak and get all that filth off of you."

"I'm liking that scenario. I'm in." He gunned the engine to show his enthusiasm.

Homeland Security, Rosemont, IL.

The next day they arrived at DHS, cleared security and took the elevator to the conference room on the third floor. They recognized the staff thus far assigned had grown again. In the conference room were a number of new players, some in uniform and others not.

Etta walked to the head of the table. Everyone took a seat. Josh hung back so that he could stare at her and dream. He was obviously still very horny.

"Good morning everyone, some of you already know me, but for our new arrivals, and task force members, I'm Etta Petrini, with Homeland Security. I have lead on this special task force. We have a much larger group of agencies represented here today, so let's go around the room and share our names and agencies. Josh, would you start."

Josh had been lost in thought trying to connect all the dots and was not paying attention to what Etta had said. He looked up somewhat surprised when he heard his name. His mind raced and he realized what she had asked. "Good morning, I'm Josh Ranalli, a United States federal employee like most of you. I'm here because I kind of stumbled onto this plot and my superiors thought I should see it through." He looked at Etta with a gleam in his eye that said, that's all you get.

While she thought he could have been a little more forthcoming she realized he was just protecting his status, as this was not normally his sandbox. She looked to the next person.

They went around the room introducing themselves. The FBI, the Air Force, ATF, and NSA, the National Security Agency, all had representatives present. There were a couple of senior agents from the Secret Service and a senior White House staffer sitting in. The new uniforms at the large conference table were from the Chicago Police Department and a couple of suburban police departments. From Chicago there was a Deputy Chief and the head of the O'Hare Airport Division. The smaller western suburbs surrounding O'Hare International were represented by their police chiefs. They did not often get called into Homeland Security and were very interested in what might be developing. Noting their neighboring chiefs were also from the O'Hare area they presumed it involved the Airport.

"Thank you all for coming this morning. From this point on everything that is said here is confidential, and on a need to know basis. I'm serious and that means not even your spouses. It must remain that way if we are to be successful."

She scanned the room to make sure that everyone was focused on what she was about to say.

"We will need your confidential support in the next fifteen days as we have identified a massive threat involving O'Hare International and the President of the United States. We have reason to believe that al Qaeda has secured twenty-nine Stinger missiles and intends to take out the President of the United States on Air Force One, to avenge the death of Osama bin Laden. As you can imagine this is a huge threat."

The room was silent. Those already aware of the plot looked for any reactions from the new members of the task force sitting at the table. They saw pursed lips and darting eyes shooting around the room. Etta continued to explain the challenge to bring everyone up to speed.

"Our initial challenge is to protect the President who is flying in here on Air Force One soon for a series of announced fund raisers. But equally important, we have to find and secure, or destroy every one of those 29 missiles. As you can imagine any of those weapons could wreak havoc on airplane traffic here or anywhere in the country. We have tracked the shipment of these weapons into the country and we have every reason to believe they are all located here, specifically around O'Hare. At this point we are trying to pinpoint where they are located."

The Chicago Deputy Chief was well aware that the president had a scheduled trip. He had weeks of planning already under his belt. He spoke first.

"Why not just have the President skip the fundraiser next week, so he won't be in jeopardy?"

"That would be the easy way to protect him, but that means we may not be able to identify the bad guys and secure all the weapons," Etta responded. "You may remember that large commercial jet that was shot down over the Ukraine, and the one that was shot down over the Persian Gulf about 15 years ago. Those were Stinger missiles, or its equivalent. Hundreds of civilians were killed with just a single strike."

Everyone at the table contemplated that deadly carnage and then processed the terror such weapons could have on air traffic anywhere in the U.S. If the terrorist's target was determined to not be coming to Chicago, then the terrorists might choose to take their weapons somewhere else.

"Right now, the bad guys are not aware that we have a handle on them," Josh said, stepping forward. He thought he'd give Etta a break for a second. "We have every reason to believe that all these weapons are right here in the area. We just need to grab them before they are used or the bad guys bug out of town. Once they leave we have a different set of challenges. I guess the 'bird in the hand' theory can be used to contain the threat."

"So let's go get the bastards," one of the suburban police chiefs said to the entire group.

"That's the plan once we get a better handle on where the weapons are physically located, every one of them. The problem is we have reason to believe they are spread around O'Hare in various houses and businesses. If we knew they were in one place we would have ended this threat a long time ago. These guys have a large team that intends to kill the president. Anyone here ever drive the expressways and roads around O'Hare?"

Almost everyone in the room nodded, except for a few of the Washington DC representatives. The group sat there conjuring up the visual of the highways and roads that surround O'Hare and their proximity to the planes arriving every thirty seconds.

Josh turned on a large projector and clicked through a number of photo images showing how low and close the planes were as they passed hotels and businesses and crossed the outer perimeter fences of the huge airport. Then he switched to a video of a number of 747's flying into the airport. The large birds were so big they didn't look like they were even moving that fast. Everyone in the room sat there mesmerized watching the screen as these huge planes roared overhead. They immediately recognized the threat to Air Force One.

"That, in a nutshell is our problem," Etta said, pointing to the fixed image of a Korean 747 just three hundred feet above the expressway and outer markers. "If you know O'Hare, you know there are neighborhoods, homes and many small businesses that abut those runway approaches. Some are just 1,000 feet from the end of the runways. We have been out there and the planes fly overhead so close that you almost feel like ducking."

Everyone contemplated the potential carnage. The Secret Service guys were squirming in their seat and looking very nervous. They were obviously contemplating pulling the plug on the President's trip just a few weeks off.

Josh saw it too. He realized he needed to convey the proposed plan of action rather than just presenting the problem. "While I'm not advocating the president be our guinea pig, we need to have these terrorists believe that he is on the way to his Chicago visit and fundraisers as preannounced. That way we can try to identify where all these twenty-nine missiles are being hidden."

The Secret Service man on the president's advance team jumped on that comment and spoke up. "I see the challenge. But we can't put the President in such danger. He'll want to do it, but that won't be an option with us."

"I certainly respect that. How about we still bring the President to Chicago as planned but we have him flown into a different airport, unannounced, say Midway, or even Gary and then chopper or drive him to his appointments on the appointed day?"

The Secret Service Director thought about that a moment and said. "That would work. But I presume you want us to maintain the charade of him flying into O'Hare?"

"Yeah, unfortunately, I think we even need a bit more. We need Air Force One to fly into O'Hare that day," Josh said. "That's the only way we will get these assholes to show themselves. They have to believe they are taking the shot to get them to haul out the hardware."

"Do you know how much Air Force One costs?" Air Force Major Chip Young said with his voice rising an octave. He was in charge of the president's plane, with the Air Mobility Command 89th Airlift Wing, from Andrews Air Force Base. "We can't just use the president's plane as a guinea pig to suck them out of their burrows!"

"I understand completely, Major, it is one heck of a big bird to use as a target. More importantly we don't want to put the crew in jeopardy either. I was actually thinking of another approach."

"I'm listening, but I don't want to think about even scratching the paint," the Major said, sounding skeptical.

"I get that, but what if your Air Force Presidential Maintenance Branch made a routine announcement in DC, that both Air Force One planes needed to be pulled out of service for two weeks for some major flight safety issues, or a major security overhaul?"

The Major looked over to his Secret Service partners, got a nod and then said, "We could do that, but how does that transfer to the terrorists? If we made a big deal about it, won't it tip them off that we are on to them?"

"Yeah, that could definitely telegraph the blow," Josh offered, "but,…. what if we made the announcement low key, say only in DC without any big fanfare . Then we let the Chicago politicians that would be getting a free ride with the President talk about the possibility they may have to cancel the fundraising events because of the Air Force One repair. The press would eat that up and before you know it everyone's talking about the grounding. When pressed by the media, the White House announces the president is still coming to keep his donors happy, but in one of the smaller presidential jets. They are all decked out like Air Force One aren't they?"

"They are, just smaller versions with of the same paint job," the Secret Service guy said. "The VP uses one and so does the Secretary of State. I think you're right, if we keep the announcement low key, no big deal, the press will find it and make a big story out of it whether we want them to or not."

"If we pull the con off, the bad guys are happy and think they are just looking for a smaller plane, which would be even easier to take down."

Again the Major looked for confirmation from the Secret Service and got a nod. "That could work. With the smaller jet we could even set it up to be flown remotely, like a drone. We could have it start out from Gary's airport, and fly the 50 miles to O'Hare at the same appointed time. That way no one goes down with the ship if a missile actually does hit the bird."

"If we could orchestrate that scenario, we can sucker these assholes to make their move. Then we swoop in and take them down and hopefully secure all those Stingers. We have some good intelligence being developed that should help us identify every location where they may try to shoot the missiles. We just have to make sure we get them all."

"So how do we know where they're hiding?" another newcomer to the task force asked?

"Good question and this is where I need all the surrounding police department assistance," Josh said. "We have identified a number of houses and businesses that are immediately adjacent to runway approaches on all sides of the airport. We will need team support to monitor them covertly, and when the time comes hit them, and hit them hard."

Etta chimed in, "You will be working with FBI SWAT teams along with your area terrorist personnel. We will all have to coordinate the take down for a specific time with all of us moving simultaneously for a grand sweep. The goal is to account for every missile."

Task force members still had questions. "But how do we identify the suspect houses or businesses. We can't raid every home on the end of every runway. There must be at least fifteen runways out there?"

"Good guess," Josh said, "there are fourteen runways out there currently if you count all approaches. When you factor in that planes come in from a variety of directions depending on the wind direction, we will have our hands full. That's why these assholes needed so many missiles, to cover all the possible in-bound routes."

The education process went on. Etta explained how the shooters would make the attempt. "We believe they plan on having spotters watch the plane's final approach from some tall buildings like the

Hyatt or Westin Hotels from the east, or maybe some commercial building roofs from the west, whatever direction the wind is blowing that day. The spotters will probably have communication by radio or cell phone direct to the shooters, they will verify the flight path on runway XYZ and then the shooter steps out of a house front door, a backyard garage, or business loading dock at the last moment and shoots as the plane passes almost overhead.

The Air Force major acknowledged that type of ground to air threat. "That would be hard to defend against because the missile travels so fast. I was shot at in Iraq, but never from such a low height. Even with the defensive measures and capabilities that Air Force One has, the aircraft would have little time to react. I would guess five seconds at 300 feet above the ground."

"So we have to get the missiles all at once. If we get the active runway shooters, the other guys may try to escape with their missiles and go to plan B. We can't let them get away and seek out another opportunity at some other airport," Etta said, "that's why we have to make this work. The FBI will coordinate with the area police departments. Chiefs, the FBI takes the lead and your guys will take direction from them. It is also important that you not share this Intel with your departments yet. If there is an increased surveillance of the areas, the bad guys will spook and then we lose the missiles."

Everyone broke into sub-groups to talk strategy. The suburban police officials got together to be briefed about the components that would be involved in their communities.

Josh walked over to Etta at the coffee table and said, "We make a good team. Heck, I even believe the bull we just sold all of them." He smiled and clinked coffee cups.

"Calm down, big boy, we haven't done anything yet."

"What do you mean? We have already saved the President from a horrific death. I've been shot at on two continents, almost been drowned in the same two places and personally saved you from drowning. We have been shot at and called pigs. I'd say we have been doing all sorts of things."

"But no definitive results yet! All we have so far is gunshot and knife wounds, my busted shoulder, and black and blue bodies! We still have lots of work to do if we're going to get all these wacko's and their pop guns."

"Ah yes, bodies, thank you for reminding me, now I have something to carry me through the rest of the afternoon." He smiled and took another gulp of coffee.

She slugged him in his sore arm and called him a pig, again!

Des Plaines, Illinois

The Des Plaines public works step-van rolled down the street towards the end of the block. The van had no windows in the back but did have all the markings of a city vehicle. Projecting off the front bumper was a six-foot boom that held a large, round metal disc with all sorts of wiring running back to the interior of the van. The whole assembly looked to be some sort of sensor that was searching the concrete and asphalt surfaces of the road. To the average person it looked like a city vehicle doing its work searching for underground conduit or sewer pipes. Every now and then a public works guy in overalls with orange reflective tape would jump out and spray some markings on the pavement.

Inside, there were three sophisticated cameras mounted on the walls of the van on each side of the vehicle. The lens poking through the metal siding of the van was small enough that they were lost in the colors of the city department logos affixed on each side of the van. Monitoring this sophisticated equipment were National Security Administration technicians. One camera took continuous video of the houses on the street. A second camera took thermal images noting any heat signatures and body counts within the walls of the subject houses. The third camera took still images of the target homes that could be used to familiarize the assault teams. Behind the technicians monitoring the equipment were two FBI agents decked out in full combat gear ready to act if the need should arrive.

The van had been making the rounds of the suburbs around O'Hare all day. In each community the city decals were switched out to allow the step van to cruise the target neighborhoods and commercial business areas slowly, without drawing any attention. The information gathered would be analyzed carefully to develop assault plans for the arrival date of the President's plane. The last thing anyone wanted to do was charge into the wrong houses looking for terrorists.

Late in the day the van was in Elk Grove Village on the west side of the airport slowly cruising up and down the blocks with runway approaches almost on top of them. Near an old carpet store and warehouse on Wolf Road directly across from the airport the technicians zoomed the cameras in on an old delivery van, tall enough to allow a man to stand up in. The vehicle was parked out in front of the recently opened store. In an earlier photo of that particular store and vehicle, they had noted the van tires were flat and the graphic signage was torn and peeling. Now the camera showed the vehicle had been fixed up and had new advertising on both sides. Someone had been hard at work sprucing up this rolling billboard and delivery vehicle.

The public works driver parked in front of the store, about thirty-five feet from the store entrance and half that for the van. All the while the cameras were recording images. The workers set out some orange safety cones to redirect traffic around the temporary work zone. They didn't know if anyone was watching them from the store as they went about their work. Together they took some measurements and then carefully sprayed some boxes and numbers in orange and red spray paint on the pavement.

Satisfied with their work, they collected the safety cones and drove off. As they did so two middle eastern men with scruffy beards walked out of the carpet showroom and to the curb. They looked at the markings but could not make out what was being done. They shrugged their shoulders to a man standing inside the doorway and returned to the business satisfied it was just the city doing road maintenance.

Washington DC., Andrews Air Force Base

A press release was issued as an internal base memo but the Communications Officer knew that it would be picked up by members of the press corps that covered the President's travel. The Colonel sat in his office as a couple of reporters that had access to the 89th Air Lift Command hangers looked over the bulletin board postings for Air Force One. They read the internal memo and took some notes about the maintenance grounding of the two massive craft.

The two reporters pulled out their cell phones and reported their findings to their editors to find out if they would need to do any follow-up. In no time they had their answer and both marched over to the colonel's office for more information.

"What's up with Air Force One, Colonel? I see you're pulling it out of service for a couple weeks of maintenance?"

"Yeah, no big deal, both birds need some updates sooner rather than later," he casually said. "We're doing it now because the President is scheduled to go overseas in about a month, and the work needs to be done, checked and certified before a long haul like that." That was all the information he was authorized to share.

"Isn't the President supposed to be going to Chicago soon?" the reporter asked, checking his calendar on his phone.

"He's still going, he'll just use one of the Air Force executive fleet. He'll probably borrow the Secretary of State's plane for the trip. He isn't using it that week and you guys know that the plane will carry the Air Force One designation if the President is on it."

"We know, but I guess it's newsworthy to pass along. Thanks." The two reporters walked off dialing their managers again.

The Colonel made a note to send another internal memo to the Director of Operations at O'Hare International Airport about the switch in equipment. He didn't know why all the intrigue had landed on his desk, but he didn't want to know. It was above his pay grade.

Schiller Park, IL.

The large jet aircraft flew over the town, east to west heading for runway 28, just two blocks from the real estate office on Lawrence Avenue. It was 2:00 am and the large 747 was probably a commercial freighter coming in from Europe. There was only a sliver of a moon in the western sky. About the only glow in the night was coming from the airport lights less than a half-mile away

Josh Ranalli and Etta Petrini sat in the back of an unmarked step van in a parking lot across the alley from the real estate office. Etta was monitoring the rear door of the building through a darkened screen window, the office was about one hundred feet away. There was no security light over the door. It had been broken three days earlier by some kid.

Josh was examining his break-in kit to make sure he had what he needed. He verified his lock pick tools were in his sleeve pocket. A small camera was wedged into the straps that would normally hold a weapon on his chest rig. The 15 Meg camera was built to take extraordinary photographs in very low light situations. They were both dressed in black fatigues and had skullcaps on their heads. Both had skintight black rubber gloves on.

An hour before they had driven past the front of the target building noting all the lights were out and no one was inside the storefront glassed office. Now they waited to make sure that the entire area was asleep and that no one was wandering the streets. There were no cars in the lot and the alley was as dark as could be expected. None of the homes in the area had inside lights on and only one garage a block down had a security light shining.

"Ok, let's do this. You keep monitoring the alley and give me a call if anyone shows up."

"Yeah, right, I'm going with you. Remember this is my operation, you're just a CIA guest checking out my domestic territory."

"I'm always checking your domestic territory, that's a given, but in this game two is a crowd. You stay here and watch my back."

Playful as always, even though the situation called for the opposite, Etta said, "I've watched your back, and front, and I've appreciated both. But I'm just protecting my interests. I'll watch your back from inside, thank you, and then you can warm my back when we get home."

Josh thought about that for a moment, and gave in, "That's almost like foreplay in my book, but I'm in for the count. You may be lead, but I specialize in this black bag stuff so you follow my lead when we're inside, ok?"

The two agents quietly stepped out of the van, closing the door but not locking it. They scanned both directions and then casually walked across the alley. Etta stood guard and Josh dropped to a knee to pick the lockset.

Etta started to whisper that she could do that faster but had to stop when she heard Josh open the door. It had taken him about ten second; so much for lock security.

Josh eased the door open and they both entered quickly into the back room, the manager's interior office. Josh signaled they should freeze. Using a small penlight he scanned the room for any electronic trip wires. They both listened for any sounds of life, whether man or dog. There were none but they held there position for two minutes.

Josh aimed his small penlight at the floor. The light bounced off the floor giving them some diffused light to see where they could step and what the surroundings had to offer.

Etta went to the other door leading to the outer office and silently cracked open the door to scan for any person who might be out there. The office was empty and the front door was locked. She noted the reverse of the closed sign hanging in the window. She shut the door and walked to the large window noting where the drapes were positioned. She looked out and seeing no one she closed the drapes.

Josh nodded and turned on his flashlight. He started scanning for any monitoring cameras or recording devices. Up to this point no one had said anything yet.

"I think we're good," Josh whispered. "So here's the plan. We look at everything very carefully before touching or moving it. Afterwards, we put it back in the same position as before. No need to let them know someone was in here."

Etta again nodded and started looking at a desk in the corner near the window. Josh went to the Manager's desk and saw that the computer was shut down. He turned on the laptop hoping he would be able to figure out the password. The machine booted up and ran through a series of prompts until it offered a password protected entry screen.

Josh flexed his fingers and thought for a moment. Now what would this asshole use as a password. He tried jihad and the computers said no. He tried Al ahu Ackbar and again the computer rejected him. He looked at the manager's business card sitting on the front of the desk and tried the first name backwards, and then the last name, Mazzoni in reverse. That was it and the computer opened up.

He started searching files looking for a smoking gun document but found none. There was a planning file but it was simply a plan for building the real estate business. He found a number of excel financial files and stuck a small stick in the computer dumping a copy of all the computer content for later analysis.

Etta moved around the office carefully examining everything. She took photos of all the listings on the map recognizing that many of the house sale and rental locations were very close to the dead end streets that they had pre-identified in their drive around surveillance. She pulled three additional small pin cameras from her pocket. These were plastic pincushion units like the one they had placed earlier on the large real estate bulletin board. She retrieved the earlier one and placed the three new ones in clusters of other pins aiming them at different parts of the office.

Two miniature microphones the size of a large nail were distributed throughout the office. One was placed near a small round conference table, wedged into the windowsill. Another was placed on the manager's desk in the bottom of a pen and pencil holder coffee mug. The third was wedged into the outer doorframe and would hopefully pick up conversations in the outer office near the front desk.

Josh was diligently copying every document he could find to his thumb drive. He signaled that he was about done when there was a sound of a car pulling in the driveway out front. They froze for just a second and then both moved to finish their work. Josh slipped his drive into a special port built into his black boot heel.

Etta went over to the outer door and cracked it open enough to see if in fact there was someone coming to the office. A car had parked almost in front of the office and its headlights blinked out. The driver's door opened and a man with a beard got out. He patted his pockets to make sure whatever was where it should be. He seemed to be in no hurry. Etta signaled Josh to hold as she was still unsure if the man was actually coming into the real estate office.

The man headed towards the 7-11 store that was one business over and still open. He walked out of view and Etta cracked the door a bit more to make sure of his intentions. She saw him pass beyond the windows. Before Josh could stop her she opened the door and duck-walked out to the receptionists counter keeping her head low.

A second man slouched down in the front seat saw the door move in the real estate office. There was supposed to be no one there. He quietly opened his car door and slid out disappearing behind the car. He called softly to his partner. They both drew their weapons.

Etta didn't see the second guy as she crept forward to the windows to make sure the first man had indeed gone to the 7-11. Once she got there looking sideways down the walk, the second guy stepped out from behind the car and pointed his silenced handgun directly at the woman dressed in black near the doorway. He was prepared to shoot through the window. She reacted to his forward movement but could do nothing as he had the drop on her. She stood, and raised her hands in surrender. The second man, inching along the darkened walkway saw his partner had stepped forward, and did so as well. He fumbled for his office keys and began opening the door.

Etta just stood there drawing the two gunmen's attention. Josh was still in the shadows of the back room but could readily see what was happening. They had both decided to not carry any firepower. That was a mistake he now realized.

Josh debated what he could do against two guns and didn't like his odds with Etta in the line of fire. As the two guys held her at bay through the window, fumbling with the key, he whispered into the outer office. "Etta, comply, don't fight. I'm staying close. I'll follow wherever they take you." With that he made sure everything was where it should be, remembered to open the drapes just as they had been, and slipped out the back door.

He locked the door, crossed the dark alley, and stepped into the van reaching for his weapon sitting between the seats. He debated going back in but thought that would blow the whole effort. Remembering the missiles he decided Etta would have to take her lumps until he could again intervene. He quickly started the engine and drove down the block and turned towards Lawrence Avenue. Crossing over, he went down a side street, and cut back through a restaurant parking lot down the street from the real estate office. Killing his lights he parked in such a way that he could monitor the situation in the office shadows.

Etta had heard Josh's instructions. His words comforted her and she tried not to follow her instinct and bolt for the back room. That would allow Josh to get away. She just hoped he planned to come back. She held steady and watched the two men open the lockset and enter.

One stepped towards her and pointed a gun at her head. The other stepped forward leering. He reached forward and backhanded her across the face, staggering her. She fell to the floor with blood streaming from her nose and mouth.

Across the street in the darkened parking lot Josh saw her go down and wished he had stayed to fight the intruders. He could have taken the two of them. He continued watching and debated literally driving into the storefront to stop the carnage but again thought of the missiles and the need to play this out for the safety of the country.

He watched and feared that he would see a gun flash as they shot the woman he was falling in love with. But that did not happen. One man continued to hold a gun to Etta's head. The other reached down and grabbed her, pulling her upright by her hair. Still reeling Etta tried to stand. The man smacked her in the gut with a closed fist as hard as he could. She went down again in a heap.

Etta pulled herself into a fetal position, trying to catch her breath. The wind was completely knocked out of her. To make matters worse she had fallen on her bad shoulder and was writhing in pain. She realized she needed to completely capitulate immediately so she wouldn't be beaten to death. She whimpered loud enough to be heard and the gun holder waived his arm across the field of fury and reigned in his crazed partner. He handed him his weapon to stop the beating. They obviously needed to find out what this woman was doing there.

He reached down and tried to assist the woman back up. She fought the effort until she realized it wasn't the boxer who was grabbing her. He dragged her over to an office chair and dropped her into it. She was a real mess, but underneath all the blood they saw that she was a pretty woman. He went behind the counter and brought out some shipping twine. He forced her forward in the chair and bound her arms together and then bound her to the chair itself. He then rolled the chair to a corner of the office to stay away from any prying eyes that might drive by. The two men looked at their captive.

"Who are you, lady? Why are you here? Who do you work for?" the non-boxer said.

Etta tried to think the situation through. Her head ached fiercely but she still had her faculties, so she tried to fabricate a story to buy time. "I need drugs and was looking for money. You make tons of money selling houses. I need a fix."

The bad ass grabbed her tied arms pulling up her sleeves looking for track marks. "Try again, lady." He reached for the Velcro pulls on her black vest and ripped them open pulling the vest over her head. Then he wrestled her black field tunic over her head and pulled out a utility knife to cut it off her body.

Tied there with only her black lace bra still intact, blood droplets from her nose continued to drip down her face between her breasts. She felt exposed and could see this was not going any place good. Where was Josh? In her heart she knew he had to be close. But she didn't want to give up the whole operation. There were thousands of lives at risk if those missiles were not found. She just needed to suck it up and play this out.

With her completely trussed up, the two men retreated to another corner of the office to debate what they should do. She heard one say that they should call Mahoud, but the other reminded him it was 4:00 am. Their job was to keep an eye on things and not create any incidents. They would take the woman to him in the morning and he could determine what was going on.

The two returned to their captive. "So we have a couple hours to kill!" He stared at the captive woman trussed up in the chair. He wanted to see what was under all that blood. He had been an Arab in America for too long. Here, all women looked better and you could see more of them. But she was a mess and that was not attractive, even to him.

Etta saw the leering in his eyes and braced herself for what was probably coming next. Damn why did she have to go out in the outer office. They could have gotten away and no one would have been the wiser. She ached all over.

The non-boxer saw his partner leering and decided the woman still needed to be alive when they took her to their boss, so he took command of the situation. "We will wait an hour and then get her in the car and go to Mahoud. Then we will be done with her. Let's clean up the mess in front. There is blood on the floor. Did you have to hit her across the face? I'll get the car and drive around back next to the door."

The man left. The boxer came over to his captive and grabbed her face to get a good look. He was used to only seeing veiled faces back home. Here he was seeing all the other parts, like at the strip clubs. He moved one of her straps off her shoulder and reached down and touched her right breast. In response, she brought her foot up swiftly between his legs and caught him right in the balls. He fell backwards howling. Then he got up and slapped her backhanded across the face.

To her surprise, he then re-arranged her bra so she felt half-dressed again. Etta figured he was afraid of the other guy and filed that away for future use. Maybe she would live through this. Where was Josh?

Josh watched the bearded man come out of the storefront and get in the car. The car backed out and went around the corner and then down the alley behind the building. Josh left the van and cut across the street between two houses. He arrived at the alleyway and saw the man park the car next to the real estate office's rear door. The man went back inside.

Josh was confident they intended to move her and this would be his opportunity. He was armed now and advanced quietly down the alley ducking in and out of doorways. He climbed on top of a garbage container and pulled himself up onto the roof creeping over to a spot directly above the rear door. Keeping an eye on the door below he prepared some plastic ties to subdue the guys when they came out.

Etta felt like a truck had hit her. She was holding her head up to staunch the bleeding from her nose. For the moment the boxer thug was leaving her alone probably because the other guy had returned. He sat there leering at her heaving chest debating what he wanted to do to her.

The non-boxer stood in front of her and again asked what she was doing there.

"I'm just looking for cash. These stores are easy pickings. There is never anyone around here at this hour. I'm really sorry, if you'll release me I'll make it worthwhile to both of you." She tried to smile through a bloody cracked lip.

The boxer sitting a few feet away got excited by that offer and smiled. He knew what he wanted. The questioner ignored her offer and repeated the question. "You will have a hell of an easier time with us than you will with my boss. He'll get the information out of you one way or another and then he'll give you to Jabir here. And I don't think either of us want to see that."

The boxer got up and walked over. Without ceremony he tore her bra from her body, completely exposing her. He threw it down and grabbed her breasts in his hands mashing them together.

Even his partner was surprised by his action. He lashed out backhanding the aggressor with a handgun catching him on the bridge of his nose. More blood sprayed out as the man went down.

"I apologize for my partner but it shows you what you can expect if you decide to remain quiet." He too stared at the woman's breasts with lust." He picked up the remnants of her black tunic and draped it haphazardly over her shoulders covering her up so his heart would stop racing.

"We must go. We will wake up Mahoud early. Get her up and don't hit her again or you will have to carry her."

The boxer glared at his partner but did as he was told. He came around the chair and grabbed the woman by her shoulders pulling her back. He touched her breasts again and then started untying the rope from the chair.

Etta tried to stand on her own so the bastard wouldn't have a reason to touch her again. She stood unsteadily and watched as the tunic fell from her shoulders again. At this point she didn't care except that it might incite them. The leader took off his jacket and draped it over her shoulders. Her front was still exposed but she felt as if he was trying. The boxer roughly pushed her towards the back door. The lead man looked out down the alley to make sure there was no one about.

Josh was directly above them leaning over the roofline. Just ten feet separated them.

The two men and the captive woman came out of the doorway

and stood between the wall and the car. Josh didn't hesitate. He leaped directly down on them hitting one on the head with the butt of his gun and landing directly on top of the other. Both went down like a bag of bricks, knocked unconscious. He also landed partially on top of Etta.

"Where the hell have you been?" was all she said, as she tried to stand with her hands still tied behind her back.

"In the CIA we get coffee breaks especially when we're on overtime," he whispered as he helped her up. He opened his utility knife and sliced through her bindings.

"I didn't mean now. Where were you when that bastard tried to rape me?" she said, as she kicked the inert body lying beneath her as hard as she could.

"I was across the street watching for an opportunity to reclaim my partner." He said this as he slipped the flexi cuffs on the two bodies and started lifting them into the car trunk.

"So you saw him smack me around with the gun and cut off my top, and smack me again. Did you like what you saw? What kind of partner is that?"

"Well, I've seen them before, remember. I saw him leering at you but I was pretty far away. You know that is a part of the job. The mission couldn't be compromised."

"You bastard, you'll never see them again! Why didn't you charge in here and pop those guys?"

"Like I said, I didn't want to blow the investigation. We still have 29 missiles out there to find. Now help me get these guys tucked in so we can blow this pop stand. Here put on my shirt. You're distracting me again."

"Bastard!" was all she said. She put on the jersey and closed the car trunk spitting on her attackers.

"I'll stay here and clean up the mess inside. Maybe we can make believe this didn't happen and the two guards decided to go on vacation. Drive these guys to Homeland and put them on ice. I'll follow once I clean up your mess."

"You Bastard! I would have come to your aid much sooner." That was all she could think to say as she got in the car and drove off.

Chicago, IL.

The morning Chicago Tribune had a below the fold story about the President coming to town for a series of fund-raisers. The seventh paragraph mentioned that Air Force One, the large 747 jet aircraft would not be making the trip, as it and it's identical partner was getting a major overhaul before a long trip overseas. It said the President would be flying in one of the smaller Executive Branch jets that had the same markings and would still carry the call sign Air Force One.

The President's schedule remained the same. He would be meeting with local dignitaries at O'Hare International Airport before travelling downtown by motorcade for an afternoon fundraising event at Navy Pier on the lakefront.

Mahoud sat at his breakfast table on Granger St. in Des Plaines. He drank some more coffee and re-read the article trying to determine what the change in plane equipment would mean. What might this change in planes do to his overall plan? Would he need to adjust the plan of attack?

The presidential plane that would be coming in was considerably smaller. He had once seen the Secretary of State's official plane fly into Lebanon. It would make a smaller target. His missile shooters would need to be more accurate. He thought about that for a while and then visibly brightened.

If the presidential craft was a smaller craft, perhaps it would not have all the defensive capabilities that the big plane had. That would be a good thing. His missiles might have an easier time taking the smaller craft down.

He made a mental note to bring more missiles to the most probable runway corridors, once the wind directions and approaches had been established that morning. While he was aware the weather and wind directions could change quickly in this windy city, he hoped they would be predictable that particular day.

Mahoud made another mental note to have his people ready to move the missiles from one location to another so he could shoot three or four missiles from a single location. Then he would double up the missiles on the opposite side of the airport as well, in case the plane was able to evade the initial volley. He would catch them as they tried to streak out of the airport killing ground.

One of his men had been charting all the arriving airport traffic patterns for the past month and more than sixty-percent of the time the plane's had been arriving east to west, coming in from Lake Michigan, flying over downtown Chicago on final approach. He was becoming more confident that the President's plane would probably do the same.

He had decided he would definitely rent a hotel room in one of the hotels near the Rosemont Convention Center on River Road. He already had the high-powered binoculars that would help him identify the President's alternate plane as it arrived at O'Hare coming out of the East. Then he would use another burn phone to advise his shooters which runway was being used for the approach, and when to step out of cover and shoot at the jet passing a few hundred feet overhead.

The target might be smaller than the famous 747, but he was convinced that it would also be easier to shoot down.

He finished his coffee and prepared to go to the real estate office. He would then make a visit to all of his safe houses to check on his compatriots and advise of this slight change in plan.

Chicago, IL.

Etta dropped off the two prisoners at the DHS building. Two Homeland Security guards met her at the back entrance. One look at her face with the dried blood and black and blue marks on her cheek and ears and they knew they had some tough customers to deal with. They also acknowledged that she had them, not the reverse. When she opened the trunk they hauled out the two bearded men and stood them side-by-side awaiting instructions.

Etta stood before the two and then without warning kicked one of them in the balls again. He crumpled to the ground again. The other captive tried to turn away expecting the same kind of kick but Etta smiled at him through her cut lip and then smacked him across the face as hard as she could. She knew this might be her last opportunity to dole out any personal justice once they went into the system. The security guards were not surprised and looked the other way.

"Take these assholes up to intake and keep them isolated and seperated. They see no one and no calls. I'll be up later."

She headed for the women's locker room. She needed to find some heavy duty Tylenol. She downed three pills and looked at herself in the mirror for the first time. She realized she should have kicked that asshole a couple more times. Maybe she would get another chance. Stripping down she saw that most of the damage was to her face. It looked like she had gone ten rounds in a boxing match. After a hot shower she tried to cover up the bruises and cracked lip as best she could.

Putting on fresh clothes was even a chore as she eased the black pants suit over her many bruises. When she was finally dressed she exited the locker room to find Josh sitting on the floor in the hallway. She was still angry he had taken his time coming to her rescue. She glared at him mouthing the word bastard for the tenth time.

Josh stood up and came over to her. He wasn't sure what he should say or do. This was beyond his limited relationship experience level. All he could think of was to blurt out how sorry he was that he hadn't intervened earlier. "Etta, I'm…."

Etta raised a hand to terminate the apology before it even started. He stopped talking and looked befuddled and unsure if he should even be there. Not sure of himself he tried to hug her but she stepped back. She was still very angry and tender in a number of places. That was the last thing she wanted to do.

He stood back silently and continued to apologize with his eyes.

"Enough." she said, to break the silence. "Were you able to clean up that mess back there? You know, all my blood on the floor?" Then sarcastically," Do we still have our cover?"

He decided to follow her lead and move on. "Yeah, I don't think our real estate terrorist will see anything out of the ordinary. They give you any trouble on the way in?"

"No," she said, again sarcastically, but less so. "Nothing I couldn't handle immediately! One of them will probably have a permanent limp and won't ever have children again, but they both deserve more than I dished out."

"Yeah, I was up in isolation and saw what an angry woman can do. Remind me never to cross you again."

"You got that right, buster." Her anger ratcheted down a couple notches. She decided he was being contrite enough. "I was just going to interview them. Want to come along, or are you afraid?"

"That's fair. Maybe I'll come along just to protect our only in-house leads. You know, good cop, bad cop. They know which one you are."

They walked to the elevator. Josh decided to push his luck. "Etta, I am so sorry, but keep in mind that had I used a heavier hand, and I wanted to, those twenty-nine missiles would have been in the wind. That would give us 29 new problems. I am truly sorry!"

"Ok, but you owe me big, mister." She smiled but the cracked lip hurt even more. "I'm not sure about you anymore."

He pouted a moment but decided not to push his luck. "Let's go say hi to our terrorists. Maybe they can share some new insights for us."

Schiller Park, IL.

With his four team leaders sitting at the small table in the back room, Mahoud talked about the change in plans concerning the President's Air Force One. He explained that they would now try to concentrate on two primary firing positions once the wind directions that day were apparent. And they would keep a couple of back-up positions if they needed them.

They discussed how the change and the movement of missiles would take place. Each man took responsibility for figuring out how to move the missiles to the new release sites at the last moment without drawing attention. This movement would also change their departure efforts to get out of town immediately after the shots were taken. Everyone went back to the drawing boards to adjust their plan.

Midway through the meeting, Kaseem drew Mahoud aside and advised that two of his security guards had disappeared. They were last seen starting their security shift the night before. It was their job to drive around monitoring all of the eastern airport properties, while two other security guards watched over the western side of the airport.

"What do you mean they disappeared?" Mohammed said. "How can they disappear?"

"They were only vaguely aware of what we are doing. They also know what we would do to them if we catch them."

"Then send out the others to make sure they have not just fallen asleep at one of the houses, and if you find them bring them to me."

He was angry but with only six days to go until the President arrived he had bigger worries about the operation. They all went back to their final planning efforts.

Federal Building, Chicago

Josh and Etta spent the early morning grilling the two terrorists one at a time. They were not that helpful at first but with the threat of an airplane ride to Guantanamo in Cuba, they spilled their guts. Unfortunately, most of the information was not new, but it did confirm the general plan for the terrorist attack.

Both Josh and Etta had the confirmations they needed to proceed. Armed with this information they could now initiate a full campaign to stop the terrorists. The better news was they could now bring the entire scope of Homeland Security and the Federal Government to the task.

They squirreled the two prisoners away on an initial charge of attacking a Federal Officer, pending a free trip to Cuba, or a federal indictment. Their car was towed to a Chicago impound lot and buried in a far corner. It would be ground up into scrap metal within the day. The two terrorists disappeared off the face of the earth.

Josh and Etta held their breath as they drove to Schiller Park near the airport to see if the two guard's disappearance would have any effect on the upcoming terrorist attempt to assassinate the President of the United States.

Pulling into the same restaurant parking lot Josh had been in the night before, they got out of their rental car and walked over to a food delivery truck that was parked against the restaurant wall.

As they entered the truck Etta looked across the street and saw that Josh could have seen her clearly getting her beating. She got angry all over again and with no warning slugged him in his sore shoulder. Having seen her take the glance across the street he knew why he was getting punched.

Two tech guys were working the truck's electronic equipment. They were monitoring the sound coming from the microphones across the street in the real estate office and watching the video feed from the hidden cameras planted in the back room.

"I don't know how you guys did with the mopes at HS, but your efforts in there last night are paying off." He pointed out the darkened front window at the real estate storefront across the street. "The microphones and cameras are working great. Everything you surmised has been pretty much confirmed by these guys. They are indeed planning to shoot down Air Force One. They even mentioned they had read about the President's 747's being grounded and that a different presidential plane would be substituted. They thought that would make their job easier because the missiles can take out a smaller plane much more efficiently."

"They're right," Josh said. "I've seen Stingers that have taken down small planes and there is actually nothing left, the explosion makes the whole craft disintegrate. What else are you getting?"

"One of the leaders, Mahoud they call him, was told that two of their guards have disappeared. He wasn't happy about it, but it isn't deterring him in his quest."

"Good, I was worried their disappearance would abort the attempt," Etta said, feeling guilty for having caused the confrontation the earlier evening.

"He's still moving forward, in fact, he's concentrating all of his assets in ten locations now, four on each side of the airport, and one north and south, the tech guy said, "They'll determine which way the winds are blowing the morning the President arrives and then shift their missiles to those locations to be sure they have all the firepower they need."

"That's great if we can trust him to do it. It will make our job easier too. If all those missiles are located in just a couple sites, we can capture them quicker," Josh said. "If…"

"So that means we should get our surveillance in place now," Etta said. "I can get us access to a bunch of HS drones that we could put up over those houses to watch for movement?"

"I like that, but not yet. Let's use old-fashioned surveillance for now. The last thing we want to do now is spook them with big brother hovering overhead," Josh said, trying not to sound like he was putting down her suggestion. He rubbed his arm where she had slugged him, and continued. "Plus, I would imagine the airport and the five to ten planes landing every minute might not like to have those birds flying in their air space."

"That makes sense. Maybe we can get some more cameras mounted in the trees around those houses to give us eyes. I could have some public works crews do some tree trimming on those blocks and get us hooked up. That way we could monitor comings and goings and hopefully see some missiles being brought in that morning. Once we do the math and count missiles, we'll have better confidence we can get them all."

"Good idea. Let's talk to the towns and the PW departments and get them in by tomorrow." Josh said. "I still like the drones but let's save them for PV day," Josh said.

All three persons in the truck looked at him questioning PV day.

"Presidential Visit Day!" he said, "in three days."

Washington, DC

The Presidents morning briefing was just wrapping up. Everyone was leaving when he asked his lead Secret Service agent, Bill Fruland to stay behind. He wanted to know more about the status of his fund raising trip to Chicago.

"So what have our people found out about the terrorists trying to shoot me out of the sky?" the President asked, lounging back in his desk chair. "Are they still in play to try and avenge OBD's death by taking mine?"

"They are, Sir, but in the last few days we have some developed some pretty good Intel and we are close to taking them down," Bill Fruland said. "We're trying to get all the stinger missiles they brought into the country. That's why we grounded your Air Force One and have publicized the fact you will be flying in another smaller jet to Chicago."

"Wouldn't that make me an easier target, in a smaller craft, Bill?" the President asked. "Are you guys trying to end my second term early?" Now he was smiling.

"Certainly not, Mr. President. I'm told they can fly the smaller craft remotely."

"So how am I getting to Chicago?" the President asked. "I'm not walking, am I?"

"No, Sir. We have you on the Secretary of State's airplane,

designated Air Force Two, for this trip. You will be flying into Gary, Indiana's airport, you'll be closer to downtown Chicago than O'Hare is. From there Marine One will take you into the city and the 'beast' will drive you to your fund raisers."

"So my sit-in Air Force One goes into O'Hare as announced, and these yahoo's try to shoot it down when it is landing? That sounds too simplistic, doesn't it?"

"Well, Sir. Perhaps to you and me, but these guys are hell bent on getting revenge for bin Laden's death. And they have the firepower to do it. That's why Homeland Security wants to play the scenario out, and hopefully scoop up all the weapons and get the bad guys at the same time. I guess there is more than a dozen in on this plot."

"Well, this would be a coup to prevent the terrorist attack, and secure the missiles, so I'm in. Just make sure that none of my family is coming anywhere near Chicago with me."

Bill Fruland stood, and walked out of the room. The President may be in, he thought, but it was still extremely dangerous to put him in harm's way. He would have to double the field team on this trip.

Schiller Park, IL

Mahoud drove towards the house on the end of the block that was almost directly beneath the jet approach route for runway 22 L. As a large 747 went thundering overhead he looked up and smiled. He watched the plane disappear and in his mind he saw it crash and burn on the other side of the expressway. Still looking up he noticed a man nestled in a cherry picker type bucket in the tree across the street. The truck said Forestry Department. The city worker was working with a long pole trimming branches that were near a bunch of electrical lines running through the neighborhood. He watched the man for a moment, as he put down the long pole and fired up a hand-held chain saw.

The man in the bucket had on dark sunglasses so the sun's glare would not hinder his work effort. He saw the man below watching him so he put on a good show of trimming branches and dropping them to the street below.

Eventually the man below got tired of starring up into the bright sun, locked his car door and walked towards the house at the end of the street. The camera that had already been wedged into a crook in the branches was recording his every move.

A quarter hour later the bucket man lowered himself to the truck deck. His partner on the ground diligently swept up the branch debris and was loading it into the grinder converting it to mulch. They then pulled their safety cones and moved the truck down the street and repeated the process on another tree. Once finished they had placed four cameras that covered all approach angles to the target house.

Less than two miles north, a Com Ed truck with a cherry picker was driving into position. After setting up some orange cones, two uniformed Com Ed employees started extending the boom to work on a power transformer pole that was at the corner of the dead end street. They went about their business in a practiced manner. Several small camera devices were strapped to the pole and aimed at the house across the street. They specifically aimed one at the side of the house, another at the front door, and one at the broken down garage next to the house.

They worked fast and efficiently and in no time had the boom box being lowered and nestled back on the truck. The two workers collected their orange danger cones and loaded up without so much as a look at the target house. As they drove down the street they made note of a late model sedan driving up. Mahoud, the ringleader of the terrorist cell was pulling up to the house.

On the west side of the airport, an Elk Grove Village public works truck parked in front of the wholesale carpet store on Wolf Road. The three workers put up a couple of ladders on both sides of a light pole and began strapping on some large signs that warned of construction work that would start in four days. As the two signs were being affixed to the pole, a small camera was wedged in between the metal surfaces aimed at the carpet store windows and front door. Another was positioned to take in the old truck that was being used in the parking lot as a large advertising billboard.

Just short of a mile south of the carpet store, a large tractor-trailer was backing its way into an alley across from an industrial building on a western approach to O'Hare. The trailer was positioned against a wall and its stabilizing wheel chocks were lowered.

The tractor then pulled away and left the trailer wedged against the adjoining building wall. Inside in the bull nose corner of the trailer a camera blinked to life. A second truck trailer was backed into a similar alley on the south-north approach to O'Hare. Each trailer was also capable of pre-positioning a SWAT strike team at zero hour.

All these cameras were fed by secure satellite to a newly established control room that had been setup in a building just south of the expressway entrance to O'Hare field. It was the Chicago police headquarters building for the entire airport. The location would draw little attention because of the constant movement of police vehicles in and out of the area. A round-the-clock team was assigned the duty of monitoring these electronic camera sites noting the comings and goings of any and all persons. All captured video and photos would be run through known terrorist databases.

The overall operation had been officially titled 'Operation Bird Strike'. The cover name would draw no attention, as bird strikes were a significant problem on airport grounds all over the world.

"So we have eyes on hopefully all the suspected launch sites. Let's hope we haven't missed any because if we do and they shoot the missiles we have even bigger problems, Etta said.

"Yeah, they could slink away to fight another day. We should start briefing the SWAT teams now so they understand the need for complete shutdown of these areas," Josh said, monitoring the many cameras focused on the houses and businesses.

"Timing will be everything. We have to wait until the last second and then come down hard, hitting them with everything we got. If we can completely surprise them, we can scoop up all of the stingers, and then we can send you home," Etta said, throwing a subtle wink across the desk at her partner.

Josh parried, "I'm starting to like it here. More action than I've seen in months in the desert. I could get used to Chicago, at least

Sugar Grove. I think I'm cut out for the quiet life."

"We'll see if Sugar Grove is ready for you, so don't make any hard decisions just yet." She winked again at her partner and went back to work writing various contingency plans.

Schiller Park

Mahoud parked his car out front and walked into the real estate office. As he rounded the counter he wondered if something was different about the office. He dismissed the thought and walked into the back room and sitting down at his desk. Again, the thought occurred to him that things seemed different here too.

He called out to the woman sitting at the front desk. "Have we found those guards yet? How the hell can they have just disappeared?"

The woman came in with her veil hanging off her shoulder as if it annoyed her. "We have searched everywhere. They seem to have vanished and they haven't returned to their rooms at the house in Des Plaines. I've got everyone searching. How do you say it, perhaps they have bought into the American dream?"

"Well, if so they would be smart to not show their faces around here again. This could be a problem. Maybe we are compromised?"

"We will keep looking. They aren't smart enough to get that far. And what do you want to do when we find them?" the woman asked. She already knew what he would say.

"Kill them, but not anywhere here. We don't need any more Arab bodies messing up the plan at this stage. Next week the President will die!"

Mohammed paused as if clearing his head and then said, "Now let's see if we can unload any of the houses we bought, we won't need them after next week. Maybe we can get some American asshole to buy one. At least we would get the earnest money."

The woman nodded her head and returned to her front counter post. She took a handgun from under her chador and placed it in a slot under the counter. She knew using it at this late stage of the game would compromise the plan, but it gave her comfort to know it was there if needed. She might go down but she would take some of the Satanists with her if they came to the business.

Mahoud pulled out a new burn phone and dialed another such phone on the other side of the airport in one of his houses. His second in command picked up after five rings, which was standard practice. When the connection was live he said, "Junior, I think we should shut down our north regional sales operation and concentrate on the east coast development, using both cities. Please make it happen, but come see me before transferring stock." He closed the phone to break the connection, and then snapped open the spine of the instrument. He placed the memory card half in his pocket and tossed the receiver in the wastebasket. He hoped the other man had done the same.

Junior understood what he was supposed to do. They had previously talked about closing down the two northern site approaches to the airport, and moving the missiles from there to the eastern approach airport locations. In monitoring and analyzing the prevailing winds for the past two months they had decided there was little chance that the President's plane would come out of the north as it made its way to O'Hare. He was very confident the President would be coming for his fundraisers flying in from the east, over Lake Michigan and Chicago's downtown. He would concentrate his firepower on the eastern approaches.

As the Air Force One jet flew overhead in the Des Plaines, Rosemont or Schiller Park residential neighborhoods he would fire multiple Stingers from multiple houses, each timed a few seconds apart. No amount of defensive measures could defend against such a barrage. The missile tracking time would be less than ten seconds from firing to impact.

He reached for another fresh burn phone and gave similar instructions to his lieutenants in the industrial buildings on the south approaches to O'Hare. In code he directed them to shut down operations and move their product to the west side of the airport at two locations on Wolf Road. This was probably overkill but if the president's plane did evade the principle missile barrage, when the plane tried to fly out of danger to the west he would follow up with another barrage of Stingers as it climbed into the sky. Either way the President would be dead, and Osama bin Laden's assassination would be avenged. This terrorist act would be a devastating blow to America, and it would rival 9-11.

With that adjustment accomplished he decided to see if he could start the process of selling his properties he would no longer need after next week.

Sugar Grove IL.

Etta and Josh pulled into her garage at 8:00 pm after a 45-minute drive from the airport. Both were exhausted from the 12-hour work day, but were also confident they were getting closer to resolving the terrorist attack puzzle handed to them.

By habit, Etta walked in throwing her car keys on the counter and headed for the bedroom to change and wash the grime away. Josh headed for the refrigerator for a beer, and then thought better of it. He walked to a wine rack where he found a nice Pinot Noir that he knew Etta would enjoy. While he wasn't much of a wine drinker he thought he'd make the effort to show he was observant and thinking of her. Plus, a good pinot was becoming a great alternative to his usual beers.

He stripped the red seal, twisted in the corkscrew and opened the bottle with ease popping the plastic cork with a single motion. He let the bottle breathe. Again he was learning. Next he headed to the refrigerator and rummaged around for the chicken breasts he had seen the night before

He opened the package and started prepping the meat just as Etta walked into the kitchen. She had completely changed to jeans and a tank top and looked refreshed and enticing. Noting her jaw was only slightly discolored and her split lip was healing nicely, he debated trying to kiss her. He decided against it. He would instead handle the dinner and let her relax.

"I'm thinking you should be waiting on this battered woman a bit more to earn back certain privileges under this roof. And I'm starving. Get cracking buddy!"

"Most certainly, my lady." He bowed and headed for the door to the deck. "Would you join me for a glass of Pinot on the deck? I'll throw the chicken on the barbie and you can regale me about anything other than work. How about telling me more about this horse rescue business."

"I'd like that," Etta said as she opened the door for him. She had lost her anger and again felt this guy could be a keeper.

After dinner, they settled on the deck with a second bottle of Pinot and talked until the stars were visible in the night sky. This far out in the boonies the stars could actually be seen away from the city lights. It was like the Drifters song, 'Up on the Roof', from the 60's, "where the stars put on a show for free'. Quietly sitting there, it became clear to both of them that this change of pace was just what the doctor ordered.

Schiller Park, IL.

Some forty miles away, Joe Mazzoni, the realtor, sat outside in his backyard listening to the roar of the jet engines flying overhead every 30 seconds. He contemplated the coming carnage that would again strike fear in America. With just days to spare until the President's arrival he had moved his chess pieces around to the various safe houses and businesses he had bought and leased. He had generated a lot of carpet sales and deliveries in the surrounding neighborhoods.

He was satisfied with the training efforts of his people and fully expected they would be successful in executing the plan. He had trained them well, like he had been trained in the Yemen sniper camp. They knew how to load, arm and shoot the Stinger missiles. They all understood they would quietly wait inside their homes or buildings until the actual signal was given to execute. Then they would simply step outdoors on the front stoop, or in the alleyway, or from the garage, and point the weapon at the jet craft flying almost directly overhead and pull the trigger. They would then drop the missile launchers and disperse from the area immediately. That was all they had to do to strike fear into the Americans.

With multiple shooting sites designated on each side of O'Hare International Airport, he knew he had the killing zones well covered from all angles. On the eastern airport perimeter he had built a crescent shaped kill zone so multiple missiles could be fired almost simultaneously from various locations filling the sky with the deadly warheads. With the President's plane being the only one in the sky on final approach, its' heat signature would draw the missiles to the kill like flies to a camel carcass.

Each of the five eastern sites had three missiles that could be launched. That would send 15 missiles spiraling up at once from a variety of locations and distances to close in on the President's lone heat signature.

If the plane survived that onslaught, he knew the pilot would immediately try to evade going to full power and elevating to escape the attack. As Air Force One tried to claw its way back into the open sky, the five west side sniper batteries would open up with 10 additional missiles launched creating a second gauntlet. To be safe he also had one missile positioned to the extreme north and south of the airport in case the smaller temporary Air Force One was more elusive and could evade all the fireworks. That left two missiles for him.

Homeland Security, Chicago

With just two days to go everyone authorized was again briefed on the status of Operation Bird Strike. The last thing they wanted was to alert the press to what was really about to happen. It was critical to maintain operational secrecy and not cause a panic.

"Thank you for your reports people. I believe we have been able to keep a complete lid on this and the bad guys don't have wind of our take down plans," Etta said from the front of the room. "All of our observation and monitoring has paid off and I think we have a workable plan in place to get all of these bastards and weapons in one fell swoop."

Josh was standing next to her at the front of the room quietly waiting his turn.

"The key for the take down to work is to move as one team. Synchronizing everything is the real challenge. Remember the FBI and Homeland Security SWAT teams take lead on each of our house and business insertions once the signal is given. No early movement, or casual drive-bys, or we may spook them. If they get wind of this operation and get away we could have them shooting missiles at planes all over the country. So we have to work at as a unified team. No exceptions."

The Chief from Des Plaines piped up and looked like he was

speaking for the other surrounding departments. "We got that, Sir, we all want these guys as bad as you do. We will do our part and follow your lead. The people in these neighborhoods are our local citizens and we want to protect them."

"Thanks, Chief," Etta said. "This will be a huge victory for America if we can pull this off without getting innocent people killed. There will be enough 'that-a-boys' to pass around for everyone."

The assault teams broke into small groups and went over their plans once more, using photo arrays, maps, and designated sniper locations. With the massive assault planned, everyone would need to know where everyone else was. They worked from detailed maps that had been drawn up. The teams knew they needed to be close but invisible before zero hour. The planning went on throughout the day.

Homeland Security Motor Pool,

Etta and Josh left the building at 10:00 am for some additional shadowing of the real estate terrorist ringleader. This time they had drawn a small compact car from the motor pool but it had dark tinted windows throughout, which would afford some invisibility in a stake out situation.

"So what are we going to change into today so this asshole doesn't recognize us," Josh eagerly asked, "I'm hoping for some short-shorts."

"It figures, you know you would really stand out in that," Etta said. "Are you a dog all the time? You need a life, or I need a cattle prod. I thought I'd change my hair and sunglasses and call it a day."

"You're no fun, ok, we'll save the costumes for after the take down, but then I get to choose outfits."

"We'll see cowboy, we'll see."

"A cowboy scene might be interesting. Me in my spurs, you in your cowboy boots, and nothing else!"

"My God, do you ever let up?" was all Etta could think to say!

They drove to Schiller Park and parked in a restaurant lot that was half full right across the street from the realtor office. A half hour later, two eastern-Mediterranean looking men came out with Mohammed / Joe Mazzoni and they all got in a red car. The two agents followed discreetly about a full two blocks back because the red car was easily identifiable in the distance. They drove east to

River Road and then turned north towards Rosemont. When the terrorists got near the convention center hotels they turned left on a side street and then into a high-rise parking deck with probably ten levels leading to the top.

The hotel parking garage was crowded so the three men kept driving up the ramps to the top level. Josh and Etta followed slowly, but parked one level below where they still had direct eyes on the elevator door at the top. The three men walked to that elevator.

Josh whispered, "Action time, I'm going to check out and bug the car. Would you consider following them to see if they meet anyone." This time he had asked instead of ordering.

She still said, "Who made you the boss?" but with a smile. She opened the door and walked towards the elevator.

Josh casually ambled up the ramp towards the red car noting there were only three other vehicles parked in the hot sun. Good, he thought, that would make breaking and entering much easier. He looked as if he was fumbling for his keys should anyone be watching and palmed a slim jim. He worked the flat blade between the door glass and trim. With a few pulls he caught the lockset mechanism popping open the door.

Making a visual inspection noting where everything was he carefully sat down and looked for anything that might offer some insight into what this guy was all about. The vehicle was pretty clean but there was a crumpled piece of paper in Arabic stuck deep between the seats. His ability to read Arabic was rusty so he took a photo of the document and re-crumpled it wedging it back where he'd found it. Finding little else he popped the trunk and found a hard shell golf bag carrier that still had a sold tag on it. The bag itself was empty but he found a high-powered set of military grade binoculars tucked in a side compartment. Inside the binocular case he found a detailed map of the entire airport noting runways and designation numbers.

'I could arrest this asshole right now invoking the Patriot Act, and get him a one way ticket to Guantanamo,' he mumbled to himself. He took some photos and then carefully replaced everything. He placed one bug in the spare tire wheel well and dropped another inside the empty golf bag. He was guessing what kind of clubs this golfer intended to carry. It would be the perfect size for a Stinger launcher. Re-checking his work, he re-locked the doors and headed back towards the ramp.

Etta had taken the next elevator down but by the time she exited the garage the three men had disappeared. She looked around and saw that a back door entrance to a Maria's Restaurant was just across a packed ground level parking area. It was lunchtime. The restaurant was tucked between some industrial buildings, and the parking garage for the hotel. It was the perfect place for a clandestine meeting.

Figuring they had used the side entrance, she walked out to the street and went in the front door. It was dark inside and she could see little so she ducked into a restroom to let her eyes adjust. She needed to see them before they saw her. She checked her appearance in the mirror and put her hair up in a ponytail and kept the sunglasses on. She would see them first.

Stepping out she walked to the Hostess stand and scanned the large restaurant while looking at a menu. They were not in the main dining room so she repeated the process in the bar area that had some booths along the wall. They were in a booth and another one next to them was open. They were buried in their menus ordering from the waitress so she walked over and took the adjacent booth with her back to the three men.

The waitress finished taking their order and slipped over to her.

"Give me a moment dear, and I'll take your order, anyone joining you?"

"Supposedly, but he may be late, I'll order for him too, and may need take out."

The waitress left and Etta scanned the menu while trying to overhear the conversation next door. She wasn't having much luck because they spoke Arabic and kept their voices down. Josh should have followed the men. Frustrated, she looked back to the menu when Josh walked up.

"Hey Babe," he said, as he walked up and gave her a kiss. He scooted her over so he also had his back to the three men in the next booth. "Thought I'd lost you. What's on the menu?"

"Figures, now that there is food involved, you come running quickly." She slugged him in the ribs with her elbow and snuggled up close. She whispered, "I don't know Arabic so listen up and see what you can hear next door."

Josh nodded and grabbed a menu as well. He made a point of being loving to his date but kept an ear focused to pick up what he could. At least he wasn't squirreled under a cot in cave for this eavesdropping. He pointed to an Italian meatball dish. Etta did the ordering as Josh concentrated on the conversation next door.

Joe Mazzoni, aka Mahoud, was keeping his voice down even though speaking Arabic. "I think we are set to do this thing," he said. "In a couple of days 9-11 will be a thing of the past. By Friday, no one will feel they can fly in an airplane anymore. America will come to its knees."

Josh wanted to get up and arrest them right on the spot but again remembered the mission. He leaned over and gave Etta a peck on the cheek. She tried to slug him again. He put up his finger for silence and listened.

"All of our carpets have been delivered and the customers are very pleased. Our new carpet layers have been trained very well.

They reported all the back orders have been delivered and installed. Everything is as planned except for the damn planes flying overhead every thirty seconds."

"Remind them that is the sound of our victory. In another day they can take out their ear plugs and leave this infernal country." Advise Jamal that I will stop by tomorrow to pick up some golf clubs. I will take them for a game I have next week. But I don't think that using them will be necessary. We will see how things go."

One of the men said he had to piss and got up from the table walking by Josh and Etta. He did not look at them.

"What will you do after Friday, Mahoud?" the third man quietly asked.

"I would like to return to my former job, Al-Aqel. After this target I would like to get back to the business of shooting, for which I was trained. I am sure that there are many more political leaders on both sides that should earn a bullet if we are to succeed."

The third man came out of the restroom and turned into the bar. Josh saw him coming and used it as an excuse to again turn and kiss Etta full on the mouth, hiding both of their faces from the terrorist. Etta saw the man too and turned to accept the kiss and embrace even though she knew they probably didn't need to do so. She hated herself for liking this guy. After the man passed by she looked at Josh and gave him a second wet kiss.

Josh looked visibly stimulated, and quietly said, "Check please," to no one in particular.

Lunches were served almost simultaneously at both booths and the talk quieted down. Etta signaled they should eat up quick and asked for a check so they could get out before the terrorists. They would reposition the car to catch the men as they came out of the garage.

A half hour later the three men drove out of the garage and headed for a warehouse on the north side of the airport, still in

Rosemont. It was the carpet warehouse. Pulling into the alley the three men parked the car near the loading dock and went inside.

Josh and Etta drove to the perimeter fence of the airport and parked the car with the hazard lights on. She had changed her hair and hat again and Josh had changed his shirt to a plaid black and white number over a black tee shirt. They got out and made a production of taking pictures of large airplanes flying overhead into the airport. Josh watched the alleyway with a small mirror he positioned on the front bumper. He would say 'now' and Etta would casually pivot and take some quick photos of the building and the guys on the loading dock. They saw that two long carpet sections were muscled into the trunk of the car and the lid was slammed shut.

"Time to blow this pop stand, little girl. Let's go." The three men drove back to the Schiller Park real estate office and into the alley behind the strip mall. As Josh drove the car by just down the street they could see the carpet sections were being off loaded. So was the golf bag carrier.

"Ok, we know where two of the missiles are located, Etta said. "You tell the watchers we need to watch for any future movement from this location as well." She liked giving him orders for a change.

Andrews Air Force Base, Maryland

The Commander of the 89th Airlift Wing was not a happy camper as his ground crew worked on the soon to be designated Air Force One jet. A cockpit crew had been working all morning re-configuring and checking the remote flight, automatic pilot features of the craft to make sure that it could effortlessly handle both a traditional landing and a steep climb fast touch and go routine as if it were being piloted. In effect, he was re-configuring a forty million dollar drone jet aircraft.

His crew was not aware of the circumstances of this exercise but he was and he did not like the thought of losing a command craft. His only solace was that it was better than losing the President's 747. That was not in his DNA.

The crew finally gave a thumbs-up clearance for the craft having checked and re-checked all systems. The Commander walked over to a mobile command trailer that would function as the pilot's cockpit for this mission. He wanted to watch the entire test flight. It looked just like a jet flight trainer with a full array of controls and monitors.

Two additional command trailers were already loaded onto C-130s and headed for O'Hare International Airport and the airport in Gary, Indiana. These forward units would actually handle the

Presidents transfer to and from Chicago.

Given the approval to spool up the craft, the grounded pilot waited for all systems to come up on mid-range parameters. Noting all systems were a go he looked to the Commander for approval.

"You have a five mile clear corridor Captain. There is a hold on all area commercial traffic in the area. Let's get this bird in the sky."

"Yes Sir." He moved the throttle back and eased the jet forward. Gaining all his clearances the grounded pilot taxied his remote craft out to the end of the runway, lined up and started down the runway. The jet handled the acceleration well and soon had the speed parameters to gently lift off and rise into the southern sky.

Gaining 10,000 feet the craft did a slow turn and brought itself around for a run at the airport runway from the north. The pilot had been told to fly the craft as if he were doing a normal landing. Once he had come in over the outer perimeter fence line he was ordered to go to full power and take the craft into a powerful climb that would allow the craft to escape the airport as fast as possible.

A number of cameras were monitoring the in-bound flight path as a number of Air Force crash trucks were standing by to deal with any flight challenges.

The jet craft with the distinctive markings came over the outer markers. Just prior to touch down the pilot pushed the throttles to full forward and the engines screamed as the plane took off at a steep 48-degree angle and turned sharply to the north..

The pilot leveled the plane off at 5,000 feet and looked over his shoulder at the Commander who had stepped back into the mobile cockpit.

"Sir, all systems functioned as expected and the bird was responsive to my every command. I'm confident that we can make this happen as expected for the operation."

"That was the plan Captain,…. that was the plan. Let's take it around again and give it another try. We have to make this look like the plane does these approaches all the time."

"Aye, aye, Sir." The Captain took the craft up to 10,000 feet again and with tower support lined the craft up again to do another pass. He did two more passes and then brought the craft in effortlessly. He was on the next C-130 heading to Chicago with all the President's ground vehicles.

Rosemont, IL.

A large section of the Donald E. Stephens Convention Center just off Bryn Mawr across from the Hyatt Hotel had been commandeered with the full cooperation of Mayor Brad Stephens. Behind closed doors a fleet of twenty industrial trucks and large step vans had been driven in over the last few days. Once inside, special seating benches were assembled and bolted to the floors of each vehicle so that a large number of FBI, SWAT and police personnel could be transferred to each threat site with minimal fanfare.

This would become the assembly point for the assault teams and support personnel and would draw the least interest because of the many trucks and people coming and going to the Convention Center and the large hotel throughout the day.

The head of Rosemont Exposition Services, Dave Houston, was coordinating the set-up just like he did for all the trade shows that came to town.

"I hope this is what you had in mind Miss Petrini?"

"Call me Etta. Yes, this is good and will allow us to give final briefings to all the assault teams. We'll need some classroom setups for the briefings too. Can we get some chairs in here?"

"I'll take care of that right away. Need any AV equipment, screens and computers? How about some sleeping cots to allow the police personnel to assemble and remain on site for the duration of

Operation Bird Strike? Our Mayor said to assist any way we could."

"What about internal security?" Etta asked. My guys are going to be pretty busy. Can we remain invisible until we're ready to roll?"

"The entire facility is at your service. We have our own security so you will not be disturbed. You ask and I'll get whatever you need. Here's my cell number."

"Thank you, Dave do all your clients get this kind of service?"

"Yes, they do. I have the best support team in the business here."

As the assault personnel assembled each group was assigned specific targets and attended detailed briefings, watched and memorized film footage of their target houses and businesses, and prepared their specific assignments.

At each target site a two-man sniper team would be covertly inserted in the middle of the night to settle in and maintain surveillance on each identified possible missile launch site, be it front porch, garage, roof window or vehicle on the property. Some would be a quarter mile away to get the right sight lines. They would be the first to engage the enemy when the missile launcher exposed itself. They had orders to prevent the launching of the missiles at all costs. Deadly force was authorized.

The morning of the operation the teams would armor up, walk the 150 feet to their transfer vehicles, and in a casual staggered disbursement would drive out of the convention center to pre-determined assembly points near their specific targets. The various vehicles were being dressed as a variety of public works trucks, electrical vehicles, buses, and road surfacing equipment, allowing them to infiltrate and blend into the neighborhoods and industrial areas.

Various personnel would evacuate the surrounding homes or businesses moving the citizens out of the area. Other attack units would assemble a block away and be prepared to swoop down once the command was given to block escape and take terrorists captive. The driver of each vehicle had specific instructions where to drive and place each vehicle to set up a defensive position for the assault troops.

Specific police units from the surrounding towns would descend on the target site perimeters to control citizen inquiry, traffic and to catch any escaping terrorist that got out of the area.

Each assault team had specific duties and objectives and had been given authority to take down the perpetrators by any means necessary. The bottom line was the missiles were to be taken and secured at all cost. Operation Bird Strike was ready to go.

Washington D.C. 7:00 am

The White House was already humming with the morning's activities. On the third floor, in the family quarters, the President picked out a power tie for the day. His Chief of staff was leaning on the doorframe asking him for the fifth time not to go.

"Mr. President, there is no reason you actually have to go to Chicago today. We can re-schedule the fundraisers for another time. Why put yourself in harm's way?"

"We've been over this before. I'm the big enchilada these crazed terrorist's want to kill, so I'll play along to make sure they think they'll get me. That forces their hands to actually pull out all the weapons, and then the cavalry swoops in and we get them all."

"Yeah, but that will happen whether you are actually there or not? Why take the chance?"

"That's the point. If I can be a part of this 'Operation Bird Strike' and we do get those damned missiles, then the public will feel safer and I get a little good news around here. There hasn't been much of that going around lately, has there?"

"Well no, there hasn't. I guess we could use some good ratings for a change." He realized that he wasn't changing the President's mind.

"You think?" The President dismissed his closest confidant and headed for the door. He stepped into the hall and ran directly into his wife.

"Not you too, I hope. I'm going to Chicago!" the President said. "Everyone thinks we have a good plan to smoke these bastards out of the weeds."

The First Lady didn't say anything. She just straightened his tie and gave him a peck on the cheek. "Call me once this whole thing is over, and don't try to be a hero. Be safe." She walked off towards her office without looking back.

The President went downstairs carrying his own overnight bag. He was aware that his Press Secretary and the Secret Service had set up press coverage for his morning departure. The whole dog and pony show was being set up for the benefit of the terrorists so they could see that he was coming to Chicago.

Stepping out of the ground level door facing the Elipse he headed across the grass and gave a casual wave to the assembled TV and news reporters as he headed towards Marine One. He climbed up the stairs, turned at the door and waved one more time before ducking inside. 'So this is what a guinea pig feels like,' he said to himself.

Schiller Park, IL.

Mahoud was up at the crack of dawn, dressed and on his way to the real estate office before the traffic started clogging up the many roads leading to the airport. He had checked into the Westin Hotel on River Road in Rosemont the evening before, but he had too many things to do to have stayed there overnight.

When he pulled into the parking lot of the strip mall real estate office, his receptionist dressed in a black burka was unlocking the front door. He backed his car up to the front door and took a hard case golf bag carrier from the trunk and carried it inside.

The receptionist' eyes gleamed as she contemplated what the day would bring. She had a new bounce in her step. She walked behind the counter and hiked her burka up exposing her black pants and tunic underneath. Clipped onto her black belt she had an empty holster. Reaching under the counter she pulled out her 45-caliber handgun, chambered a round and nestled it into her hip holster.

Mohammed carried his golf case to the back room and kicked a roll of carpeting open so that it unraveled across the floor. Picking up the Stinger launcher and a missile that was taped to it, he loaded it into the golf bag carrier. Adding a few golf clubs he wrapped the single weapon of war with the war clubs of golf to prevent the contents from rattling around. He zipped the travel cover and shook the whole assembly noting that no metal on metal sounds came from the contents.

Finished with his packing, he wondered what golfers saw in such a silly game of hitting a small white ball around a course. Still, he took great satisfaction in knowing the President would die partially because of his golf bag carrier. He decided to load the carrier back in the car trunk before additional people began parking in the lot outside.

Across the street in a donut shop parking lot, Josh and Etta slumped in their car munching day old donuts and sipping on burned coffee. Josh was glad this escapade was coming to a conclusion.

"You know, I've come full circle. I started my cop career sitting in patrol cars eating donuts. These could actually be from the same batch."

"How can you be so relaxed right now?" Etta said, as she again slugged him in the arm. Bad coffee went flying. "Today is the day they try to kill the President. That bad guy just loaded a deadly weapon in his car disguised as a golf bag and all you can think about is donuts?"

"Well, they are pretty bad donuts, don't you think?" He waited for an answer but she just slugged him again.

"I envy you. I'm a nervous wreck that something will go wrong and you act as if you don't have a care in the world." She was angry that he was so relaxed.

"I don't like to kiss and tell," he said, mischievously. "But I got laid last night and there is nothing that could beat that. It was one fine lady who I could easily spend my life with." He tensed up presuming another slug in the arm was on the way.

Etta directed a stern look to her left and tensed her fist. "Loose lips sink ships sailor. Button that talk and honor the lady, or I'll encourage her to tear you a new one."

"Oh, I love such dirty talk. Hey, it looks like he is rolling. I hope it's back to the hotel so we can get some more room time across the hall."

Etta slugged him again. She hoped his arm stung from the blow.

Stephens Convention Center, Rosemont

The tall dock door at the back of the Convention Center of Hall A opened slowly. Shielded from the street by 10 foot high drapes, the first truck, an Elk Grove Public Works truck drove out of the garage area and started its journey towards the west side of O'Hare Field. It had the farthest distance to cover to get into position to be ready when the President's plane was scheduled to arrive.

Once the vehicle was in position a number of workmen in hard hats and safety vests set up a series of orange cones to re-direct traffic and began their day's work. Just three hundred yards away was Al's Carpeting warehouse.

Two blocks away in a separate pick-up work truck three men in surveyors gear set up another work site. While one man set out safety cones and surveyors equipment, the other two carried long boxes and disappeared behind a building. Climbing the back stairs to the roof they duck walked to the perimeter wall and set up a snipers nest to monitor the front and back of Al's Carpeting. As they set up, a couple of swarthy looking men came out the front door of the carpet shop and wrestled a roll of carpeting into the Al's Carpet truck parked in front close to the street. Only one man returned to the store. The spotter scoped the truck and saw a roof access door was opened up. Watching he saw the man in the truck bed raise his head out of the window and look around.

"Gotcha buddy. Hey Cade, zero in the truck in front. See the guy peeking out of the top of the truck roof."

"That's one of our targets," Cade said. "Get me a good distance on that truck. I bet its 420 yards."

"Switching to heat sensor. We can even take him out inside the truck if I can get a strong enough heat register. If not, you'll have to wait until the gopher pops his head up."

"Roger that. It's like old times in Kandahar."

A second truck with Bensenville Electrical markings rolled out of the Convention Center and headed for the southwest side of the airport. Inside was a complete assault team sitting quietly checking each other's equipment. They had gone over their assault plans and were confident they could take down these amateurs.

Over the next hour eleven other trucks with various town and city markings left the Center and headed for their target sites in Schiller Park, Rosemont, Des Plaines, Elk Grove Village, Bensenville and Chicago.

Westin Hotel, 10th Floor

Josh and Etta had the room directly across the hall from Mahoud and his burka secretary. Josh was laying on the bed watching Etta. She stood at the door using the peephole to monitor the room directly across the hallway. Every time she would look over at him on the bed he would silently pat the bed beside him, raise his eyebrow and smile. She'd send him an exasperated look and go back to her peeping.

"How can you be so damn calm, a terrorist attack is about to happen involving the President in the next hour?" she whispered. "You're out of your mind. Is this what you do in the field before you pull that sniper trigger?"

"Pretty much, because I'm a trained professional. They taught me how to remain calm at all times. They always said to relax first, then go to battle. Thus, I'm pacing myself and relaxing before it gets crazy. You ought to try it." He patted the bed again.

She knew he was wound up tighter than a hardball.

But Josh continued the patter probably to stave off nervousness.

"We both know the timing of the President's arrival. It's not due for another hour and ten minutes. We have some time to kill. That asshole is not going anywhere now. He's obviously the spotter. Come on, lay down and take a load off. Maybe we can think of something to do for an hour?"

"You couldn't last an hour if your life depended on it!" She stuck out her tongue and went back to her peephole.

"But I'd certainly like to try," he said, as he pouted for her benefit. She was not watching.

"I'll tell you what, I'll come over there for this terrorist watch."

Josh rolled off the bed and walked to the door. He molded himself to her backside and reached around to fondle her breasts. He breathed in her fragrance giving her a kiss on the neck. She didn't respond.

"You're incorrigible." She gave him a hard thrust with a hip butt that sent him flying backwards. "We'll have time for that later lover boy, after we get these bad guys."

He realized he had pushed her about as far as he could, given the circumstances.

"With your bodily encouragement, I'll take that as a future IOU date. I work better when I have a definite goal and a more focused outlook. So let me have a look through your peephole M'lady... Even that sounds dirty!"

He looked through the security eyepiece and saw nothing but another door. Bored he turned away and said, "It's not fair, I bet he's across the hall jumping on that burka babe. You know the eyes can drive you crazy when that is all you can see."

"As I said before, you're incorrigible." Staring through the eyepiece, she smiled at her prospects if she made it through the day.

Gary, Indiana

The President's back-up 737 jet, approached from the south and made a perfect landing on the north to south runway. It immediately taxied to a pre-arranged hanger that could accommodate the whole plane out of sight from any eyes on the highways passing by the airport. The President was now within thirty-five miles of Chicago as the crow flies.

Across from the hanger an electronics team climbed the steps of the 737 and entered the cockpit to make a series of safety checks to again test the remote control system being pressed into service. Captain Tony Young still sat in his pilot's seat not yet ready to give up his command. He watched as Air Force technicians hooked up an array of electronic modules that would fly the plane remotely. He didn't like that he was losing his seat to a machine. He had in fact offered to pilot the jet craft into O'Hare Field himself. He was still confident he could evade any missiles being shot up his ass. He was a former Air Force pilot that had flown F-16's in the first Iraq war. He was used to missiles being shot up his ass and thought he could better handle the craft in this kind of situation. But the President had overruled him, wanting no lives lost in the effort to capture the terrorists and the deadly weapons.

The electronics team communicated with the pre-positioned trailer that was parked next to the main Control Tower at O'Hare.

Systems lit up and a pilot sitting in the trailer asked for permission to take control of the plane. Captain Young acknowledged the request, but he also threatened the guy if he damaged the craft. He climbed out of the pilot's seat and exited the cockpit shaking his head.

Once all personnel were clear of the plane an aircraft tug coupled up and pulled the plane from the hanger. Once the hanger doors were again closed the remote pilot started his pre-flight plan and eventually turned over the starboard engine to spool up. Command did not want the plane sitting on the tarmac for any longer than necessary because too many people might see it and question what they were seeing.

The airport had been temporarily shut-down to all traffic and the newly designated Air Force One was given priority permission to use Runway 22 to the northwest. The plane taxied to the end of the runway, and with instruction from the Tower, revved its engines to full power.

It raced down the runway and took off without incident turning east away from Chicago. The plan was to run it out over Lake Michigan and then do an about face for a western run into Chicago and O'Hare.

O'Hare International Airport

Secret Service personnel were on alert in the Main Control Tower monitoring all activity as the air traffic controllers were clearing the sky of all plane traffic in a hundred mile circle around the airport. Planes inside that distance on final approach were being brought down on all four runways from east to west. Other planes flying to Chicago still outside the one hundred mile radius were instructed by the air traffic controllers to enter a holding pattern that would spot them at pre-determined elevations in a vertical pancake stack circling one hundred miles out from O'Hare. Planes would be stacked up waiting for the all clear signal once the President's plane had landed.

With the predominant winds coming out of the west on this clear morning, the few scheduled departing flights still on the ground were directed to take off from the same four runways heading east to west. The early morning rush of incoming and departing planes had slowed and the three planes still sitting in the bullpen were waved ahead to take off and clear O'Hare airspace.

Other planes that had already left their gates were directed into holding areas where they would wait until released for departure. The planes still sitting at the gates were advised to hold as well. In most cases passengers were not even told it was for a Presidential arrival. To them it was just another delay they would have to deal with.

Once the last few arriving planes had touched down and taxied to their gates, and the three departing craft had been sent on their way, the airport went into lockdown awaiting the President's arrival.

Passengers in the terminals began to figure out what was happening and many stood at the windows of the terminals watching for the President's signature blue and white jet, known as Air Force One, to arrive in Chicago.

River Road, Rosemont

River Road runs north and south through Rosemont between the Stephens Convention Center and many hotels and office buildings serving the business sector. Many of these large office towers and hotels are ten stories and higher. Because of the thousands of workers and travelers in these buildings there are numerous highrise parking garages that hold over one thousand vehicles on a daily basis.

Earlier that morning two windowless panel vans had approached two different parking garages in this Rosemont corridor. One van had 'Susie's Catering' magnetic signs on each side panel and the other van was marked as ABC Electronics. The catering vehicle entered a multi-level garage behind a cluster of high-rise office buildings north of the Kennedy Expressway leading into the airport.

The other ABC electronics van entered the Hyatt Parking garage adjacent to the Rosemont Convention Center, which was directly south of the highway leading into O'Hare. Above and between the two large garages jet aircraft on final approach flew past every thirty seconds.

Both panel vans drove up the ramps in the busy garages looking for parking space. The lower levels were packed and they continued upward eventually finding parking slots two levels below the open exposed roof level. Each driver found a relatively dark corner location against the open-air walls and backed their vehicles in leaving enough room for the rear panel doors to be opened against the concrete half-wall. The drivers got out of their vehicles and walked away. They walked towards the elevators that would take them to ground level, but after a few minutes they each doubled back and entered different vehicles that were on the same level. But these were cars that looked east through the open half-walls.

They settled in, turned on their burner phones and put their seats in a reclining position. Almost invisible outside the car, they watched to the east as plane after plane came thundering by passing between the two garages just 300 feet above.

Westin Hotel O'Hare

In the twelve-story Westin Hotel adjacent to the merging lanes of the Kennedy ramp and the I-90 entrance to the airport, a man on the tenth floor opened the door of his east facing suite, carefully stepped out and walked down the hall.

"Damn," Etta whispered as she watched through the peephole. "He's moving, he just went down the hall."

Josh jumped up from the bed and was all business. He grabbed his sport coat to cover his weapon and raced for the door. Opening the door a crack, he looked down the hall in the direction of the man, only to see him at the end of the hall on the west side of the Hotel overlooking the airport. He was carrying large binoculars.

"He just went into another room on this side of the hallway. What the hell, why didn't we know about that?" he whispered, clearly spooked. He resisted the urge to open the door and charge down the hall.

"He must have registered that room on another day under a different name," Etta said quietly. "So now what?"

"I don't know. I guess we could go down there and smoke him out. But he doesn't have the Stingers with him, they're still across the way with burka lady," Josh said, as he tried to clear his head.

"So let's break in and get the missile first and then grab him as well," she said.

He thought a moment. "That would work, but he may be the official spotter, the one who gives the signal and go order himself. Remember we need to catch all these assholes in the act. If one of them gets a message out to the other locations then we have to deal with the Stingers disappearing into the wind? No, we can't do that." Josh looked confused and again shook his head to clear his thoughts. "The good news is we've learned they have a second hidey-hole! That may complicate our takedown but at least now we know it's there."

Down the hall Mahoud went to the window and trained his military grade binoculars on the airport a half mile away. The image was clear and looked close through the lens. He scanned the runway and tarmac areas. Everything looked as he expected they should with the President's plane due to arrive. He scanned the east runways and noted there was a short line of planes queued up ready to depart west. No other planes were lining up. They had shut ground operations down before the President's arrival. He then looked at the terminal that was closest and could see a lot of travelers standing at the windows looking out. It excited him that so many people would actually witness the death of their President. All was well. He tucked the binoculars under his jacket and went into the quiet hallway and padded his way down to his spotter's suite.

He let himself in with his key card and silently shut the door. Upon entry he looked at his compatriot standing in the window with binoculars and realized she had changed while he was gone. No longer wearing the black burka, she was in tight black jeans and boots and had a stylish jacket draped over a low plunging blouse. He liked what he saw but shook the thoughts from his mind. He needed to concentrate on the task at hand. In the next half hour he would fulfill his deadly mission.

He took out a new burn phone and began sending texts to each of his shooters in the primary houses, businesses, and parking garages underneath all of the east to west runway approaches. Connecting to the first site he typed, 'On schedule, east to west primary, soon, switch'" The code words had been pre-determined. He punched the end button, took the SIM card out of the phone and snapped it in half and put it in his pocket. He snapped the phone in half and threw the two parts into different plastic bags. He knew his shooters would do the same. Additional phones were lined up on the table to make the other calls. He worked his way through the multiple locations.

He advised the terrorist teams on the west side of O'Hare that they would be secondary shooters should the President's plane get through the initial barrage of missiles. Each site knew that changed the approach they would use but they had drilled for this possibility and responded with a simple 'Understood'.

Mahoud walked to the window with his binoculars and started scanning the eastern skyline looking for a distinctive airplane that would have the markings of Air Force One. He reminded himself that the plane would be smaller than he had originally planned for. But that was ok because the smaller craft would be easier to shoot down. The President would soon join Osama bin Laden.

The former burka woman took a second set of glasses and started scanning the eastern sky as well. They said nothing. Mahoud wanted to take another look at the woman's low cut blouse but he knew that his mind would wander. There would be time enough for that after they had shot down the President.

Des Plaines

At Al's Carpeting Warehouse across the road from the Allstate Arena two men emerged from the loading dock carrying two long carpets on their shoulders and loaded them into a step van. The sniper sitting on a rooftop a block away zeroed in on the two men but did not shoot. It was still too early. He radioed the command center and advised his assigned SWAT Team the bad guys were on the move in a van. The SWAT team loaded into a windowless step van marked as a Jimmy John's Sub Shop delivery van, and pulled out of an alley two blocks away. They knew which direction the carpet van would have to go since the other exit road had been blocked with public works crews tearing up a road. They would tail the van from a distance and see what they were up to.

The carpet van headed towards the Airport but turned right on Higgins Road. They drove to an office building and entered the parking garage driving up the ramps. The assault team followed at good distance once they realized where the van was going. There was only one way in and out. As the assault team driver rounded a corner inside the garage he noticed a series of white SUV vehicles lined up near a building entrance door.

"I'll be damned, look at that," he pointed to the SUVs, "these guys have balls. This building is the U.S. Fish & Wildlife Agency offices. I guess that would be a good cover."

The carpet van went all the way up until they were one level below the open upper deck. One guy jumped out and went to a parked car that had been sitting in a dark corner. He started the vehicle and moved it to another close by parking slot. The van backed in. It was now parked in a shadowed corner of the garage level seven, just a few steps away from an open half wall that looked to the south, towards the airport.

The three men in the carpet van prepared the single Stinger missile they had inside the van making sure the battery was fully powered up and ready for a go signal should it come. A large jet thundered overhead and as they looked out through the garage concrete wall. They measured the distance and realized it was perhaps just two hundred feet above their position and less than 300 hundred yards away. They reported their readiness with a short pre-determined text on a burner phone. They were prepared to react just seconds before the President's plane would be overhead. Their missile would accompany another from the carpet store on the other side of the runway approach. The two weapons would catch the plane in a deadly crossfire.

The assault team recognized they were getting closer to the upper most levels and found a parking spot near the stairs to the different levels. They parked backing in and the driver remained in his seat with the engine running. His task was to block any escape attempt with his vehicle. The other members of the squad dismounted, readied their equipment, and duck walked to the stairwell. They carefully climbed the concrete stairs to the next level. Luckily the door to the level had an observation window they could see through rather than hooking up a small camera cable to pass under the door. They did not see the van on this half-level so they advanced upward.

On the next level the team leader took a quick glance through the window and spotted the van on the other end of the deck in a dark corner. He saw movement as well. The team decided on a plan of attack and carefully eased the door ajar enough to allow three team members to slide through on their bellies. Their cover was a row of parked cars.

Two more team members went up another flight of stairs and checked out the deck. They found they could advance and worked their way across the deck until they were directly over the terrorist van. Silently they secured rappelling ropes to a couple of parked cars, hooked up their harnesses without making a sound and prepared to attack the terrorists from above.

Over Lake Michigan

The remote pilot in the trailer parked next to the main control tower monitored his forward-looking cameras and could see the Chicago skyline rising over the horizon in the distance. Though remote he felt that he had complete control of the craft.

Using his radio he conversed with the O'Hare Control facility, which was actually located in Aurora. Il. about thirty five miles southwest of the actual airport.

The plane would shortly be on final approach and would be turned over to the actual control tower. He was advised all air traffic had flown out of the control area or was on a ground freeze until Air Force One was safely on the ground.

In his remote control van beneath the main control tower, he verified all systems were green and gently toggled his joystick left and right to be sure that he had complete control of the 737 with the President's light blue color scheme. All systems were a go!

On a closed channel, he verified with his co-pilot, also in the van, that all of the plane's defensive measures were at optimum parameters and ready to be deployed once an active threat was identified. Both pilots knew they would have only a few seconds to react and defend the plane before being shot down. No pilot wanted to lose their ride even if they were in a remote trailer parked safely on the ground.

Schiller Park

The assault team assigned to a small home just north of Lawrence Avenue had moved into their positions two hours earlier. A two-man sniper team had slowly worked their way across a rail yard and settled into a small railroad storage building just one hundred yards from the target house. They had a good field of vision for both the front and back doors of the house and the entire garage should the door open. They had orders to shoot if any missiles were presented.

Other members of the team were down the street working on a water main break that had been dug up the night before. Each had body armor on beneath their work clothes and had weapons ready within a foot or two in toolboxes or under pipes stacked next to the hole. Each member of the team was taking a turn in the muddy hole to keep things real.

Communications was kept to a minimum but the sniper and spotter advised the rest of each site team any movement or situational change.

"Heads up. We have movement at the back door. A tall man with a beard in a green shirt and a woman in a black burka are walking across to the garage. Both are verified as being on our target list."

"Roger that."

The two people walked to the garage and pulled up the door

manually. A single old van was parked in the center of the two-car garage. They both got in the vehicle but did not start the car. While the garage was dark, the spotter could see movement with someone climbing into the back of the van.

"We have a potential shooter in the back of the van. Doesn't look like they are driving anywhere. That would potentially place at least one missile in the vehicle in the garage. We have him in our sights now. We will take out van tires if they try to move."

"Roger that, if they go active we will assault the front of house and push through and announce our back door exit."

"Copy."

Everyone, both terrorist and assault team, hunkered down waiting for the call that would announce the 737 was coming into range and on which runway approach.

Des Plaines

The house at the end of the block looked out at a 20-foot wooden wall that separated the residential neighborhood from the Tri-State Tollway. It was also under a canopy of mature trees that blocked out the bright sun. Traffic was always heavy and you could hear the cars and trucks whizzing by even though the solid wall was there to deaden the sound.

In a heavy clump of bushes a block away a camouflaged sniper team sat comfortably inside the greenery monitoring the front and side entrances to the old dilapidated house and garage. They had arrived before first light and were deeply burrowed in sharing the bushes with an army of mosquitos. They were scanning back and forth watching for any movement in the windows. Every now and then a curtain would be drawn back a couple inches and a set of eyes would scan the streetscape.

Behind the house down both blocks heavily armed police squads were silently going house-to-house and moving people out of the danger zone. They took them to a bus where the situation was explained. So far all the neighbors had cooperated without any protest.

As the neighborhood was cleared the assault team advanced house by house until they were assembled behind a six-foot tall solid wood fence just forty feet from the target home. They silently checked their gear and waited for an entry signal.

Chicago, Over Lake Michigan

The familiar blue and white 737 approached downtown Chicago and passed over the Hancock Building on Michigan Avenue heading for a straight in approach to O'Hare International Airport. The pilot toggled his controls to again verify he had complete control of the planes remote instruments. He began his landing process and hit the switch to lower the wheel assemblies. Once they were locked into position he again checked his control board to make sure that the airframe drag performance differential was not affecting the craft's stability, nor preventing him from taking evasive action. The plane responded as it should have and he was confident that he could make this landing without incident.

Eight miles west Mahoud continued to scan the eastern sky from the Westin Hotel. He zeroed in on the lone plane in the east and centered it in his field of vision. His compatriot drew in her breath as she too found the aircraft in her binoculars.

"There it is! Mr. President is right on schedule. Right now I would say it is lining up for a landing on 27 L bringing him right over our position. Keep watching the approach and let me know if it deviates from that path. The wings will dip if he is deviating from that path and runway. I'm making the calls."

Mahoud immediately reached for the first burner phone lined up on the table and began making the short five second connections.

His voice trembled as he gave the go ahead to the primary teams. He then advised the other teams of their secondary back-up roles should the plane survive the gauntlet. Once he had called all the terrorist teams with their orders, he picked up a powerful walkie-talkie that was programmed on a dedicated wavelength. Each of his teams had a similar unit and would turn on the power at the last second. No one would say anything. Only Mahoud would give the signal at the last moment to step out and shoot at the President's plane. The other would just listen for the go signal and then perform their duties.

Once they had released their deadly projectiles their jobs would be done. They would drop the weapons and clear out. Each terrorist group had an escape plan driving out of the area.

Mahoud walked to the window and balanced the binoculars in one hand and the walkie-talkie in the other. He was as excited as he could be and the binoculars slipped from his grasp as he tried to locate the plane, which was now just a mile out from the hotel. Realizing he didn't need the binoculars anymore he let them lay and concentrated on the descending plane in the distance.

Even though it was daytime the planes landing lights were switched on and helped to illuminate the flight path. He watched in awe as the plane swooped in flying on a path that took it directly over the Kennedy Expressway.

On final approach the remote pilot throttled back his engines as he continued to drop out of space on a pre-programmed trajectory. Ahead, his forward screen captured the flashing strobe lights at the eastern edge of the runway directing his flight towards the appointed runway. All remote systems were functioning as planned.

The active passive defensive measures on board Air Force One were designed to react automatically to any kind of missile threat. A series of defensive measures would protect the plane from attack. Defensive flares would be automatically fired away from the craft responding to a threat. These flares would burn bright as metallic chaff exploded out and away from the fuselage creating all sorts of metallic images and false heat signatures that would confuse any missile homing devices and minimize the rockets kill power.

The remote pilot was confident that the defensive systems would work as they were designed. And that he would land the craft safely.

Westin Hotel on River Rd.

Mahoud tried to moisten his dry throat and watched as the 737 came in lower than even he thought it would. Timing was everything. He patiently waited to bark the final order to shoot. He knew that seven terrorist's sites were now spooled up with their missiles, poised to kill the President. He knew that a minimum of eight missiles would be fired on his command.

"Now, shoot!" was all he said into the walkie-talkie. He dropped the unit and sprinted for the door. He opened the door and charged down the hallway towards the corner room. As he ran he pulled out an electronic room key.

The hallway end room faced southwest towards the runway approach and would give him a clear view of the passing plane as the various missiles sought out the quarry. Slamming the door shut he ran to the sofa opposite the bed and picked up another missile launcher that had already been loaded and turned on.

Balancing the missile with one hand he took his Glock 17 from his waistband and blasted four shots at the large window corners blowing the glass out of its casing, sending it showering down to the parking lot ten stories below.

He stepped forward and aimed his shoulder man-pad at the passing airplane and pulled the trigger sending yet another missile on its path to kill the President. He too wanted the personal satisfaction of having killed the President of the United States to avenge the killing of Osama bin Laden!

Westin Hotel

Josh and Etta had been monitoring the approach of Air Force One on their radios linked to the Command Center and knew the countdown was just seconds away. As they prepared to yank open the door and attack the terrorist leader across the hall, they saw their man bolt out the room door and race down the hallway.

Without hesitation Josh opened the door and charged after the man who had a forty-foot lead. Etta was about to follow her partner but then realized the woman was still in the room across the hall. She reversed herself and moved towards the door to confront the female terrorist. Since the door had slammed shut but was probably not double locked, she aimed her gun at the two hinges and fired. Both shots connected and the hinges lost their ability to do their job. Using a high kick she knocked the door in and charged in assuming she would run into resistance.

The woman in black had been about to follow her leader out the door and was about to open the door when the shots blew the hinges off. She collapsed against the wall and waited for whoever would be charging in.

Josh was racing down the hall full tilt when the room door slammed in front of him. As he got closer he heard four shots and then a loud whooshing sound. With a full head of steam he slammed into the doorway. The doorframe cracked and the door gave way as he tumbled into the room searching for a target.

Parking garages off the Kennedy Expressway

On both sides of the Kennedy Expressway two separate terrorist teams had stepped out of their respective vans and pointed their Stinger missile launchers at the blue and white Boeing 737 that was passing overhead just three hundred feet above them and two hundred yard out. They started tracking the craft in their missile sites and prepared to pull the trigger that would shoot the craft down.

Coming out of the shadows with weapons drawn the two FBI assault teams announced their presence and attacked the vans. Two separate sniper teams did not hesitate upon seeing the actual missile units and took out the shooters immediately knocking both men to the ground before they could pull the trigger device. The tactical units advanced from car to car expecting a firefight from the remaining terrorists but received little resistance.

Two gunmen in the spotter car opened up with handguns but were cut down immediately by the superior firepower of the assault unit. The cars were riddled with bullets and the two occupants died quickly. The FBI assault team advanced to prevent any other terrorist from picking up the weapons and trying to finish what they had started. Descending like locusts they secured the area in a matter of seconds. The assault team leader barked into his radio that site D was secure and two missiles had been secured.

In the Communications command center a large blackboard was immediately updated with the information. Only twenty-seven missiles still needed to be secured.

A moment later the Assault team on the other side of the expressway reported that they had secured their site as well and had secured one of the two missiles. They reported that one bird had been fired at the plane before the shooter could be taken out. The black board was again updated as the command unit waiting for additional reports to come in.

At the house in Schiller Park adjacent to the railroad tracks, the assault team had an easier job because the plane had not come in directly over the house they were assigned to. The home was about a mile south of the actual runway being used by the President's plane. The terrorists had boldly walked out the back door towards the garage to link up with the crew that was sitting in the garage.

As they prepared to unleash their missiles in the general direction of the airport to add to the turmoil that was being created, the FBI sniper settled on his targets and took two shots at the men in less than three seconds. Both men holding missile launchers went down. He had already received clearance to shoot to eliminate the threat.

At the same time the assault team breached the front door of the house with flash-bang grenades and rushed into the residence surprising four additional people, two men and two women. Pushing through they engaged the four in a short firefight and secured the premises. Pre-announcing they were coming out the back door they gathered the rest of the terrorist group. The team leader called in that Site F had been secured and two missiles were captured.

Almost the same scenario happened in the parking deck on the north side of the airport across from the Allstate Arena. The assault team there had advanced from car to car without being seen and when the terrorists started to load up their vehicles to pull out, the FBI team advanced just as two officers repelled down from the deck above to join the party. The terrorists were completely surprised and gave up without a fight. Two more weapons were secured and the information was reported.

The carpet store in Des Plaines received their shoot order and prepared to step out on the alley loading dock between buildings to release their missiles in the general direction of the airport. They planned to put the missiles in the air to seek out the only jet engine heat signature that would be in the area.

The Assault team had stealthily approached the alley dock moving from dumpster-to -dumpster once the signal had been given. As the two shooters stepped out they announced their presence. Both shooters looked dumbfounded. One dropped his launcher and put his hands up before being cut down. The other terrorist ignored the challenge and aimed his missile skyward. He received a snipers round in the side of his head for his effort. In crumpling to the ground his finger pulled the trigger and the missile left its tube. It travelled fifty feet and blew up a metal dumpster at the end of the alley showering everyone with metal shards and garbage.

The two terrorists in the building saw what was happening and rushed out the front of the store to get away from the carnage. They jumped into a car as the assault team sent withering firepower at the vehicle. They still managed to pull away and started down the street only to run into a roadblock created by a bus parked across the street. Des Plaines and Rosemont Police manned the blockade and with a strong display of firepower the two terrorists stopped and opened their windows sticking their hands out in complete compliance. The team leader called in his action report.

Air Force One

As soon as the missile threat lit up on the plane's cockpit dashboard, and in the remote pilot's van on the airport tarmac, the plane's automatic defensive measures went into action. Upon sensing the threat to the aircraft, defensive chaff flares were jettisoned out from the fuselage to the left and the right. They burned brightly as they hurtled in all directions away from the craft creating false images of the plane's heat signature coming from the hot engines. The flares burned so intensely the heat-seeking missile's electronic homing devices were confused by the array of multiple hot spots and choose to lock on and chase any one of them rather than the plane itself.

At the same time the defensive mechanisms were firing off, the remote pilot took control and started flying evasive maneuvers with the plane. With Air Force One's wheel assemblies already down and locked in position, the plane's ability to change course, to dip and roll, or claw for elevation was severely limited. Still, the pilot knew he had to save the plane so he retracted the landing gear and dipped the plane forward, and then rolled the wings to the left and then right changing the planes signature in the sky. At the same time he advanced the throttles and clawed for the sky.

A second array of defensive chaff flares were catapulted from the fuselage just as a missile tore into the left jet engine housing blowing it cleanly off of its wing struts. While the engine exploded and fell away the wing remained momentarily stable and the pilot wrestled with the aircraft as it shuddered and continued to climb.

The plane started to careen over to the right as the wing weight of the craft had been dramatically altered. The remote pilot fought to maintain control as he tried to keep it air worthy to cross over the airport outer markers. If he was going to crash he wanted to be on airport grounds and minimize damage to the surrounding neighborhoods.

Tri State Tollway

Chicagoans heading north and south on the Tollway and Mannheim Rd. driving past the Airport entrance ramp saw a bright flash of light in the sky above them. They were drawn to the bright light in the sky and startled to see a plane with an engine breaking away from the fuselage. They were even more horrified to see the planes colors with the familiar blue and white markings that would suggest the craft was Air Force One.

The plane's engine was hurtling away from the craft but because of its forward motion the huge engine was flying as much forward as it was falling down. Drivers screeched to a halt and pulled over to avoid the falling debris. Drivers behind these cars that were not as observant started smashing into the cars in front of them causing chain reaction accidents that started backing up north and south. The drivers that could pull over got out of their cars and watched the plane's demise above and the traffic mayhem surrounding them.

The large Rolls Royce engine kept tumbling forward as much as it dropped and cleared the expressway only to come crashing down on a large inflated soccer field that was just west of the expressway. The engine housing weighing some ten thousand pounds hit the inflated roof and tore a huge hole in the dome, causing it to deflate like a balloon as the air escaped.

The jet craft rolled to the right as the loss of the engine weight created a huge weight differential. To those watching below it looked like the pilot was trying to compensate for the engine loss but the entire fuselage continued to roll and drop from the sky. The plane almost rolled vertical on its one good wing as the pilot tried to stabilize the craft. As he fought to regain control he realized the craft was going down and he started estimating if he could make it to the airports outer markers. He committed to doing just that and advanced the throttle on his only engine to push the craft the three thousand feet.

At that moment another missile smashed into the right engine heat source and hit close enough to the fuselage that it blew a gaping hole in the body of the craft. The plane was breaking apart and started falling out of the sky. The plane came down like a spear and crashed into a car rental facility on a frontage road. The plane still traveling in excess of one hundred miles per hour plowed through hundreds of rental cars that were lined up. The fuselage exploded from the impact and the fireball from the aviation fuel started a domino effect of exploding cars. The entire conflagration lit up the afternoon sky.

People inside the airport terminals who had been watching for the President's plane to land stood there stunned at what they were witnessing.

Westin Hotel

Etta charged into the room searching for her quarry and was immediately set upon by the woman in black. The woman jumped on her from behind and at such close quarters there was no shot to be taken. Both women went down in a heap on top of the door rubble. Though surprised, Etta was the first to twist out of the bear hold from behind and spring to her feet. Both women stood and looked around for their weapons knowing the first one to find theirs would win the prize.

Then the terrorist recognized the woman standing before her as someone who had once been in her real estate office. She smiled wickedly as if she would enjoy this challenge to upset their plan. Etta saw the gleam in her eye and recognized she had her hands full.

As Josh scanned the room lying on the floor he saw the man throw the Stinger missile launcher at him. He ducked. The man took one look at Josh and started running towards the window just fifteen feet away. Spreading his arms he jumped out of the window. Josh was stunned, but realized the guy had on one of those newly developed squirrel type para-suits that assisted a jumper in flying. Josh didn't think twice. As a trained paratrooper he ran for the window and launched himself out into the sky as well. While he didn't have a parachute he knew that he would drop quicker than the squirrel suit guy would and he could catch up to the fleeing terrorist. He wasn't going to get away after launching that missile.

The Iranian woman ripped off her jacket and advanced in a wrestlers crouch looking like she knew what she was doing. Etta didn't want to wrestle. She had to cover her partner. She scrambled to the left off the door rubble to get more solid footing. Then she attacked, rushing the woman rather than waiting for her to advance. They collided and flipped over a side chair. Etta saw the chair coming and was able to roll freely over it while the black-clad terrorist took a severe jolt to the kidneys and went down hard. Etta searched for her weapon but still could not locate it. As the furious woman got up rubbing her back, Etta sucker-punched her in the nose, and the woman went down again. Etta looked around for her gun.

Josh tucked his arms tightly to his body after jumping out the window and directed himself towards the terrorist gliding down below at a slower pace. With less wind resistance he caught up with him before they had past the sixth floor. Josh landed on the terrorists back and grabbed both arms holding them open to see if he could gain any directional control. The last thing he wanted to do was steer him into the hotel six stories off the ground. Even with the double weight the squirrel suit still had some maneuverability and slowed their descent.

Josh looked over the flying squirrel's shoulder and noticed a large pile of aggregate piled up that was being used for the highway construction next to the hotel. That was it. He needed to fly the squirrel into the peak of that sand pile and hope that it would break the fall enough to allow them to slide down the hill to safety.

Etta jumped on the downed woman and committed to the wrestling after all. She grabbed an arm and pulled it behind her to get a cuff on the squirming wrestler. She succeeded in cuffing her left hand but then got thrown off doing a header, landing in a heap. Now the terrorist was up and swung the cuffed hand in an arc catching Etta in the shoulder drawing blood. She went down as blood whipped into her eyes. The advancing woman punched Etta in the face and she went down again.

Falling back Etta shook her head violently from side to side to get the blood out of her eyes. In so doing she spotted her gun lying beneath a coffee table. Feigning fear she rolled that way and reached under the table to gather in her weapon. The woman was again advancing, this time with a knife that she had pulled out of her boot.

Grabbing her personal weapon she knew she had racked a round in the chamber before entering the room. The terrorist with the evil eyes started to pounce on Etta as she pulled the weapon out from under the table. The woman stopped, recognizing a gun trumped a knife in any fight. Still lying on her back Etta aimed and shot her center mass twice. The woman dropped like a stone, but so did the advancing knife in her hand. Etta rolled to the left as the knife grazed her ear and fell to the floor. The woman fell on top of her, bleeding out.

Etta squirmed out from under her and checked to be sure she was dead. She was, so Etta ran out the door and down the hallway just as two security guards came running down the hall on the report of shots fired. Etta yelled over her shoulder "Homeland Security, Call the police!" She sprinted into the room at the end of the hallway where the door had been shattered expecting to find Josh and the terrorist. Not finding anyone she looked out the blown out window and then downward hoping for the best.

Josh wrestled with his magic carpet rider and steered the duo towards the sand pile. Both men hit the pile just shy of the peak and passed through the sand like a knife passes through concrete. After plowing through the sand in an explosion of dust both men separated and continued their downward trajectory rolling down the twenty foot pile of aggregate. At the bottom they rolled in different directions with Josh smashing his head into a large backhoe bucket and Mahoud rolling into a bush.

Mahoud was the first to stand although unsteadily. He looked around to gain his senses and spotted the crazed man who had jumped on him as he descended. He reached for his gun but it was no longer there. He looked for another weapon and spotted a four-foot piece of lumber acting as a wheel chuck on the backhoe. He picked up the board and advanced on the unconscious man.

Etta looked out the window and saw the two men below. One was staggering towards Josh who looked to be unconscious, if alive at all. She didn't hesitate, she screamed, "Homeland Security" and fired two shots downward at the advancing man. Shooting from over 150 feet above she realized she couldn't hit the man but she wanted him to know she was trying. The two 9mm bullets slammed into the pile creating sand eruptions between Josh and the advancing man. She fired twice more and while not hitting him, she got his attention.

Mahoud looked up at the room he had flown out of and saw a woman aiming a gun at him. He dropped the board and turned to run.

Etta fired twice more and then turned and ran down the hall. Two more security guards were advancing with weapons drawn at the sound of gunfire. Etta flashed her Homeland Security credentials again and gave a cliff notes summary of what had just occurred. She pointed out the dead woman lying in the room and threw them her HS business card before sprinting for the elevator.

Outer Markers, O'Hare International Airport

The remote pilot in the large trailer parked beneath the Control Tower, fought the controls of the President's plane. As the plane shuddered and started to do a barrel roll dipping its dead wing towards the fast approaching ground, he watched his forward monitor to see if he would make it over the outer markers. Then, realizing he didn't have enough speed and altitude to clear the car rental lots and the limousine holding pen, he shut down all systems remaining to hopefully minimize the conflagration that was about to happen.

The plane slammed through the last fence line and catapulted through the runway marker lights, which vaporized from the concussive force. Air Force One immediately exploded in a huge fireball and continued sliding and grinding itself into the thick pavement as it traversed down the runway. This ignited the leaking fuel pouring out of the dismembered wings of the dead airplane.

The President's plane maintained its upright stature with the two wings acting as rudders until they too lost their ability to grip the fuselage and capsized inward towards the fuselage adding to the conflagration. A thousand feet down the runway the plane came to rest burning brightly in the afternoon sky.

In the terminal buildings across the tarmac people stood with their noses to the windows stunned by what they were witnessing. They could not believe that the blue and white Air Force One had been shot out the sky in front of them. The President must have surely died in the crash landing they witnessed!

Rosemont, IL.

Mahoud staggered towards the parking lot behind the hotel and found his car, which was close to the exit of the lot. He gunned the engine and hit two parked cars backing out and racing down the lane. He drove through the parking lot gate lift at 40 mph splintering the wooden barrier as he careened onto a side street across from a McDonalds. He turned west towards a small park and then immediately turned into an apartment complex. He could still see the Westin Hotel in his rear view mirror.

Driving slowly he figured they would come looking for him fast enough. They could have seen what kind of car he had driven away in. He drove slowly to not draw attention while he looked for someplace to park and hide. He finally found a spot next to an extended length heating and cooling work van. He turned off the engine and slid down in the seat to hide in case that madman was still following him. He wiggled out of his squirrel suit and stuffed it in the back seat while trying to comprehend what had just happened. What the hell, how could they have known he was in the hotel? Then he remembered that his accomplice was still back there. He hoped she had gotten away without having to jump out of the tenth floor window like he did.

His mind was a blank as he tried to comprehend what he had done and what his terrorist team might have accomplished. He wondered if his missile had hit the president's plane. At the same time he sat there waiting for his world to end. Figuring he had a better chance of surviving if he wasn't acting like a crazed killer, he tried to calm down. He wondered if any of his missile teams had hit the President's plane and turned on the car radio and found an all-news station.

A reporter was breathlessly stating, "We are breaking into regular programming to advise that something big is happening at O'Hare International right now. As you know, the President's plane, Air Force One, was scheduled to arrive in Chicago about this time today. Near O'Hare we have been receiving a number of conflicting reports of a plane crash. There are sirens and police cars racing all over the place, and we just received word that the airport has been completely shut down."

"Jessica, sorry to interrupt, but we just had a driver on the Kennedy call in to report he had seen a man literally jump out of the top floor of the Westin Hotel at O'Hare and hurtle to the ground. As he gawked at the sight, a second man jumped out of the same window and landed on top of the first guy before they hit the ground. That is unconfirmed but could that be what is causing all the commotion?"

"Thanks Emily, but I think it is more than that, we just received another unconfirmed report that the President's plane, has come under attack by unknown parties, as Air Force One tried to land at O'Hare. They believe that missiles had been fired at the president's plane. We have just received another report that the plane has been hit by at least one missile and the plane has exploded."

"The phones are lighting up here at the station. Another driver on the Kennedy says he saw an explosion on a plane approaching O'Hare. He also advised one of the plane's engines was ripped away from the wing when the missile slammed into the left side of the craft. The engine exploded and tore loose. He said the engine started catapulting through the sky and smashed into that large inflatable indoor sports bubble in Rosemont. I've seen that bubble from the Tri-State Expressway interchange. It right next to that women's softball stadium. This eye witness report is unconfirmed but we have a crew heading that way right now."

I just received another unconfirmed report that the President's plane has been reportedly hit by a missile, or multiple missiles as it was trying to land at O'Hare from the east. We are trying to confirm that with airport authorities now."

Rosemont Apartments

Mohammed listened carefully to the conflicting and sketchy reports he was hearing. He hoped what he was hearing was the case, and he was pleased with himself since he had gotten his missile off. He would be able to claim credit for the kill with his elders. But now he needed to get away because he still had two additional missiles in the car trunk. He would try to do more damage to America's sense of air security and safety.

As he thought about his next step, a laborer in white coveralls stepped out of the apartment building in front of the car and headed for one of the vans he was sandwiched between. He immediately saw an opportunity to escape. He would become a heating and cooling repairman.

The terrorist waited until the man had walked between the vehicles and unlocked the van sliding the door sideways. He exited his car at that moment and asked the guy the time. The workman had his head inside the van rummaging around for something and checked his watch. At that moment, Mahoud hit him hard with his handgun on the crown of his skull. From the crunch, the terrorist realized he hit him hard enough to kill him. A casualty of jihad.

He reached for the van keys and his own as well. Opening his trunk he hauled out the two wrapped stinger missiles and placed them in the back of the van. Leaving his car unlocked with the keys on the dash board, he hoped someone would steal it and drive away, leading any pursuers on a wild goose chase.

Then he quickly drove away from the apartment building and out to Higgins Road and then west to Mannheim Road/ Hwy 12. Trying to drive casually he headed south on Hwy 12 on the road that would take him right past the airport runway that the President's plane was landing on.

He passed through the remote parking lots area and came to a stop amidst all sorts of traffic backed up on both sides of the road. People had pulled over to the sides of the road in both directions and many were standing outside their cars looking into the airport. As he stayed in the far left lane where traffic was still slowly moving he looked right and could see huge billowing clouds of black smoke drifting into the sky. He knew black smoke denoted aviation fuel burning as he had seen it many times in the Middle East.

Inching forward he finally saw what everyone was looking at. The burning wreckage of a Boeing 737 was still fully engulfed in flames reaching 50 feet into the sky. Seven massive yellow airport fire trucks had surrounded the plane and were shooting foam and water on the burning plane with huge water cannons. It looked like they were slowly gaining control of the crash site. He could clearly see the nose and tail fin of the aircraft in the quarter mile distance burning in the bright afternoon sun.

The people standing next to their cars along the highway were silent and despondent. They were trying to contemplate what had happened. The President of the United States had been shot out of the sky by terrorists.

Not wanting to draw attention he continued to drive forward in the lane that was still moving. He would have liked to stay and savor the terrorist act but he knew moving along would allow him to fight another day. As he passed the carnage, he saw more billowing smoke on his left. This smoke was more white than black and he could only guess what else was afire. He fumbled with the radio and tuned in that same radio station to see if he could find out more about the terrorist act.

The talk show radio program was in a full frenzy as the lead talk host tried to make sense of what had happened. His hope was to bring some order to the delivery of this breaking news. Additional reports were coming in every second.

"While we have many conflicting reports we can tell you that the President of the United States was scheduled to be in Chicago today. As his plane, Air Force One, was on final approach into O'Hare International Airport from the east, a number of missiles were fired at the aircraft from a number of different directions. At least two of the missiles connected with the President's plane. The plane sustained enough damage to be literally shot out of the sky. It crashed into the end of East West Runway at 1:15 pm this afternoon. We do not know the status of the President nor the people traveling with him. When we have additional information and confirmation of the facts we will report them to you."

Another newscaster offered another report.

"When Air Force One was shot at, one missile ripped into the fuselage of the craft near the rear tail wing assembly and another missile connected with the left engine mount. The missiles may have been a stinger type missile, a ground-to-air offensive and defensive weapon that homes in on the heat signature of an aircraft. These types of weapons have been used in war zones for thirty years and can be devastatingly effective especially when aimed at low flying planes.

The missile that took out the left engine effectively blew the engine off the wing and it fell away causing damage on the ground. It hit the Rosemont Sports bubble near the airport tearing a massive hole in the bubble going in and then back out again on the southern side of the massive tent structure. It then kept going sliding through a street and into a parking lot amongst all sorts of government vehicles causing explosions. We have reports that a number of major fires are raging in the sports bubble and behind the government building. We are told the building houses Homeland Security, the DEA and the Immigration Agencies."

Reports continued to pour in.

"We have also been officially advised that the terrorists that coordinated this attack on the President and America were positioned in a number of house and businesses in communities surrounding O'Hare Airport. Various community police departments, along with Homeland Security, and the FBI are rounding up these terrorists as we speak. Citizens are asked to stay indoors as these perpetrators are presumed armed and dangerous."

Mahoud sat in the massive traffic jams that were everywhere near O'Hare. No one was moving. Everyone was tuned to radios and many people had poured into restaurants and stores with televisions to seek more information. He debated doing that himself, but realizing they knew where he had been for the actual attack, he feared that they had his photo as well and it might shortly be on every television screen in America.

He drove slowly south on Mannheim Road looking for some place to ditch the van that had gotten him away from the scene of the attack. He decided to drive to Midway Airport on the south side of Chicago. He could park the van in one of the parking lots there in a dark corner and then break into another car late at night to find a new ride. He headed south listening to the news reports.

Rosemont Convention Center, Operation Headquarters

Josh had a huge knot on his head bandaged with gauze wrapped turban style. The irony was not lost on him. At least Etta was not giving him a hard time. She looked pretty beat up too and had a bandaged ear and cuts on her face. But she had gotten her target in the firefight. He was advised he had a concussion that required medical treatment but he waved the medical personnel aside. He insisted that Etta drive him back to the mission headquarters where they both needed to be. He was still angry he had not caught the ringleader and he wanted to get back in the action.

As they pulled into the temporary convention hall headquarters they saw Dave Houston, the Convention Manager pushing some lockup cages into a number of draped cubicles that had been set up. They were being pressed into service to lock up the terrorists that had been captured and brought in. These man size cages were usually used to store valuable trade show equipment and computers on the show floors at night. There were twenty cages in all. The twenty cages had been spread out along the hall's outer walls with pipe and drape curtains surrounding each one. As the terrorists were brought in with black bags over their heads they'd been individually locked up one person per cage. This would facilitate the individual interrogations that were already on going.

Josh and Etta parked and walked over to the tote board in the center of the large hall. They saw that thirteen terrorists had been rounded up, nine others had been killed in the firefights, and six others sustained injuries in the assault requiring medical care. A triage area had been set up in the back of the large hall.

The key numbers they were searching for were the stinger missile counts. They saw that twenty-seven missiles had been accounted for. Eighteen missile launchers and missiles had been captured by the various SWAT teams. Two other launchers had malfunctioned when they were fired. Seven of the missiles had been fired at the President's plane, three of which had connected with the craft. Doing the math they both realized there were still two missiles in play. And they both knew who had them.

Etta and Josh turned their attention to the status of their assault teams. The tote board held those numbers as well. Luckily, there were no fatalities but the overall assault team had sustained nine gunshot wounds, with three SWAT team members in critical care.

Having surveyed the numbers they asked for an update on the status of Air Force One. Television links had been established in the hall and all the major network and news feeds were being carried on a table full of monitors. All the local networks had rushed to the scene in the past half hour and were broadcasting from mobile trucks in and around O'Hare International Airport. They were breathlessly reporting the crash landing of the President's plane but were not saying anything about the status of the President himself.

Just then the various television stations almost simultaneously interrupted their own coverage announcing breaking news.

"Breaking News. We have just received confirmation that the President's Air Force One craft has indeed crashed on Runway 27L at O'Hare's International Airport. The craft was hit by a number of missiles fired at it while attempting to land this afternoon, less than an hour ago. The plane crashed into one of the rental car lots and passed through the limousine lot and the outer marker lights on the runway before erupting into flames on the end of the runway. Emergency teams are on site and we will have more information as soon as we can get it."

Every person viewing held their breath waiting for further news.

"We have just been advised that the President was not aboard the craft, and in fact has been here in downtown Chicago. He is about to hold a press conference on this terrorist attack. We will now cut to the President of the United States."

"My fellow Americans. Within the last hour the United States was attacked by a cell of terrorists that planned to assassinate me and send the United States into turmoil. They failed to meet their objective. I am pleased to report that we have rounded up over twenty-five conspirators that took part in this terrorist attack. The good news is that they missed the mark and only shot down a drone Air Force One standing in for my usual 747 plane. There was no loss of life in today's attack at O'Hare International Airport."

"The reason that we have been successful in foiling this terrorist plot on U.S. soil is that we were aware of their plan over four months ago. With our under cover intelligence assets in the Middle East, and Yemen specifically, we were able to gain valuable insight about the plot and plan accordingly. For a variety of reasons it was thought that letting the plot proceed was the best way to capture the terrorists and more importantly to capture these dangerous missile systems that they planned to utilize. These weapons of mass destruction could have caused irreparable damage to our country. We made the decision to go after and capture all of the weapons before they could be deployed throughout the country.

Please know that I am completely safe, as no one was actually in the plane. It had been flown into Chicago like a drone. Most important, all of our strike teams have been accounted for. While some injuries did occur in capturing these terrorists I am told that none of them are life threatening. They are all safe and the missiles that were not utilized have been secured.

There will be more information made available by the White House and our strike teams as soon as we can draw all the information together. God bless you and God bless the United States."

"Great," Josh said, as he headed towards the car. They drove out of the Convention Center towards the Homeland Security headquarters building tucked behind the expressway interchange at the entrance to O'Hare International Airport. "Didn't anyone mention to the President that there are still two missiles unaccounted for out there? Why did he say the threat is over and everyone can relax?"

"I agree with you, but it actually makes sense," Etta said. "Every press outlet throughout the country is showing video of Air Force One burning on the end of that runway and people all over the country are watching this attack unfold on the television. He needed to calm fears right away. Can you imagine what happens if those fears aren't settled? The stock market goes crazy, people become obsessed with the fact that flying isn't safe. They'll say 9-11 is happening all over again. Then the economy suffers and people are afraid to travel. He had to get in front of the story right away."

I guess you're right, but we still have two missiles in play. And we haven't caught their squirrel flying ringleader. Holy shit! Look at that, the sports bubble has completely collapsed."

As they drove down the street to the HSD building there were four Rosemont fire trucks parked haphazardly in the street right of way. Weaving through the trucks Etta took out her credentials and showed them to police officers cordoning off the roadway in front of the Homeland Security building. As they turned the corner to drive into the parking lot they saw more fire trucks surrounding ten DHS and Immigration vehicles that were burning as if one. In the middle of the heap they could see the flaming outline of a large airplane engine.

"Well, at least we know what happened to the engine that got blown off by that one direct hit," Etta said.

"Yeah, I'm guessing the engine first slammed through that sports bubble and then slid across the street into your parking lot. I hope no one was hurt when that huge hunk of metal came hurtling through."

"Park here. We may not be able to get back out if we don't. We need to update everyone and then spread out to find that bastard.

They ran into the building and in the DHS conference room they got another update. A be-on-the-lookout, BOLO, had already been issued on the leader and the vehicle he left in. All airports, bus stations, and train stations were on the look-out for the sole terrorist still on the loose. Every police agency was looking for the terrorist.

Josh was beside himself having lost the terrorist at the hotel. His head throbbed with pain but he chose to ignore the pain so he could back in the game.

Just then a report came in that a man had been found dead beside a car in an apartment parking lot in Rosemont, directly behind the Westin Hotel. Josh contemplated what might have happened and headed for the door. It was his guy switching cars and killing someone in the process. He knew it. Etta read the same report and followed him out the door. They drove to the apartment parking lot in the shadow of the Westin Hotel and showed their credentials. The local police were investigating the death and had initiated a canvas of the adjacent buildings to determine what had happened.

One man, a tradesman working in one of the apartments came

forward to say he was working with another guy in the apartment who went out for a smoke and never came back. He advised that his work truck had been parked near the other guys work van and was no longer in the parking lot.

Etta and Josh surmised their terrorist suspect had jacked the work truck and asked what trade the missing worker had been in. Etta looked up the name and number of the heating and cooling company and called to get a license number, the coloring of the van, and a photo of the corporate name painted on the vehicle. Another BOLO went out within minutes to all agencies throughout the area. Josh and Etta jumped into their vehicle and started canvasing the area to see if their terrorist had stayed in the area.

Driving around was difficult because so many police agencies had piled into the area to assist. As Josh and Etta debated what they should do next they received a call from headquarters that an Illinois State Trooper had just reported seen the missing BOLO van going south on I-294 near I-55. He was driving north so he was unable to follow on the divided highway.

"Looks like he's trying to get out of Dodge, Etta stated, as she headed for the Interstate on ramp. "We have to catch up or he'll set up shop at some other airport and take out another plane."

"I'm not so sure," Josh said, "I've hung around these crazed jihadists long enough to know they aren't afraid of dying. Just the opposite, they are insistent on meeting their maker and all those virgins. It's like they have a death wish. No, I think he not running, he going to try and complete his mission!"

Etta looked at Josh recognizing he was right. "So what does he do next? She asked."

"Well, he's in a van driving away from the scene of the crime, south it sounds like, and you have to figure he has a radio. Our news radio folks are blabbing all sorts of information on the terrorist attack, so I figure he's up to speed on the fact that the President is not dead. He already knows that it was a set-up and that is just pissing him off to no end. He knows that we picked up or killed the rest of his crew, so he's thinking of a way to complete his mission, even if he has to die in the process."

"Desperate man, with nothing to lose," Etta stated out loud as she drove south weaving in and out of traffic. "That's the worst kind to deal with. So where do you think he's heading?"

Josh thought about that for a moment ignoring the car lurching back and forth as Etta raced down the expressway. "I know where I'd be going!" Josh exclaimed, as Etta shot across three lanes of heavy traffic.

"Look at the facts, he's heard the President is alive and still in Chicago. He's heard the same bulletins we heard. He's going to go finish the job. He's heading for the lakefront and knows the President's Marine One helicopter will take him out of town to the Gary airport where Air Force One is located. That is what I'd do, I'd create a second chance to complete the mission. If that failed I'd race for Gary's Airport and try to get close enough for another shot. He is going to try and shoot him down again."

"Ok, but how the hell will we be able to find him along 25 miles of lakefront property between Chicago and Gary? Talk about a needle in a hay stack?"

"I agree Etta, it's a long shot but it is all we have until we get better info. Head towards the lakefront and let's see if we can narrow down the possibilities. And we monitor headquarters and see if they can feed us additional info."

She gave him that look that said 'who is making all the decisions again'? At the same time she knew this was probably the best course of action if they wanted to stay in the game. She again crossed three lanes of traffic to catch the off ramp from I-294 to I-55 narrowly cutting off a big rig. "So how is the head, can you do this?"

"A cracked noggin is the least of my worries!" he said. "My head is throbbing, but that's the adrenelian pumping. We can't let this maniac take another shot. I'll take some aspirin later." Passing through the toll and circling through the interchange Etta entered a congested I-55 heading towards the city.

South side of Chicago

Mahoud was nervous because he was outside his plan, but he was also determined to complete his mission. He was willing to die in the process. So he would devise a new plan. He headed down 55th street through a neighborhood of small Chicago bungalows. He had been told many Chicago police officers lived in this part of town because they could afford the housing stock. He drove carefully and minded all the rules of the road. Arriving at Midway Airport he pulled into the massive parking deck just clearing the warning that his vehicle may be too tall. He heard the roll tube gently drag across his van ceiling.

Once inside he carefully looked for a dark corner that would shield most of the van from searching eyes. He found such a corner near the back where one of the ramps to the upper decks sheltered much of the view of the van. He wedged his van in backwards so it looked less like a van and more like a car.

He sat in the cab listening to the radio. New reports explained the President had actually flown into the Chicago area on another Air Force One that landed at the Gary, Indiana airport just thirty miles south of Chicago. The President had flown to Chicago's downtown by helicopter on Marine One. He had attended his fund raising events and was now resting comfortably at his private residence on the south side of Chicago.

He sat there thinking about what had transpired. The plan had failed. The President was still alive. From reports he figured that the rest of his team had been captured or killed. He was now alone. He also figured there was no way he was going to escape this city. They would eventually catch up with him and his missiles. That could not happen without at least trying to finish the job he had started. He needed a new plan.

He pulled out his phone and got a signal. He googled background on the President. He quickly found what he was looking for, the address of his Chicago home residence. It was an old mansion in Hyde Park. With the address known, he switched to a map program and started analyzing where the Marine 1 helicopter could possibly pick up the President, and what flight paths that pilot would most likely take to get the President out of Chicago to the Gary Airport, almost directly south of the President's home. Expanding the map program he could see the house was only a few miles east of his current location.

Mahoud scrutinized the map switching back and forth from the road map to the actual satellite views. Zeroing in he realized the area would be crawling with authorities protecting their President, so he looked for the most unlikely site to set up his shooting nest. He found what he was looking for and plotted a detailed route to get him there quickly.

Climbing into the rear of the van he rummaged through the equipment and found three cans of white spray paint. It was the same color as the van itself. He could buy himself some time by over spraying the heating and cooling name on the van. It wouldn't stand up to scrutiny but it might buy him time. In the shadows of the dark parking garage corner he stepped outside and started spraying over the name on the exposed side of the van. It took two cans of the white paint to cover the large sign.

Next, he broke in to the silver mid-size car sitting next to the van. It would allow for the easiest transfer of his carpeted missile launchers. Using a tire iron he broke out the drivers' window and reached in unlocking the door. He transferred his two rugs to the back seat and threw a tarp over the weapons.

Next he climbed into the vehicle and reached down to hotwire it. It was something he had been trained to do and he had no problem starting the vehicle. He went back to the van to look for any other item that might prove useful in his final quest. He found a water bottle and a half-eaten sandwich which he took, as well as two jackets, one heavy, and one light.

Taking the car's parking lot ticket in the dash storage bin, he pulled a cap down over his face and drove slowly out of the garage to the check-out kiosk and paid in cash telling the lady to have a great day. Once on 55th Street he turned east and crossed Cicero Avenue and under the Orange line rail tracks. He cut over to 59th street which looked to be less traveled. He knew this would take him towards the lakefront and his last chance for redemption.

Chicago

Josh and Etta drove on I-55 all the way into the city and pulled off as they got to the McCormick Convention Center complex sprawling the lakefront for a quarter mile. They would await better information and then be in a better position to act on any intelligence they received.

Etta pulled out her mobile connected I-Pad and decided to see where the President actually lived. She knew he was on the far south side in Hyde Park, but she had never been there. Josh watched from his seat and visualized what he would do if he was planning to shoot down the President's helicopter.

Both of them first looked at an overview map that took in Chicago's south side and showed all the way to Gary's Airport to the further south. Etta found the address in question and then zoomed in to show the south Greenwood residence.

"Let's look closer at the lakefront area. I presume the President's helicopter would pick him up somewhere near the water where they could land safely and also control access in and out. Once the President was on board the pilot would go directly out to open water to neutralize any threat coming from the ground and neighborhoods."

Etta searched the Lake Michigan waterfront scanning for a suitable landing zone for the president's helicopters. There would be at least two, one as a back-up. She walked the screen visual from north to south following the contours of the lakefront. Josh just looked over her shoulder and occasionally asked her to zoom in or expand out to see surrounding terrain.

Etta's phone buzzed and she got word that the van had been spotted near Midway Airport and an intense search was underway.

"Josh you may be right. They spotted the van near Midway and they have half of the police force converging to scour the neighborhoods and areas around Midway. He may be trying to shoot down a civilian craft with the weapons he has remaining."

"I still vote for the President and the lakefront. I know how these guys think. I've been in bed with them for too many years. He's going to keep pursuing the President. I'll bet my career on it!"

They went back to scrutinizing the south side waterfront feeling more confident that they were on the right track. Almost directly east of the President's house, a half mile away, they found a large lakefront park. Checking the satellite view they saw that there was a peninsula effect with no trees projecting into the lake.

"I think this is where the President's helicopters might land to pick him up. Zero in."

"Yes, please," Etta said, giving him the look that he knew well now.

"Yes, please, I apologize, I usually work alone. And I don't listen to myself. I'm thinking like a sniper now, Etta. I'm searching for a kill shot, just like he'll be doing. Once I figure that out then we'll know where to zero in and look for the son-of-a-bitch. I'm sorry."

"Apology taken, .you've never shared that with me before. I feel like I've entered your inner sanctum. It's kind of an intimate moment. Almost like foreplay. I'm getting excited!" As soon as she said it she was embarrassed. Etta zoomed in even more as asked.

"No time for foreplay now, young lady, but if that does it for you, I'd like a rain check after this is over?"

"We'll see, … well see."

Josh concentrated on the task at hand.

"So, that could be the LZ but it involves a circuitous land route for his vehicles through city streets and the neighborhoods. If that is the pick-up LZ, then he would head straight out into the lake about two miles, and then turn south for the Gary Airport. Once the helicopter is that far out it would be a harder target to shoot out of the sky. It could be done but Marine One has all sorts of defensive capabilities just Like Air Force One has. Our terrorist would have to shoot at the helicopter before it gains too much altitude or it flies too far out or the missile would fail to connect. That's why the lake front is where he'll take the shot."

Etta backed the screen out again to get an overview perspective and pointed at something else. She had an opinion too.

"Josh, what about this. Washington Park is even larger and much closer to the President's residence. It would involve only a five block ground run from the house. And the middle of the park has a huge open field that could be defended while the helicopter swoops in and out?"

"Great observation. Are you thinking like a sniper or the Secret Service? It makes sense to minimize the ground transportation exposure with a bad guy still loose. I'm guessing the Secret Service is working overtime and wants to get him out as fast as they can."

He was listening. Etta scanned the Washington Park perimeter and found that the University of Chicago Midway Plaisance was a wide greenway boulevard leading from Washington Park all the way to Jackson Park and the lake. She pointed out the corridor leading to safety.

Josh was impressed. "This is kind of like foreplay for you isn't it?"

"We're partners right, isn't that what partners do? They help each other. It has nothing to do with foreplay. But if that turns you on, so be it, just don't let it ruin your aim."

"All I meant is your right, Etta. I told you I've been in the desert too long. Sorry. How about we check on the extraction plans with the Secret Service, if they'll share them. They have to be spooked with the stand-in plane being shot down. Just tell them we need to know exit strategy and timing."

"Just so you know, that was going to be my next call," she said smugly, and grabbed the phone.

Josh kept scanning the lakefront map on the screen. He was on board with her theory. He was already looking for a place he would set up to take the shot that could take down the President. He had to think like a terrorist in order to stop this lunatic.

He followed the possible route the Marine One helicopters would take. On the satellite image he noted there was a small boat harbor in Jackson Park that was packed with at least 50 moorings. Remembering how the Canadian terrorist had fired on them from a 45 foot fishing boat without any warning, he zeroed in to see that this would be a good site to lay low until the last moment, pop out from beneath deck and shoot a rocket.

Using the litmus test that he could make such a thing work if he had to down a helicopter overhead, he made a series of notes and moved on to look for other sniper nest opportunities. He found two more boat basins at the southern part of Jackson Park, but they would be further south of where the helicopter would be when it headed out into the lake.

Scanning even further south the land became industrial with old factories, grain storage facilities. They were too obvious to be shooting sites and would be covered by police swarming the area once an exit timetable was established. He followed the shore line all the way to Gary's Airport and decided the land was too industrial and open for any bad guy to lay in wait for the president's helicopter. No, he would blend in, bide his time and step out to take the shot just like they did at O'Hare.

Etta got off the phone looking perplexed.

"You were right, they're spooked, alright. Hell, I'm supposed to be in charge of this Task Force and they didn't want to share exit strategy even with me. Had to go up the food chain to get some answers."

She paused and flashed a smile.

"So I win! They are planning to take the president home in an hour and are planning on using Washington Park for the LZ. They will be leaving at 5:00 pm before it gets dark. The helicopters are currently in Gary and will come north just before the President's motorcade leaves the house and goes to Washington Park. They will use that University of Chicago greenway to get to Jackson Park and then out into the lake and on to Gary.

So I win!"

"Well, good for you and us, your supposition was correct." He bowed to her insights.

"Our supposition," she said, emphasizing the word our. "But that doesn't get us any closer does it?"

"Actually it does. I've been trying to figure out where I would shoot down the President in this scenario. The question is, would our guy think the same way?"

"Well, you've been right so far. You said he wouldn't quit and bug out. That he would try to complete the mission, and he would head over here to do it. With a sighting near Midway, I think he is doing just that. So what's next?"

Etta's phone buzzed again. It was headquarters relaying more information. As she listened to the update she took notes. Josh went back to the satellite maps and worked it out in his head what he would do.

"Our guy is heading this way. The search at Midway found the van in a long-term parking garage, buried in a second-floor corner. One side had been painted over to cover up the heating and cooling sign, and there was broken glass on the ground next to the vehicle.

They presume he took a car that was parked next to him. So again, you're right.

"Ok, were still on point. And I think I know how he'll try to do this. So I think he is going to set up and shoot from here."

Josh zoomed the satellite image in close enough to a boat basin that had about 50 boats moored at a series of docks.

Etta looked confused and challenged the site, "Why there?" she asked.

Josh zoomed the satellite image back out and Etta could see the boat basin was in Jackson Park within spitting distance of the Lake. It was directly east of that wide University of Chicago greenway boulevard that led back to Washington Park where the President would board Marine One.

"You haven't been wrong yet. So that's as good a guess as any."

"It's not a guess. It's where I would set up. Just like that Ponzi scheme assassination in New York where we met. It's what a killer would do to maximize his chances."

She remembered back to meeting Josh in New York when she thought he was a smug bastard. She shook the thought out of her head and simply said, "Let's go."

Hyde Park

Mahoud drove the silver La Crosse east from Midway and headed for the lakefront. As he passed Washington Park he glanced left and noticed all sorts of police activity. There were barricades being set up and police cars were making all parked vehicles move or get towed. He stopped for a moment to think about what he was seeing. Looking at his phone map he saw that the President's residence was less than a half mile away. He realized he would get another chance and drove on towards the lake front.

Driving through the University of Chicago he noted the same police build-up. Entering Jackson Park he turned south on Cornell Avenue, which circled the entire park, to distance himself from the police presence. He took Hayes Drive over to Lake Shore Drive and turned north and then entered a cloverleaf to the yacht basin. He parked in a half-filled lot.

Pulling out his handgun he screwed a silencer on the end and tucked it in his pants pulling his jacket closed. Walking out onto one of the piers he walked with a map in his hand until he found a lone man kneeling on his open deck. No one else was visible in the surrounding area.

"Pardon me Sir, could you assist me. I'm trying to find Henry Jackson's boat?"

The man stopped varnishing his wood deck and turned to help the inquirer.

"Come aboard, young man,…..Jackson, you say. Not sure I know that name. Let me get my directory and see if we can find him." He stepped down the stairs to the salon below.

Mahoud stepped aboard and took a quick look around to see if anyone was watching or had paid attention to his inquiry. There was no one visible on any of the surrounding boats so he moved under the canopy. He pulled out his silenced weapon.

"I don't see a Jackson listed," the elderly man said, as he climbed the stairs.

Mahoud made one last scan of the immediate area and shot the man through the heart. The silencer did its job and the noise was no more than a chirp in the confined space of the deck salon. The elderly man cooperated in death by falling backwards and down the stairs disappearing from sight. Mahoud sat down and started drinking the man's lemonade that was sitting on the table. He casually looked around to see if anyone was looking. No one was even visible even though there were many cars in the parking lot. He stepped downstairs and dragged the body further into the forward berth.

Looking about he found the foul weather boat covers that were used to seal up the boat when not in use. Taking the primary salon tarp he rolled it up and carried it topside. Casually he stepped off the boat and headed for the car. Once there he wrapped the large tarp around one of the Stinger Missile launchers in the back seat along with one shell and threw it over his shoulder to carry back to the boat. He planned on using one missile and would hold the other in reserve if he needed to take another shot later.

Once back on the boat he prepared the missile for a launch sequence and laid it out on the bench seat opposite the captain's chair. He covered it with his two jackets. He then took the salon weather tarp and started buttoning up the boat so it would look unattended and sealed up.

Below deck he opened all the port holes so that air would continue to flow with the tarp buttoned up so the heat would not ripen the dead boat owner. He waited to kill the President.

Hyde Park

The Secret Service team did a final check before the President was to be transported to Washington Park, and the temporary Marine One landing site. The twin helicopters were in-coming and would arrive in ten minutes.

Police had completely locked down the Washington Park site. A large grassy area had been circled with crowd control fence sections to designate the landing site.

All surrounding streets had been blocked off and the motorcade would have clear sailing from the residence to the park LZ. Sniper teams were on the roofs of all the tall buildings in the area searching for possible targets.

To the east, out over Lake Michigan at an elevation of 2,000 feet, the lead Marine helicopter pilot radioed the two craft would be touching down at the appointed time. They were nine minutes out.

The Secret Service Team started moving the President in a tight phalanx formation, from his front porch the thirty-five feet to the presidential limousine. Once the President was safely inside, the motorcade started rolling onto 51st Street heading west.

The President's limousine was sandwiched with four Secret Service black SUV's on all sides. Out front there were two Chicago police cruisers, lights flashing. Behind were two more cruisers, for the six-block trip to the temporary LZ in Washington Park.

Approaching the Northeast corner of Washington Park the President's motorcade drove over the curb and proceeded across the lawn into the center of the park's baseball fields. It was a large clear space, devoid of trees and obstacles that would allow the Marine One helicopters to fly directly in, and then just as quickly elevate and leave the park with their passenger.

Jackson Park Boat Basin

Josh and Etta drove down Lake Shore Drive and entered the parking lot of the Museum Shores Yacht Club in the Jackson Park boat basin. They parked between two other cars and ducked down to minimize being seen inside the vehicle. Josh rifled around in his duffel bag and pulled out a set of binoculars. He started scanning the many boats and parked cars in view. The yacht club building was rather small and looked like a converted Quonset hut with a few tables and chairs surrounding the building. No one was sitting around enjoying the late afternoon sun setting in the west

Etta checked in with command central and advised where they were, so they would not get shot at by curious cops. She asked if they had any better information on the sole terrorist's location. Was he still unaccounted for?

"Be advised the car he may be driving is a 2012 silver La Crosse. The owner showed up at the Midway Parking Garage while we were still processing the crime scene. The license tag is # KLR 1011."

Josh immediately started scanning the parking lot for any silver vehicles. He spotted two cars that matched the general description but could not see the plates. He pointed them out to Etta.

"Be advised we may have spotted the vehicle in a boat parking lot in Jackson Park on the lake front. We will investigate and report back."

The cars were both parked near the middle of the lot across from the longest pier.

"The guy could be in one of the cars," Josh said, as he continued to scan the boat basin, or maybe in one of the boats. That is where I'd set up a shot. Ok, it's my turn to step out and take a look."

He took off the bandage wrapped around his head and reached for a White Sox ball cap in his bag. He also pulled out his weapon and chambered a round. He put two extra magazines in his jacket. Turning to Etta, he handed her the binoculars.

"If you will cover me from here, I'll do a perimeter search. First, I'm going to walk over to that rest room and take a look from that vantage. Then I'm going to stroll down to the middle pier and walk out like I own the place. Can you scan with the binoculars and see if you see any movement?"

"I appreciate how you asked instead of ordering me. Yeah, I can do that, but you be careful, Ok?"

"If I see the son-of-a-bitch I'll let you know by phone. Let's open a line between us, and turn on the speaker function so I don't have to pull it out of my pocket."

He put on his dark sunglasses, grabbed his go bag and climbed out of the car. He didn't look around but instead started walking to the restroom building. His path took him past the one of the silver cars. Approaching carefully, he noted the license plate was not the one they were looking for, if he even still had the same car. He noted a baby seat in the back. Not stopping, he entered the men's room and found a vented window that allowed him to look out across the boat docks unseen.

"Etta, the first silver car was not our guy's ride. It had a children's seat in the back. I'm not seeing anything out of this vented window. Just some out of shape rich guys working on their expensive boats, and a few women sunbathing. Maybe that warrants a further search?" he joked.

"Yeah, right. The President's life is in jeopardy and you're looking at bathing beauties. Get on with it buster. Remember you can't pee in there forever. That would be unusual, even for you."

"You're right again, I guess the ladies can wait. I'm going to check out the center pier and split the basin in two. And I'll check out the other car. Cover me."

"Roger that," she said, "But I'm going to check out the last pier on the right. I've already scanned everything else. I can look like a boater too, maybe even a bathing beauty! I'll cover you from there. You concentrate on the other end."

"Be careful and don't be a hero. You'll fit right in with those bathing beauties/"

"Is there any other way?" she said.

"Said the girl with a black and blue body that is smoking hot!"

She giggled. They were hunting a deadly terrorist and this guy just never let up. He was one cool customer. She headed towards the pier on the right

Josh exited the brick outhouse and casually headed for the dock in the middle. As he crossed the parking lot he walked past the other silver La Crosse. Getting closer he saw the license plate was the one they were looking for. Trying to remain cool he realized he was thinking like a terrorist. As he passed the car he saw that a grey blanket was stretched across the back seat covering something.

"Etta, our guy may be here. The license matches. Be on alert." He checked his weapon in his belt and flipped off the safety.

"Ok, so we know he's here somewhere. Now we just have to flush him out."

As he approached the gated entry to the various docks he stopped when he heard a helicopter beating in the sky off in the distance. He looked up as the constant rotor clip became louder. He saw that it was actually two helicopters and they were flying in close formation. It was the President's ride.

At the three-foot high gate to the pier he saw that it was already open so he walked through like he knew what he was doing. Heading down the wood ramp he waved to an imaginary person and behind his sunglasses scanned back and forth searching for the terrorist.

Jackson Park Boat Basin

Out over the Lake two identical brownish green Marine One helicopters flew straight west towards the Jackson Park beach and went feet dry passing over Jackson Park heading towards the University of Chicago campus and Washington Park.

Mahoud heard them coming. He knew that sound well from years of fighting in Iraq. It normally would have required him going to ground, diving for cover and trying to become invisible from the air. If successful you would live to fight another day.

But here it was the sound he had been waiting for. He ducked his head out from the tarp and looked up. He could see them thundering overhead from east to west. His two targets were flying in formation just five hundred feet above his head. Perfect targets for a missile just like the ones he had fired in Iraq.

His guess had been correct. They were going to retrieve the President and would most likely re-trace their steps to get him out over the water of Lake Michigan in the next ten minutes. That would minimize the danger to the President as they headed south to the Gary Airport and safety.

He ducked back under the tarp and prepped the Stinger missile. He loaded the deadly shell and started spooling up the battery mechanism. He knew the procedure well having taught twenty of his men how to load and launch the man-pad Stinger missile. As he worked he figured they must have all have been caught or killed by now. He was the last chance to make this a successful mission. He would not only avenge the death of Osama bin Laden, he would avenge the deaths of his fellow fighters.

With the weapon auto spooling up to full power he set the missile launcher down next to the tarp and unbuttoned enough of the grommets so that he could push through them easily at the last second and shoot the weapon downing the President's helicopter. This was his chance for retribution!

Jackson Park Marina

Josh moved carefully but tried to act as if he was out for a boating excursion as the helicopters rushed by overhead. Seven boats down the ramp, he saw a man's head pop out from beneath a boat tarp, perhaps drawn by the sounds of the helicopters above. He watched as the two helicopters flew overhead heading west making a good amount of racket because they were low and moving fast. He then lowered his view and saw a man he thought he recognized.

Josh waved casually, like an old friend and kept walking forward. The man did not wave back. Instead he ducked back under the tarp.

Josh had found his terrorist. He was far enough away that he could advise Etta they had located the guy.

"Etta, I got him. He's in the seventh boat out on this pier. It's him. It looks like he may have recognized me."

"Copy that. How do you want to handle this?" I can cover from here."

She ducked behind a boat and got the attention of a family sitting on the next boat over. She flashed her badge and told them to get below deck. She showed her handgun and they immediately did as they were told. She took out her binoculars and scanned over to the seventh boat. No one was in sight.

Mahoud was terrified. He was so close to accomplishing his mission and now a guy who had tried to buy some real estate from him and jumped on him at the Hotel was walking down the pier towards him. He had to be an agent. He kept his head down, grabbed his gun, and edged towards the side of the boat where the tarp had been unfastened. With a quick glance he could see the man was now just three boats down the deck and still advancing.

Etta watched as Josh advanced. She saw movement in the boat and saw a man push back the tarp with a gun in his hand.

"Josh, gun!" was all she could yell out.

Mahoud poked his head out and without warning shot twice at the advancing man. The first bullet missed high but the second shot caught Josh in the upper left shoulder area. The bullet smashed into his shoulder missing his heart and a major artery by less than an inch. The impact knocked Josh down on the wooden deck. The wind was knocked out of him and he laid there for a moment before realizing he was still in the line of fire. He rolled left behind a plastic boat foot locker rolling over his shoulder wound. Blood was oozing out on his shirt and dripping on the wooden deck beneath him.

Etta saw Josh go down hard. She realized he had been hit by gunfire although she had heard nothing. Without a moment's hesitation Etta fired an entire twelve shot magazine at the terrorist's boat from her vantage point.

The .45 caliber bullets tore into the boat splintering the fiberglass and smashing the tempered glass windows. She had to draw the guy's attention away from Josh. Mahoud was about to poke his head out again and finish the job when the bullets came flying in from another direction. He ducked back down. He crawled over to the shattered window and tried to see what he was up against. Across the way a woman poked her head out and started shooting again, this time with well-placed shots meant to hit him. He recognized her too. It was the damn business woman who was with the guy at the real estate office.

They were both agents chasing him. That was how they had

foiled the O'Hare plot. Now he was angry. Mahoud didn't know what to do. Should he save himself, or wait for the prize that would be flying over in minutes. How could he escape and still kill the President.

Josh was down but still conscious. He heard Etta firing from the other pier and thanked God he had a partner for a change. He pulled out his weapon and put it on full automatic. He reached over the wooden foot locker and emptied a full magazine of seventeen shots from his 9 mm Italian pistol at the boat just thirty feet away. That would keep the guy's head down. He ejected the magazine and slammed another home and then took stock of his wound. He was alive so it had missed his heart. It was only moderately bleeding so he assumed it had missed an artery.

He looked over the box and saw the guy stick out a silenced weapon to shoot again. He reached over the box and started unloading another magazine each slug hitting the target boat. He hoped Etta was ok and would be able to take the guy down because he could feel himself drifting off.

The terrorist knew he had hit the agent so he turned his attention on the woman. Now she was the more immediate threat. He kept his head down and without hesitation reached for the missile. If he could get away he had another missile in the car.

He shouldered the missile launcher while sitting on the floor and made sure it was spooled up and ready to fire. He reached up with his gun and shot four times at the boat two piers over. That would keep her head down. Then he crouched below the blown out window, stood up and shot the missile at the boat the woman was hiding behind.

Etta had ducked when the four covering shots came in her direction. She knew the shots were meant to keep her head down. Instead, she popped up to send a volley his way. Her intent was to keep his attention on her, not Josh.

Centering her gun she was about to shoot again when she saw him raise a Stinger missile and point it at her. A fraction of a second later the missile flashed in her direction. Being fifty feet away she knew she was about to die.

The missile was not homing in on any heat signature. It was just flying straight at a target mass that was in its way. On contact it would explode in a ball of fire taking the boat to its grave right in its' boat slip.

In that moment Etta had Josh on her mind and wasn't about to throw in the towel. She pulled the trigger on her weapon and dropped it on the pier. At the same time she arched her back and dove into the water behind the dock.

The missile made contact with the flying bridge and exploded ripping the entire upper structure from its hull. Had it hit lower on the side of the hull it would have immediately sunk the vessel. But it didn't take out the whole boat.

Etta saw it coming and dove backwards into the ice cold water fearing for her life. She knifed through the blue green surface and dove as deep as she could. The boat's explosion and resulting concussion in the water knocked her senseless. Summersaulting through the water she slammed into a thick wooden pylon below the surface. The impact knocked the breath out of her and she blacked out for a moment, drifting downward in the icy depths.

Mahoud poked his head up to see the explosion blow the boat apart. In the smoke and fire he could see no woman trying to shoot back. Turning his attention back to the guy on the dock he grabbed his gun and stepped out onto the dock. Approaching the man he realized he too must be dead.

Pointing his weapon he walked up to the inert figure laying on the dock. There was a nice round wound in his chest close to his heart. He looked dead but Mahoud viciously kicked the man anyhow to see if there was a reaction. The man did not flinch or move.

He kicked again and the man fell into the water. He watched him sink from site. Satisfied there was no threat he ran to his getaway car.

Etta came to sinking into the muck beneath the deck. She realized she was drowning. Her ears were ringing from the blast, but she was alive. Getting here wits back she looked up and could see the surface above her. Mustering the will to live she pushed her feet into the muck and used her arms to pull for the surface. As she broke the surface she bumped into a short ladder to the deck. Struggling up she saw a man running off the other pier and into the parking lot.

She was too late to stop the terrorist running away. But she wasn't too late to save Josh. Picking up her handgun she hobbled down her dock and rushed over towards Josh. When she got there she could not see him and presumed he was in the water. Without a second thought she jumped back into the icy water again and dove down. The water was churned up and cloudy, but she thought she saw something. Pulling in that direction she ran into Josh before she realized it was him, floating in a cloud of red.

She grabbed him by his Kevlar vest and started pulling towards the surface seven feet above. He was not assisting and his body weight was slowing the process. They both broke the surface and gasped for air spitting water from their mouths.

Two men who had witnessed the shootout came running up and started pulling the inert man out of the water laying him on the pier. They then both reached down for the woman and hauled her up. She kneeled down next to Josh.

"Don't you die on me you son-of-a-bitch! You're the best thing that has happened to me. You can't die now, you bastard." She pounded on his chest.

Sputtering water and coughing, Josh croaked, "That will kill me before the bullet does," He blinked water out of his eyes and reached up to stop her from pummeling him again.

"Oh my God, Josh, you scared the crap out of me."

"And you're dripping ice cold water all over me. Did you go swimming too?"

She laughed to break the tension. "Twice, that asshole used his missile to blow my cover boat out of the water. That's two times I've been shot at with those damned missiles. He got away."

He looked down at his chest wound. Confirming what he saw, he asked her to turn him over. "Turn me over and see if there is an exit wound. That would actually be good news."

She gingerly turned him on his side and saw another larger hole in his back. "Yeah, it's a through and through. From the amount of blood I'd say it didn't hit anything too vital. You'll live and have another scar to decorate that body of yours."

Josh smiled weakly. The men surrounding them stared at the bleeding man lying on the dock with a wound in his chest. Etta looked up hopefully and one man had the sense to pull out his phone and called 9-11. Another man in a swimsuit stepped forward stating he was a doctor. He asked for towels and other people ran off to get them.

"Doc, I'll live. Have you done triage before? Just stuff some gauze plugs in both holes to slow down the bleeding and throw a wrap bandage around the shoulder to hold everything in place. I'm going after that lunatic."

The Doctor understood what was being requested, but cautioned that was not a good idea. Josh waived the concern off and said, "just do it," and then "please".

While they quickly bandaged up Josh, Etta borrowed a phone and called headquarters reporting in and requesting assistance. She was told the President had just transferred to Marine One and would shortly be in the air.

Josh struggled up and they headed for their car. He knew where this bad guy would go to finish the job. He wouldn't be far away. He'd be on the beach to take one last shot at the President.

Etta drove. Josh rode shotgun and gave directions. "He'll be over these hills and across the lakeshore drive hiding somewhere to take one last shot as the President flies overhead." Josh said pointing towards the lake.

"How do you know that? He's probably just trying to get away like a sane person would."

"That's the problem, this guy is not sane, he is certifiable, and intent on getting his target. He'll keep trying until someone stops him for good. Right now that is you and me!"

She drove out of the parking lot onto the drive and crossed three lanes of traffic. There was a three foot retaining wall paralleling the drive preventing drivers from stopping or getting to the lake.

Etta slowed and put on the emergency lights, immediately starting a traffic backup on the drive. People were honking their horns and yelling at the car causing the back-up. Josh reloaded his gun with a new magazine and stuffed a backup magazine in his Kevlar vest. He struggled out of the car door. People stopped honking when they saw a man brandishing a gun. Etta got out and also brandished a weapon in plain sight. All the cars became silent. Josh and Etta jumped over the retaining wall and disappeared into a wooded area heading for the beach.

They moved cautiously. They had time on their side until they could hear the Marine One helicopters approaching. That would be zero hour. Coming out of the trees heading for the beach they spotted the silver car. The car was empty.

"How do you always guess right, are you clairvoyant?" Etta whispered, sounding annoyed. How did he always get this spy crap so correct?

"I told you this guy was committed to seeing his virgins as a martyr. I'm just thinking like he would if I was as committed to a mission. He's close,.... this is the flight line for the choppers coming out and he knows that. Heads up, I'm sure he will defend his position to the death. So let's oblige him." They continued to walk the tree line to stay hidden. Up ahead they saw a public bathhouse building.

Jackson Park Beach

The terrorist was hiding in a bathhouse looking out the vented window above a stall. This was not how he hoped his plan would end. He had promised he would take out the President as revenge for the killing of Osama bin Laden. He was prepared to die in his effort to kill the man that had ordered the Seal team mission into Pakistan.

He hoped that no one had seen him enter this concrete bunker. He checked his handgun and made sure the magazine was fully loaded. He would save one bullet for himself so he could meet Allah. Then he turned his attention to the single missile he still had with him. He checked it carefully and spooled up the mechanism so that it would be ready to fire when he heard the helicopter coming. He realized there would be two helicopters coming out, and that concerned him. Which one would carry the President? He would have to make a decision as he only had one Stinger missile left to fire.

He cracked the entrance door to look out to the north and could see the Chicago downtown skyline in the distance. No one seemed to be around. That was good. He was about to ease the door closed again when he saw movement in the trees above the beach.

He was incredulous, it was that same damn man and women who confronted him back at the boat. He was sure he had blown the woman out of the water. He was also sure the man had died when he kicked him into the water to drown. But they were both still alive and pursuing him, yet again. He should have taken the time to put bullets in both of their brains when he had the chance.

He realized that he was not going to get away. These people were relentless and were coming for him no matter what. In that instant he knew what he had to do. He would try to remain in hiding until the last moment when the helicopter was flying overhead. He would not try to engage them which would expose his position. Then he would step out into the line of fire, acquire the helicopter, and release the missile. If he was not dead by the time the missile left its tube, he would drop the unit and defend himself. He desperately wanted to see the actual shoot down. It is what he had promised his leaders.

Just then he heard the reverberations of the approaching helicopters far off in the distance, but coming his way. He grabbed his launcher and missile, made sure it was ready and stepped to the door to await his shot.

Etta and Josh were advancing carefully when they heard the rotor wash of the helicopters off in the distance. The President's Marine One helicopters were on the move, making a dash for the relative safety of the waters over Lake Michigan. Once out there they could fly a safe distance from shore and make a beeline for the south and the Gary, Indiana Airport where Air Force One was idling waiting for its passenger.

Josh and Etta zeroed in on the bathhouse as it was the only place that would afford some measure of cover for the terrorist to make his final attempt.

"Josh, we don't have much time left. The birds will be here soon. We can't let him take the shot," Etta said, as she raced from tree to tree with her gun drawn.

"I know, he has to be in there, Josh said. "It's the only cover in the area. I think we have to draw him out, and then take him out. How much ammo do you have?"

"I have two full magazines and a half load," Etta responded. She reversed magazines slotting the full load.

"I've got three full mags. .How about we carefully start firing at the building shooting at the doors and the vent windows to see if we can spook him out. But save enough ammo so if we do have to engage him, we still have firepower."

Both federal agents nodded to one another and started aiming at the block building. Etta had a better sight line to the bathhouse vented windows and concentrated on them. Josh had a direct line to the doors of the men's and women's bathrooms. They started laying down a barrage of bullets slamming into the building. Etta was only forty feet behind the building and zeroed in on the window slots concentrating her firepower. With her third hit the bullet ripped the screen from its slot. She decided to concentrate her shots through the hole in the wall opening. She presumed it would ricochet around inside and cause mayhem.

Josh concentrated on the doors and particularly the men's room door. He too was about forty-feet away. He stitched five rounds into the metal doorway all at head level. Made a nice little circle about the size of a man's head. If the indentations showed on the inside of the door, he figured the bad guy would know he meant business.

Just moments after hearing the helicopters and seeing his pursuers Mahoud was ducking from rounds being fired at the building. They had found him, he thought. He dived behind a metal toilet stall. Just then a slug ricocheted off the wall and slammed into the divider. He was now worried he would not see the helicopter before his life ended. He had to do something to buy himself time. He decided to return fire.

He crept over to the doorway and pulled it open enough to slide his gun through the narrow gap. He searched for a target in the tree line. Spotting the man he tried to aim and pulled the trigger. The suppressor was still screwed on and the gun almost silently coughed as it discharged. The bullet tore into a tree just inches from the man's head.

Josh didn't hear the shot as it left the chamber but he felt the concussion of the bullet slamming into the tree just behind his head. He hit the deck and yelled out to Etta.

"He's in there and still shooting with that silencer. See if you can work your way around to get a different angle on the men's room door. Let me know when you are in position."

"Are you OK? Or did you get shot again?" she said as she shot twice more into the vent hole she had created. Then she started ducking behind trees and moving to a new position. When she got there she signaled Josh that she was in position.

"Ok we have him boxed in. If he shows his face we blast away and take him out. We have to prevent him from getting out in the open to take a missile shot."

"Roger that," she whispered back. But I'm running low on ammo. How about you?"

"Me too, but we can't let him know that. Conserve but be prepared to lay down a lot of lead if he does step out with that launcher on his shoulder. No questions, we take him out!"

"Ok by me, I'm tired of this bastard. How's your shoulder?" Etta asked.

"I'll live although I may need a new shirt. Red is not a good color on me."

Etta rolled her eyes and then aimed at the door and pulled the trigger letting the terrorist know they were still there.

As the bullets hit and further stitched the metal door, the terrorist was now terrified himself. He was desperately trying to figure out his very limited options to still use the Stinger missile. He looked around and realized that there was water pooling on the concrete floor dripping from the roof. He looked upward and saw daylight poking its way through the wooden slats.

Desperate for a plan he searched the room and found a large plastic waste container. Pushing it to the spot beneath the ceiling hole he climbed up and started trying to break the wood slats from the roof. One large plank broke off when he put his full weight on it. He crashed to the floor with the eight foot board.

Using the thick board as a battering ram he started smashing pieces of roof and saw the gap widen. He knew that if he could fire the launcher through the hole the Stinger missile would shoot up but also would adjust to acquire its target seeking the heat signature of the craft. He stopped twice to open the door slightly and shoot into the woods where the man had last been. That would hopefully keep them at bay.

Josh saw a couple of pieces of the wood and shingle roof pop up and splinter and realized the terrorist was not giving up. He might not have to even step out of the building. He intended to shoot the missile through the gap in the roof. That meant he would have to go in. He formulated a plan.

Etta saw the wood splinters popping up as well. She watched as Josh advanced on the building and got his attention by whistling. She signaled she understood what he was doing and walked her fingers towards the building signaling her approach as well.

Josh tried to get her to hang back but knew that she would decline. He signaled he was going up on the roof and she should guard the door should he come out. She thumbed her magazine ejection button, checked the number of rounds she still had in the magazine and slammed it home again. Moving towards the door she got within twenty-five feet and laid down in the sand near a sidewalk edge providing a culvert of cover. If he showed she would take him out.

Josh could hear the helicopters approaching and knew he had to act. As he got to the building wall he saw a metal locker that afforded a three foot high platform. From there he could reach the roof without too much noise.

Etta could see what he was doing and decided to draw the terrorist's attention to the door with a couple of well-placed shots. The bullet impacts hitting the metal door reverberated through the bathhouse.

At that moment Josh threw his good arm up to catch the roofline and swung his leg up and over. He could feel his wound oozing blood but ignored the pain as he heaved himself up. The noise of the low flying helicopters seemed to cover his noisy climb.

Inside the bathhouse the terrorist was trying to shake the impact sounds out of his ears so he could hear the helicopters approach. He had decided that the second helicopter would be the one carrying the President. The first would be a decoy and he would concentrate on the second.

Josh pulled himself up as quietly as he could towards the gap in the roof. It was now large enough to stick the missile through the opening. The helicopter noise level was increasing. He knew he only had seconds to end this drama. He inched closer to the opening and using his good arm he pointed his weapon into the hole and fired.

The bullets slammed into the concrete floor and ricocheted around the room.

Mahoud ducked as the bullets flew about and returned fire shooting through the roof at whoever was up there. He could hear the helicopters getting closer yet.

His shots hit the ceiling but with the suppressor on the gun the bullets power was greatly reduced. They tore into the ceiling but did not break through.

Josh heard the shots slam into the ceiling below and rolled away from the hole to protect himself. The roll took him over his bad shoulder and he lost his balance sliding down the roof and off the building. He landed on his back and the wind was knocked out of him.

Etta saw him fall and got up from her prone position and charged the building.

Mahoud heard the man fall off the building and grabbed his missile. He stuck his gun in his belt and climbed on the waste container. The helicopters were very close based on the noise level. They were also very low. He pointed the missile launcher through the hole in the roof and waited. Holding the launcher was a two-handed job. He concentrated on looking out the hole in the roof to see if he could see the helicopters in the sky as they passed. He was confident that he could still finish the job.

Josh lay crumpled on his back with a leg twisted under him at an unusual angle. He had lost his gun in the fall. He looked around and saw it just a few feet away. He groaned as he tried to roll over and move towards the weapon. His leg would not cooperate. He rolled over and started crawling pulling himself with his elbows.

Etta, on the other side of the building could not see Josh but decided she had to stop the terrorist. She raced forward and prepared to push in through the door and shoot the terrorist. As she got within ten feet of the bathhouse door, with the first helicopter literally passing overhead, she heard the explosive whosshing sound of the missile being fired through the roof. He had gotten the shot off. Where was Josh, she thought as she hit the door and pushed through.

Marine One

The Stinger missile had been fired from its launcher and ignited immediately searching for a heat signature to seek out and kill. As soon as it launched, it located two heat signatures in its sky. One signal was stronger than the other and it locked onto that craft.

The lead Marine pilot was about to announce the craft was going feet wet out over Lake Michigan when the emergency klaxons went off. A threat to the aircraft had been detected and all the defense systems were automatically activating. He had trained these scenarios for years and immediately followed procedure. He veered to the right almost flipping the helicopter on its side. He knew his partner craft would go the opposite direction. His job was to clear the immediate airspace as fast as possible and claw for elevation.

At the same time he announced the emergency on his radio microphone advising command and all of his passengers of the threat. Hopefully they were all seat-belted and not walking about because they would be in for a rough ride.

Automatic defensive measures immediately went into action. Chaff cylinders were ejected from multiple ports on both sides of the fuselage shooting out thousands of small shards of metallic confetti in multiple directions to confuse any incoming missiles about the actual whereabouts of the helicopter. This chaff sent out at various distances would muddy and expand the heat signature of the craft as it flew out of the target zone.

A multiple of radar screens on the pilot's console was tracking any threats that could be identified as they continued evasive procedures. The pilot kept climbing as fast as the GE engines could spin the rotors. A second set of chaff cylinders ejected from the craft as the pilot swung the craft to the left now that the distance between the two Marine One helicopters had been widened.

Jackson Park Beach

Etta hit the metal door so hard with her good shoulder that she started falling as she entered. Her right gun hand started searching for a target. She had already put her finger on the trigger even though she had been trained not to until an actual target was acquired. In the half-light of the late afternoon sun she could not identify the terrorist location as she hit the floor. He was nowhere in sight

Mahoud was still standing above her on the waste container and as such was six feet in the air when the woman came crashing in. He drew his handgun from his belt and calmly shot down at her from his perch. His first shot missed as the woman sprawled on the floor. He wobbled on his perch and aimed again.

Etta heard the shot come from above her as she hit the floor. Her training kicked in and she rolled over towards a corner of the room. She sighted her quarry and still lying on the floor she shot upwards catching the man standing above her in the upper thigh. Blood started gushing out of the wound.

He crumpled to the floor physically landing on her before she could get another shot off. He still had his gun in his hand and pointed it at her head. The suppressor was right in front of her eyes. She surrendered and without being asked dropped her handgun.

Josh was dragging himself towards the men's room door when the first two shots had been fired in the restroom.

Marine One

The first Marine One helicopter didn't have time to evade the threat before the Stinger missile ripped into the body of the large green craft just underneath the rotor assembly and engine housing. The hottest signature on the craft.

The massive helicopter blew up in a horrific explosion and bright flash of light. The craft broke apart at about 600 feet above the lake. The flaming wreckage exploded outward in a thousand large and small pieces and started drifting down towards the lake below.

The bulk of the craft came down haphazardly and smashed into the water sending up spray in all directions, and then quickly disappeared beneath the surface.

There were no parachutes in the sky, just flaming shards of helicopter and smoke from the explosion drifting from the site.

The second Marine One helicopter continued its' evasion tactics as it moved out further, hell bent on getting away from land and to the relative safety of the lake. It did not return to the scene, as that was not protocol. It continued its journey straight east out towards the open lake. Three miles out it turned southeast towards Gary, IN. as fast as the craft could fly.

Jackson Park Beach

The explosion was loud and unmistakable. Mahoud was furious he had not seen the explosion but at least he knew that the missile had connected with one of the helicopters. Now it was up to Allah to determine if his mission had been successful.

He stared down at the woman on the business end of his gun and debated pulling the trigger pointed at her throat. She had pursued him with the man all day long. She had prevented him from being successful until the last few minutes. He should kill her right now and then make sure the guy is dead as well, he thought, as he stared at her, waiting for her to twitch.

Then he realized he was still alive and in control of the situation. He could still get away and claim credit for killing the President. She would be his hostage. He slowly got up holding the gun aimed at her forehead. Rising, he ordered her to stand. He quickly frisked her hating to touch an infidel woman at all. She had no other weapons.

Ordering her into the corner he moved to the door and cracked it open to see if the man was still out there waiting for him. He saw the man's body lying in the sand just outside the door. He wasn't moving at all. His leg looked bent backwards in an unnatural position. He was out of action, Mahoud thought.

Opening the door he moved his gun to direct the woman through the door and followed her out at a distance using her as a shield.

She moved out and saw Josh lying there, his face half buried in the sand. He was not moving and she couldn't see him even breathing. Perhaps he was dead, she thought.

It would now be up to her to stop this terrorist.

She moved as if she had given up and was pushed forward with the gun still aimed at her head. Moving towards the inert man's body he casually slid sideways and moved to put an insurance bullet in Josh's head. Now, three steps beside her, she did not hesitate. She rushed him like a Chicago Bears tackle burying a shoulder under his arm and pushing through him from behind. Both went down hard and she drove his face into the sand as she reached for his weapon. Coming up with a face full of sand he struggled for gun control but then threw it away out of reach, and twisted his body to fight off this determined woman. He slugged her in the jaw with a right and was winding up his left when she head butted him with everything she could muster. His head snapped back.

Mahoud was stunned by her aggressive attack. Women didn't fight men, they cowered and feared for their lives. He tried to get his head to stop ringing and shook her off of him, standing unsteadily. Gathering his wits he dove for the gun laying in the sand and came up in a crouch trying to draw a bead on the woman again. He was angry and had had enough. He pulled the trigger.

Etta saw it coming and dove into the sand next to Josh's inert body, but caught the bullet in her calf on the way down. The blood spurted from the wound turning the sand beneath her red.

The terrorist smiled as he realized he had won. He readjusted his aim to finish the job. He started to pull the trigger again.

At that moment Josh rolled over on his bad arm and aimed his handgun at the terrorist standing almost directly above him. He squeezed the trigger and fired four times, stitching the terrorist from top to bottom; head, heart, torso and groin. The terrorist fell to the sand face down and did not move.

Josh groaned and reached for Etta.

"Well it's about time you got back in the game. I thought you were dead," she said, gently slugging him in his good arm and giving him a victory kiss.

He groaned again. "Hey, you're supposed to be on my side. Is that a way to treat your partner? Are you ok?" He rolled over again to take a look for himself.

"I caught one in the leg, how bad does it look?

"It's a real bleeder" Josh said. He paused and then said, "Take off your blouse and I'll wrap it up for you." He smiled brightly as he said it. "You know I have been doing a lot of these wounds today."

Etta just rolled her eyes and was tempted to slug him again. Instead she just settled back into the warm sand, and said, "I wonder if we still have a President?

Gary, Indiana Airport

Marine One, the one still in the air, came in hot off Lake Michigan directly towards Air Force One as it sat spooling up its engines. Surrounding the large blue and white 747 were all sorts of police cruisers at the four corners. Security and Secret Service personnel were stationed in an inner circle near the landing zone waiting for their boss to arrive.

As the Marine One helicopter hovered above, it flared its rotors and settled down just one hundred feet from the stairs leading to the open door of the jet aircraft.

Once the helicopter had touched down with the wheels chocked, the rotors started slowing down. The door was then popped open and a Secret Service detail went up to the door and surrounded the President who had a Kevlar raincoat on buttoned to his neck. Two attempts had been made on him in one day. He looked ashen and troubled by all that had taken place. Moving in a tight phalanx formation the security team walked him to his plane and up the satirs with the taller security men in the rear to further screen the back of the President's head and torso.

The door to the huge craft was closed and the plane started rolling before everyone was buckled in. All other traffic was on hold and the plane taxied to the runway and took off for Washington, DC.

Once airborne, two F-16 fighters settled in on either side of the craft and provided aerial protection. The three craft simultaneously turned east and disappeared into the evening clouds.

Sugar Grove, Illinois

Etta limped out the back door of her home onto the wood deck that surrounded the kitchen. She was balancing two mugs of hot coffee in one hand as she maneuvered into the morning warmth. She had gotten rid of the crutches after a week and was doing a much better job of getting around.

Josh sat at the round table with half a glass of orange juice in his hand. He pushed it as far away as he could with his good arm. "Any chance we're going to graduate to something a little stronger soon? This health food is going to destroy my carefully cultivated digestive system."

"I'm just trying to get that carefully cultivated digestive system of yours trained to eat regular healthy food, rather than all the crap you have consumed for years."

"Does that mean you'll allow me to stay here for a while? I'd like that, but only if you promise not to slug me anymore. Not many guys have girlfriends that chase and kill terrorists for a living. And beat up their own partners."

"Girlfriend huh, that's news to me. Did I miss something? I don't remember any commitment discussions. Besides, you work overseas, and I work here stateside. How would that commitment stuff work? And I doubt phone sex is anything to look forward to. I hear the distance thing can be a bummer?'"

"Well, ….while you were debriefing last week, I made a couple of calls to my boss at Langley. I told him I had finally exceeded my personal quota of sand in my ears, bullet holes in my manly body, and scars from overseas adventures. I suggested that I might need to transfer agencies before my body completely breaks down. He said he understood and would see what he could do to find me some stateside desk that I could drive. I then asked if that desk could be here in Chicago. He said he'd look into it. He also said to get well because he would really like to meet you."

"Wow, that's the most complete sentences you have ever strung together," Etta said. "But that doesn't really answer my question about commitment. So are we boyfriend and girlfriend now?

"No,…. after what we went through I don't think that is enough, just being friends, even if it is friends with benefits." He gave her a big smile. "By the way I think we may be healed enough to restart that benefits stuff. I'd like to suggest blowing through the boyfriend – girlfriend phase completely and moving on."

Etta sat there and raised an eyebrow.

A very pretty eyebrow, he thought. He reached into his arm sling and pulled out a ring box handing it to Etta.

"I'd get down on one knee but you would probably have to help me get back up. Etta, would you marry me?"

Etta was shocked, but she was also in love with this rough desert rat. She had been to hell and back with him. He was a true partner through thick and thin. More importantly, they were both alive because they had relied on one another.

She hadn't loved anyone for so long she was worried she might not ever meet the right guy again. But Josh was the right guy. He made her smile, something she rarely done, and he did it all the time.

And she was actually getting used to his lame humor and loved his gentle touch.

She had decided weeks before that he was a keeper. She couldn't think about a better ending. So she simply said,

"Yes, but, I'll reserve judgement on the punching!"

CPSIA information can be obtained at www.ICGtesting.com
Printed in the USA
LVOW11s0239021115

460694LV00001B/35/P

9 781478 761907